DAMAGED
INTENTIONS

DAMAGED
INTENTIONS

MIKE OMER

THOMAS & MERCER

Text copyright © 2022 by Michael Omer
All rights reserved.

Published by Thomas & Mercer, Seattle

www.apub.com

Amazon, the Amazon logo, and Thomas & Mercer are trademarks of Amazon.com, Inc., or its affiliates.

ISBN-13: 9781542032520
ISBN-10: 1542032520

Cover design by Faceout Studio, Spencer Fuller

Printed in the United States of America

DAMAGED
INTENTIONS

CHAPTER 1

They were coming.

He stumbled in the dark house, eyes darting frantically, sobbing in fear. How long did he have? An hour? Maybe less. And he knew what they'd do to him when they got there. He tried not to think about it, but he knew. He'd heard enough testimonies, seen enough photos. *Please, God, don't let that happen to me.*

He found the toolbox on the top shelf in the garage. As he yanked it, standing on his tiptoes, the lid opened, a screwdriver tumbling, hitting his head. Hissing in pain, he set it on the floor. He rummaged inside, the rattling of metal objects echoing in the dusty space. *Come on, come on . . .* He upended it on the floor, the loud clattering making him wince. Did anyone hear it? The neighbors? A random passerby, already calling the police? Or maybe *them*?

There! He grabbed the pliers, and rushed out of the garage, heart thudding in his chest.

First to get the GPS tracker out. He knelt on the floor, trying to recall the schematics that he'd memorized. But it was difficult to concentrate, his breathing erratic, his mind filled with the brutalities they'd inflict on him when they got here. The burns. The mutilations.

He took a deep breath, forced himself to focus. This was the moment to prove himself. To show what he was worth. Hours of training, of memorizing, of preparing for this moment.

Yes, he remembered now.

Pinching the hidden tracker with the pliers, he yanked, tearing it out of its socket. Trembling, he got up, went to the bathroom. When he tried to discard it in the toilet, he dropped the pliers instead. *Damn it, damn it!* He fished the pliers out, flushed the tracker.

Now for the microphone. That one was farther in the back, harder to reach.

As he was trying to wedge in the pliers to reach the microphone, something flickered in the darkness. A patch of white light, a cell phone. He picked it up, and stared at the screen. A new message.

Red_Queen: Caterpillar, you there?

Caterpillar was not his real name, of course. But online aliases were the disguises they all wore to muddy the waters, camouflage their scent. He had to answer, to mislead anyone who was listening, watching, making notes. Finger quivering, he typed, I'm here. His finger left a smear of blood on the screen, a red, sticky stain. His DNA and fingerprint.

Red_Queen: Did you see the thread they posted earlier? About those kids?

He wanted to smash the screen, to yell at Red Queen that this was not the time, that they might be coming, that he could be compromised. Instead he forced himself to tap the answer, calm, short, no spelling mistakes.

Caterpillar: Busy. Will check later.

He turned off the screen, grabbed the pliers again.
Which one was the mic?

The bottom-right first molar. He tugged the chin, positioned the pliers inside the loose jaw, clutching the tooth. A strong tug and he yanked it out, tumbling back, landing on his ass. He felt the blood on the floor soaking into his jeans.

Back to the bathroom, his posture more steady. Let the tooth tumble into the toilet without dropping the pliers this time. It left a red, smoky trail of blood as it clattered to the bottom. He flushed it.

He allowed himself to smile. He'd done it. Gotten one of their agents. He was the first one to ever succeed. They'd been fighting this shadowy group for over three years, and sometimes it felt like this battle was hopeless. That the powerful cabal of those twisted bastards was completely untouchable. After all, the Circle controlled the government, the army, the police, the media. What could a paltry group of average people do against something like that?

But maybe there really was a reason he was chosen, along with the others. This was proof; he'd done it.

He'd killed one of the enemy. And if he could get one of them, then together, they could finish the rest.

Turning around, he stared at his face in the mirror. Disheveled, smeared with blood. But victorious.

He washed his hands in the sink, leaving red smears on the white porcelain, thinking of *them*. Trying to figure out how they would act. They'd probably try to contact their agent soon. See that he wasn't responding. Tracking the GPS might lead them on a wild-goose chase throughout the city's sewers. He had some time. Not too much; it wasn't smart to underestimate the enemy. But enough to cover his tracks.

Returning to the living room, he switched on the light, and paused. For the first time, he could really see what he'd done. The smears of blood all over the floor. The body, lifeless, eyes vacant. The jaw open wide, two teeth missing, traces of blood and gristle left behind.

Dizzy, he leaned against the wall. He did what had to be done. This was war, and he'd been chosen to protect the innocent, the helpless.

Wars could get bloody.

A sudden uncomfortable thought. What if he'd gotten it wrong?

What if the teeth he'd removed didn't contain the tracker or the mic? Maybe there was a mistake in the schematic, an intentional error, an act of counterintelligence by the enemy.

Trust no one. Always think ahead.

The tracker and mic could be in any of the remaining teeth. He still had a lot of work ahead of him. He knelt by the body for the third time, grabbing another tooth with the pliers.

He hesitated. This was insane.

After all, there was a hammer in the toolbox.

CHAPTER 2

A bad memory's smell could crawl up your nostrils and settle in your mind for hours, for days, for weeks.

Abby Mullen stared through her rental's windshield, trying to breathe deeply, to fill her nose with the smell of the car's air freshener. Pine, maybe, or some other poor imitation of a plant's scent. It didn't help. The stench she'd been smelling for the past week, that she'd been dreaming about, that haunted her days, didn't dissipate.

People often raved about how smell triggered their memories. How the aroma of cinnamon brought back Sunday morning with Grandma and her homemade muffins. Or how the fragrance of a fresh bouquet made them recall a vivid springtime picnic.

But hardly anyone ever talked about how the smell of disinfectant made them remember holding their father's hand in the hospital as he faded away. How the stench of rotting meat brought back that childhood moment when they came upon a dead dog in the woods and confronted death for the first time.

No one ever talked about smoke. Suffocating, all-consuming smoke, and the memories it brought with it.

Abby sat in the driver's seat, jaw clenched. Part of her a grown woman, a mother of two, a lieutenant in the NYPD. The other part a seven-year-old girl, stumbling through a wooden corridor hazy with smoke.

She coughed, eyes half-closed and streaming. Muffled screams through the barred door, a woman begging to be let out. Mommy? Or someone else? She had to let them out.

The walls radiated heat, an inferno on the other side. And dozens trapped there. Locked inside by her. She'd made a mistake; perhaps she'd misunderstood. But she would unlatch the door and . . .

"Abihail, get away from there!" Eden screamed behind her, coughing herself, sounding scared, desperate. But she didn't understand—there had been a mistake, and Mommy and Daddy were shouting for help.

The door was just a few steps away, Abihail reaching for the latch to let them out.

A hand on her shoulder, yanking her back, twisting her.

She screamed in anger and fear, trying to pull away.

And then an explosion, the force of it thrusting her away, a sudden searing pain on the back of her neck, flames engulfing them . . .

Abby's hand involuntarily went to the scar on her neck, and she let out a shuddering breath. She felt the tough patch on her skin, a reminder that she wasn't a child anymore. That the fire, the event that was dubbed by the press the Wilcox Cult Massacre, was decades in the past.

And now, for the first time in over thirty years, she was in North Carolina, back at the location of the Wilcox Family's compound.

The large wooden structure that had housed their chapel, the offices, the mess hall, and Moses Wilcox's bedroom was gone, of course. It had burned to cinders, and any remains had been cleared away long ago. The three large dormitories that had housed all of them were gone as well.

Instead, a large granite rectangular memorial stood by the road. Behind it, a few trees, completely bare. They were maple trees, planted in memory of the people who'd died in the fire. She'd seen the pictures of this memorial during the autumn, the vibrant red of the trees' foliage contrasting with the memorial's somber tone. Now the effect was lost—the trees matching the sky and the slab of granite, all in shades of gray. Gray, like smoke.

She stepped out of her rental and walked over to the large stone. She traced the granite's rough surface with her finger as she read the inscription.

In memory of the fifty-nine innocent souls whose lives were cut short on the twenty-third of April, 1987. Nine of them were eight years old or younger.

Below the inscription, four columns of names.

She scanned the list quickly. *Martha Richardson* and *David Richardson* were in the middle of the third column. Her mother and father.

Thinking back, she tried to picture them. Her mother, with whom she'd spent a lot of time, picking flowers in the field, or making bouquets for the flower shop, she could picture easily. Blonde, like Abby, and her hair cascaded all the way to her waist. She gathered it in a ponytail, not bothering to hide the feature that hounded Abby to this day—her big ears.

Her father was a different matter. She could recall holding his hand during grace—it was large, and always extraordinarily warm. The skin was scratched—a result of working with thorny flowers all day long. But beyond his hand, she remembered nothing at all.

Another name at the bottom of the column. *Moses Wilcox.* For a moment she stared at it, jaw clenched. Then, frowning, she looked closer. She'd thought the names had been written alphabetically, but if that were the case, Moses would have been in the fourth column, near the end of the list. She quickly realized why that wasn't the case—for the last eight victims, only the first names were inscribed, for some reason.

Having found her parents, she reread the names, finding others she remembered. Eden's parents. Isaac's mother—his father had never joined the cult. Hanna, who'd worked in the kitchen and would often bake cookies for the children. Eric, who'd lumbered around, always staring strangely at her, scaring her.

She was surprised at how many of the names she recognized—people she hadn't thought of for more than thirty years. And . . . there was some sort of a mistake.

The man who'd driven the truck that carried her mother's bouquets to the flower shop was named George. And though she scanned the list four times, she couldn't find his name. There was another one, George Fletcher, but he was Eden's father, and Abby knew for certain they weren't the same person.

She took out her phone and dialed Eden.

"Hey, Abby." Eden's voice was cheerful, a far cry from the terrified, desperate woman whom Abby had helped two months before.

"Hi." Abby's eyes went instinctively to Eden's parents' names as she talked to her. "Listen, I just got to the memorial."

They'd discussed this before Abby had flown to North Carolina. The recent reunion of the three survivors of the Wilcox Cult Massacre—Abby, Eden, and Isaac—had raised some unanswered questions and stirred dark, forgotten memories. Abby wanted to investigate further. Eden and Isaac weren't as thrilled with the idea. They preferred to leave the past behind. Nevertheless, Eden had told Abby to update her if she found out anything.

"How does it look?" Eden asked.

"I don't know. Like a memorial stone. There's a list of names here." A short silence. "Yeah."

"I wanted to ask you—do you remember George? Not your dad—the other George."

"The one who drove the truck? Sure. He used to let me drive with him sometimes."

"He was there until the . . ." Abby cleared her throat. "Until the end, right?"

"Yeah . . . I'm pretty sure he was. Why?"

"I think they forgot to put his name here. Do you remember his last name?"

"No idea. I was just a kid." Eden sounded almost defensive.

"Yeah. We all were. Okay, thanks."

"Did you meet that guy yet?"

"No. That's my next stop."

"Okay. Good luck."

"Thanks. I'll call you later." Abby hung up the phone, and looked around. Then she picked up a small stone from the side of the road, and placed it on top of the memorial. She ran her finger through the curvy *M* letter on her mother's name.

Then she stepped back into the car and turned on the engine, bracing herself to meet the person who shared with her one of the worst moments of her life.

CHAPTER 3

The house was in a sparsely populated street where the trees outnumbered the houses twenty to one. The grass in the yard was spotted with tiny fluffy white flowers, giving it a fairy-tale feeling. A gray-haired man sat in a wicker chair on the porch, smoking. A large golden retriever lay by his side, head resting on his front paws, his eyes shut.

Abby stepped out of the car, and approached the man. "Excuse me—"

"They're all in the back." The man gestured with his hand, the cigarette held loosely between two fingers. "Just round the back. See if you can find yours."

"I . . . what? I'm looking for Norman Lewis?"

"Yeah, that's me. I told you, check the . . . oh, never mind, let me show you."

He got up, groaning, hand on his lower back. The golden retriever jumped in excitement and followed Norman Lewis, who shuffled slowly to the back of the house. Confused, Abby walked after them. After turning the corner, Norman stopped by a large pile of shoes and stared at it. Abby joined him, and gazed at the shoes too. The dog looked up at her expectantly, wagging his tail.

They were a sorry bunch of shoes, mangled and muddy. There were all kinds and shapes—a few sneakers, a child's boot, a woman's red high heel.

"That one?" Norman pointed at the red high heel. "Looks about your size."

"No, um . . ."

"Don't see it here? You don't happen to have the other one, do you? I'll keep a lookout for it. He sometimes buries them before bringing them here, so it might take a few days."

"Mr. Lewis, I'm not here about a missing shoe. My name is Abby Mullen? You told me to drop by anytime this week?"

"Oh!" His eyebrows shot up. "You're that NYPD cop. I didn't think you'd actually show up."

Abby raised her hands in an embarrassed "here I am" motion.

Norman lowered his gaze back to the pile. "It's been worse for the past few days. There was a rainstorm last Saturday, so the streets got muddy. Everyone leaves their dirty shoes outside their house, and it's party time for Cooper here." He shrugged. "Ah, well. Let's go inside."

He led the way to a cozy, small living room and sat on a couch that was probably older than Abby. She sat on the only other chair in the room, a rocking chair. Cooper curled up on the rug between them, and let out a long sigh.

"Can I get you anything to drink? Coffee? Tea?" Norman asked.

"No thanks, I'm fine."

"Apple juice? Beer? Just water?"

"No, really, I'm good."

He settled back. "Ever since my wife died, two years ago, Cooper began stealing people's shoes. I don't know if it's a weird coping mechanism or if he thinks that the shoes he fetches will make me feel better."

Cooper raised his head at the sound of his name. Abby leaned forward and scratched his head, and he wagged his tail, thumping it on the floor. As far as shoe fetishists went, he was the cutest one Abby had ever met.

"At first he only brought left shoes. Nine left shoes. I thought the dog is a sort of genius. Did you ever hear of a dog distinguishing between left and right shoes?"

"I haven't." She grinned at him. He seemed to be happy with the company, and she dreaded dredging up the past and ruining the moment. She decided to give it a couple of minutes.

"But then he brought some right-side shoes, too, so I guess it was just coincidence. Brought me a clown shoe once. Thirty inches long, and purple. Are you sure I can't get you anything to drink?"

"No thanks."

"Suit yourself. So what brings an NYPD officer to Ayden?"

She sighed. "I wanted to ask you about something that happened long ago. The fire at the Wilcox compound."

"Oh." His face darkened.

For a second, Abby almost felt like saying that she actually had lost a shoe, that that was why she was there. Instead she said, "You were there, right?"

"I was there," he said heavily. "What's your interest in it?"

She hesitated. "My name used to be Abihail."

He gaped at her for a brief second. Then his mouth went slack, the blood draining from his face. "My god," he whispered.

"You remember me?"

"Girl, I forget a lot. I managed to forget the anniversary with my wife three times in a row. But I will never forget anything about that day. Believe me, I've tried."

Abby smiled at him sadly. "I'm glad. Because I was hoping for some answers."

He pursed his lips for a few seconds. "You know what? I think that *I* could use a drink. Wait here."

Cooper got up and followed Norman as he left the room, but then paused and glanced back, as if unsure if he should leave the guest unsupervised. He turned around and walked back to Abby, then rested his nose on her knee. She scratched his head, and he shut his eyes in pleasure. When she stopped, he began buffeting her arm with his nose until she relented and scratched his head again.

After a few minutes Norman returned, holding a beer bottle in one hand, a steaming mug in the other. "As long as you keep scratching him, he'll never let you go." He handed her the mug. "Cinnamon tea. It's cold outside."

"Thanks," Abby said politely, and sipped. She was surprised at how marvelous it tasted. Cooper pushed her hand, demanding more petting, and she spilled some tea on herself.

"Cooper, out," Norman told the dog, opening the front door.

Cooper stared at him with a hurt expression.

"Go on, out."

The dog let out a long-suffering sigh and plodded out through the door. Norman shut it behind him, and sat down.

He took a sip of his beer. "So this isn't really about a case, is it?"

"Not really."

He nodded. "I always wondered about you three, you know? Where you ended up. Back then you looked so . . . lost. I even tried to find you once, but they wouldn't tell me where you were."

"I went to a foster family, and they ended up adopting me."

His face brightened slightly. "That's good to hear. Any idea what happened to the other two? Eden and Isaac?"

"Eden has her own family now. Isaac is an accountant." General facts, skirting over darker truths. But Norman narrowed his eyes, a shrewd spark in his gaze. He wasn't fooled.

"So," he said. "What did you want to ask me?"

"Well . . . I was wondering about our conversation. On the phone. I know there are transcripts. I've read them. I wanted to ask . . . is there anything that doesn't appear in the transcripts?"

"Like what?"

"Like how I seemed to you."

"You sounded terrified. You had a gun to your head."

"Did I cry?"

He hesitated. "I guess you did."

"You guess? You said you remember everything about that night."

"Yeah, but I couldn't see you," Norman pointed out. "The line was bad; there was a lot of interference. Like I said, you had a gun to your head. What seven-year-old wouldn't cry?"

A seven-year-old who didn't actually have a gun to her head. A seven-year-old who just repeated the lines that Moses Wilcox told her to say.

"I told you we were in the mess hall, with all the other congregation members," Abby said. "Could you hear them?"

Norman frowned. "I think I remember I heard crying in the background."

"Sixty-two people in a crowded room. They would have made noise."

"I don't think so. That Moses Wilcox had a gun. I think they were afraid to talk."

"All you remember is some crying?" Abby prodded.

"Yeah."

"Okay," Abby said heavily. She took a moment to drink from her tea.

She'd been hoping for something else. That he would say that she blubbered on the phone. That he heard screaming for help in the background. Her memories of that night were hazy and confused. Until recently, she'd believed they'd all been in the mess hall together. That Moses had held a gun to her head, instructing her on what to tell the cops.

But a couple of months ago, after meeting Eden again, she began remembering things differently. Eden, Isaac, and she had been in a different room than the rest of the congregation. Moses had told her to talk to the cops, to tell them that they had to stay away because he held a gun to her head.

"Tell them about the gun." His finger pressing against her temple, just like a gun. "Tell them all sixty-two of us are together."

And then he left the room. And when she talked to the cops—to Norman, who now sat with her, nursing his beer—she repeated what Moses had told her to say. Even though he didn't actually hold a gun to her head. He wasn't even in the same room. And then, after she ended the call, she walked over to the door of the mess hall, latching it like Moses had told her to. Locking the rest of the congregation inside.

There was no way to be really sure, but everything Norman said now seemed to corroborate those memories. She'd played a part in the fiery death of those fifty-nine people, her parents among them.

She blinked, clearing her throat. "I was at the memorial earlier. Some names don't have a surname."

"Yeah. We didn't have a list of the people in the cult . . . I mean, the congregation."

"You can say *cult*."

"I think that some of the members were drifters from other states. People came and went. The bodies were . . . well, you can imagine. A lot were in a pretty bad state. Hard to identify. We asked around; people knew most of them. And you kids gave us some names. Later some families came forth, identifying their loved ones. But eight of them we never properly identified."

"That's right. There was a name missing. George something."

He raised his eyebrow. "No, it's there. George Fletcher."

She shook her head. "There were two Georges in the cult. George Fletcher and another one."

"Not as far as we could tell. Maybe he left before that day?"

"He didn't. Could he have survived the fire?"

"No one survived except for the three of you."

"It must have been chaotic. It was dark, there was a huge fire, smoke everywhere. Maybe you missed—"

"There were fifty-nine bodies. And three survivors. Sixty-two. All accounted for." He leaned forward. "Why do you think there was another survivor?"

"I told you, there was another guy named George. He doesn't appear on the memorial."

He looked at her intently. "Why did you want to talk to me? You didn't come here because of the memorial. You called me over a week ago. What is this about?"

She weighed the question in her mind. Finally she decided to take the plunge. "After the night of the fire, Isaac and I stayed in touch. He wrote me a few letters; then I started writing back. Later we wrote emails. And in the past few years we've been chatting, almost every day."

Norman said nothing, holding her gaze. She could see the cop that he used to be. The cop who knew that when someone talked, you *listened*.

"He even sent me pictures. You know, *This is me with my foster parents. This is me on the bike I got for my birthday. Me and my date going to the prom,* that kind of thing. Anyway, a few weeks ago Eden and I decided to pay him a surprise visit. I found out his address, and we went there. And he's not the guy I've been in touch with."

Norman raised his eyebrows. "You mean you got the address wrong?"

"I got the address right. The Isaac we met was the kid I grew up with, the third survivor from the fire. The person I've been writing to wasn't the same guy. He looked different in the pictures. And Isaac, the real Isaac, hadn't heard from us in thirty years."

"You think someone pretended to be Isaac?" He squinted, his tone incredulous.

"Yes."

"Why?"

"That's what I want to find out."

"And you think whoever did this was in the Wilcox cult?"

"He knew some things that only people who grew up in the cult could know. Only things that people who knew me back then knew."

"There are people who left the cult before the fire. There's that guy who wrote the book."

"Leonard Holt," Abby said. Leonard had written an autobiography about his time in the Wilcox Family. He'd left a year before the fire. "And there were a few others who left throughout the years. I guess it's possible."

"Well, it wasn't this George guy; I can promise you that." He got up. "Wait here a second. I have something you might be interested in."

He left the room. Abby took another sip of her tea—lukewarm now. She put it down on the coffee table. From somewhere in the back of the house, she heard something tumble, followed by a string of curses.

"Is everything okay?" She stood up.

"Yeah, I'll be there in a moment." Norman's voice sounded strained.

A sound of incessant scratching accompanied by a high-pitched whine came from the front door.

"Can you open the door for Cooper, please?" Norman shouted.

She went to the front door and pulled it open. Cooper stood in the doorway, a shiny black high-heeled boot in his mouth. He dropped it at her feet, then looked up expectantly at her, wagging his tail.

"Thank you, I don't know if it's really my style." She picked up the boot. "You got the size right, though."

He panted happily, tongue lolling.

"Oh god, another one?" Norman groaned behind her.

She turned around. He held a dusty cardboard box. He put it down on the floor, and held out his hand. Abby gave him the boot.

"Looks expensive too," he muttered. "Covered in drool. I hope its owner won't be like the lady from last week. How am I supposed to replace something she bought in Paris?"

Cooper padded inside, clearly satisfied that his job here was done. Abby shut the door.

"This box has pretty much all the papers I collected about the Wilcox cult fire," Norman said, pushing the box toward Abby. "Reports, interview transcripts, pictures. There's even an interview with you in there. Not that you said a lot."

Abby knelt by the box, opening it. Stacks of papers, yellow with age. She thumbed through them. Witness interviews. A memo from the FBI. Autopsy reports of victims. Her eyes skirted sideways as she uncovered an image of a body, burnt black. A bunch of news articles. A copy of Leonard Holt's book.

"I kept collecting these even after I retired," Norman muttered, scratching Cooper's head. "I don't even know why."

"Some cases stick with you," Abby said distractedly, thumbing through the newspaper articles. Pictures of the burnt compound, headlines describing the "Shocking Wilcox Cult Massacre," "Three Survivors from Horrible Fire." And then . . .

"Oh," she whispered.

"What is it?" Norman asked.

It was an article dated months before the fire. An interview in the town's paper with a local florist who'd won an award. It described him as a man from a nearby Christian congregation.

And a photo.

She raised her eyes to look at the old man. "That's my dad."

CHAPTER 4

When he was stressed, Caterpillar clenched his jaw at night. In fact, he didn't just clench it; he would grind it, his teeth scraping against each other, over and over and over. A former girlfriend had told him it was a ghastly sound, that she could hear his teeth pulverizing themselves to dust. She'd wanted him to go to the dentist, which he refused to do.

He didn't trust dentists, even then. Before he knew the truth. He had sharp instincts.

Still, lately it was one stressful day after another, and he woke up each morning with a pounding headache and an aching jaw. He wasn't relaxed, like he should be after a night's sleep. His muscles were tense, his entire body rigid.

He groaned as he got up and plodded to the kitchen. Made himself a pot of coffee. He'd make a new one every morning, extra strong, and he drank it throughout the day, often making a second pot in the afternoon. Coffee helped his mind stay sharp, helped him see the patterns.

It was all about patterns.

Sipping from his cup, he stared out the window, at the backyard. Some of the flowers in the garden were wilting. He frowned, his expression mirrored in the windowpane. Because of his position, the flowers seemed to almost crown his translucent reflection. A wreath of dying flowers. He snorted at his own morbidity, and ran his hand through his thin brown hair. Though he was just shy of forty-five, he thought he looked younger. But the stress of his daily routine was beginning to affect him. He seemed pale, and tired. He needed a shave.

He left the kitchen and went to his desk. He placed a sheet of paper on the desk's surface, then put his cup on top, to avoid coffee stains. Then he turned on his laptop and dived in. That was how he thought of it lately, not as *browsing* or *reading the news*—weak phrases that made it sound like a quick pastime. The struggle was hectic and intense; it took different shapes every day. If you just "read the news," you didn't have a real idea what was going on. You were one of the masses, a sheep, what he and the rest of the Watchers liked to call a "sleepy Alice."

No, to really *know* what's going on, you had to dive in. With your entire body, entire mind. Swimming through the endless online data available. Sifting truth from lies, reality from illusion.

A single click, and multiple browser windows opened on his screen. Twitter, Facebook, the *New York Times*, CNN, Fox News, *TMZ*, *People* . . . that was where you started. And from there, you had to feel your way through the miasma.

First things first: he logged into the Watchers' forum and skimmed the new posts that had popped up since he was there last. He'd logged off the night before at around three a.m., and it was now nine. Six whole hours had passed. An eternity.

And the forum had been busy.

Caterpillar loved logging in every morning. He wasn't fighting this war alone. They were a team. An army, really, with hundreds of soldiers scanning the net twenty-four hours a day, fishing for intelligence, for things that stood out. For patterns.

A new thread had popped up, discussing an earthquake in Puerto Rico that had knocked out the power. Some deluded Watchers thought that the earthquake itself had been manufactured by the secret technology of the cabal. Caterpillar rolled his eyes. As if natural disasters had never occurred before civilization. The power outage—now, that was something else. Were they expected to believe that the electricity of the entire island was so easily knocked out? A member pointed out that the electricity of Puerto Rico was supplied by the Puerto Rico Electric Power Authority, which had been *privatized* in 2018. Who owned it? Who gained from shutting down the power? Sometimes asking questions was more important than answering them.

Oh, that was interesting. A new comment in the uncovered-agents thread.

No one knew who the members of that shadowy group that controlled everything were—the Circle. They maintained complete anonymity, working through shell corporations and hundreds of agents. But the Watchers had a list of probable agents who worked for the cabal, with varying degrees of certainty. The governor of Utah was an agent, as was the deputy attorney general of the United States. Two judges on the Supreme Court were almost certainly agents, with three more possible agents, guaranteeing the cabal complete power over any decisions made there. It was often hard to figure out who was an agent and who was manipulated to act through the two Bs of the Circle—bribery and blackmail.

Nothing angered Caterpillar more. Men and women sold humanity every day because they were greedy or weak. He knew that if the Circle ever approached him, he would laugh in their faces, no matter how much they offered.

And the Watchers weren't helpless. They could intimidate those agents and accomplices, bombarding them with emails and messages and phone calls. They could let them know that someone was seeing them for who they really were.

The new post was about Sofia Lopez.

Sofia Lopez was supposedly the mother of an eleven-year-old boy who'd been shot and killed by a rancher after the man mistakenly thought the boy held a gun. Shocking, terrible. Until you looked closely at the facts.

A portrait photo of the boy circulated in the media. It was one of the Watchers who realized that the child was similar to a child in a cereal commercial from two years before. Similar? Once you looked closely, you could see it was definitely the same boy. And was the actor's name Lopez? No, it was not. Once they noticed that, a lot of additional pieces fell into place. A photo of the ranch in the *Times* was clearly manipulated—a part of a tree's shadow was cropped. And the rancher in question was in the middle of a legal fight with none other than the *federal government* over their new restrictions on his access to a nearby local water source.

When you asked the number one question—who gained—the answer was right there to see.

Sofia Lopez was no more a grieving mother than Caterpillar was a ballet dancer. She was one of the Circle's agents. And someone had just found her address, phone number, and email. All were posted on the uncovered-agents thread.

Caterpillar got up, pacing through the house, feeling the rage building up in him. This was even worse than usual. The Circle and their agents cynically using the one thing that bonded everyone. Empathy. Who wouldn't sympathize with the pain of a grieving mother? Who wouldn't tear up at the thought of that sweet, smiling boy? How much was the bitch getting for her sob act? More money than Caterpillar would see in a lifetime. He went to the garage, glancing at the guns on the shelf. Got them just last week, and looking at them made him feel better.

He returned to his laptop and logged onto a website that let him send emails from a temporary address. He generated a new email address, a string of letters and numbers sent through the dark web, impossible to trace back to him.

Clicking the compose button, he took a second to figure out what he wanted to write. No need to be subtle. All caps. **WE KNOW WHERE YOU LIVE.** She'd get the message. He opened Google Street

View, found Sofia's address, and took a screenshot. A nice close-up shot of the bitch's house. He attached it to the email, and sent it to the email from the forum. Other Watchers would do similar things. They'd call her and threaten her, and she'd realize that she should never have taken the cabal's money.

He smiled, satisfied. He used to feel powerless, his life puppeteered by forces beyond his control. Since he'd started Watching, he'd wrestled his control back.

Switching to YouTube, he viewed a thirty-five-minute video of a popular Watcher, who outlined in detail how aborted fetuses were used to produce food for cattle in Florida. He repeatedly said that his viewers shouldn't trust him. They should do their own research.

That was part of what Caterpillar loved with the Watchers. Unlike the media and politicians, none of them insisted that they had the monopoly on knowledge and expertise. Knowledge was everywhere. All you had to do was look and do your own research. First and foremost, you should trust yourself. This was how the Watchers protected themselves. They knew for a fact that the Circle had people in their forums and chats masquerading as Watchers. But these bastards couldn't do anything, because Watchers were trained to do their own research and never take the word of anyone else.

A headline on Fox News caught his attention. In a recent press conference, an NYPD police chief commended the efforts of his officers in arresting eleven suspects in a drug-ring bust in Queens. Quick quiz, ladies and gents: How many were reportedly arrested the day before?

That's right. Nine.

Had the police chief made an innocent mistake? Or was it a Freudian slip, acknowledging what Caterpillar had claimed the day before on the forum? That they'd arrested more than nine people, and that some of the people arrested "disappeared."

There was a rush when things clicked together. You didn't get it every day. Some days you were just piling unanswered questions, mismatched parts to that one-billion-piece jigsaw puzzle out there. But then a fact would align with a theory, and two unrelated events snapped with a third, creating one whole. And at that moment, you could glimpse how everything worked. The blueprints to your rotten civilization.

And you saw how one small group of people managed to manipulate everything, control the lives of everyone in this country, shaping world events.

It was as clear as day.

CHAPTER 5

Abby's flight back to New York was less than two hours long, and it was impressive how much discomfort and angst could be crammed into such a short time period. Her fellow passenger was both sweaty *and* talkative, which seemed somewhat unfair, because a person should really choose. And how could anyone even get so sweaty in January, in a freezing air-conditioned airport? It was a mystery.

The entire flight was accompanied by turbulence, and every few minutes the plane seemed to plummet about a thousand feet, leaving Abby's guts way up in her throat. And Mr. Sweaty would giggle and say, "Now *that* was a big one," every single time. He asked the flight attendant for some tomato juice halfway through the flight. When she handed it to him, another bit of turbulence hit, and half the tomato juice ended up in Abby's lap.

When they finally landed, Mr. Sweaty bid her farewell in a manner that hinted they were best friends now, and for one ghastly second, Abby thought he was about to hug her. And then, when she'd left the infernal plane behind her, it took her over thirty minutes to remember where she'd parked her car.

She was about to burst into tears at any moment.

Steve, her ex-husband, called as she was driving out of the airport and told her that he would drop the kids at her place and fix them dinner. So she could drive straight home and not worry about it. It was a surprising, thoughtful gesture, and due to Abby's fragile state of mind, it made her recall some of their better times together.

Finally home, she hauled her carry-on out of the trunk of her car. It weighed about ten pounds more than it had before, after she'd stuffed all the papers she'd gotten from Norman into it. She planned on going through everything later that evening.

She opened the door, and for a moment stood in the doorway, blinking. Samantha and Ben sat on either side of Steve on the couch, and he was showing them something. It seemed like something from a different life, one in which she'd never divorced, their family still intact. They all raised their heads as she stepped in, and Ben bolted from the couch, running to hug her.

"Mommy!"

She smiled and knelt to hug him, the last few hours momentarily forgotten. Being hugged by her boy was still one of the best things in the world, and she was aware that this experience would dwindle in the coming years. He was eight, hurtling toward his teens. How many more years of hugs did he have in him? One, possibly two? Better enjoy them while they lasted.

He finally drew back and began speaking excitedly. This was a habit of his, whenever he came back home after spending a few days at his father's house. He needed to bring Abby up to speed regarding every moment she'd missed. Unfortunately, his excitement always led to the collapse of grammar and punctuation, making his speeches somewhat incomprehensible. In addition, he loved walking in circles as he talked, which always made Abby dizzy.

". . . and then Dad took us for ice cream and I chose chocolate and the park was full of ducks and bread I gave them and then a swan came but I didn't have any more and I thought that he would cry but Daddy said that they have peanuts for brains and it was this big and jumped and then I found a rock I still have it I'll show you it's oh and then . . ."

"That sounds very exciting," Abby said, making her way to Sam, who now stood up as well. "Hey, sweetie." She gave her a hug. A mother-and-fourteen-year-old-daughter hug, which was awkward, rigid, and far from satisfying.

"Hey, Mom," Sam said. "How was your flight?"

The question brought Mr. Sweaty back to Abby's mind. "Pretty awful—there was a lot of turbulence. It's good to be home. And how was your stay at your dad's?"

"It was fine." Unlike her brother's, Sam's summaries were concise. Perfect grammar, though.

"Anything interesting happen at school?"

"Not really. Oh, some big shot from the police came by today, to give us a lecture about drugs. Maybe you know him." She paused. "I don't remember his name."

"He must have made quite an impression on you, then. Was it a good lecture?"

Sam shrugged.

Abby sighed and glanced at Steve. "Thank you for dropping them off."

"Sure." His expression was strange, also something from the past. He hadn't looked at her like that in a long time. A photo album sat in his lap—their wedding album. That was what he'd been showing the kids when she'd gotten home.

"You're looking at old photos?" she asked.

Steve glanced down at the album and snapped it shut. "Yeah, um . . . Sam wanted to see some old photos. And I remembered where you kept the albums. I hope that's okay."

It wasn't, not really. She didn't like the idea of Steve poking into her stuff. But she was tired and confused, and he did really help her with the kids, so she just smiled. "Sure."

She turned toward the kitchen. "I really need a cup of tea. Do you want one, too, Steve?" She left the rest of the sentence, *before you leave*, hanging unsaid.

"No thanks," he said behind her.

Her favorite mug was on the counter, not in its usual place. She grabbed it.

Steve's voice, suddenly urgent, came from behind her. "Oh, hang on, Abby—"

A *thing* inside the mug. A hairy *thing*. A mouse, eyes open wide, mouth ajar, poised to leap. She screamed, letting the mug drop onto the counter. It fell sideways as she scrambled back, her mind blank. The mouse, surprisingly, stayed inside the mug.

Both Steve and Ben showed up in the kitchen.

"Sorry, Mom," Ben said, looking guilty. "I was thawing Pretzel's meal, and I couldn't find the regular plastic box."

"Guh," Abby commented. Pretzel was Ben's pet snake. He ate mice, which were kept frozen in the fridge, next to the regular human food. Because Abby's life was a series of terrible compromises.

"He wanted to put it in one of his cereal bowls," Steve explained. "Can you believe it? But then I found this chipped mug in the cupboard, and I told him he could use this instead."

Her favorite mug. She'd gotten it from her mom. Perfect shape, perfect size, the lip of the mug not too thick or too thin. Yes, it was chipped; that was what happened when you used the same mug almost every single day for years. Her. Favorite. Mug.

"It's okay, right, Mom?"

"Yes, of course it's okay." Abby's voice was so brittle she thought Ben would certainly notice.

But he didn't. The obliviousness of youth. "You know what Dad calls them?" Ben asked. "Mousicles. Isn't that good? Like Popsicles, but—"

"Ben, I think your mom needs a moment of peace," Steve said. "Why don't you go feed your snake."

"I'll wash the mug later, Mommy, I promise."

"No need," Abby said faintly. "I think you can use it from now on." It used to be her favorite mug. Now it was a mouse-thawing mug.

"Sorry," Steve said when Ben left. "I was about to warn you. Good thing I stopped him from putting it in a cereal bowl, huh?"

"They ate dinner, right?" Abby's patience was gone.

"Yeah, I made spaghetti. I suggested that he could thaw the mouse in the microwave, but he said you don't allow it."

He wasn't leaving. And for some reason he kept talking. What was he—

She now realized what the expression on his face was, and why it looked so familiar. She hadn't seen that face in years. Not since she'd found out about the affair. This was his apologetic expression. He'd messed up somehow. And this wasn't about the mouse.

She folded her arms and looked at him.

He wilted under her stare, his shoulders sagging. "I should tell you something."

"Uh-huh."

He glanced behind him, as if to reassure himself that none of the kids were nearby, then lowered his voice. "Sam asked me why you flew to North Carolina."

Abby's gut tied itself in knots. "And what did you tell her?"

"I told her what you told me, that it was related to a case."

"Good."

"But she . . . do you know that thing she does? Like how she says the right thing, and makes this weird face, and keeps . . . I don't know. Keeps making you talk? And she can get you to tell her stuff . . . I think our daughter might have Jedi powers."

"She doesn't have Jedi powers," Abby said through gritted teeth. "What did you tell her, Steve?"

"I might have said that you were born in North Carolina," Steve said wretchedly.

"Okay . . ."

"And that something terrible happened to you when you were a child. I figured that could be the reason you went there, right? The memorial of the Wilcox—"

Abby slammed her hand on the counter. "You told Sam I was born in the Wilcox cult?" she hissed.

"No! As soon as I realized she didn't know about it, I shut up, I swear. But she became really weird after, and kept asking to see old photos." He spread his hands helplessly. "I always assumed you told the kids about it. You said you'd tell them when they were older."

Abby turned away, the tears that had threatened to show up finally materializing. "I didn't tell them yet."

"You really should have, Abby." A shift in his strategy and tone there. No more apologetic Steve. Now he was patronizing, reprimanding Steve. Oh god, this was really not the time. Not in the kitchen, next to all these sharp knives.

"I'll tell them when I decide to," she said through gritted teeth.

"I don't like keeping secrets from my—"

She whirled at him, and her stare made him clamp his mouth shut. Good. She apparently could still do that when she really needed to.

"I'm really sorry, Abby," he finally said again.

This reminded her of how much she *hated* Steve's useless apologies.

"Fine," she said. "I'll handle it."

"Okay." There was a short pause. "I swear, she's a Jedi Knight. She was like, *These are not the droids you're looking for,* and I was like—"

"Thanks for dropping the kids off, Steve," Abby said.

"Yeah. Good night, Abby."

She heard him say goodbye to the kids, and then the front door opened and closed. Then she let out a shuddering breath. She could really use a cup of hot tea right now.

But first she'd have to choose a new favorite mug.

CHAPTER 6

The tweet from the NYPD's chief of detectives showed up at exactly half past seven in the evening. Caterpillar noticed it just three minutes later.

It was seemingly innocuous, the kind of random tweet that a sleepy Alice would never even give a second glance. It read, *During the holliday nine suspects involved in drug ring Caught by our joint drug enforcement force.*

But, of course, it had to do with that arrest that had initially caught Caterpillar's attention. And when he scrutinized it, he realized it had two mistakes in it. *Holiday* was misspelled, and *caught* was capitalized. Two mistakes in one tweet.

Sure, everyone made spelling mistakes. Caterpillar wasn't any different. But was he expected to believe that the NYPD's chief of detectives made *two* mistakes in the same public statement? This was a man who had people whose *entire job* was to proof his public statements.

These mistakes had to be intentional. A signal.

Excited, he opened the forum browser tab, set to post about it, then hesitated.

It was common knowledge that the forum had been infiltrated by agents. There were threads discussing it, even sometimes downright accusations of this or that forum member. If he posted his discovery too soon, exposing his hand to the cabal, they would change course, leaving nothing but fog in their wake.

No, this might be too important.

Instead, he opened a private chat he had with a handful of Watchers. A group they'd formed a few months before that he trusted implicitly. He pointed out the tweet, and the strange mistakes, and asked what they thought it meant.

It was 7:38 p.m.

Dennis's room smelled of feet and mildew and food gone bad. He wanted to open the window, but a stack of boxes full of papers blocked the way. Dad had said he'd move them somewhere else, but that was three days ago, and it still hadn't happened. Nor would it happen anytime in the near future, Dennis knew. When his father placed his things somewhere, they stayed there. Just like the pile of newspapers at the foot of his bed. Or the tangle of cables on his desk. Or the bags with the old clothes on the floor. Or the empty plastic containers behind him.

Dennis sat hunched by his desk, staring at the laptop. To his right was a pile of boxes full of his own old toys, which his father refused to throw away. To his left, a pile of leaflets that he had accidentally knocked down, which was slowly scattering all over the room. He had, he estimated, eleven inches of extra space to move around in.

He was used to sitting hunched.

One of his old friends had posted an image on Instagram of himself eating at Wendy's with a bunch of guys from class. Most of them used to be Dennis's friends when he was younger. Now he was fourteen, and they didn't text him or talk to him anymore. When had they started avoiding him? Glancing at each other with meaningful stares when he invited them over?

It had been a year, for sure. Maybe two.

He coughed, a series of dry coughs, the dust in his room tickling his throat. What was that smell? It drove him insane. It was probably more than one thing.

A message popped up on one of his chats. His other life. His online life, where no one knew who he was or about his dad. No one ever saw his house, the yard with the tumbling piles of garbage, his own room and its slowly diminishing space. No one even knew how old he was. For them, he was another Watcher, his nickname Dormouse.

It was their private group, an excited message from Caterpillar, his fellow Watcher. He had found something. Two mistakes in one tweet. Dennis's interest was piqued. He completely agreed with Caterpillar's assessment. This *couldn't* be accidental.

But unlike his room, Dennis could organize it. Find the patterns that were there. He was good at it. As far as he knew, there was no one better.

A message had been encrypted in the tweet. A message meant for some people, invisible to others. What was it?

He ran the tweet through a few decrypters, trying to see if there was a simple code there, but found nothing. Then he focused on the two words with the mistakes. Those were the words that the chief of detectives was underlining.

Holiday. Caught. What was special in these two words?

He needed to pee. The bathroom was down the hall from his room, only a few steps away in a regular world. But in his home he would have to roll the chair carefully back so that he could extract himself. Then circle around the bags of clothes, trying not to slip on the flyers that were strewed on the floor. Open the door—it didn't really open all the way, there was a box blocking it, but enough so he could wedge himself out. Then walk down the hall, flattening himself to the left wall because the right wall was stacked with milk and egg cartons. If he knocked those down, his dad would freak, and he'd have to stop and restack them before resuming his journey. Then move the stack of newspapers that blocked the door to the bathroom, effectively blocking the hallway but enabling him to enter the bathroom.

He could hold it in for a while longer.

Holiday. Caught.

There were scrambled words hidden within those words. He unscrambled them, creating order in chaos.

Idaho and Utah. Two states.

He posted it in the group's chat. He'd decrypted the message. The time was 7:43 p.m.

◆ ◆ ◆

Alma didn't believe in conspiracy theories. They struck her as idiotic. Flat-earthers? Those crazy people who bought into David Icke's shape-shifting reptilians? You wouldn't catch her believing any of that crap.

She hadn't been interested in the Watchers either. Not at first. Not until she'd found out about the children.

It started when she'd watched that documentary about the sex trafficking of children. She'd cried all week, thinking about that. Then, when she talked to one of the other mothers on the school board, the mother mentioned the cabal, explaining that they were behind the majority of the sex trafficking, and that it *went on right under their noses.* Alma rolled her eyes, but her friend smiled and said, "Don't take my word for it. Do your own research."

That caught Alma's attention. Who in this day and age told you to make up your own mind? Everyone wanted you to adopt *their* mindset, their way of thinking.

So Alma did her own research. About the cabal, nicknamed the Circle, and the Watchers. Finding YouTube videos and articles and flowcharts and lectures. She'd spent five or six hours every day, for weeks, reading about it, doing her own research. And to her horror she found out that it was true.

But there was a silver lining. She could fight it. Alongside other people who'd found out the truth.

She finished cleaning up after dinner, trying to ignore her son's argument with her husband about playing the Xbox in the evening. Her phone blipped, then blipped again. She checked it, read the messages from Caterpillar and Dormouse.

Utah and Idaho? That rang a bell.

She went over to the computer. Her daughter was watching a video about making slime. Truly the pinnacle of humanity—the development of computers, photography, the internet, all so that her daughter could spend her time learning how to create slime at home. As if slime was a desirable effect and not something you wanted to avoid.

"Honey, I need the computer."

"The video is almost over."

It was not almost over. There were seven minutes of slime to go.

"I need it for something important."

"This is important."

Alma inhaled through her nose. "Get off the computer. *Now!*"

Her daughter got up and stomped away furiously. Alma sat by the computer and opened her document. It was password protected. The Circle had hackers who could steal your files, and Alma wasn't taking chances.

She entered the password, and scanned the list. Utah and Idaho. A girl had disappeared in the mall in Utah two weeks ago. A boy had never come home from school in Idaho over six weeks ago.

Two children missing. And now a Circle agent hinted at those cases.

This was a message to the Circle's customers. The people who bought children for sex. This explained why they used the public platform of Twitter.

Her heart thumped as she copied the links to the related news articles and pasted them on the group's chat under her own alias—Red Queen. It was 7:48 p.m.

◆　◆　◆

Zachary sat in front of his laptop, in his bathrobe. He hadn't worn actual clothes in three days. The perks of being unemployed. He ate potato chips, oily crumbs dropping from his lips and fingers onto his exposed stomach, while watching his own latest video.

On screen, a woman groaned as a man pounded her from behind. The man was a porn actor. Zachary didn't really care who it was. The woman was Natalie, who had sat across from him in high school four years ago, during English classes.

Natalie didn't know about this video. In fact, if anyone would have asked her, Natalie wouldn't recall having sex with this man at all. Because she hadn't.

The video was a product of what people called "deepfake." A video that Zachary had created using random porn and several pictures of Natalie from their yearbook and from her Instagram page.

It was one of his best so far.

He had one for most of the girls who had gone to school with him. For some of them, he'd created several.

One day, when he finished creating his collection, he'd send his videos to every guy from school. Maybe he'd also send them to the girls. And to the girls' parents. It would be his ultimate revenge for the way those bitches treated him all those years ago.

Ever since getting fired, he spent all his time creating lots of these videos, as well as doing his own research about the Circle, those bastards who controlled everything. The Circle, he knew, had gotten him fired. Several of the Watchers agreed with him. The cabal got people fired all the time. Those people had reasons to get the unemployment rates up. For them, he was a statistic. A number in their damn spreadsheet.

But he would expose them. He would get his vengeance.

Then again, he almost had to thank those assholes. Being at home had prodded him to start his own side business. Say a guy got ditched by his girlfriend. And he was pissed. All he had to do was send Zachary a few photos, and Zachary would create a nice video for him. His ex-girlfriend with two men. Or six men. Or women. Whatever. As long as the dude paid, Zachary would deliver the goods. For a small fee, Zachary would also upload the videos to a bunch of porn sites.

Revenge paid better than working at Walmart.

His phone kept bleeping. Zachary picked up a few crumbs from his belly with his finger, licking them one by one. Then, still sucking his fingers, he checked the messages. According to his friends in the Watchers group, the Circle was signaling to their pedo customers that two kids were up for sale. Psychos. The question was where and when. When was easy. There had been chatter in the forum that something big was about to happen on January 9, which was the very next day, at 11:00 a.m. It had to be this.

But where?

He checked the Twitter feed of that cop. Right there online for the world to see, and no one lifted a finger.

It was then that his eye caught a tweet from just two hours before by the same guy. *Went to Christopher Colombus High today to talk about the dangers of drug abuse. Our future is our children.*

Another spelling mistake there. It was *Columbus*, not *Colombus*. And the tweet was posted exactly two hours before. Two hours. Two children. *And* he ended the tweet with the word *children*. A few months ago, Zachary wouldn't have given it a second thought, but he now knew how these guys communicated. He was familiar with their codes.

He typed excitedly to the rest of his group. They were five— Caterpillar, Red Queen, Dormouse, Jabberwocky, and of course himself.

He'd chosen the best nickname—Hatter. As in the Johnny Depp version, the badass creepy one, not the dumb, fat, Disney-cartoon version.

They had their location. Christopher Columbus High.

A high school. And in the city, no less. Zachary thought about it. About his own high school. About the girls, and the way they'd treated him. He wondered about Christopher Columbus High. Would it be the same? Full of stuck-up teenage girls?

He imagined barging in there. Kicking down doors, his friends backing him up. Yeah. His lips curled in a smile.

We should check it out, he wrote.

On the monitor, a final groan, Natalie's face a mask of ecstasy. The time in the corner of the monitor was 7:56 p.m.

◆ ◆ ◆

Caterpillar's heart pounded as he tapped on his phone excitedly. They'd cracked it! They'd figured out the message.

A high school. Typical Circle strategy, twisted and inhuman. Bring their pedophile customers into a school full of children. Probably to whet their appetites before the actual sale, then jack up the prices. Perhaps the Circle would even suggest further transactions—a kid from the school for an additional hefty fee. Nothing was impossible with these people.

This was a once-in-a-lifetime opportunity to unmask the Circle. If they could interrupt the trade, save the kids, maybe catch the agent who intended to sell them, then everyone would finally see that the Watchers had been right all along.

They couldn't tell the police. The Circle practically owned the police. Hell, the message came from the NYPD brass.

He could post about it in the forum, but then the cabal would know that they'd found out, and they'd call it off, take the kids somewhere else.

No, Hatter was right. They had to check it out themselves. The school was only two hours away. He could drive there tomorrow morning, scope it out. Maybe someone from the group would join him. They all lived in the vicinity—that was one of the purposes of this specific group. A cell of Watchers who lived close enough to help each other in person, if needed.

He asked them. Both Hatter and Red Queen said they could be there. His eyes went to the bag on the floor. The guns. Just for safety.

They had deciphered the secret message and had an action plan.

It was 7:59 p.m. Less than half an hour since the NYPD chief had tweeted about the arrest.

CHAPTER 7

Sam lay on her stomach on the bed, head resting on her right arm. She gazed at Keebles, her dog. The white Pomeranian spitz crouched, tense, her eyes locked on the crack underneath Sam's dresser. She'd been frozen in that pose for the past ten minutes. Sam knew what she was looking at. Five days ago, Sam had been eating M&M'S in her room. One red M&M had dropped and rolled underneath the dresser. Keebles had been eyeing that M&M ever since, waiting for it to roll out again. So far, it hadn't obliged. But Keebles could wait.

As she often did, Sam wished she were a dog, with dog problems. The main concerns being when the next meal would show up, if there would be a walk soon, and what her nemesis, the vacuum cleaner, was up to.

Instead, Sam struggled with a secret her parents were keeping from her.

She'd known for a while there was something. If you paid attention, you noticed the little things. A moment of silence and furtive exchanged glances when she'd asked Grandma about Mom's biological parents. The way Mom touched the scar on her neck when Sam asked her about her childhood. The time Sam needed baby photos of her parents for school, and only Dad had one.

Lately there had been other things. In the past weeks, Sam had awakened three times in the middle of the night because of her mom's screams. Each time it had been a nightmare, which her mom persistently claimed she didn't remember. Or her mom would be in the bathroom, and when Sam listened carefully, she could hear her crying.

And whatever it was, Sam knew that the adults in her life all kept it from her. Tiptoeing around the edge of something that shouldn't be mentioned.

Here was the thing. When no one talked, when the truth was kept from you, then every terrible thought, every speculation, became a possible reality. Maybe her mom didn't want to talk about her biological parents because they'd died from a genetic disease, one that her mom had recently found she was carrying. Maybe her mom hadn't been adopted at all—she'd been kidnapped by Grandpa, and the police had finally caught on to him. Sam spent hours every night conjuring up nightmarish scenarios, drawing and painting them in her mind, until she felt as if her rib cage were being crushed.

And then that trip to North Carolina. The moment her mom had talked about it for the first time, Sam could feel something was off. First of all, since when did her mom leave the state for a police case? Come to think of it, since when did her mom even work on a case? Mom was in charge of the NYPD's crisis intervention training. Sure, they'd call her to manage an active crisis, but not to investigate a case. The whole thing stank.

Keebles suddenly tensed, probably reacting to something the elusive red M&M did.

Sam grinned at her dog's alert pink tail. She'd colored it a few months ago, and the result was so adorable that she'd kept it up. Once she even thought of sprinkling glitter on it, but Mom had a fit, saying that the glitter would end up all over the house. Which was probably true, but it would have been *so* worth it.

"Keebles!" Sam called her.

The dog swiveled in that manner that only Keebles could, a complete 180-degree turn in one millisecond. Then she hopped onto the bed, sniffing Sam's cheek, her nose wet and cool.

Sam scratched behind Keebles's ear. "Who's a good girl? Who is it? Who's a very good girl?"

Keebles stared at her in fascination, enthralled by the mystery. Someone in this room was a good girl. A *very* good girl. Who could it possibly be?

"You are! You are a good girl!"

Keebles did a little dance, tail wagging, tongue happily lolling. Apparently she was the good girl. This was the best outcome she could have hoped for.

Sam sighed again. If only she were a dog.

If Sam had had any suspicions regarding the North Carolina trip, they'd ballooned once she'd mentioned it to her dad. He'd broken eye contact almost immediately, fidgeting like Ben sometimes did when her mom caught him taking his vile spider somewhere he wasn't allowed to. It was just a matter of getting the truth from him.

After watching her mom do it endless times, Sam knew all the tricks. Repeat the last words Dad said back to him. Ask him endless open-ended questions. And Sam had tricks that Mom didn't. For example, if you told him he did something better than Mom, he instantly began talking. It was like magic. "Wow, Dad, you make spaghetti so much better than Mom," and BAM—you got a ten-minute lecture about how his friend from college taught him to make spaghetti, the secret was the basil and garlic in the sauce, and sure, Mom had other great qualities, which were never mentioned specifically. And from there, you just had to tug the conversation in the right direction.

It had taken Sam less than an hour. Mom had been born in North Carolina. And something had happened to her there.

With no specific details forthcoming, she was forced to let her imagination fill in the blanks again. She checked the time. Not late enough. Ben would still be awake, and her mom would never talk in front of him. Sam would have to wait for him to fall asleep. Because tonight, she was resolved to get some answers. To find out what had happened to her mom all those years ago.

CHAPTER 8

The suitcase, full of distant, painful memories, sat on the floor. Abby stared at it for a long minute, then hefted it onto the dining table and opened it.

The top item within it was the one she'd looked at last—the newspaper article with her father's picture. He stood smiling, bouquets of flowers behind him. He seemed tall, with a long, full beard and thick eyebrows. His eyes were soft, kind. The caption below read, David Richardson, owner of the local shop Magical Garden.

She tried to bring forth any memory of him. Perhaps she recalled a hug? A moment when they trimmed a bouquet together? She wasn't sure. She had such vivid memories from her childhood, but her father had somehow slipped through the cracks in her mind, leaving almost nothing behind.

She read the article for the fifth time since leaving Norman Lewis's home in North Carolina. It was a short piece, of the sort one would expect in a local paper, praising the colorful bouquets and David's kind disposition. The journalist mentioned that David was married and had one daughter. During his very short interview, her dad quoted the Bible, a quote she knew well. "Consider the lilies of the field, how they grow; they toil not, neither do they spin."

A quote favored by Moses Wilcox in his sermons.

She put the article aside, and slowly emptied the suitcase onto the table. She put the book about the Wilcox cult aside. Then she sorted the paperwork into different piles. Witness statements and interviews in one pile, various newspaper articles in the next, a third pile of police reports.

A very large pile of autopsy reports.

She counted the autopsy reports. Fifty-nine, like Norman had said. She read the names on each of the reports. Only thirty-three were positively identified. George Fletcher was fifth from the bottom. No autopsy report for another George.

She started with the interviews of the three survivors. The name on the top one was Abihail Richardson. That was the name Moses Wilcox had chosen for her, and it made her skin crawl. No one had called Abby by her birth name, Abihail, for years. No one, that was, until two months ago, when she'd met Eden again.

Skimming the first few lines of the transcript of her own interview, she tried to recall it. The words awoke no memory, no emotion. She'd apparently remained mostly silent, answering occasionally with monosyllables. A social worker had been present, and terminated the interview after a while. There was no follow-up.

She flipped the page, and a few photos tumbled out, catching her by surprise. She tried to catch them, managed to grab one clumsily, crumpling it slightly. The photos were part of the report detailing her injuries. The photo she held in her hand was a close-up of the burn on the back of her neck. She bent and picked up the other two. One was a photo of the backs of her hands, scratched raw in multiple places. Those scratches were a result of her frequent aggressive handwashing—a practice of the Wilcox cult.

The third photo was of her as a child, in the police station, sitting down, hands in her lap, staring at nothing. One of her ears protruded from underneath her golden-blonde hair, making her look even more helpless and lost. There was no official value to that photo; it didn't document anything physical, and there was no good reason for it to be in the report. It was as if the photographer, after taking the photo of her injuries, had glimpsed another, deeper hurt and tried to document it as well.

Putting down the photos, she opened the thickest folder in the pile. The initial report. She thumbed through it. A summary of fifteen pages describing that hectic night. A sketch of the scene. And a thick brown envelope. The envelope had multiple strips of tape holding it shut. At some point, Norman had probably decided to make sure that he would never be tempted to open it again. Abby held it in her hand, feeling its weight, already guessing what she would find inside.

She tore it open and carefully felt inside, her fingers sliding on the glossy paper. Photos. She took them out.

The first one was of the remains of the large room, debris everywhere, smoke and ashes curling in the air. And bodies. Dozens of broken, burnt bodies everywhere. The next photo was even worse—a close-up of an unrecognizable blackened body, discarded in the corner of the room. And then a third photo of several bodies piled up by a closed door. The next was a couple, charred beyond recognition, found in what could be a last embrace . . .

She shoved the photos back in the envelope, letting out a long, shuddering breath, her eyes tearing up. Damn it.

She couldn't let the past creep up on her like that. She would have to power through the paperwork, forcing herself to separate the documents from her memories, her grief and guilt. And to do that, she needed coffee. It was past ten in the evening, and she had three or four hours of work ahead of her.

She went to the kitchen and fixed a pot of coffee, knowing well that she'd regret it later. Once she'd finished with her night's work, she'd try to sleep, only to find that her mind was fully alert. Then she'd finally fall asleep at half past five in the morning, only to be awakened by the alarm clock. And then she'd have to go throughout the day feeling like hell, with her partner, Will, making endless *Walking Dead* jokes.

But the alternative was not drinking coffee, and that didn't sound fun at all.

She didn't want to go back to the dining room table. She could feel the stacks of papers on it looming behind her back. Instead, she poured herself a cup of coffee and sipped it, looking outside her window. A soft drizzle pattered on the sidewalk. She let herself think of nothing, filling her mind with the sound of rain. A brief moment of pleasant static.

But she couldn't keep the thoughts away for long, and they came crawling back. Something about the photos she'd seen bothered her. It jarred with her memories, feeling out of place. What was it? And where was the other George? Was he the man pretending to be Isaac for years? Why would he do that?

She took out her phone and opened her chat with "Isaac." A long chat, with hundreds, maybe thousands of messages back and forth. In the past weeks she'd scrolled through the chat several times, reading the messages, horrified and revulsed. Realizing how much information she'd given away to this impostor, thinking she was talking to a child-hood friend. And now that she knew the truth, she could see that the information went almost only one way. She would tell him about her life, and he would provide her comfort, ask her for details, almost never talking about himself. The perfect listener. She should have realized it years before. After all, as a police negotiator, she did the same every day. After they'd discovered the truth, both Abby and Eden had tried to message the other Isaac, the impostor. But he'd already realized that they'd figured out the truth. They'd told him they were coming to see him, after all. And he knew what would happen once they met the real Isaac. He ignored all their messages after that.

She wanted to prod him, to shock him out of his silence. She sent him an image of the memorial stone. Then she added the text, **one name missing.**

She waited for a minute for him to react, but nothing happened. The message had been sent, but there was no indication that he even saw it.

Putting the phone away, she turned back to the dining room, her heart leaping with fright as she glimpsed the figure standing there.

Oh, it was only Samantha.

Her daughter stood next to all those things from Abby's hidden past. She held a stack of papers in her hands.

No, no, no . . .

"Sam?" she said softly.

Sam raised her eyes from the page, meeting her stare blankly. It occurred to Abby that she hadn't heard Sam's creaking bedroom door, or the girl's usually loud footsteps. Had Sam sneaked out of her bedroom intentionally?

"I never knew that the Wilcox congregation had been dealing drugs," Sam said, her voice steady. She put the paper she'd been reading on the table—one of the newspaper articles that Norman had clipped and saved for all those years, covering the massacre. "I mean . . . I guess I knew they did something to draw the attention of the cops, but I never gave it much thought."

"Sam . . . it's late." Abby stepped over to the table.

"I wanted to talk," Sam said. "Hear about your trip." She put down the rest of the papers. The interview transcript with Abby—Abihail—from all those years ago. The photos of seven-year-old Abihail. Sam had homed in on the things that Abby had been looking through. At least she hadn't opened the envelope.

Abby stood in a verbal minefield. Another parent would have tried to lie, or feign anger, or play dumb. But Abby's negotiator instincts kicked in. If you had nothing to say, silence was probably best. Instead of saying anything, she picked up the autopsy reports and the brown envelope and placed them carefully in the suitcase. Whatever happened, she didn't want Sam looking at the countless photos of charred human bodies.

"This is you, right?" Sam tapped the photo.

"Yes," Abby answered softly. Sam had seen photos of her as a child before, though none of them this young.

"You were in the Wilcox congregation."

Abby met Sam's eyes. "The Wilcox cult. I was one of the survivors."

"Your name used to be Abihail?"

"Yes."

"Why did you change it?"

"Moses Wilcox named me when I was born. I started hating that name." Abby thought about it. "Also, teachers at school kept mispronouncing it, and kids made fun of it. I asked Grandma if I could change it, and she agreed."

"How old were you?" Sam kept her face blank, but Abby wasn't fooled. Behind that calm facade, a hurricane was brewing.

"I was seven, the night of the fire," Abby said.

"Seven," Sam echoed. "You always told me that you were adopted as a baby. That you didn't remember your biological parents."

"Twice," Abby blurted before she could stop herself.

"What?"

"I didn't *always* tell you that. I told you that twice." It was easy to remember. Because it was easy to remember when you lied so blatantly to your child. Not the harmless lie, telling them that Santa would find a way inside even though you didn't have a chimney. A lie that you knew was wrong. That you knew you'd one day regret.

"Does it matter if it was twice or twenty times? You let me think . . ." Sam shut her eyes and took a deep breath. Holding the torrent back. "Why didn't you tell me the truth?"

"At first you were too young, and then—"

"No. Don't bullshit me. There are ways to tell small kids about this. For example, you could say, *Mommy grew up in a bad family.*" Sam changed her voice, mimicking a sweet, patronizing tone. *"But then one night, there was a fire, and Mommy escaped, and Grandpa and Grandma adopted her, and they were all happy because Mommy finally found a family that loved her."*

"Okay," Abby said, her throat clenching.

"You told me how babies came into the world when I was *four*. You could have found a way to explain this. You're supposed to be good with words."

"I didn't want to talk about it."

"Let's talk about it now." Sam folded her arms.

"Okay, but lower your voice. I don't want Ben to wake up."

"God forbid he hears the truth."

"Sam, please."

"Okay, fine," Sam said, her voice quieting down.

"I was born in the Wilcox cult," Abby said. "We called it the Family. My parents were recruited in the late seventies. They married after joining the cult. The cult leader, as you probably already know, was named Moses Wilcox."

"Why did you say *recruited*? It's not the army."

"People almost never *join* a cult. They get recruited. They get manipulated, and are slowly pulled in." She saw the look in Sam's eyes. "I know how it sounds . . . you think that anyone who joins a cult is dumb. But that's very far from the truth. Cult leaders don't want dumb people. They want smart people that will help run the show. Your biological grandma was a pediatrician, and your grandpa was an engineer."

"Was it . . . like . . . horrible?"

"For some. Not for me. Some of it wasn't great. There were a lot of sermons, and Moses Wilcox made us wash our hands all the time. For hours. Until our hands bled."

Sam's eyes widened, tearing up.

"But I loved the people," Abby said. "And the cult gave me purpose. So it was a good feeling."

"What kind of purpose?"

"Sam, I don't think we should talk about all of this right now—"

"What kind of purpose, Mom?"

Abby sighed. "I was supposed to grow up and bear the Messiah's offspring. Supposedly they would have wings and protect us in the apocalypse."

Sam looked pale. "The Messiah . . . you mean Moses, right? He planned on using you like some sort of breeding, um . . ." Her lips trembled.

"Yes, but he never touched me," Abby said hurriedly. "The police found out about the drugs. There was a siege, and then the fire broke out. And everyone died."

Some truths could remain hidden forever. Sam would never know that *she* was the one who'd locked the room where the entire congregation was staying, following Moses Wilcox's instructions. That it was *her* fault they couldn't get out when the fire started.

Abby smiled at Sam, a broken smile. "And then Grandpa and Grandma adopted me, and we were all happy because Mommy found a family that loved her."

Sam didn't smile back. "I asked Dad why you went to North Carolina, and he wouldn't tell me. And you know, I asked Dad about your adoption once, and he told me to ask Mom."

"I told him that when you grew older—"

"And Grandma straight up lied to me once. I asked her how you were when you were a baby, and she said you were very sweet."

"Look, Sam—"

Sam clenched her fists. "You didn't just lie to me. You told everyone else to lie to me. I'd expect lies from *you*. But Dad? And Grandma?"

Abby felt like Sam had punched her in the gut. "You talk like I lie to you every day," she said, her voice trembling.

"Close enough."

"I don't lie. Except for—"

"I ask how was your day, and you say it was fine, but I can see that it wasn't. I ask why you and Dad broke up, and you say you just didn't love each other anymore, and that's bullshit; even Dad told me about his affair. When Grandpa had a heart attack, you told me at first that it was the flu—"

"Okay." Abby slammed her hand on the table. "I lie, okay? I'm not perfect. Sometimes I lie."

Sam stared at her in disgust, a tear running down her cheek. Then she whirled and walked away.

"Sam."

Sam closed her bedroom door behind her. She didn't even slam it. She wasn't throwing a tantrum. It was the real thing.

CHAPTER 9

Christopher Columbus High School was a somber rectangular structure that brought back memories from Caterpillar's own school days. Orange-brown walls, windows with thick iron grilles and dusty panes. The few students he glimpsed had the shell-shocked faces that came with the realization that the holidays were behind them.

He circled the school a few times, examining the layout. Three stories; the windows on the bottom floor were barred. There were a few entrances to the school, but all of them were shut. In the back, the school's yard and basketball court were fenced.

He drove farther before parking the car a few blocks away. He switched off the engine and took out his phone. The chat already had a few new unread messages, and he skimmed them. Red Queen and Hatter were here already. He tapped a response, telling them where he was, and asked them to come over to his car. There was no need to tell them to be careful, to make sure they weren't followed.

He waited, scanning the street, checking the mirrors. He felt exposed, wished he had tinted windows. Every passerby could be a Circle lookout or an agent who'd somehow followed him. He fought his instinct to hunch in his seat, and leaned back, twiddling with the radio. There. A couple walking toward him. The man pointed at his car, the woman nodded, and they hastened their steps. Caterpillar's hand went to his pocket, feeling the reassuring presence of his gun.

The man opened the front passenger door and slid inside, the woman joining them in the back.

"The Circle cannot reach us," the man said.

Caterpillar swallowed, his throat dry. He completed the phrase. "They can't stop what's coming."

"Caterpillar?" The man offered his hand. "I'm Hatter."

It was strange, meeting Hatter for the first time. In a way, they were already very close friends. They chatted with each other every day. Hatter was one of the strongest people that Caterpillar knew. Fired from his job for no apparent reason, handed one injustice after another, he'd still managed to land on his feet, and now had a lucrative job as an independent video editor. He was loyal, and he knew who his friends were. And who were his enemies.

"Good to finally meet you." Caterpillar shook the man's hand. Hatter's grip was strong; he was one of those people who thought you had to squeeze hard when you shook. He was large, hair cropped short, with a thick, wet lower lip. He seemed younger than Caterpillar had thought he'd be, perhaps in his early twenties. When Caterpillar's hand was finally released, it was clammy.

"And you're the Red Queen," Caterpillar said, glancing backward.

Red Queen often seemed timid on the forum, but Caterpillar wasn't fooled. When they talked about what the Circle did to children, she would work herself into a rage. Her descriptions of what she'd do to those men if she could find them often made him smile.

He clumsily twisted his hand to shake hers, and she took two of his fingers, smiling, looking tense. She was about his age, midforties. She was blonde, her nose weirdly small and sharp, like a tiny pencil. She wore bright-red lipstick, hoop earrings, a thick pearl necklace.

"I can't believe we're finally meeting," she said. "You can call me Alma."

Alma smiled at Caterpillar. He had a kind face, and she felt relieved. When she'd met Hatter earlier, she'd instantly felt intimidated by his brusque and hostile demeanor, and was worried that Caterpillar would be the same. But Caterpillar seemed almost gentle. Fluffy chestnut-brown hair and matching warm brown eyes.

She'd known Caterpillar for over a year, and they'd shared many intimate conversations. Despite his acting tough in the forum, she knew he was a gentle soul. His wife had left him not long ago, shattering his heart. He refused to talk about it, and Alma could feel how much it had hurt him. Perhaps, now that they'd finally met, she could help him open up about it, get it off his chest.

"You know," Hatter growled, "we use nicknames for a reason. Telling us your name is stupid and careless."

"Sorry," Alma instinctively said. "But, I mean . . . now that we finally meet in person, I can see who you are. I can trust you. It's not like you're Circle agents."

"It's not *about* that," Hatter snapped. "What if they capture us? They could torture us. We can't divulge what we don't know, right?"

"You're right; I didn't think about that," she said meekly.

He was absolutely right, but he didn't have to be so mean about it. She didn't like Hatter, though she did her best not to let it show. His posts on the forum were always a bit creepy. Whenever they exposed a female Circle agent, he would call her the c-word. And he'd once said about one of them that she "deserved to be raped." Someone told him that was out of line, and Hatter pointed out that the Circle did that to kids, so they surely deserved the same. It had devolved into a very loud argument, and he hadn't said that again. But still. Alma remembered that.

"I checked out the school just before you came," Caterpillar said.

"Yeah," Hatter said. "I walked by it earlier. I was just telling Alma that I figured out the best place to watch it from."

"Watch it?" Caterpillar said, surprised. "Aren't we going in?"

"They won't let us," Hatter said. His voice had a sharpness to it, and a drop of spittle shot from his mouth, spattering on the dashboard. He didn't seem to notice.

They were talking to each other, and she felt excluded from the conversation, in the back of the car. She agreed with Caterpillar. Those poor kids were in that school right now. She imagined them, scared, crying for their mothers, not knowing the horrible fate that might await them. Her heart clenched tightly. No. They had to go in. They couldn't let those children suffer a second more than what was necessary.

"I thought we should go in too," she said, in a half whisper.

"Look, like I said before, the front door is closed and there's a buzzer," Hatter said impatiently. "They won't buzz us in. The side doors will be locked. It's better to wait for the pedos to show up."

◆ ◆ ◆

Hatter's fists were clenched in his pockets. Something in Alma's voice grated on him. It was a sort of nagging, complaining voice. And why had the stupid cunt told them her name? Did she think they were playing a game?

He glanced backward at her. She was dressed like a grandma. Pearl earrings, baggy sweater. Fake-looking bright-red lipstick that did nothing to make her look better.

Hatter had always thought she was much younger. He'd imagined her around his age, and kinda hot, like that chick from the Tarantino movie. He liked talking to her on the forum, even if she sometimes got all huffy about something he said. But meeting her in real life turned out to be a disappointment.

"The pedophiles could be inside the school already," Caterpillar said. "We finally have some good intel. I say we go in, have a look around. If they don't let us in, we can find a good spot and wait."

Caterpillar, at least, acted like a pro. Hatter gave him a long look. The guy seemed sharp and focused. They were both among the more experienced Watchers in the forum, and Hatter was glad to have this man watching his back. Still, it wasn't like anyone had made Caterpillar boss.

"Look, I don't mind going in, but how are we going to do that?" he asked. "Knock on the door and just ask them to buzz us in?"

"Well, we can hang close to the front door," Caterpillar said. "I bet people go in and out all the time. Once they open it, all we have to do is just step inside. It's not like they'll tell us not to."

"That doesn't sound like much of a plan," Hatter said.

"Open the glove compartment," Caterpillar said. "There's something there for both of you."

Hatter frowned, then pulled it open. It took him a moment to figure out what he was looking at. His eyes widened. Two guns. He took one, felt its weight in his hand.

"Oh no," Alma blurted from the back. "We don't need those."

Hatter took the other one, held one in each hand. Imagined himself walking down the hallway, guns blazing. Behind him, Caterpillar and Alma, walking in step. Everyone fleeing as the three of them strode through the school, looking for some pedos to shoot.

"It's a last resort, just for protection," Caterpillar said. "We don't know how many there are."

"Yeah," Hatter said, heart beating fast, jaw clenched in a tense smile. "Yeah, okay, let's do it."

CHAPTER 10

September 26, 1988

The smell of fried chicken seemed to permeate the entire apartment, teasing Neal. It whispered tales of that crunchy surface, the juicy meat within, salty potatoes.

His stomach rumbled, and he wished, like he did every day, that his dad would get home already.

It was a strange, torturous routine. Neal was not allowed treats in the afternoon so that he wouldn't ruin his appetite before dinner. But they couldn't start dinner without Neal's father. Dinner was a meal that a family ate together. And there was no knowing when his dad would show up. Sometimes he'd be home by five, and on other days, he would arrive only after nine in the evening.

"Mom," he said piteously. "I'm *starving*."

"Your dad will be home soon." His mom smiled at him.

"Can't I have just a bit?"

"No, I want us to eat together."

He couldn't figure it out. They never talked as they ate. Maybe Dad would ask Mom to pass the salt. Or his mom would snap at him that he should sit up straight. But surely this was not what his mom had in mind.

"But, Mom—"

"How about we read a little more while we wait for Dad?"

"Okay," he agreed instantly before she changed her mind.

"Come on." She patted the couch by her side.

He jumped onto the couch, already burrowing into his mother's side. There was only one proper way to read with his mom. He snuggled under her arm, and she hugged him closer, enveloping him in her warmth. She leaned over to the table and picked up their book, flipping the pages.

"Where were we?" she asked.

"Alice became very small, and then she ran away from the puppy." Neal shut his eyes, imagining Alice as she ran away through the tall stalks of grass. He could always imagine everything his mom read to him.

"Right." His mom scanned the page and began to read. Alice had just met a caterpillar smoking a hookah.

"What's a hookah?" Neal asked.

"It's a thing you smoke."

"Like cigarettes?"

"No . . . more like a pipe," his mom said vaguely. She cleared her throat and resumed reading. "'At last the caterpillar took the hookah out of its mouth and addressed her in a languid, sleepy voice.'"

"What's languid?"

"I think it means sort of sick."

"The caterpillar was sick?"

"No, I don't think so."

"Maybe he was sick because he was smoking. At school they said cigarettes can make you sick."

"Maybe. Now let me read. '"Who are you?" said the caterpillar.'"

His mother changed her voice when she did the caterpillar's voice, making it thick and booming. A shiver of delight ran up his neck. *This* was what he loved best when his mother read to him. The way she did the voices. He could already read himself, but it was difficult, and he couldn't do the voices like his mom did.

Mom kept reading, Alice and the caterpillar talking. Alice's voice was high and childlike, and the caterpillar sounded like Neal's gym teacher.

And then, halfway through their conversation, Dad came in. And the air in the room seemed to change.

Sometimes, once every week or two, when Dad came home, he was very angry. Neal could tell it instantly, by the way Dad slammed the door behind him, and how he would drop the bag on the floor. And also by the way his mom seemed to tighten.

"Hey, hon," she said, and her voice sounded almost like Alice's voice in the book. Too high. Not Mom's regular voice. "Glad you're home; dinner's waiting."

He ignored her, stepping into the kitchen. Neal heard the fridge open, then that sharp hiss as Dad opened a can of beer.

Mom stood up, and glanced at Neal mutely. He knew instinctively that dinner would wait for a bit longer. And that maybe tonight they wouldn't eat it together as a family after all. She went to the kitchen.

"How was work?" Neal heard her ask.

"I got fired."

"Why?"

"Cutbacks. It's bullshit. There were no cutbacks. *They* wanted me out. That's what happens when a guy insists on safety. They don't like that. I made things complicated for them."

Neal had heard that tone before. He didn't know who "they" were, but Dad would always snarl when he said it. Sometimes "they" wanted more taxes. Or "they" were turning the neighborhood into a shithole. Or "they" raised the rent because they were greedy.

"Maybe you should talk to your boss tomorrow," Mom said. "Tell him that—"

A sudden, muffled thud. A sharp cry from Mom. Neal curled into the corner of the couch.

"It's done!" Dad shouted. "Do you want me to crawl back there, let them step all over me? Is that what you think I should do?"

Mom didn't answer, and Dad kept hollering at her. Neal couldn't bear it. He snatched the book and ran to his room, shutting the door, hiding in his bed under the blanket. Even with the door shut, he could still hear his dad's muffled screams. They had screwed him. They wanted to humiliate him. He wouldn't give them the satisfaction.

Neal was terrified of them. He shut his eyes, listening to his dad's words, trying to imagine who they were, but he couldn't. It wasn't like the stories Mom read to him, images he could easily conjure in his mind. They remained in perpetual darkness, turning the country to hell, and hiring illegal immigrants, and stealing honest people's livelihoods, and ruining television, and turning Christmas into a way to take people's money.

Trying to shut away his father's screaming, he opened the book and began reading, each word an effort.

"Who are you?" said the caterpillar.

CHAPTER 11

Abby stared blurry eyed at her monitor, wishing she'd called in sick. Last night had been even worse than she'd initially predicted. After her conversation with Sam, she'd gone over the papers, but couldn't focus on anything. She kept thinking of things she should have said to Sam during their conversation, or things she should have said before she'd gone on that trip, or even before that. Years before. The Ghost of Christmas Past was apparently still hovering in January, and lacking mean-spirited rich men, it had chosen Abby to torment instead. After hours of reading police reports and interview transcripts, she'd shoved all the papers into her briefcase and gone to bed. There she spent a few more sleepless hours, planning and fine-tuning her conversation with Sam in the morning.

Which all amounted to nothing. When Abby had woken up that morning, after two hours of sleep, Sam had already been gone. She'd left a note that said that she would grab a ride to school with the parents of her friend Fiona. She didn't answer her phone.

Now Abby sighed and decided that she wouldn't get any proper work done this morning, no matter what. She rummaged in her bag and took out the brown envelope. She took out the photos and flipped through them again.

She'd done that several times last night, and though they were still painful to look at, it had become bearable. She went through them slowly, searching for whatever had bothered her the night before. Was it someone she recognized in the photos? Perhaps something missing?

She paused when she reached the photo of the bodies piled by the closed door.

A closed door. The memory flashed in her mind.

The door was just a few steps away, Abihail's hand already raised to remove the latch, to let them out.

A hand on her shoulder, yanking her back, twisting her.

She screamed in anger and fear, trying to pull away.

And then an explosion, the force of it thrusting her away, a sudden searing pain on the back of her neck, flames engulfing them . . .

The door had exploded. She remembered looking back. Seeing the blaze, Isaac dragging her away.

She took out the sketch of the scene from her bag. It was large and noted the triangulated location of each of the bodies within the mess hall and the kitchen. Four bodies were piled by the kitchen back door, lying inches from each other.

The kitchen back door.

Of course. There was a back door to the kitchen so that they could easily carry food inside and dump the trash. And the bodies were piled around it. They were trying to get out. But they couldn't. The door was locked.

In the past weeks, ever since she'd recalled the events from that night, she'd thought that she'd trapped the congregation in a room with no way out. But there *was* another way out, and someone else had locked it. In all probability, Moses Wilcox, just before he'd set the fire in the kitchen. And the entire congregation burned to death, except for the three surviving children.

And George, the missing name from the memorial. Where was George?

Perhaps he wasn't there. Though that made no sense. Everyone was accounted for. Fifty-nine dead, and three survivors. A total of sixty-two.

Unless there weren't fifty-nine dead. The gas canisters in the kitchen had exploded, leaving total chaos in their wake. It was possible that the medical examiner had made a mistake—the majority of autopsies were performed in the local morgue. They were not equipped to handle disasters like that. She'd skimmed the autopsy reports last night, but she'd have to do it again today, be more thorough.

She shook her head. Her mind was foggy; it was hard to think straight. She needed to talk this over with someone. She briefly considered Eden, but brushed the idea off. Her fellow survivor didn't want to remember that night again.

No. Someone else. Someone she trusted. Someone she could lean on.

CHAPTER 12

Detective Jonathan Carver struggled with the station's coffee machine. It was clogged yet again, third time this month. As far as Carver was concerned, the problematic coffee maker was the bane of the 115th Precinct—worse than the commander's obsession with paperwork, or the weird smell in the men's room, or even, y'know, crime in all its forms.

No one except Carver cleaned the damn thing; that was one of the problems. And it was about twenty years old. Carver couldn't figure out why the commander refused to get a new one. All cops needed a steady supply of caffeine to do their jobs.

He was unplugging the downspout hose when Dillard and Anderson stepped into the small kitchenette.

"Hey, Carver," Dillard said. "Did the coffee machine stop working again?"

Carver rolled his eyes. Dillard had a way of asking questions that should have been rhetorical, except he always waited for an answer. He grunted in response.

"Well? Did it stop working?"

"Yes, Dillard, it stopped working. Do you think I'm doing this for fun?"

"Well, no. I thought it stopped working."

Carver got the valve out and washed it in the sink, while Anderson and Dillard hovered behind him, waiting for the magical machine of life-giving fluid to resume working.

Carver's phone blipped. He inserted the valve again and glanced at the screen. A message from Abby. Hey.

He smiled. Hey :) How was your trip?

It was weird. Can we meet tonight? I need to talk to you about it

Sure!

He and Abby were taking it slow. Very slow. Almost sluggish, really. Though he wished things could move faster, he knew that Abby's entire life was in turmoil right now. For her, he was willing to wait with no demands of his own. They'd gone on a few dates. She'd invited him to dinner twice, once with her children. She'd introduced him as her date, blushing as she said so. Samantha, her fourteen-year-old daughter, had grinned at him, bemused, while the younger boy shook his hand, his face serious.

". . . don't want those crazies around a school," Anderson was saying.

"What crazies?" Carver asked, reattaching the hose. "MS-13 tagging the high school again?" The gang targeted one of the precinct schools and kept spraying the number thirteen on its walls. The commander had the patrols driving by every hour, but still the bastards kept coming back. It was like swatting away flies.

"Nah, not our schools," Dillard said. "Dispatch just got a notification from the feds. That crazy Watchers group decided there's child slavery going on in a high school up in the 109th."

"The Watchers?" Carver frowned. "What, those conspiracy theorists?"

"Yeah. Apparently there's been a lot of chatter in their groups about it this morning, and the feds are monitoring them," Anderson said. "They're worried some of them might show up in that high school. So now they're sending someone to check it. Like we don't have enough real problems without a bunch of nutjobs making shit up."

Carver screwed the back of the machine in place, frowning. "The 109th, huh? What's the high school's name?" Abby's daughter's high school was in the 109th.

"What was it? Christopher Columbus High?" Anderson asked Dillard.

Carver put the screwdriver down, feeling uneasy. "I gotta go."

"What about the machine?" Dillard asked. "Hey, Carver, what about the machine?"

But Carver was already on his way out. He was overreacting. It was probably nothing.

Probably.

CHAPTER 13

Anyone looking at them would think they were a couple of parents picking up their kid early. Or at least that was what Caterpillar hoped.

He and Alma stood in front of the school, a few steps away from the main door. The chill outside was nasty, a biting cold that crept down your collar and through your shoes, becoming a constant nagging ache. He wished he had a hat, or gloves, or thicker socks. Alma's nose and ears had turned pink, and she kept shivering.

How long had it been? Five minutes? Ten? Too long. Their plan wasn't working. He felt exposed. Whenever he put his frozen hand in his pocket, it'd meet the gun, cold and heavy. In the car, the gun made him feel powerful. Out here, if a cop stopped to frisk them . . .

They were a couple waiting for their kid, he reminded himself. And it was important; it would be worth it. He imagined the kidnapped children, held somewhere in this school. Perhaps the basement. And those desperate parents, just waiting to hear about their children. Had they lost hope? How would they feel when Caterpillar showed up with their kids, safe and sound? He imagined their faces, awash with gratitude. His hands on the kids' shoulders.

The school's main door opened, and a woman with square spectacles who was wrapped in a large coat stepped out. He moved instantly, as if he'd been walking toward the door all along, trying not to rush as the door began to swing shut. His eyes were fixed on the passage to the school. It shrank quickly, becoming a tiny gap, a crack.

He caught the door, his fingers shoved in the inch-thick crack, and smiled at the woman. She smiled back, hesitantly. He was ready to explain if she asked who he was. His son had gotten in a fight again. They'd called him, saying that he should pick him up. The words were already on his lips, a rushed, panicky speech.

She just took another look at Alma and him, and walked away.

He exhaled, his heart pounding in his chest. He could almost hear his own pulse, a steady thud . . . thud . . . thud. He pushed the door, holding it for Alma as she stepped through, taking her time.

And then Hatter was there, walking quickly, one hand in his pocket, joining them, the three of them inside, letting the door shut behind them.

He hadn't seen a school from inside for quite some time, the white-lit hallway, the somber brown-orange classroom doors, the line of lockers.

"Okay, we're here," Hatter said in a low growl. "Where to now?"

Where would the cabal be doing their business? The basement sounded likely, but maybe they'd do it in an unused classroom? Would they have the audacity to utilize the auditorium? He had no idea. For some reason he hadn't thought this far ahead. He'd assumed that once they were in, they'd see some clues. Furtive-looking men, hurrying somewhere. Perhaps children crying.

He looked around, then quickly lowered his face, heart thudding faster.

"Cameras," he whispered. "Keep your faces hidden."

"It doesn't look like anything's going on here," Alma said. "Maybe we should step outside."

"What did you expect?" Hatter asked, his voice gaining that sharp, ugly inflection again. "A sign that says *Pedo market this way?*"

They had to keep moving. "The security cameras," Caterpillar said. "If we can check the footage, maybe we can find them."

"And how do we do that?"

"We should check the secretary's office. I bet they monitor it from there."

"Oh yeah? And they'll just let us watch it?"

"We can check. If they ask us to leave, we'll get out."

He searched for someone to ask where the secretary's office was. Perhaps a student. His heart wouldn't stop thudding, and every thud vibrated somewhere in the school. A steady, powerful drumbeat.

◆ ◆ ◆

Thump . . . thump . . . thump . . . the steady beat of the drums vibrated in the music room as Samantha drew the bow across her electric violin. They'd been playing for the past hour, all the band skipping their classes to gain precious practice time. They were working on their cover of "Black Betty," one of Sam's own favorites. Usually when they practiced, her mind was consumed by the music, all her endless thoughts and anxieties gone, leaving behind the rhythm, the music.

This morning, her mind was too crowded, the thoughts clunking in her head, getting between her and the tune. She kept missing her cue, and her music was off.

Her mother had grown up in a cult. The Wilcox cult. She was one of the only survivors.

How had they kept it from her? Dad, Mom, her grandparents. For all those years? All those times she'd asked about her mom's biological parents, getting noncommittal responses or outright lies.

The beat of the drums shifted, turning chaotic, the tempo rushing forward to the tune of Sam's hectic thoughts. The fanatic cult. The night of the fire. Her mom, just a child, in the midst of it all.

She'd skimmed the book about the Wilcox cult she'd found in Mom's things. Then she'd googled it. Before last night, she'd known only the most basic facts. There was a cult, and almost all the members had died. Another horrid story like Jonestown or the Branch Davidians. Now she knew a lot more, maybe too much. About Moses Wilcox's many wives. About the cult members' fervent belief that the end of days was coming, and that Wilcox's many winged children would protect them in the holy war that would follow. About the night of the fire.

Mom had a burn scar on the back of her neck. When Sam had once asked her about it, Mom had said that she'd gotten it as a baby, before she'd been adopted. But that wasn't the truth, was it?

"Come on, Sam!"

The frustrated bark snapped her back into focus.

"Sorry," she blurted. Fiona and Ray stared at her. The blood rushed to her face. "I wasn't paying attention."

"It's *your* precious solo," Ray pointed out.

"I know! I'm all over the place today."

"Maybe we can try doing the guitar solo instead," Ray suggested.

Sam exchanged glances with Fiona, their drummer. Fiona rolled her eyes and stuck up her drumstick like an enormous middle finger pointed at Ray. "*Enough* about the guitar solo, Ray?" she said. "Our version has a violin solo after the drum solo—that's the whole point? Otherwise we're just another dipwad band playing the same forty-year-old hit?"

"Fi, shut up, no one asked—"

"Suck my stick, Ray?" Fiona managed to perform a deeply obscene gesture with her drumstick. "Can we just play?"

Sam grinned at Fiona, who winked at her and hit her sticks together, setting the tempo. One-two-three . . .

◆ ◆ ◆

"Sir," the woman said, her voice laced with contempt. "I can't help you. I don't even understand what it is you want."

Caterpillar's jaw was clenched tight. Both his hands in his pockets, the right one clutching his gun. The secretary was probably in her fifties, black hair with strands of gray, lips pursed in dissatisfaction. She could help them save lives with a few taps of her fingers, but she preferred to admonish him as if he were one of the school's students.

Behind her, he could see out the window to the street. The office was on the top floor; it had been easy to find once the student they asked had pointed the way.

"Look, I told you." He kept his voice low, controlling his temper. "We've been monitoring communications of a criminal group, and we have reason to believe that they're using *this* school—"

"Are you with the police?"

"No, ma'am, we're an independent organization. We just need you to check the security cameras and—"

"I just did before you walked in here. I saw nothing out of the ordinary."

Was she lying? Playing dumb? He thought of the kids crying somewhere in this school. He had no time for this bullshit. "We would prefer to be the judge of that. If you can show us the footage, we'll be on our way."

"If you want to see the footage of your child, you need to submit a request, and we'll get back to you."

"Maybe we should leave," Alma said nervously behind him.

Was the secretary working with them? Or one of the many manipulated by them? How could he tell? "You don't understand; this isn't about any one child."

"Thelma, are these people bothering you?" a gruff voice asked.

Caterpillar glanced behind him. A large man wearing a brown jacket had entered the room, eyes narrow, suspicious. A teacher? Or perhaps someone from the school's security? Caterpillar felt a tug of panic. Was *he* working with them?

"No, Mr. Ramirez, it's fine. I think they were just leaving."

"Yes," Alma said.

"No," Hatter snarled. "We weren't." He walked around the desk, towering above the secretary. "Show us the damn security footage."

She looked up at him in shock and fear. "I'm sorry, but—"

"Show us!" Hatter roared.

Ramirez hollered, "Hey, get the hell out—"

Alma shouted something. Caterpillar stood frozen, eyes wide, fingers squeezing the gun's grip. Hatter moved fast, hand arcing, smacking the secretary hard, the gun cracking against her head. She gasped, falling from her chair. Ramirez moved forward, shoving Caterpillar. Caterpillar pulled his hands from his pockets to defend himself, one holding the gun.

A sudden blast, a shock that ran through his arm. Ramirez stared at him in shock, and Caterpillar realized he was pointing his gun at the man. He was about to say something like *don't move* or *freeze before I shoot*. But no, it was already too late.

The man collapsed, Alma screaming, the secretary moaning on the floor, a trickle of blood running down her face, and the phone was ringing, and everything sounded muted after that ear-shattering gun blast.

Sam frowned as she heard a loud thump, out of sync with the drums' rhythm. What had that been?

She forced herself to ignore it; her solo was coming up, and she wouldn't give Ray another reason to complain.

"No," Alma muttered. "No, no, no."

The phone was still ringing. Hatter yanked it from the cord and slammed it on the desk, shattering it. For a second, the room was almost quiet, aside from Alma's muttering, and then there was a scream. A woman stood in the doorway, eyes wide, looking at the room, taking in the groaning secretary, the fallen teacher. Her eyes locked on Caterpillar's; he was already moving, his gun turning to point at her, when she bolted out of the room, still screaming.

Caterpillar knelt by Ramirez, whose eyes gazed vacantly at the ceiling, lips moving, blood bubbling from his mouth. Maybe he was trying to say something. Caterpillar couldn't hear him. All he heard was the screaming, and Alma's hysterical voice, and his own thudding heart, and that strange accompanying rhythm from somewhere nearby.

"Alma, shut up!" Hatter barked. "Guys, take a look."

He stared at the secretary's monitor, ignoring the woman lying by his feet.

Caterpillar forced himself to stand. Dazed, he walked over to Hatter, took a look at the monitor.

It was the security footage they had been desperate to see. More than a dozen different cameras throughout the school, displaying hallways and various rooms.

And they were all teeming with students and teachers, running in panic.

"Sam, stop for a second. There's something wrong with the sound," Ray said.

"What?" Sam raised her bow from the violin.

Ray frowned. "For a second, the violin sounded like . . ."

They locked stares, Sam feeling the chill spreading in her chest. They could all hear it now.

". . . screaming."

Hatter stepped out to the hallway, watching the screaming students running past him. A blonde teenager with nice cleavage took one look at him, the gun in his hand, and her face twisted with fear. She turned, running the other way. More joined her. All of them running away, afraid of him.

He smiled. That rush that he'd felt since he'd pistol-whipped that old hag was growing, a sensation he'd never felt before. He wasn't helpless anymore. He was the one in control.

Aiming his gun, he squeezed the trigger.

Bam! Bam! Bam! Each explosion sending a jolt through his arm. Hysterical screams, girls darting left and right, as if that would help them if he decided to take them down. Bam! Bam!

Someone grabbed his wrist, yanked it sideways. He roared, threw a punch at his attacker, heard the crunch as it hit the man's nose.

It was Caterpillar. The man stumbled back, looking dazed.

"What are you doing?" he spluttered.

"They're warning shots, you idiot," Hatter said. "I was shooting above their heads."

"You could have hit someone!"

"You should talk, asshole. You're the one who shot that teacher."

"It was self-defense! He was coming at me!"

"Yeah? Well, you sure screwed us with your—"

"You're a real psycho, you know that? Why did you hit that woman?"

"Shut up," Hatter spat, trying to listen above the din of screaming kids.

"I was going to convince—"

"Shut the hell up!"

Caterpillar's jaw snapped shut, blood running from his nose, trickling past his lips. Hatter listened carefully. Already? No, it was impossible.

But there it was. Above the noise around them, sirens blared.

◆　◆　◆

"What the hell is going on?" Ray asked, his voice trembling.

They'd all heard it. The blasts, the screaming. Kindling a fear that each and every student in this country kept somewhere in their heart. Sam had talked about it, and thought about it endlessly, with her

75

friends, or at class after each additional catastrophe. What would she do if it happened? What *should* she do? The instructions kept changing. *You should run. You should hide. You should lock yourself inside and wait for help. Never trap yourself somewhere you can't get out of.* Could they trust the teachers to protect them? Would the police show up on time?

Questions that she preferred to stay unanswered. She didn't want Christopher Columbus High on that list, with the names that everyone knew. Virginia Tech. Sandy Hook. Santa Fe. Columbine. Stoneman Douglas.

She approached the door.

"Samantha, wait," Ray said.

She raised her hand to shush him. The music room had no other exit. They couldn't stay here. For the past few years the instructions had been to *run.* Get out of the building as fast as possible.

Opening the door, she stared outside.

Saw the two men, both of them armed, one of them with blood running down his face. The other one, large with cropped hair and meaty lips, turned around to look straight back at her.

And raised his gun.

CHAPTER 14

Carver's radio crackled as he got off the Grand Central Parkway.

"Christopher Columbus High School, possible shots fired, possible shots fired." The voice belonged to a female dispatcher, cool and measured. But Carver could hear the edge in her tone.

A response, rife with static, came immediately after: "Central, three-seven-five, on my way."

Carver snatched his mic. "Central, delta-five-oh-nine, on my way."

He hit the lights switch, and the familiar red-and-blue lights flickered on the lower rear window. He gave the siren a few quick pulses, and vehicles in front of him edged sideways, giving him just enough space to squeeze through.

"Come on, come on," he muttered as he zigzagged between the cars, fingers clutching the steering wheel, squeezing it. He turned on the siren again as he approached a red light, his body humming with tension. A quick glance to either side—it was clear, and he shot through the intersection, heard the honking, a squeal of breaks; perhaps he'd misjudged it, but the intersection was behind him now, and the road was open, and he could floor it.

The engine screamed as he hurtled down the street, the siren now blaring full time, and the radio crackled because there were more shots fired, and a report of a man down, and he thought of Abby, and of Sam, and he pushed those thoughts away.

◆ ◆ ◆

Caterpillar stood frozen as Hatter raised his hand, pointing the gun at the girl in the doorway.

"Don't!"

The door slammed shut. Hatter turned to face Caterpillar, his mouth twisted in a sneer. Caterpillar's eyes were watering, his nose throbbing in pain. Had Hatter broken it?

"We need to get out of here," he muttered.

"Too late," Hatter said. "Don't you hear that?"

He did; of course he did. The sirens were getting louder, and closer. How had the police shown up so fast? It had been barely a couple of minutes.

"Get away from that!" A screech, from the secretary's office. Alma.

Caterpillar turned, stumbled back into the room, nearly slipped on the puddle of blood. There was someone else there now, a man, standing frozen on the far side of the room. The secretary knelt on the floor, by the phone that Hatter had smashed, holding the handset limply. Alma waved her gun back and forth erratically between the man and the secretary.

"Put the phone down," Alma said, her voice tight. Her face was pale, eyes wide with fear, her hand trembling.

Caterpillar took a step toward Alma, and pointed the gun at the man. He glanced at the door through which the man had entered. The principal's office.

"You." He tried to keep his voice steady. He tasted blood. He was bleeding freely from his nose. He swiped his mouth with the back of his hand. "Stay there."

The man, his face slack and pale, leaned against the wall, hands already raised.

Glancing at the secretary, Caterpillar said, "Get up."

She stared at him. Blood trickled from her forehead, a nasty purple bruise materializing where Hatter had hit her. She didn't seem to have heard him.

"Get up!" he barked again, pointing the gun at her.

She scrambled to her feet.

"Get over there." He motioned at the principal. "Stand against the wall."

He didn't know what he was doing, but he had to stay in control, before things got any worse. He couldn't have these people calling anyone. Couldn't have them giving away their location, their descriptions.

Alma's breathing was fast and heavy. She sounded as if she was about to cry.

"What are we going to do?" she whimpered. "What are we going to do?"

Caterpillar had no answer for her. "Hatter, get in here!" he shouted.

There was no response.

"Hatter?" He peered out into the hallway.

Hatter was gone.

A block away from the school, traffic came to a standstill. Carver's siren blared, and the vehicles around him tried to make room, but there was nowhere to go. He drove his car onto the sidewalk and switched off the engine.

His vest was in the trunk of the car, and he put it on, tightening the straps. A sea of faces looked at him from the motionless cars on the road, and he could spot some cell phones aimed his way. None of it mattered.

He took off down the street, hardly feeling the weight of the vest, the hammering of his heart, the burn of the chilly air as he breathed it in. He already spotted the flickering lights up ahead, a patrol car that had reached the area before he did.

Children were spilling from the school's front door, faces morphed in panic, their screams carrying over the wind. Damn it, damn it! He pushed himself harder, his feet flying on the sidewalk. His portable radio was crackling, dispatch calling for reinforcements.

He hit the shoulder mic. "Central, delta-five-oh-nine, I'm at the location," he screamed above the wind, above the pain in his lungs. "We need to clear the street."

"Copy. Reinforcements on their way."

Spotting a uniformed cop by the school's entrance, he ran toward him. The cop was shouting at the hysterical kids, trying to impose order. Some listened; some didn't. A kid stumbled, fell, was almost trampled. Someone helped him to his feet. Carver glanced at the school, the endless row of windows facing the street. He glimpsed movement through some of them.

"I'm Detective Carver," he shouted at the cop as soon as he was within a few yards of the man. "We need to get these students away from those windows. We need them to gather over there." He motioned at the basketball court by the school. There weren't any windows facing it.

The patrol cop, a young man not much older than the kids spilling from the school, nodded and turned to the crowd. "Everyone move over to the court!" He motioned with his hands at the basketball court.

A few students looked around helplessly, tearstained faces and shocked eyes. A dozen or so ran to the court, but the rest were still spilling onto the sidewalk and even into the street.

Carver cupped his hands around his mouth and took another lungful. "Hey!" he shouted. "All the teachers, over here. We need to get everyone to the basketball court. Do it now!"

His voice carried over the screams and the sirens. There was a shift in the crowd, a few adults shepherding the kids around them, following the patrol cop's frantic motions.

"Do we know what's going on inside?" Carver shouted at the cop.

The cop shook his head. "Shots fired. I heard kids saying they saw someone with a gun."

Carver pressed his mic. "Central, delta-five-oh-nine. Sighting of a shooter in the school."

"Copy that. Adam ten on its way."

Adam ten was the truck of the Emergency Service Unit in the area. They were trained to handle these kinds of situations. Carver looked at the cop. "Make sure *everyone* is gathered at the court. And try to clear the street. I'll go help the stragglers."

He skimmed the crowd for a few seconds. He just wanted a glimpse of Samantha's smooth brown hair to reassure himself. But there were hundreds of students, and he couldn't spot her. He had no time to look. With one final glance at the mass of stumbling, crying kids, he turned to the school's front door.

◆ ◆ ◆

Abby sat by her desk, staring at the photos in her hand, trying to conjure up memories.

"Abby."

Abby's partner and friend, Will Vereen, stood by her chair, towering above her, casting his long shadow on her desk. Flustered, she flipped the photos facedown on her desk, then pushed her chair back and swiveled it to face him.

"Will, sit down; you're blocking the sun," she said with a nervous smile.

He didn't smile back, which made her own grin evaporate.

"We got an alert," he said. "There's a reported shooting at Christopher Columbus High. ESU is on its way."

The words took a moment to register. "That's Sam's school," she whispered.

Will nodded. He knew; of course he knew. That was why he'd come over to tell her.

"Any casualties?" She swallowed. It was hard to talk. Hard to breathe.

"We don't have any information yet."

She was out of her chair, keys snatched from the desk, everything forgotten. Already dialing Sam, she strode toward the exit, her loud heartbeats matching her quickening steps. The phone call went straight to voice mail.

"Sam, call me as soon as you get this message." She hung up, already half running. She had to get to Sam.

"Do you hear anything?" Fiona whispered.

Sam shook her head. The music room's walls were padded with cloth and acoustic foam to soundproof it. Normally, Sam and her friends would complain about the terrible soundproofing that felt as if it almost *amplified* the noise outside the room. But now the padded walls sucked all the sounds away, making it impossible to hear anything.

Sam put her ear to the door. Could she hear anything? Anything at all? Maybe a siren in the distance. Was that a scream?

When that man had pointed his gun at her, she froze.

Then she'd pulled back, slamming the door. She'd been sure he'd come after them. But he hadn't.

Not yet.

He could be standing on the other side of that door. Pressing the gun to it. Inches away from her head.

"I don't think anyone's out there," she whispered.

They were trapped in this room, no way out. But they were also protected, for the moment. They'd pushed a large desk and a few chairs against the door. And the three of them crouched behind the stacked furniture.

What next? What next? She thought of their ALICE drills. No windows, no way to get out. They should hide, and get ready with something to throw at the shooter, or something they could hit the shooters with. What could she use? Ray's guitar? The drums' cymbals? None of this would work. In the active shooter drills, they were usually in class. There were things they could grab. Some of the teachers placed baseball bats behind the classroom doors, just in case. They'd never done drills in the music room. Never without a teacher to tell them what to do.

What did ALICE stand for? Alert, lockdown . . . she couldn't remember the rest. Her mind was buzzing; she could hardly think.

"We should make a run for it," Fiona said.

"No way," Ray whispered. "We wait. There's no way they can get in."

"They can get in, if they really want to," Sam said. She checked her phone. No signal. There never was any signal in this room. She tried to dial her mom anyway, got nothing.

"We should wait for the cops," Ray hissed.

It was tempting to crouch there behind the door, with their weak blockade, and wait for help. But that man was out there. With his strange, creepy smile and his deadly firearm. He *knew* they were in the music room.

They would have to leave soon.

◆ ◆ ◆

"This is the police. Everyone out. Run to the basketball court," Carver shouted. His voice echoed in the hallway, accompanied by terrified screams and sobbing.

A young teenage boy limped past him, his glasses askew. A couple of girls followed soon after, one of them stopping to point behind her.

"I saw him over there," she blurted. "He had a gun."

"Okay. Go to the basketball court," Carver repeated. He pulled out his own gun, advancing down the hallway.

Someone was sobbing nearby. Carver homed in on the voice, heart hammering. A classroom door stood ajar, and he pushed it, tense.

A young boy, maybe fourteen years old, crouched huddled behind a table. When Carver stepped in, the boy's eyes widened, registering the gun. "No, no!" he screamed, raising his hands to protect his face.

"I'm a cop," Carver said. "You need to get out of here."

He approached the boy and helped him stand up. The kid's pants were wet.

"What's your name?" Carver asked.

"M-Micah."

"Micah, everyone is gathered on the basketball court. Let's go."

Carver led the boy out of the classroom and to the front door. As he did, he caught movement down the hallway. He whirled, protecting the boy with his body.

A girl in a wheelchair rolled toward him. Carver hurried over to her. Her lip was bleeding.

"Are you hurt?"

"I was knocked off my chair," she said, wincing.

"I got you." He pushed her over to the exit. He had to wheel her around a discarded backpack. "Can you take it from here?"

"Yeah." She grabbed the wheels and began propelling herself outside.

The noises from the street were deafening. Screams, sirens, honking. The school's interior was eerily silent in comparison.

"Did you see anyone else left behind?" Carver asked.

"I don't know. Everyone was running, and I fell. I hit my head. I heard the coach shouting, trying to help kids get out. I don't know if he's there." Her lips trembled.

"You're good. Just join the rest on the basketball court."

She wheeled herself out. Carver turned around, listening intently. More footsteps. He took a few steps toward the sound, searching.

A man turned the corner of the hallway. Large. Cropped hair. Something in his hand.

"Don't move!" Carver shouted, pointing his gun at the man.

The man immediately leaped back. Carver's finger squeezed the trigger, but he hesitated for a fraction of a second, thinking he could be a teacher.

The man disappeared around the corner. Carver ran after him when he saw movement. A gun pointed his way.

A loud blast shook the hallway, and Carver flattened himself against the wall, aiming his gun, shooting back. The shots echoed in the tight space, deafening. His ears were ringing, eyes locked on that corner, searching for the hand holding the gun, but it was gone.

◆ ◆ ◆

Caterpillar watched the security footage in horror, saw Hatter as he tried to get out, leaving him and Alma behind. And then the stranger appearing on a different camera, helping a girl in a wheelchair.

And then the shoot-out. He heard the shots, a series of explosions, watched it on the screen, Hatter appearing on one of the small frames, the other man, probably a cop, showing up in two different frames.

And now Hatter was running away, back the way he'd come. He'd disappear from view on one camera, reappear in another, his face pulled in a grimace.

The cop still stood, gun aimed at the corner. He stepped slowly forward, gun steady, unwavering.

Hatter was leading the police to them.

"We need to leave," Caterpillar said to Alma.

"We can't." Her voice sounded like glass splintering, each syllable fractured. She stood by the window, peering outside. "There are already two police cars outside."

"You!" Caterpillar barked at the principal. "There's a back door to this place, right? I saw it earlier. Which way to the back door?"

"It's . . . you have to go to the first floor . . . cross the gymnasium . . . I . . . you go left . . . ," the principal stammered.

"Forget it, they'll be at the back door too," Alma cried. "We're trapped!"

He looked at her, then at the man lying on the floor, bleeding, looking pale.

"This man needs help," Alma said, voice trembling. "We need to get him to a hospital. We'll tell them why we were here. We never meant for this to happen."

Caterpillar nodded. She was right. They should give themselves up. What did Hatter think he was doing, shooting like that?

No, the cops would understand. He would tell them. About the kidnapped kids. And . . . and . . .

The police were controlled by the Circle. If they turned themselves in, they were as good as dead. He knew that. Alma knew that. No, there had to be another way.

He glanced at the monitor. The cop had turned the corner. Hatter was nowhere in sight. Maybe he'd found a place to hide. Or maybe he'd managed to get out.

"How do I activate the general-announcement thing?" he asked the principal.

"The what?"

"You know! The intercom! The thing you use for general announcements?"

"The PA system?"

"Yes! The damn PA system. How do I use it?" Caterpillar aimed his gun at the man, his hand shaking.

The principal swallowed. "Please . . . I'll show you."

No sign of the shooter. Carver hesitated. He needed to pull back. ESU was on its way, and it would be able to handle this much better.

But the girl in the wheelchair and that boy, Micah, probably weren't the only kids left. He couldn't leave other kids behind. He took another step, and another. Feeling exposed, knowing that the shooter could be behind any door. If there really was only one shooter. The guys back in the station had mentioned a group of people. Maybe there was more than one. Maybe—

A loud, shrill electric squeal. "Attention, attention." A jumpy voice, full of edge and corners, echoing everywhere. "We have the principal here. And the secretary. If you don't get out, we will shoot them."

Carver gritted his teeth. *We.* More than one, then. He kept moving forward.

"I'm not kidding! Get the hell out. Tell him! Tell him to get out!"

And then another voice, terrified. "Yes, please get out. They have guns."

Tell him *to get out.* They had eyes on him. Carver looked around. Spotted the security camera. Damn it.

If they were watching the security footage, they'd be in the administration section.

He took one last look at the camera, the lens staring back, unblinking. Finally, he retraced his steps, toward the exit.

CHAPTER 15

Abby did her best to create a mental wall between her job and the rest of her life. It wasn't easy; most cops ended up letting police work seep in. There was a reason the divorce rate of cops was so high. But usually she managed quite well.

And now her job collided with her life, bringing that paper-thin wall down. It was brutal, and jarring, and it snatched her breath away.

Samantha's school. A place that Abby had already visited dozens of times, dropping off her daughter on her way to work. A building she viewed as a part of life's dependable routine. She never really gave it much thought, which only went to show that in her mind, it was *safe*.

It was far from safe right now. With sirens screaming everywhere, a chopper somewhere above, an ESU van on the sidewalk's curb. She flashed her badge to get past a uniformed officer who blocked the road, rerouting traffic.

Abby had been in crisis management for a long while, and it was all part of her everyday life. But not here. And suddenly those ESU officers, fanning out around the school in vests and helmets, felt wrong, out of place, ominous.

She checked her phone for the hundredth time. She'd tried to call Sam, and messaged her, Are you okay? The message was still unread. Putting away the phone, she parked her car and got out, looking around her.

A familiar face. Carver. What was he doing there? The school wasn't in his precinct.

He was talking to Mrs. Pratchett, the vice principal, a thin woman wearing a gray jacket and a long brown skirt. Abby strode over, taking a deep breath, trying to collect herself.

"Carver," she said. Her voice came out shrill, the fear laced in it for anyone to hear. "What's going on?"

He turned to face her. A few years ago, Abby's adoptive dad, Hank, had had a heart attack. Abby and her mom stood in the emergency room, waiting. When a doctor finally stepped out, calling their names, Abby had studied his face desperately. Trying to figure out if this was the face of someone with bad or good news. In those few seconds before he told them that Hank was fine, she'd registered every part of his expression, trying to assess what it meant. He wasn't smiling—that wasn't good. He had a frown—but maybe it was because he was busy. His lips were tight—bad news? Or was it just his professional face? His eyes seemed weary, but it was probably the end of his shift.

Now she felt that need again, to read Carver's expression, to figure out if he was about to tell her something terrible. His deep-green eyes reflected worry but not outright fear. His brown hair was disheveled, but he didn't seem to notice.

"Abby," he said. "We're still trying to piece it together. There was a shooting, and from what we can tell, the shooters weren't from the school."

"Any casualties?" She wanted him to say there weren't. She wanted all of this to stop.

"We don't know yet. We're trying to make sure that all the kids are safe. This is what I was discussing with Mrs. Pratchett here."

"We've gathered all the kids on the basketball court," the vice principal said. "And we're verifying their presence according to the attendance system. We have only four students unaccounted for."

"Which students?" Abby's throat clenched.

"Frank Howard, Barry Johns, Lisbeth Reynolds, and Ruby Allen."

Abby exhaled, feeling the relief flooding her. Sam was all right. She turned toward the basketball court, already stepping away to find Sam, hug her forever.

"The shooters inside have hostages," Carver said.

Abby froze, turned back. "The missing kids?"

Carver shook his head. "Not that we know of. They definitely have the principal and the secretary. They threatened to shoot them if we didn't pull out."

"They threatened to shoot the hostages? Who talked to them?"

"No one. I was inside. They used the PA system."

"Which means they're in the principal's office, right?" Abby said, turning to the vice principal.

"Or my office," the vice principal said. "Or they were using the secretary's microphone. She has one too."

"Did they say anything else?"

"No," Carver said. "They let the principal speak, and he repeated what they said. Told me to get out."

Abby wanted to know the exact phrasing and how they'd sounded. But that could wait. "Do we know who they are?"

"I saw one of them. A big man, cropped hair, wearing jeans and an overcoat. He shot at me, and I shot back, but he got away. According to a few statements I got from students, there are either two or three of them; I'm not sure yet. But just before the shooting, dispatch was notified by the FBI that there's some online chatter on the Watcher forums regarding the school."

"The Watcher forums?" Abby frowned. She was dimly familiar with the Watcher conspiracy theorists. They'd been gathering momentum for quite some time, and according to an article she'd read a few weeks before, they numbered over a million "adherents," as they called themselves. Of course, all you had to do to be an adherent was share their memes on Facebook or Twitter. A few celebrities had touted their half-baked theories, and there had been a minor national shock when a congressman had said he supported what they were doing.

"The FBI are following their chats?" she asked.

"Yeah," Carver said. "A few months ago a man in Oklahoma threatened to bomb the local library. It turned out it was a result of Watcher-related theories. The bureau classified them as a domestic terrorism threat."

"Okay," Abby said, eyeing the ESU van. "I'll go have a word with—"

The vice principal's phone rang. "Sorry," she said. "Parents have been calling . . ." Her words faded as she glanced at the phone screen, eyes widening.

"What?" Abby said.

"It's the principal's office!"

"Wait!" Abby said hurriedly, reaching for the phone, but the woman had already accepted the call.

"Hello? Henry?" she said breathlessly. Then her expression froze, the fear etched on her face. She listened for a few seconds, then whispered, "Okay."

She offered the phone to Carver. "It's one of them," she said, voice trembling. "He wants to talk to the cops right now."

Carver exchanged looks with Abby. She hesitated only for a fragment of a second before taking the phone from the woman's hand.

"This is Abby." Her voice was low, calm, slow. The voice of a person in control. "Who am I talking to?"

CHAPTER 16

Caterpillar sat with the phone's handset to his ear. He couldn't use his own cell phone, not if he didn't want to give the police and the FBI his full identity, including his social security number, his home address, and his goddamn favorite cereal. But he didn't dare sit by the principal's desk, in full view of the snipers and the chopper flying outside. So he sat against the wall beneath the windows, hidden from sight, with the phone cables stretched to their limit, the phone itself dangling a few inches above the floor.

"This is Abby," a feminine voice said. "Who am I talking to?"

"I said I want to talk to the cops," he barked into the phone. He glanced through the doorway at the hostages, sitting side by side. Alma aimed her gun at them. Someone moaned; he wasn't sure if it was one of the hostages or Alma herself.

"I'm a cop." She sounded relaxed, at ease. Did she even understand what the hell was going on? "What's your name?"

"You tell those cops out there that if anyone, I mean *anyone*, enters the building, we're going to shoot the hostages, you got that?" He would. He really would. They were probably working with the Circle. Selling children. He had a moral right to threaten their lives.

"Yes, I understand." Her voice remained steady, unwavering. "No one will enter the school. We don't want anyone hurt."

"Good." The dangling phone pulled at his wrist; his arm was getting tired. "We're armed, we have hostages, and we can see you on the security cameras, so just stay the hell away."

"That's understood. It sounds like things are very tense there, and I have to tell you, people are really worried here too. We all want this resolved without anyone getting hurt."

"Then stay away. And don't try anything funny, like cutting the electricity or the phone lines. We know how the police operate, you got that? Don't mess with us."

"Absolutely. Can you tell me your name? I want to know what to call you when we talk."

"You don't need to, uh . . ." His voice broke. From the corner of his eye he saw the principal move his hand.

"Don't move!" Alma screamed. "I'll shoot! Don't you move!"

"Hey, don't move a damn inch!" Caterpillar shouted, aiming his gun at the hostages.

The principal flinched, freezing in place. The woman on the phone said something, but Caterpillar didn't catch it.

"What? What did you say?"

She answered him; he heard the syllables, but his brain couldn't connect the words. He was about to vomit. His nose throbbed, the taste of blood on his lips, the world spinning. Damn it, where was Hatter? The police were going to break into the building at any moment. They'd throw a flash grenade inside, then storm through the windows. He'd seen it in the movies a hundred times. If they did that, he would shoot the principal. He would shoot the secretary. He would take as many of the bastards as he possibly could.

The woman—Abby—repeated her words for the third time, her voice completely steady. "It sounds like you're having some sort of problem over there. Is everyone okay? Are you hurt?"

"I'm . . . yeah. No, I'm fine." A drop of blood spattered on the floor. Damn it. He wiped the blood from his lips and gently touched his nose. The pain made his eyes tear up.

"Is anyone else there hurt? Any of your friends?"

"No, listen, everyone is okay—you just go tell the other cops to stay away."

"How are Henry and Thelma? Are they okay?"

"Who?"

"Henry is the principal, and Thelma is the school's secretary. They're with you, right?"

He glanced at the doorway. Thelma sobbed, a large bleeding bruise on her forehead. Beyond her he could glimpse the feet of the man he'd shot. Ramirez. "They're fine." He swallowed, his throat clenching. "They're here, so don't try anything funny."

"You're saying that Henry and Thelma are there with you, and that you want the police and everyone else to stay away, because you don't want anyone to get hurt."

"Yeah, that's right!" His voice was hoarse. He realized he was shouting. He lowered his voice, cleared his throat. "That's right."

"Okay, I want to update the commander here, but people are really worried. How can I reassure them that Henry and Thelma are okay?"

He gritted his teeth. "One of the cops heard the principal on the PA system earlier."

"One of the cops heard Henry on the PA system?"

"Yes! I let Henry . . . the principal talk to him on the PA system."

"I'm really glad you did that. How will I find this cop?"

"Look, you get someone to . . . just . . ." He clutched the handset, squeezing it hard. Every second that ticked by felt like an hour. He had to get them to stay away. "Just ask them, okay?"

"Okay, but it might take some time, and I don't know if I'll manage to find him. I want to be able to tell the commander that Henry and Thelma are fine."

Caterpillar blinked a tear of frustration away. His nose throbbed. "They're okay. You can take my word for it."

"I believe you. You sound like an honest man. But the commander will ask me how I know that they're fine, and if I tell him that I took your word for it, he'll never buy it."

She was right. Hell, the police commander would probably prefer to believe that the hostages were dead. That they could storm the school, clean this mess up. "Okay, you know what? Hang on." He motioned at the principal. "Get over here. Now!"

The principal's eyes skittered from Caterpillar to Alma.

"Do what he says," Alma said. "Slowly."

Caterpillar aimed his gun at the principal. The man got to his feet and shuffled over, his eyes never leaving the gun.

"Sit down," Caterpillar said. "Not too close." His heart hammered. What if the principal tried to wrestle his gun from him? He would shoot the man.

But the principal just sat down, a few feet away.

"Here," Caterpillar said, handing him the phone. "Tell the cop that you're all fine."

The principal took the phone from Caterpillar and pulled it to his ear. The cable wouldn't go that far, and he had to lean forward to talk. "Hello? This is Henry Bell. I'm unhurt."

He paused, listening, and then said, "Thelma got hit on the head . . ."

Caterpillar raised his gun threateningly. The principal's eyes widened.

"And, uh . . . Carlos Ramirez is here too . . ."

Caterpillar snatched the phone back. "You got that? They're fine. You get everyone to stay back."

"I really appreciate that you let me talk to him." Abby sounded grateful. "It seems like you want to do the right thing."

"Sure," Caterpillar said, his breath steadying. "Tell everyone to stay away. I don't want anyone to get hurt. And get that chopper out of here."

"Everyone will stay back. And I'll get that chopper away, but that might take some time, because I don't think it's a police chopper; I think it belongs to a local news channel."

"Whatever, just get it out of here."

"I'll tell them," Abby said. "Who should I tell them I talked to?"

"I'm hanging up now." His hand shook from the effort of holding the dangling phone. "You just tell them."

She said something else, but he let the handset drop. Then he crawled to the phone's base and hung up the call.

CHAPTER 17

"You'll get us all killed."

Sam ignored Ray's terrified whisper. She grasped one side of the desk, Fiona grabbing the other.

"We don't want it to drag on the floor and make a noise," she told Fiona, her voice low.

Fiona nodded grimly. They lifted the desk and shuffled it aside, moving it away from the door. The door budged slightly, and for one terrifying second, Sam thought the man with the gun had been waiting outside all that time, that he was about to burst in. But the door remained shut.

She put her ear to the door again, heard nothing. Very slowly, she turned the doorknob, opening the door a crack, and peered outside.

The hallway was empty.

She stepped through the crack, breath held, eyes skittering back and forth, searching for movement. In the distance, she could hear a screaming siren, honking, a helicopter flying somewhere, all sounds muffled and far away. She took a few steps forward, wincing as even the lightest footstep made a sound that echoed in the empty hallway. Behind her, she heard her friends' heavy breaths, and realized she was still holding hers. She let out a long, soft exhale.

The music room was on the school's top floor. To get to the exit, they would have to take the stairs, go down two floors.

She led the way, none of them saying anything, trying their best to stay quiet. As they stepped closer to the secretary's door, she heard something else. It sounded like sobbing.

The door was open, and she glanced inside.

A woman stood inside, facing away. A wave of relief washed over Sam at the sight of another grown-up, someone from school, and her mouth opened, about to say something. But the words died before leaving her lips.

The woman was aiming a gun. Sam shifted slightly, the rest of the room veering into sight.

Mr. Bell and Mrs. Nelson sat side by side, backs to the wall. Mrs. Nelson's face was smeared with blood. And just across from them someone lay on the floor . . . Mr. Ramirez! Curled and motionless. Amid a pool of blood.

Sam had never seen so much blood. Her head spun. Oh god, she was about to faint. She leaned on the wall, inhaling softly, biting her lip as hard as she could. They had to keep moving, but her feet were planted in place. She couldn't budge. Couldn't pull her eyes away.

Another man moved into view, stopping by the window, shutting the blind with one hand, a gun in the other. He was the man she'd seen earlier, the one with the blood running down his face. The lower half of his face was completely smeared, giving him a gruesome, terrifying appearance.

Mrs. Nelson's eyes widened as she noticed Sam. She let out a tiny gasp.

The woman with the gun turned around.

And Sam bolted down the hallway.

◆　◆　◆

"Hey!"

The shout made Caterpillar whip around, gun raised, pointed at the hostages. But Alma stared at the doorway, her body frozen, mouth agape.

"What is it?" Caterpillar asked. "Did you see something?"

"I saw someone out there!"

"Was it Hatter?"

"No . . . I . . ."

Caterpillar took two strides over to the security footage and skimmed the tiny camera feeds, looking for any movement. There. Three kids running down one of the hallways. He searched for anything else, saw nothing.

"Just a few of the students," he told Alma, eyes still on the screen.

"I thought . . . I thought it was . . . for a moment I thought . . ."

He knew what she'd thought. The same images were running through his own mind nonstop. Men with full body armor and assault rifles storming down the hallway. A flash grenade tossed inside the room. A sudden bright light and then blurry forms rushing at them, shooting to kill.

"Just kids," he said, half to reassure himself. "We need to keep an eye on those security cameras all the time."

It was impossible, and he knew it. They had to watch the feed, but they also had to watch the hostages, and talk to the cops, and get the word out to their fellow Watchers, and close the blinds and barricade the windows against snipers . . .

His heart hammered as he watched the kids running. On their way out. Escaping this hell. If only he could join them.

Another figure, shifting into view on one of the feeds.

Hatter.

Caterpillar watched as the kids moved through the school, disappearing from one feed, reappearing in another. And Hatter on another feed, his back to the camera, lumbering down a hallway, head turning left and right.

And then they all stepped into the same screen.

Sam was a few yards away from the main door when he appeared, stepping around the corner of the hallway, standing between them and the exit. Sam stumbled, her run screeching to a halt, as he turned to face them, expressionless. Circles of sweat stained his blue shirt. His lower lip protruded, a sheen of saliva on it. His eyes were beady and dark, and glared straight at her.

A gun in his hand.

He raised it, and for a fragment of a second, Sam stared directly down the barrel.

She turned and bolted back the way she'd come, Ray and Fiona by her side. When they did shooter drills, the teachers told them to zigzag, that it would make them harder to hit. But now as she ran, hearing his footsteps behind her, all she wanted was to get away as fast as possible, and zigzagging suddenly sounded dumb.

The gym. There was another door to the outside by the gym. She let her feet fly, the hallway a blur. A quick glance back—he was still behind them, face red with effort, but they were getting away. He wasn't shooting them. He was trying to catch them.

"Gym," she blurted to her friends.

Fiona was falling behind, her face twisted in fear. Ray's jaw was gritted tightly, each breath a hiss through his clenched teeth. Sam turned left, and her friends followed.

And there was the gym, and the exit. It was shut, but it was usually unlocked during the day. Just seeing the door gave her a jolt of adrenaline. Nearly there. Fiona whimpered, and Sam willed her to run faster, to keep up. They were faster than him; they were almost out. The sirens were clearer now, their screaming hardly muffled through the double doors.

She crashed into the door, turning the handle, pushing. The door rattled, staying shut.

Sam pushed harder, her mind screaming at her to move, *move*! But the door was locked, safety a few inches away and out of reach.

A burst of agony in her scalp, her head pulled back. She shrieked as she was shaken this way and that, her eyes tearing up with pain. He'd grabbed her by her hair and was now jerking her left and right, pulling her away from the door. A sudden tug made her stumble sideways, slam into the wall, spots dancing in front of her eyes. She fell to her knees, gasping.

More screams, a crack, a muffled groan of pain.

"All of you, on the floor, or I shoot!" The shout was loud, angry, out of control.

Something slammed her back, and she slumped to the floor, sobbing. In the background, Fiona screamed, and Ray gasped in pain.

From her position on the floor she saw the crack under the door, and a thin sliver of tantalizing sunlight.

CHAPTER 18

A wave of relief washed over Abby as the negotiation truck inched through the crowded road toward the area the police had cordoned off. Abby glimpsed Will Vereen behind the wheel. She'd phoned him as soon as the call from inside the school had ended. She waved him over to the area that she'd saved for the truck—a few yards away from the mobile command center.

The area in front of the school had transformed completely. The flicker of red-and-blue emergency lights was everywhere, accompanied by the sound of police radios and the rotors of the helicopter above. ESU officers in full ballistic gear—vests and helmets—were gathered on one side, while patrol officers were ushering civilians away. Everywhere she looked, people were holding cell phones, filming the excitement, to upload online and score a bit of momentary social media fame.

Captain Franco Estrada, the commander of the 109th Precinct, stood by the command truck, wearing a vest, talking to one of the cops. Abby strode over, and as she approached them, his loud voice boomed over the din.

". . . reroute the traffic to 149th; I don't want any more cars getting within two blocks of this school." He glanced at Abby and motioned for her to come over. Then he turned back to the cop. "And wear a vest. I don't want you here without a vest, you got that?"

The cop nodded and walked away.

"Lieutenant Mullen, right?" Estrada said. Though his hair was jet black, his trimmed beard had turned silvery gray. He had a frown that Abby suspected was perpetual. It probably came with the job. Although she lived and worked in his precinct, she'd only met Estrada a couple of times before and had never talked to him in person.

"Yes sir," she said.

"You talked to the people inside?"

"Yeah, they phoned the vice principal from a landline inside and asked to talk to the police."

"And you just happened to be here?"

"My daughter goes to this school."

His frown deepened. "Is she okay?"

She was, according to the vice principal. But Abby had a constant tugging fear in her heart that would dissipate only when she saw her daughter with her own eyes. And Estrada's question made that fear expand, breaking Abby's concentration.

"Um . . . yes." She blinked rapidly. "All the kids are accounted for except for four of them. I have their names."

"But as far as we know, they're not the hostages."

"No. We know of three hostages, all from the school's staff."

"How do we know about the hostages?"

"I managed to get them to let me talk to the principal for a few seconds."

Estrada raised an eyebrow. "Well done. Can we call the people inside?"

"The phone they used is offline, and they're not answering any other number. I have the vice principal's phone. I expect they'll try to call us soon."

"Good." He checked his watch. "It's now ten forty-seven. I want you in the command center at ten past eleven for a briefing. You're the negotiations commander for now. Get a team ready."

"Okay."

"I don't want this to end with ESU storming the school, Lieutenant." She swallowed. "Me neither."

"Good. And I don't want to see you out here without a vest. Tell that to your team. Vests on everyone."

"Got it." She returned to the negotiation truck, which had just parked. Will jumped off. "Abby, is Sam—"

"Sam's okay." She pushed the lingering anxiety away. She had to focus. "We don't have a lot of time, and we need to get working. Estrada is the incident commander; I'm the negotiations commander."

"Okay," Will said. "Tammi's in the back, already working on the intel board."

"I want to see what—" The phone in her pocket rang. The vice principal's phone. She raised a finger, motioning for Will to wait, and took the phone out. The phone number blinking on the screen wasn't identified. Could be one of the hostage takers, calling from their cell phone.

She took a deep breath and answered. "Hello."

"Mrs. Pratchett?" The voice was female, high pitched, half-hysterical. "This is Lorna, I'm Penny Smith's mother? She's in the tenth grade. I heard there was a shooting in the school. Is Penny okay? She won't answer her phone."

"Lorna, this is Lieutenant Mullen," Abby said. "Mrs. Pratchett is busy, but your daughter should be fine. I have to keep this line free—"

"Can I talk to her? Was there really a shooting? Is anyone hurt?"

Abby walked over to the back of the truck and climbed inside the familiar work space. One wall at the rear had an enormous whiteboard, on which Officer Tammi Summers was scribbling. On the far end stood a desk with two phones and a radio.

"Lorna . . . how did you hear about this?"

"It was on the parents' chat. Can I please talk to Penny? Just for ten seconds. Why isn't she answering her phone?"

Abby massaged her forehead. If it was on the parents' chat, all of them were probably trying to call someone who could tell them what was going on. This phone would ring nonstop. And she had to keep the line free.

She motioned for Will. "Get Carver," she said. "He's outside."

"Hello?" Lorna said. "Are you there?"

"Sorry, I have to hang up." Abby ended the call. She turned to Tammi. The young officer seemed unusually pale. "Are you okay?"

Tammi swallowed. "Yeah. I was working on the negotiation board while we were driving. It was a mistake. I got a bit carsick."

Abby knew the feeling. She'd done it herself a few years before, had almost thrown up when they'd arrived at the location.

She scanned the board, still mostly empty. In an hour or two, the entire thing would be covered with intel, and the entire space would smell like a whiteboard marker.

"I printed out some information about the Watchers," Tammi said, handing her a stack of pages. "We don't know if those people are Watchers, but for now, it's a decent assumption."

"I want to know how many people we're dealing with," Abby said, skimming the text. "Some of the kids or teachers have seen them."

The rear doors opened, and Carver stepped inside, Will following him.

"Hey, you needed me?" Carver said.

"Are you doing anything?" Abby asked.

"No, this isn't my precinct. They asked me to stick around to give them a statement."

"Can you do me a favor? Show Officer Summers here where the teachers and students are. And while you're there, tell the vice principal to contact each of the parents and update them. I can't have them phoning here." She hesitated, feeling that weight tugging at her heart again. "And can you please tell Sam to call me? I need to hear her voice."

"Sure, no problem."

Abby glanced at Tammi. "Take statements from anyone who saw anything. Descriptions, anything they might have said or done—you know the drill."

Tammi could also breathe some fresh air while she was at it. Abby didn't want the officer vomiting inside the truck. Judging by the relieved expression on Tammi's face, a similar thought occurred to her.

Abby's own phone rang. She glanced at the display. Steve. Damn it. She raised her eyes and told Tammi, "Let me know as soon as you have anything solid."

Tammi nodded and followed Carver out. Abby took a deep breath and answered her phone. "Steve."

"Abby." His voice was tense, panicky. "Debra's mother from Sam's class called me, there was a shooting incident at their school? Do you know any—"

"I'm at the school. We're still looking into it."

"I tried calling Sam, but it went to her voice mail. Is she okay?"

It was the third time in ten minutes that someone had asked her if Sam was okay. But coming from Steve, it was much worse. Although Steve had been an underwhelming husband, he was a good father. And in his voice, Abby heard her own gnawing fear. She'd tried to call Sam several times as well, reaching her voice mail every time. She kept reminding herself that Sam turned off her phone in class. That in the chaos after the shooting, she must've forgotten to turn it on.

"Sam's fine," she said. "The vice principal told me she's accounted for. As soon as I talk to her, I'll tell her to call you. I need you to pick up Ben from school. I know it's early, but—"

"Absolutely, I'll pick him up right now. What do you mean, as soon as you talk to her? Where's Sam right now?"

The vice principal's phone rang. Abby glanced at it. The display read *Henry Bell Office*. The principal's phone. It was them. Steve's voice still yammered in her ear, and was the last thing she needed right now.

"I have to go, Steve. I'll tell her to call you." She hung up and slid the phone into her pocket. She turned to Will, holding up the vice principal's phone. "It's them."

For a second none of them said anything. The phone kept ringing.

"I had a good rapport with him last time," Abby said. "I'll be primary negotiator. You'll be secondary negotiator. I need you to listen in."

She wished they'd already routed the principal's line to the truck's phone. That way, she could talk easily, with Will listening in with his own pair of earphones, recording the call. But right now, they'd have to do it the old-fashioned way. They stepped close to each other, their heads touching, with the phone between them. Abby took a deep breath, her heart thrumming.

"This is Abby," she said.

"I told you to get that helicopter away from us!" The man's voice was angry and fearful, but not as bad as before. Good. Abby needed him calm. She needed him to feel that he was the one in control of the situation, and that they were all working together to resolve everything.

"I'm sorry," she said. She needed to start by defusing his anger. "Like I said, it might take some time. I need to convince the commander, and then he needs to talk to whoever is in charge of the—"

"I don't care, just get it done!"

"How can I make the commander see that this needs to happen?" She injected helplessness into her voice, while keeping it calm. Get him to think of her as a lowly cop who has little influence over her almighty commander.

A second of silence. He was thinking of an answer, trying to solve her own problem for her. "Tell them I will shoot the hostages if the chopper doesn't fly away."

A bad threat, and she needed him to think of it differently. She rephrased his sentence. "You want me to tell the commander that as long as the chopper gets out of here, everyone will stay safe?"

"Yes, I just . . . listen, we really don't want anyone to get hurt. But that chopper is freaking us out, okay?"

"What about that chopper is worrying you?" She knew what was on his mind.

"We don't want to see it, okay?"

He was worried the chopper could have a sniper that would shoot him at any moment. Time to remove that concern from the table. And the best way to expel fear was to bring it out in the open. Fear shriveled in sunlight. "We would never risk the lives of Henry and Thelma and Carlos by doing anything rash."

"Wouldn't you? You've done it before."

She was sure he could give her examples, and she couldn't get bogged down in arguing about alternative facts. "It seems like you're worried we're going to break in at any moment. What makes you think that?"

"We know how the people who run the show think. They don't care about anyone getting hurt or dying. They want to clean up this mess."

It really did sound like this guy believed the Watchers' paranoid theories. She had to distance herself from the people he thought of as the enemy. "It sounds like *you* care. And I care. I don't want anyone to get hurt."

She held the phone away from her face and partially blocked it with her hand. That would give him the impression that she was talking to people around her. She shouted at no one, "Guys, I *told* you to stay back! Everyone take a few steps back. And tell them to get that chopper away from here; it's making everyone nervous."

She paused for a short second, then said to the man on the phone, "Sorry. I want us to work together to keep everyone safe."

"If you get those people to do as we say, no one will get hurt." He sounded much calmer. A man who was regaining his control. They were getting somewhere.

Abby let her voice become slightly more upbeat. The voice of a friend. A confidante. "You sound like a good guy. How did this all happen?"

CHAPTER 19

Caterpillar sat at the principal's desk, fingers tight around the phone, his knee jumping nervously. He had hardly even blinked in the past hour, constantly turning his head this way and that, searching for movement, a threat. He'd blocked the window with a file cabinet and had closed the blinds, but it hardly made him feel any safer. They could still blast through. Or they could crawl through the air vents, or fill the building with a toxic gas. The Circle had done it before.

"Hello?" The soft, calm voice came from the phone. "Are you there?"

Abby, he decided, was not a Circle agent. Not that it mattered much—the chief of detectives was, and he would want to silence them. The only reason they weren't dead yet was that there were too many witnesses out there. Caterpillar had peered out the window earlier, had seen the street from above, numerous people filming with their phones. Good, at least that kept him safe.

"We didn't mean for any of this," he said, his voice hoarse.

"What happened to get us into this situation?" Abby asked. She sounded curious. She really wanted to know.

"Listen, we just came to check this place out, okay?"

"Check this place out?"

"Yeah. We had reliable information that there's a child-sex-slaving-ring operation right here in this school." The phone line crackled. Was someone listening in on this call? The Circle had people in all the phone companies. He'd have to remember to be careful, not to give anything important away. "We were going to catch them in the act. We didn't want to hurt anyone; all we're doing is saving the kids."

"You came to the school to save kids from a horrible fate." She sounded sincere, but he remained wary. People said you had to give a person the benefit of the doubt, but that was because they didn't know any better. Doubt was not a benefit; it wasn't something you automatically deserved. If people wanted trust, they had to *earn* it.

"That's right—we wanted to stop this vile trade. Those psychos are selling kids, you know? You have no idea what they're capable of."

"You know, I'm a mother," Abby said. "I have two young kids, and the thought of sexual predators keeps me awake at night. If I knew that children were about to be trafficked, I would have done anything to help them."

"That's what *I* felt. I wanted to help those kids. I never wanted anyone to . . ." The image of his gun shuddering in his hand, that man dropping to the floor. He'd lunged at him; Caterpillar had acted in self-defense. That man could even be working for them. It had been impossible to avoid. "I just wanted to help."

"Who gave you the information about the kids?"

"No one *gave* it to us. I wasn't *told* to come here." He tensed. What was she hinting? That he'd been manipulated somehow? "We figured it out. We outsmarted those bastards."

"Then you and your friends were resourceful enough to find out about it by yourselves. And you came to check if it was true. That was all you wanted to do. To save those children."

"Exactly! But we didn't know that it would get out of hand. It wasn't my fault that . . . I mean, we wanted to look at the security tapes and—" That chopper outside sounded closer, the sound of its rotors getting incredibly loud. They were coming for him!

He shot to his feet, the phone tumbling from his fingers, and dived to the floor. His gun? Where was his gun? He'd left it on the table. He lunged up, grabbed the gun, aimed it at the hostages through the doorway. If the sniper shot him now, he would take them out—he would take them all out.

The chopper sound faded away. He grabbed the phone. "You tell them to stay back, you hear me! Stay the hell back!"

"We're all staying back," Abby said. "We don't want *anyone* hurt."

"Yeah? Well, that chopper was damn close."

"Hang on," Abby said. It sounded like she tried to muffle the phone with her hand, but he could still hear her as she shouted at someone. "Hey, you! Get back, I told you, stay away from that building! And find the commander—I want this chopper on the ground, you got that?"

Caterpillar exhaled, eyes darting around the room. Every few seconds, he'd pause his stare on the air vent, searching for movement. Nothing there. He'd keep checking. He'd have to push the desk over to block the vent. They'd have to block all the vents in these rooms.

"Sorry," Abby said. "It seems like you're under a lot of stress. We need to think together how to make things easier."

"I just wanted to save those kids," he repeated, his voice cracking.

"I absolutely understand that. You're a compassionate man, and it's important to you to do the right thing. You put yourself at risk to save innocent children. I wish more people were as caring as you."

"Yeah, and look where it got me."

"How did you find out about the trafficking?"

"I'm part of a group. I don't know if you've heard of it." He hesitated, not knowing if he should tell her. But she'd find out soon enough anyway. "The Watchers."

"I think I heard about the Watchers!" She sounded surprised. "Did you guys have anything to do with the arrest of Harvey Weinstein?"

"Yeah, we're the ones who figured it all out," Caterpillar said guardedly. "We look out for corruption, trying to help people who can't help themselves. There's a small group of people . . . a cabal, and they're pulling all the strings."

"A cabal?"

"Yeah, that's right. Do you know who I'm talking about? You're working for them."

"Why do you think I'm working for them?" She sounded confused.

He let out a tense laugh. "Because almost everyone does. Especially the police. You might not know it; you might think you're just a cop. Whatever you do or say, you're just following orders, right? But whose orders? What agenda are you actually advancing? If the NYPD is in the cabal's pocket, then everything you do is for them."

"So you're saying that anyone who is not aware of this cabal might actually be working for the cabal. And the Watchers are trying to fight that?"

"Exactly. And we found out some stuff yesterday. There was a message in code, and a few of us broke the code together. And we decided to meet up and check it out."

Movement outside the room. He shifted to get a good look at what was going on, and his heart skipped a beat. Hatter stepped into the secretary's office, pushing a boy and two girls in front of him. The boy had a split lip, while one of the girls had a large bruise on her cheek. The kids looked dazed, eyes staring ahead, unfocused. One of the girls was sobbing.

"I have to go," he said weakly. "Keep everyone away from the building, okay?"

"We need to keep talking," Abby said. "And figure out how to keep things under control."

"You keep everyone away from us. Things here are under control, as long as no one comes close, you got that? I'll call you later."

"Okay. Who should I tell my commander I was talking to?"

"You just tell him you talked to the guy inside. That should be enough."

"I want to tell my commander that we're making progress, but he won't believe me if I can't even give him a first name. You know how it is."

Did it matter? That was why they had online aliases. To keep them safe. "I won't give you my name, but you can call me Caterpillar."

"Caterpillar, okay. When will you—"

He hung up and went to the door. "What the hell are you doing?"

Hatter smirked at him. "I heard you tell the cops on the PA system that we have hostages. Good idea. I found a few more. I don't know if the cops care about these old assholes." He tipped his head toward the principal and the secretary. "But they wouldn't want the kids to get hurt."

Caterpillar swallowed. He'd painted them as the good guys for the past ten minutes. And now Hatter was threatening children. "No one's going to hurt the kids." He exchanged looks with Alma, who nodded, looking pale.

"We'll see. It depends on what the cops do," Hatter said. "We were lucky. The door they tried to escape through was locked. But we need to lock the rest of the doors. Shut all the windows. This place is huge; we need to make sure the police don't get in."

"The police can break the doors if they want to," Alma said, her voice trembling. "We need to surrender—"

"No one is surrendering," Caterpillar barked.

"Damn right," Hatter said. "And the police won't just come in, right? That's why we have these." He shoved the boy toward the other hostages in the corner. The boy stumbled, falling to the floor.

"Stop that," Caterpillar said. "There's no need to—"

"Don't tell me what to do," Hatter spat.

Caterpillar walked over to him. "We need to work together, all right?"

Hatter glowered at him, and Caterpillar realized that the younger man was much taller than him. He seemed to tremble, not out of fear but as if barely holding back his rage. His face was pink, his eyes bulging.

"You were right," Caterpillar said. "We need to lock all entrances to the school right now. And make sure the windows are shut. On the bottom floor, the windows are barred, but the police can storm us through the windows on this floor."

Hatter prodded the two girls toward the rest of the hostages. Now all five of them sat against the wall. The girls clutched each other for reassurance. Caterpillar wanted to tell them there was nothing to worry about. They would never hurt them. They were there to *help*.

But he also needed the girls to stay afraid so that they wouldn't try to run.

A sudden sound startled Caterpillar. It was a guitar, playing some sort of song. Was it a video playing on the computer? No. It was a ringtone.

Hatter hurled himself at the hostages. "Whose phone is that?" he shouted. "Where is it?"

Caterpillar grabbed the secretary's handbag, upending it on the desk. A jumble of stuff tumbled out, scattering everywhere—a wallet, sunglasses, lipstick . . . and there! A phone. He snatched it off the table, but it clearly wasn't ringing—the screen was dark.

The ringtone kept going, coming from the corner of the room, from one of the students.

"Where is it?" Hatter was pawing at the goth girl.

"It's not mine!" she shrieked. "Don't touch me!"

"Here, it's my phone," the boy said, pulling it from his pocket. His hand trembled as he offered it to Hatter.

Hatter snatched it away just as it stopped ringing. And then it started again. Hatter tapped on the screen, and the ringtone stopped instantly.

"Phones," he snarled. "All of you give us your damn phones."

The other teenagers hurriedly got their phones out of their pockets, and Hatter snatched them away, turning them off.

"My phone is in my bag in the office," the principal blurted.

"I'll get it," Alma said, her voice tight.

"You." Hatter kicked the principal's leg. "Where are the keys to the school?"

"I . . . I don't have them."

Hatter kicked him harder. The man cried out.

"They're in the top drawer of my desk," the secretary blurted.

Hatter rummaged in the drawer and took them out. "I'll be back in a minute. Watch the security feed, and let me know if anyone's coming." He stepped out of the room.

Caterpillar looked down at the hostages, then cast a furtive glance at the man who lay on the floor, blood smeared on the tiles around him. How had it come to this?

CHAPTER 20

"I have fourteen minutes before the meeting with the mayor and the chief of police," Estrada said. "So we'll keep this brief."

They sat around a long metallic table within the mobile command center. Abby had taken off her vest when she sat down, hanging it on the back of her chair. Baker, the ESU commander, kept his vest on and seemed completely comfortable in it. A detailed blueprint of the school was spread out on the table.

"Agent Kelly is our FBI liaison." Estrada gestured at the agent. "He'll debrief us on what the bureau has so far."

Abby had worked with Kelly a few months before. Since the last time they'd met, he'd apparently decided to grow a goatee. The decision seemed ill advised. His facial hair was thin and patchy, and a bare spot right under his chin made it look like the two parts of the beard were trying to escape each other.

He leaned forward and cleared his throat. "This morning, one of our analysts noticed a flurry of activity on one of the Watcher forums. There was a lot of back-and-forth about sexual trafficking of children in a high school in New York. There was some debate in the forum about the date and time, but the majority of the forum agreed that the event was supposed to take place this morning."

"And why, exactly, did they think that?" Estrada asked.

"A member found a few spelling mistakes in a Twitter account of a police official. The Watchers perceived this to be intentional, a signal by the so-called cabal that he's working for. And when scrambling these words—"

"Jesus Christ. Forget I asked." Estrada groaned.

"Usually these things blow over pretty quickly, but in this case there was an indication that a local group had, um . . . deciphered this yesterday and were in fact intending to take action."

"Do we know the identity of the people in the local group?"

"Not yet, but we're working on that. All indications hint at a small group. Less than ten members. We alerted NYPD, and we tried to contact the school, but no one answered the phone. And then we got the reports about a shooting."

"Any idea how dangerous these crazies are?"

"The Watchers conspiracy group is estimated to have over a million adherents in the United States alone. They have it all, from bored twelve-year-old boys to eighty-year-old grandmas." Kelly shrugged. "My wife's uncle is a so-called Watcher, and meeting him at Christmas is always a delight. Unfortunately that group also includes some well-armed extremists; some have been previously incarcerated. Last year we arrested a Watcher who'd constructed several pipe bombs at home. I don't know yet if this is the kind of people we're dealing with here."

Estrada turned to Abby. "You talked to one of them; what's your impression?"

"I think the people we're dealing with here are incredibly dangerous, but not because they're aggressive," Abby said. "The core emotion that's propelling them right now is definitely fear. He's not gunning for a fight; he's demanding that we stay back and threatens to harm the hostages if we don't. This siege is not one that he saw coming, and right now he feels trapped and afraid. And while his fear is running high, the hostages' lives are at risk. To make matters worse, he's very suspicious.

He believes that the police want all of them dead. The phrase he used was *clean up this mess*."

"The Watchers' core belief is that law enforcement agencies are controlled by the secret cabal," Kelly said.

"Then what can we do to work with that?" Estrada asked.

"First of all, we need to reduce his fear and give him a feeling of control," Abby said. "I'd suggest pulling that chopper away if we don't need it. I'm establishing a rapport with him and working on shifting his perception of me. As a first step, I need him to trust my intentions, think of me as his ally within the police. As far as he's concerned, I've already heard about the Watchers and how they exposed Harvey Weinstein."

"How they what?" Estrada massaged the bridge of his nose.

"The Watchers claim to be the ones that unveiled the truth about the Weinstein sexual abuse cases," Abby said. "They think of it as one of their big wins."

"And you think he won't see right through your claims to believe him?"

"Probably, at first. But people want to be believed. And these guys want an ally. I also made it a point to stress that he's a compassionate guy who wants to do the right thing. Hopefully, hearing that I think of him as a compassionate guy will make him try and match that expectation. It'll help throughout the negotiations."

"Good. Did you get anything from him?"

"I have an alias. He said I can call him Caterpillar. Considering the strange choice of an alias and the fact that he offered it up pretty quickly, it's probably a nickname or an online username."

"We'll check the forums," Kelly said.

Abby nodded and glanced at Estrada. "It's worth checking the license plates of all the vehicles parked on adjacent blocks."

"We're already on that," Estrada said. "Looking for any car that doesn't belong to the school's staff or local residents. We're also pulling the footage from security cameras in the area. What can you tell me about the hostages? You talked to the principal."

"Just for a few seconds. I think some of them might be hurt. When I talked to the principal, his tone indicated that he wanted to say something about Carlos Ramirez, but Caterpillar snatched the phone away. Henry did mention that Thelma Nelson was hit in the head."

"Can we get them to release the wounded hostages?"

"I'll try, but for now I seriously doubt it. There's zero trust between us."

Estrada glanced at Baker. "What if we need to break inside?"

Baker pointed at the blueprint. "The administration wing in the school is on the top floor, in the eastern part. This here is the principal's office, and the adjacent room is the secretary's office. They've closed the blinds in those rooms, and barricaded the windows by pushing furniture against them. We know that they're using the landline from the principal's office."

"I think that's where they're keeping the hostages," Abby said. "When we first talked, he was yelling at the hostages to stay still."

"According to the vice principal, that's also the only place they can monitor the security cameras," Baker said. "So I believe they'll barricade themselves in there. Unfortunately, the security camera coverage is pretty thorough. Unless we kill the electricity, they'll see us coming."

"And if we take out the electricity, they might kill the hostages," Abby said. "They've said as much."

"I'd hoped that the security feed is on a cloud, which would let us see what they're seeing, and also to modify it, essentially rendering us invisible, but apparently it's a closed-circuit system, so no luck there. Striking fast and hard is our best shot. We can rappel from the roof and break through the windows. I think the window in the secretary's office isn't well barricaded." He tapped on the blueprint. "We might manage to take them out without any of the hostages getting hurt, but it's risky. However, we're working on constructing a replica of this section of the building back in the academy. Once we're done, we'll have a team start simulating a break-in. We need Mullen to buy us some time while we work on that."

Estrada checked his watch. "Okay. I want a brief status update from both of you in half an hour. Mullen, I want you to establish a way to contact them. There's no way we can resolve this if they won't answer the damn phone when we call."

CHAPTER 21

Shouts and shrill yelling. Sam's head throbbed. A metallic scent, a bitter taste in her mouth. The light was too bright. It was hard to breathe, and the room smelled bad, and somewhere a siren still screamed, and it all came at her at once—she wanted it to stop, stop, stop!

She squinted as she looked around her. A large smear of blood on the floor, and Mr. Ramirez lying there, motionless. Mr. Bell and Mrs. Nelson sitting next to Ray, eyes wide with terror, and all those strangers shouting at each other, holding guns, waving them. Everywhere she looked, someone was hurt. Fiona's lip was bleeding, and Mrs. Nelson's forehead had a gruesome gash, and one of the men's noses was bleeding, the blood running down his face to his chin and shirt and dripping to the floor, and Mr. Ramirez, oh god, his chest . . .

She shut her eyes and took a deep, shuddering breath. And another. With her eyes shut, she no longer felt overwhelmed. She ignored the shouting, and bit her lip hard, drawing blood. A sharp, clear pain she could focus on. She concentrated on the pain in her lip, shutting her eyes, trying to take deep, steady breaths.

After a few minutes, the world became bearable, that overwhelming sensation from before dissipating.

She listened to the two men and the woman arguing, raising their voices, talking over each other, their words blending into one unintelligible shouting match.

"Didn't have to shoot in the—"

"Who took the first shot? Not me, asshole, so why don't you—"

"We need to get that man to a hospital, or he might—"

"School kids now? What were you thinking? You're going to—"

"I told you to stop moving!"

She opened her eyes slowly. The light still hurt, like a jagged shard in her skull. She looked down at Mr. Ramirez. His shirt was soaked in blood.

"Excuse me," she said softly.

"The Circle are going to send the cops to wipe us out—"

"Not as long as we have the kids here—"

"Excuse me!" she said loudly. The two men were still yelling at each other, ignoring her, but the woman glanced her way. Deathly pale, nose red from crying, the gun trembling in her hands.

"What?" the woman snapped at her. "What is it?"

"The nurse's office is down the hall," Sam said. "Mr. Ramirez needs bandages."

The woman gaped at her.

"I know some first aid," Sam added. "I can bandage him, maybe slow the bleeding."

The woman blinked, then nodded hesitantly. "Okay. Come on." She turned to the two men, who'd finally stopped screaming at each other. "Caterpillar, I'm going to get some bandages for this man here. This girl will show me where the nurse's office is."

Caterpillar? Sam looked at the two men.

"Okay," the man with the broken nose said. "But be right back." He made an attempt to clean the blood from his face with his sleeve, smearing it onto his cheek.

"If she tries to run, shoot her," the other guy said, not even glancing in their direction.

Sam's guts turned to ice. She glanced at the gun in the woman's hand. "I won't run," she whispered.

"Okay." The woman placed a hand on Sam's forearm and led her out of the room. "Which way?" she asked.

"Here." Sam turned and began walking very slowly down the hallway. "It's the third door on the left."

"Hatter didn't really mean that," the woman said as they got farther down the hall. "None of us want to hurt you."

Sam took another step, and another. What would Mom do? Start with the basics. "My name is Samantha."

"I'm Alma." The woman said this without thinking twice. She wasn't trying to hide behind some weird nickname like her friends.

"Alma, you don't seem like the other two."

"What do you mean?" There was an edge to Alma's voice.

"You wouldn't take hostages or shoot innocent teachers or—"

"You have no idea what you're talking about. My friends wouldn't do that either. We never intended any of this to happen. All we wanted was to help." Alma's voice rose.

"Help?"

"Be quiet." Alma's lips trembled. She quickened her steps, her fingers digging into Sam's forearm, dragging her.

"Okay." Sam cursed herself. Mom would never have done that. She'd skirt around the big issues, not attack them head on. To make any kind of bond here, Sam had to do this right.

They reached the door to the nurse's office, and Alma pushed it open. She stepped inside, dragging Sam with her.

The sterile white room was free of the chaos outside. No discarded notebooks or backpacks that had been left behind. No sobbing or screaming. No blood. If it weren't for Alma's bony fingers around Sam's forearm, and the gun in the woman's hand, Sam could have pretended that this was just another day at school, going to the nurse's room because of stomach cramps or a headache.

Alma let go of her arm. "Get what you need, quickly." Her voice was steely, cold, but underneath that facade was a distinct tremor. The woman was terrified.

"Okay." Sam turned to the medicine cabinet. For a few seconds she stared at the rows of supplies, wondering what the hell she was doing. She'd done a two-day course of first aid during the summer because Mom insisted. She didn't have a clue what half of these things were.

Dad's favorite mantra was "gotta fake it till you make it." He'd grin proudly when he said it, as if he'd just come up with the cleverest sentence ever. His goofy smile would always make her roll her eyes. Now she wished he were here, grinning, being his annoying self. Wished he could tell her what to do.

There, on the top shelf. A roll of bandages. And some alcohol. Mr. Ramirez lay in the other room, bleeding. She had to hurry.

But she also had to stall. To get to know this woman better. The more they talked, the harder it would be for Alma to pull the trigger, if it came to it.

"While we're here, we should get something for Mrs. . . . for Thelma," she said.

"Thelma?"

"The secretary? She got hurt."

"Oh, right."

"And for your friend. Um . . . Caterpillar? We should get him something for his nose."

"Good idea." Alma walked over to the file cabinet. She opened the top drawer. What was she looking for? Sam glanced at the gun in Alma's hand. What if she made a grab for it?

But the nurse's desk stood between them. She could never do it fast enough. She recalled Alma's grip on her arm. The woman was stronger than she looked. And Sam's head still pounded; every movement drove a spike of pain through her skull. No. She wouldn't be able to wrestle the gun away. She turned back to the supply cabinet.

"Alma, are you a mother of one of the kids at school?" Sam ran her fingers along the supplies, pretending to read the labels.

"No. My kids don't study here."

"Oh, you have kids?" Sam kept her tone casual, curious. Injecting a bit of warmth. "How old?"

"My daughter, Frances, is ten years old. And Kyle is eleven."

"Oh, wow, one year apart?" Sam vaguely knew that this was considered tough for the parents, though she wasn't sure why. "Isn't it hard?"

"It was at first." Something crept into Alma's voice. A softness. "God, first two years after Frances was born, I hardly slept a wink. But it was worth it. They're such good friends now." She slammed the drawer and opened the next one.

"I'd love for my brother to be closer to my age." Sam's mind churned as she kept her tone casual. Names. Names were important. They made things personal and real. "But Ben's only eight. He's obsessed with animals. Did Kyle like animals when he was eight?"

"Frances did. Still does. Kyle cares mostly about his Minecraft world." Alma let out a sudden sharp sob and wiped her eye. Then she slammed the drawer loudly and opened the next one.

Sam's heart fluttered. She'd made the woman upset. But no, maybe this was a good thing. Alma was thinking about the world outside. She probably wondered if she'd see her kids again.

"I'm sorry," Sam said. She kept her tone honest, warm. "This must be so hard. You had no idea things would turn out this way. You were probably supposed to be back home in the afternoon, to be with your kids."

"I thought I'd be home by noon," Alma whispered.

"Home by noon?" Sam had learned this from Mom. Repeating a person's words almost always made them talk more.

"Frances has ballet at four. And Kyle is always hungry when he gets home; he doesn't like the food in the school's cafeteria. And now . . ." Alma's voice broke.

"Is there any way I can help?" Sam asked, shutting the supply closet.

Alma turned to face her, her eyes watery. "Yes, I think there is." Her tone was almost hopeful.

This was it. Sam had broken through. Now Alma would perhaps suggest that if they let her and the other hostages go, then Sam could tell the cops that this was all a big mistake. Or maybe she would let Sam go, and Sam could tell the cops everything. Or at the very least, Alma would let her talk to her mom.

Whatever it was, Sam knew that it would have to come from Alma. She couldn't afford to push now. "Sure." She smiled. "What do you need?"

Alma took a few steps toward Sam, eyes wide, excited. "Do you know where the Circle are keeping those kids they were going to sell? They have to be somewhere in this school. Once we find them, we can all leave."

CHAPTER 22

Caterpillar's nose kept throbbing, a dull ache that wouldn't stop. His shirt was spattered with drops of blood, and he kept wiping his lips and chin with his sleeve. His nostrils were clogged with mucus or blood or whatever, and he had to breathe through his mouth.

How bad was it? He took out his phone, turned on his camera, and checked himself in the screen.

He could hardly recognize himself.

It wasn't just the nose, though the red, swollen thing looked terrible. Apparently he hadn't properly cleaned all the blood from his face—he had smears of dried blood all over his right cheek. His eyes were bloodshot, both of them bruised in the corners. His hair was disheveled. He looked deranged.

The nose seemed twisted, and he tried to prod it gently to straighten it. A piercing flash of pain shot through his skull, accompanied by a horrifying crunching sound. He let out a moan.

"What's your problem?" Hatter grunted. The man sat in the secretary's chair, his eyes locked on the screen—watching the security camera feeds.

"You broke my damn nose," Caterpillar snarled.

"Quit whining. It was an accident. I felt someone trying to grab my gun, and I reacted. You're lucky I didn't shoot you by accident."

Caterpillar was about to snap back, but decided to stay quiet. What was the use? Arguing wouldn't turn back time. Their bad decisions from earlier felt as if they'd happened years before. Now they were stuck with the consequences.

He closed the camera app and logged into the Watcher forum, where he skimmed the posts. There were *dozens* of new threads discussing the incident, and the moderators were chasing their own tails, trying to tie them all together into one megathread. So far they were unsuccessful. He wanted to post something himself, to give them an update from inside. He bit his lip as he considered it, imagining the responses, the praise for their actions. The Watchers flocking to their cause.

No. The police would be reading the forum posts as well. It was unsafe. Maybe later, after he had a better handle on things. For now it was best to stay quiet.

"I need to call that cop again," he said instead.

Hatter glanced at him. "Yeah? What are you going to tell her?"

What *was* he going to tell her? Sure, things had gone badly. But he could still use the cards they'd been dealt and strike a winning blow at the cabal and their horrific actions. If only they could find some additional evidence of what they'd already uncovered, they could show the world the truth—Caterpillar and his associates were trying to stop a sickening trade of children, and the events that had transpired were the result of self-defense.

He glanced at the four hostages sitting in the corner of the room. "What if we demand that they look into the trade of the children from this school?"

Hatter snorted. "What? The police? Why would they do that?"

"We can offer to exchange hostages if they do a thorough investigation." A spark of excitement shot through Caterpillar. This could be done. "I bet the entire city is watching this on the news, right? Maybe the entire country. They won't be able to ignore our demands. People would be furious."

"Don't be an idiot. The police are assholes, the bitch you talked to earlier included. You think we'll tell them to investigate this thing that we *know* they're involved with, and they'll just roll over and agree? They'll tell you to stuff it up your ass."

Caterpillar gritted his teeth. "What's *your* idea, then?"

"We tell them to organize a car for us. No, you know what? A private helicopter. And some cash. We get on the helicopter with the hostages, and we get the hell out of here."

"They'd never agree to that!"

"Why wouldn't they? We have six hostages here. Even if this guy over here dies, that's the life of five hostages, one of them the principal of the school. Say we ask for two hundred thousand for each hostage. That's one million, and it's peanuts for these guys. All they want is for all of this to go away. My idea would make that happen."

"What about the trafficking of the children? Don't you want the world to know—"

"It's not going to happen, you dumb asshole!" Hatter roared at him. "Get that into your thick skull. They won. Again. We have to make the best of a shitty situation. One million dollars can get us far in Mexico. We can buy three nice houses, live the rest of our lives like—"

"What's going on?" The sudden voice from the doorway made them both whirl. It was Alma and the other girl, who held two bags.

"Just talking about our next steps," Hatter said, voice low. He fixed his stare at the girl. "What do you have there?"

To Caterpillar's surprise, the girl met Hatter's vacant stare and gave him an apologetic smile. "Nothing much. Basic first aid." She walked over to Caterpillar. "I brought you some cotton for your nose. And I found some painkillers." She rummaged in the plastic bag until she found both items and handed them to him.

"Oh, thanks." Caterpillar blinked.

"Can I bandage Mr. Ramirez?" she asked.

"Um . . . yes. Do that," Caterpillar said. He stared at the bag of cotton and the ibuprofen box in his hands.

The girl crouched by Mr. Ramirez and gently unbuttoned his bloody shirt.

Alma motioned for Caterpillar to come over. He joined her, and they stepped into the hallway.

"I talked to Samantha about the missing kids," Alma said, her voice barely above a whisper.

"Samantha? That's the girl's name?"

"Yes. And the other one's named Fiona. The boy's name is Ray. Anyway, she said she hasn't heard about any kids being trafficked here."

"That's not surprising. They wouldn't involve the students."

Alma nodded. "But she said she can show us around the school. She knows about a few private corners they could be stashed in."

Caterpillar glanced at Samantha warily. The girl had opened Mr. Ramirez's shirt and was now unrolling some gauze, her face deathly pale. "I don't like it."

"I don't like any of it," Alma said. "But if we find them . . ."

"Yeah." If they found the kids, it would change everything. "Hatter thinks we should demand a private chopper. And ransom. Escape to Mexico or something."

Alma's eyes widened. "We can't do that. It won't work. And even if we did, I'm not leaving my family behind."

"Yeah, I'm with you. I'm going to talk to that cop again. But I won't mention that bullshit."

"You have to buy us some time. We can find those kids."

Caterpillar said nothing. Another option occurred to him. What if they'd made a terrible mistake? What if the kids had never been here?

What if all of this had been a trap set by the cabal to take down the Watchers?

Buying time wasn't enough. They had to strike back.

"I don't trust Hatter," Alma said.

"Yeah. Me neither." Caterpillar glanced at the room through the doorway.

Hatter, completely motionless, stared at Samantha. His lips were twisted in a way that made Caterpillar think of a large toad. He wished he hadn't involved the man in all of this. But wishes couldn't change the past.

CHAPTER 23

April 5, 2015

"I'm sorry. We did all we could, but . . ."

Neal stared at the nurse's expression as she kept talking, each word dismantling the tower of hopes and dreams he'd been building for the past five months.

"We couldn't find a pulse. The fetus just . . ."

Just that morning they'd been talking about a name. Last night he'd checked out baby cots online. A week ago he'd walked by a playground, and a vivid image of walking there with his child had popped into his mind.

"She probably stopped—"

"She?" he interrupted.

The nurse's eyes widened. "The fetus, I mean," she stammered.

"The child . . . it was a girl?" Last checkup, they'd told the doctor they didn't want to know the gender. They wanted it to be a surprise. And there it was. Surprise.

The nurse turned pale. She gave him a quick nod. "I'll, um . . . you can go in." She hurried away.

He shuffled into the room, an assortment of medical instruments and monitors lining the walls. Jackie lay on the bed, a turquoise blanket draped over her. Her eyes were open and vacant, staring at nothing. She didn't look at him when he came in.

"Hey," he whispered.

A slight tremor in her lips. No other response. Three days ago she'd told him that she hoped their child would get her nose and not his. Did she know it was a girl? He hoped not.

He walked over to her. Her hand was dangling, lifeless. He took it in his, gave her a tiny squeeze. "I'm sorry, sweetie."

"Me too," she mumbled.

When she'd called him earlier, telling him she had cramps, neither of them was very concerned. Jackie had had cramps repeatedly in the past couple of months. They'd gone to the doctor every few days, only to find out that everything was fine.

Which was why, when his boss had delayed him on his way out, he thought nothing of it. There was some urgent paperwork to be done. It couldn't wait. No big deal. He did the paperwork. Finished it in less than an hour. But then there was a problem with a traffic light on the way home, and he got stuck in a jam for more than thirty minutes.

When he'd gotten home, there'd been a spot of blood on Jackie's pants, and she'd been moaning in pain.

Watching her now, he felt the guilt swelling inside him. This was his fault. If he'd only told his boss to shove his paperwork. If he'd taken a different route. Maybe they could have saved his girl. And Jackie wouldn't have been lying here right now, her eyes dead.

Earlier, during lunch break, a coworker had told him to enjoy his last days of freedom, and Neal had laughed.

Giving Jackie's hand another squeeze, he said, "I'll go get you some things from home, okay?"

Her eyelids fluttered. She said nothing.

He hurried out of the room.

The nurse was outside in the corridor, talking to a doctor. As Neal stepped out, she glanced at him, then lowered her voice. The doctor frowned, then turned and gave Neal a long look before turning back to the nurse, whispering something to her.

What were they talking about? A sudden suspicion pierced the waves of guilt that threatened to consume him. He walked toward them, and they both stopped talking and strode away.

They'd been talking about him. About Jackie.

About their girl.

Something they didn't want him to hear. Didn't want him to know.

The guilt was fading away now, replaced by something else.

Had this really been something that couldn't have been prevented? *Every single time* they'd gone to the doctor before, everything had been fine. What had happened today?

He suddenly, wildly, thought of his boss. Since when was paperwork urgent? Urgent paperwork? That wasn't even a thing. And that traffic light. He thought back to all those countless days he'd driven back and forth on that road. Had the traffic light *ever* been broken before? Never.

Then why today? What had happened today?

That look the doctor had given him. Like he knew something.

The guilt had dissipated completely now. This hadn't been his fault. He wasn't sure who was responsible, not yet. But he was sure of one thing. Someone was to blame. And it wasn't him.

CHAPTER 24

Abby sat in the primary negotiator's seat, her earphones on. The line in the principal's office was still busy, as was the line of the secretary's office. Abby tried both every few minutes. If the people inside didn't answer soon, she might have to try to speak through the bullhorn, asking that they answer the phone. She hated the bullhorn. It instantly gave an aggressive edge to everything she said.

Will sat beside her, the second pair of earphones on his neck. He flipped a page in the initial summary Tammi had printed regarding the Watchers.

"Some of their theories are pretty involved," he muttered. "It'll be difficult to steer the discussion with this."

"We don't actually need to steer the discussion when it comes to the Watcher conspiracy theories," Abby said. "We use it to create a rapport, to give them the feeling of recognition."

"But their theories inherently distrust the police. We can't build trust like that."

"'The police' is a big, terrifying, abstract thing. But they'll be talking to Abby and Will, their friends within the police."

Will glanced at her skeptically. "This is not a jonesing addict suffering from hallucinations. This is just a theory. We can prod them to see that it makes no sense."

Abby raised her eyebrows in surprise. "Why?"

"Because if we break it, we make them see there's no good reason to stay in there. The reason for them being there doesn't exist anymore."

Abby shook her head. "You're right. This isn't a hallucination or a delusion. It's more like a religion. You don't go telling a religious extremist holding hostages that his god doesn't exist."

"This isn't a religion." Will smacked the papers in his hand. "It says here that the Watchers believe that Michael Jackson was assassinated by the cabal because he tried to expose them. That's not—"

The phone rang. Both of them froze. Abby glanced at the display. They'd managed to get the cellular company to reroute any calls that came to Judith Pratchett's phone from the school straight to the line in the negotiator van. And the call that was ringing was from the principal's office line.

Abby waited for Will to place the headset on before answering. "Hello?"

"Is this Abby?" Same voice. It was Caterpillar again.

"Yes. Caterpillar, I'm glad you called; people here were getting worried. How are you holding up in there?"

"We're fine." He sounded wary, but not as frightened and manic as before. "So long as the police keep away from the school, nobody will get hurt."

"Absolutely. I really appreciate your efforts to prevent this thing getting out of hand. I know that you want people to see your side of the story, and I will do my very best to explain that you were trying to help those kids. But I'm worried about how it'll look if someone gets hurt."

"As long as you stay away, there's no reason for that."

Abby waited for a second, then said, "Henry said that Thelma hurt her head. So I'm concerned about her safety. A head injury could become worse without medical attention."

"I think she's fine. That's not why I called. I want you to do something for me."

Abby glanced at Will, feeling that mix of relief and trepidation. In every crisis, demands changed the conversation. They gave the negotiator valuable information about the subject's state of mind. They also indicated that the subject was looking forward and wasn't just stuck in the terrifying now. Sometimes, when the demands were simple, they could be met, to foster goodwill.

More often than not they were difficult to comply with. And *that* had to be handled very carefully.

"How can I help with your situation?" Abby asked.

"You know that message on Twitter I told you about? The one with the code?"

"I remember. You and your friends managed to decode a message that helped you figure out about the sex trafficking of the kids at school. Which is why you decided to help those children."

"Exactly." He sounded satisfied. "The message came from the NYPD's chief of detectives."

"The chief of detectives?" Abby echoed, injecting surprise into her tone.

"We want his admission. We want him to announce publicly that his message had been sent with the intention of attracting potential customers. We want him to admit that he was instructed to do it. We want to expose those bastards once and for all."

An impossible, insane demand. But it was definitely something that she could work with. First of all, she needed to change the tone. The demand came angrily. Caterpillar wanted to hurt the shadowy cabal he imagined was pulling the strings. Anger was a dangerous motivation that made people dig in, refuse to be flexible. But Abby could reflect his words back to him, make him see his own demands in a better light.

"I want to make sure I got it right. You want the chief of detectives to admit to what you discovered, that his tweet was about child trafficking. Because once he does that, people will realize that you were right to act, and that you only did what you did to save those children."

"Yeah, that's right."

"If we manage to shed light on it, people will definitely understand your actions. Especially if no one got badly hurt."

A slight pause there. "Right."

"The thing that concerns me is that if someone *is* badly hurt and we don't get them help, it will make things look bad. After all, you were trying to *save* lives."

"Yeah." He cleared his throat. "Thelma . . . she's okay. But there's a guy here who's hurt. It wasn't our fault. It was an accident."

"Okay. What can we do about that?" If she suggested a solution, Caterpillar would refuse, suspecting a trick. She needed him to suggest one.

"I guess he should get some help soon. But first I want that admission."

"About that. There are a few things I need to do to make that happen. I'll have to get some additional proof, because it's not likely he'll just admit it if I tell him to. I'll start digging, but that means I have to get permission to check the police database. I'll need to question the school's faculty and a few people close to the chief. I'll need to get a court order to instruct Twitter to give us some information about that tweet, like who read it, and cross-reference it with known sexual offenders. And I want to check forums of sex offenders that focus on children, and see if there's been any chatter about this. But that might mean working with the bureau, so I have to find someone I can trust there."

"Uh . . . okay."

Abby leaned back in her chair. Her right ear was squashed. Her glasses were trapped underneath the earphones and dug into her temples. She adjusted the earphones. "All that would take time. I'll need you to be patient and put up with the stress for a while longer. In the meantime I will keep everything in control here, if you keep things in control there. That means you need to control both your friends and the other people with you. How can you do that?"

"My friends will agree to that. They want people to see the truth. And the hostages are fine. One of them is bandaging Carlos right now, and it looks like she's doing a good job. And the rest are doing as they're told."

"That's good. I'll also need you to leave the line open so that I can call whenever I have an update on my investigation."

"I don't want people calling here, threatening us, or trying to tell us to surrender."

"I promise that won't happen. It's just so that I'll be able to update you, or in case I have a question regarding the investigation."

"Yeah, okay."

"Okay. I'm concerned about Carlos. This might take a while, and I don't want his situation to get any worse."

"He's being taken care of. He's fine."

"Once people realize why you did all this, it would present you in a very positive light. But if Carlos is badly hurt—"

"I said he's fine." He was getting impatient and defensive.

She decided to back off. She would bring Carlos up again in their next call. "How about everyone else? Is anyone hungry or thirsty?"

"We'll take care of that. You just do what you said." The line went dead.

Abby removed her headphones and placed them on the table. She took off her glasses as well, letting the world turn into a soft blur. She let out a long breath.

"We definitely need to prioritize getting Carlos Ramirez out of there," Will said.

"Yeah." Abby put her glasses back on. "Did you notice how he talked about the hostage bandaging Carlos? He said 'one of them' at first, and then 'she,' talking about her in the abstract."

Will nodded. "But Thelma was mentioned earlier in the conversation by name. It's someone else. And I think I heard someone in the background. Hang on."

He fiddled with the recording panel. Abby hadn't heard anything in the background. The primary negotiator had to focus on the dialogue, listening closely to the subject, constantly thinking about the best way to navigate and influence the conversation. That meant that the rest—background noises, small mannerisms, changes in tone—often faded away. It was the second negotiator's job to pay attention to the details.

"There." Will hit play.

Abby heard herself say, "How can I help with your situation?" Caterpillar answered, talking about Twitter. And in the background . . . something. She frowned. Will rewound, then adjusted the sound so that Abby's and Caterpillar's voices were dimmer, the background noises enhanced. He pressed play again. And there it was. A sharp sob, someone saying, "Oh god." A high, feminine voice. And Abby was almost certain it had been a young girl.

"One of the students?" she said.

"It sounds like it, right? A girl."

Abby glanced at the list of the missing kids on the whiteboard, even though she already knew the names by heart. "So it was probably either Lisbeth or Ruby."

"She could be the one who was bandaging Carlos. We can check with the parents, see if any of them knew some first aid." Will rewound the recording a few seconds earlier. "There's something else. Listen to his tone here."

Abby listened as Caterpillar said, "That's not why I called. I want you to do something for me." Will stopped the recording and looked at her.

"He lowered his voice," Abby said.

"Exactly. He didn't want to be heard. I think his associates aren't on board with his demands. He's talking from the principal's office, right? And we think that at least one of them is watching the security camera feed in the secretary's office. He lowered his voice so they couldn't hear him."

"You're probably right. We could use that to—"

The back of the cabin opened, and Carver stepped inside, Tammi following him. The moment Abby saw Carver's expression, a shard of fear pierced her guts.

"What did you find?" she asked.

"We have descriptions of the three intruders," Carver said. "They asked a kid how to get to the secretary's office on the third floor. And we have some useful statements from staff and from other kids. The hostage takers are using handguns, and only one had a bag with her, so they probably have very limited ammunition. But we have some bad news. It's about Samantha."

"Is she hurt?" Abby shot up from her chair, her gut clenched. "Where is she?"

"She isn't with the rest of the kids," Carver said. "She's missing."

"But they checked the names," Abby blurted, glancing at the list of names on the whiteboard, as if she'd missed the name of her own daughter.

"They'd checked all the names according to the attendance system," Carver said. "But Samantha wasn't present in any of her classes today. I talked to a friend of hers who said that she sometimes skips class to practice with her band. None of the kids in the band are present. And none of them are answering their phones."

Abby's head spun, and she recalled that girl who'd said *oh god* in the recording. A girl who, she now realized, sounded a lot like Sam's friend Fiona. And Sam knew some first aid.

Her daughter was inside the school.

CHAPTER 25

The sticky blood soaked into Sam's jeans, and she felt it on her skin constantly, a cloying, sickening feeling. She pushed the sensation away from her mind, just as she ignored the guns around her, the occasional whimper from her friend, the creepy stares she got from Hatter.

Mr. Ramirez's breathing was labored, and a trickle of blood ran from his lips. The gaping hole in his chest was covered in frothy blood. It hissed whenever he inhaled. The bullet had probably punctured the man's lungs.

Sam was in Mr. Ramirez's chemistry class. She hated it, even though he constantly tried to explain how beautiful chemistry was. Fiona and Sam used to say that Mr. Ramirez probably watched periodic table porn in secret. They'd laughed their asses off, talking about the elements that really turned him on. Now, as she thought about it, a sob hitched in her throat. She shouldn't have said that. He'd just been trying to get them to enjoy what he was teaching.

She'd brought some alcohol pads from the nurse's office, and she used several to clean the wound gently. Each pad turned pink within seconds, and she discarded them one after the other, wishing she'd taken more.

What next? Just placing gauze on the thing wouldn't work.

"Alma," she said, her voice low. "I need you to check on your phone how to bandage a chest wound."

"I thought you knew what you were doing," Hatter said. "The way you talked, I figured you're practically a surgeon."

Sam glanced at him, adopting an apologetic expression. "I did a first aid course, but we didn't really cover bullet wounds, and I think his lung is punctured."

He kept his eyes on her, his lower lip bulging out. She held his gaze for a bit, then looked away. Unlike his two friends, this guy didn't seem worried by the situation. In a way, he was almost relishing it. Was he enjoying the danger? Or did he get a rush from holding people at gunpoint? Sam had no idea. Her best bet was to keep away from him. Alma, despite her insane delusions about some sort of nefarious group of people who controlled the world, was easier to talk to.

"I think it's called a sucking chest wound," Alma said, reading from her phone. "Um . . . it says you should tape some sort of plastic over the wound. You can use the packaging of the sterile bandages."

"Is there, like . . . a video or something?" Sam asked desperately.

"I can look—"

"How about you do what Alma told you?" Hatter barked at Sam. "The guy's a goner anyway. You want to play doctor, go ahead. But you're not turning this place into nursing school."

"Hatter," Alma said. "We should do our best to—"

Hatter whirled and stood up, fists clenched. "What's up with you and this girl?" he snarled. "Are you becoming *friends*? Are you trying to screw with us, Alma? Do you think that when this is over, this girl will tell the police that you weren't a part of all this?"

"N-no."

"Because if I remember correctly, you aimed your gun at these people. And when I said we shouldn't go inside, it was *you* who said that we should."

Alma's lips trembled, and she lowered her phone slowly.

Sam turned her back on them, focusing on Mr. Ramirez. The sterile bandages were stored separately, each in a white plastic package. She carefully opened one so that the plastic didn't tear too much. Then she wiped the plastic with an alcohol pad, hoping it was enough to properly sterilize it. She placed it flat on the gaping wound. He groaned faintly, his eyes still shut. Sam prayed the man was truly unconscious. She couldn't even begin to imagine the agony he was in otherwise. Grabbing the roll of tape, she tried to fasten the plastic wrapper with a piece of it, but it kept slipping off.

"I need someone to lift him up while I tape it," she said.

Hatter got up from his chair and crouched by her. He looked down at Mr. Ramirez, then grabbed the man under his armpits and propped him up roughly.

"Thanks," Sam said. She began unrolling the tape to wrap around Mr. Ramirez's chest. That forced her to lean closer to Hatter, their heads inches from each other. His heavy breath brushed her cheek, the smell of blood intermingling with a pungent odor. She focused on the tape, making sure it didn't twist as she fastened it. Hatter inhaled as she turned her head away from him. She did her best to ignore his presence, managing to wrap the tape once around the body. All she wanted was to be done with this. But she knew it was not enough.

"I, uh . . . need to bandage him as well," she said.

"Go ahead," Hatter said.

Wrapping the bandage was worse. She had to do it several times, the proximity to Hatter almost impossible to bear. Once her forehead brushed against his cheek. Blood was already seeping underneath the dressing, turning the white cloth purple. His skin was cold. Too cold? She had no idea. His breathing was faint and labored. Her eyes filled with tears, and she didn't know if it was because she was scared of Hatter, or because she knew that Mr. Ramirez was dying, or maybe because it was all just too much. She sniffed, and kept unspooling the bandage, doing her best to bind his wound as tightly as she could.

Finally, she was done. She fastened it shut and drew away, letting out a shuddering breath. She took another alcohol pad and wiped the sticky blood from her hands.

Hatter lowered Mr. Ramirez to the floor and, without saying a word, sat back down in front of the computer, staring at the screen.

Sam buttoned Mr. Ramirez's shirt. Once she was done, she inspected him for any other wounds. His pants were soaked with blood, and she carefully checked them, searching for holes. The outline of his wallet and his phone bulged from his pockets. Did his wallet have photos of children? Did his phone display a missed call from a wife or a close friend? She exhaled. She'd done what she could.

All this time she'd acted out of need, each task following the last one. Now, with nothing left to do, she felt lost. She returned to the corner and sat by Fiona. She took one of Fiona's hands, their fingers intertwining. Fiona gave her hand a light squeeze. Sam glanced at her friend, giving her a hint of a smile.

Would they one day talk about this moment, like they talked about everything else? Using phrases like *Oh, and you remember how . . .* and *I couldn't believe that . . .* like they did with all their shared memories? Sometimes it felt to Sam that she and Fiona spent almost all their time talking about stuff that had happened before. That day Fiona cut Britney's pigtail with scissors in first grade. Or that time Sam accidentally walked in on Mrs. Heroux, their French teacher, kissing someone's father. Or how in second grade Fiona intentionally threw up in class to avoid an upcoming math test. Or that time when they were five years old and hid underneath Fiona's dad's desk, each of them eating a large piece of paper to see what it tasted like.

And now this. No matter what, she couldn't see them talking about this day. Not even if they all came out unharmed. She leaned her head on her friend's shoulder, trying to find solace in the touch.

The second man—Caterpillar—stepped out of the principal's office. "I talked to the cop and bought us some time."

"What about the private helicopter?" Hatter asked.

"I didn't talk to her about that yet," Caterpillar said. "I did all I could to stop them from storming the building."

"You talked to her for ages!" Hatter snapped. "What the hell did you talk about? The weather?"

"I'm still trying to figure out if we can even trust her." Caterpillar raised his voice. "Do you want me to offer a hostage trade-off after ten minutes of conversation?"

"You better not be trying to cut some sort of deal with her," Hatter said.

"You know me better than that," Caterpillar said.

Growing up in a house with parents whose marriage was falling apart had taught Sam to listen closely while pretending not to hear. Every time Mom and Dad argued, Sam would walk around the house like a deaf ghost, making no noise, hardly breathing, ignoring the raised voices, the accusations, the eventual screams. At first she'd hide in her room under the blanket, waiting for it to stop. But when it kept on going, she'd learned to live with it. She'd learned to listen to every word, somehow believing that if she understood what was going on, she could stop the next fight. She could stop Dad from leaving.

Now she listened again in the hope that knowing what was going on could help her get out of this safely.

Hatter stared at Caterpillar for a few seconds, then seemed to relax. "So? Do you think we can trust her?"

"I don't know yet, but she isn't one of the agents we know about. And she sounds like she genuinely doesn't want anyone hurt."

"Yeah? What's her name?"

"Abby."

Fiona gasped, and Sam squeezed her hand hard, her own heart thudding. Mom was the one talking to Caterpillar on the phone. Did she know that Sam was a hostage? Would it change how her mom negotiated?

She allowed herself to feel hopeful. Mom was there, trying to get her out safely. And if anyone could do it, it was her mom.

CHAPTER 26

When Sam had been eight, Abby had taken her to the mall to do some shopping. Sam needed new shoes. It took them forty-five interminably long minutes to find the right pair—white, with a pink sparkling stripe. Abby, relieved and exhausted, stood in line to purchase them. Sam was beside her. And then she wasn't.

It happened so fast. Abby looked around, first confused, then annoyed. And then anxious.

And a few seconds later, terrified.

Sam had disappeared.

She was shrieking for Sam repeatedly, running all around the store, and outside, and back inside, everyone staring at her, looking around them, asking her if her child was missing, and yes, of course her daughter was missing, and someone asked what he looked like, and Abby stared at them until she realized they thought that Sam was a *boy* and she shrieked that she was a girl, just a little girl, her name was Samantha, did anyone see where she went . . .

And then there she was.

There was another pair of shoes she liked, with a *purple* sparkling stripe. She'd decided to check for herself if there was a pair her size, and walked off into the storage room in the back.

That moment was seared in Abby's memory. That feeling of absolute heart-stopping terror. Occasionally, at night, she'd dream of that moment, and wake up, breathing heavily, and see that she was in bed, that it had been just a dream, and that Sam was in her own bedroom, and on that day she'd been fine, she was only gone for a few terrible seconds.

Now that feeling had returned. The seconds ticked by, and the sensation didn't abate.

The not knowing.

The desperation.

The breathlessness.

The fear.

". . . think that all three children are in the school," Will said.

Abby blinked and looked at him, realizing that she hadn't even been aware that he was talking.

She and Will were in the mobile command center with Estrada. Will was briefing the commander. Abby was . . .

Abby was trying to remember how to breathe.

She was trying to remind herself that when done right, hostage situations usually ended nonviolently. She was trying to remind herself that Sam was a smart girl. She was trying to keep away all those names of terrible events, the Platte Canyon High School and the West Nickel Mines and Ruby Ridge and the Wilcox massacre and the Sacramento hostage crisis and . . . and . . .

"Do we know if they're being held hostage?" Estrada asked. He was talking to Will, but glanced briefly at Abby.

You didn't talk like that in front of the parents. Parents didn't get the details. They were assured that "we are doing everything we can" and that "we have a lot of experience in these kinds of situations." You didn't tell the parents that you didn't know if their kids were being held hostage or if they were cowering in a classroom, terrified of being found. You didn't tell parents that you didn't know who the men holding their kids were, and all you had was an online nickname. You didn't tell the parents that the men had only guns and limited ammunition, but it was still more than enough to kill their kids, and the rest of the hostages, several times over.

You didn't tell the parents all that.

"We don't know for sure, but we believe we've heard Fiona Brock's voice in the background of the last phone conversation," Will said.

"Okay," Estrada said. "I was notified that of the other names of missing kids, Lisbeth Reynolds showed up at her home. And Barry Johns turned up a few blocks away. He ran, got lost, and hid in an alley. So two of the four missing kids are accounted for. We don't know about the other two yet."

What if Sam had decided to run back home, like Lisbeth had? There was no one there. What if she was in her room right now? Abby took out her phone, about to call Sam again. Her finger hovered an inch above the screen. A terrifying image bloomed in her mind. Sam hiding under a desk somewhere in the school. An armed man walking past, Sam holding her breath so that he didn't hear her. And then . . . her phone ringing.

Abby let out a faint gasp and put the phone down. Sam would never have walked home without telling anyone, like Lisbeth. And she would have called by now, if she could.

The slight movement made both men turn to face her.

"We've made some progress in the negotiation," she said. She tried to keep her voice steady, but it was useless. Her vocal cords were clogged with tears of fear, tight with tension. Every word came out hoarse, uneven. "We bought ourselves a lot of time, and they will keep the landline free for our calls, so for now we can talk to them whenever we want. They also verified that Carlos Ramirez is there and is hurt, and it sounds like they'll agree to get him some medical attention, though we haven't established anything concrete yet."

"What do they want?" Estrada asked.

Abby let Will summarize it; the effort of saying a few simple sentences had almost been too much. She'd have to postpone the next conversation with Caterpillar, get her shit together first.

Estrada listened, leaning forward, lips pursed. As soon as Will finished, he exhaled softly and cleared his throat.

"Okay, so we have some time," he said. "We need to decide how to switch negotiators."

Abby blinked. "What?"

"We can't have you negotiating with these people while they're holding your daughter hostage."

"But they don't know she's my daughter. It shouldn't impact the way they're handling this." She glanced at Will for encouragement, but he didn't meet her gaze.

"This isn't about what *they* know," Estrada said. "You can't perform this negotiation. Not while your child is at risk."

No, she was the *only* one who could do this. She couldn't trust anyone else to do it right and save Sam. She had to make that abundantly clear. "With all due respect, sir, I think this is more about me being a woman and less about how I do my job. You only say that because I'm a *mother*. But if I were a man, you would never tell me that."

Estrada stared at her, surprised. She'd been shouting, standing up, her fists clenched. When had that happened?

"This isn't about you being a mother," he said softly. "I have three children, Mullen. If any of them was inside that school, I would go to pieces. If anything, I'm astounded how well you're holding up. But you can't possibly be the negotiator."

She sat back down. "Switching negotiators is always dangerous. I already have a rapport with these guys. I've made a lot of progress. If we switch now—"

"You gave us a good reason to explain the switch," Will said.

She turned to him in disbelief. "What?"

"You told them that you're going to investigate their claims, right? You made it sound like you're going to do it all on your own. They'll understand if you aren't available to talk to them while you do it."

"Will, you know I can do this. If anything, Sam being there will only serve to focus me. And we don't even know that she's a hostage. What if we switch and she shows up out here two minutes later? We'll be jeopardizing this negotiation for nothing. We can't afford to do that."

"This isn't a discussion, Mullen," Estrada said. "And it's not your call, or Vereen's. It's mine. I want you to switch, and do it as soon as possible."

"But—"

"Vereen." Estrada turned away from her. "I want you here in twenty minutes for a briefing with Baker from ESU. We're done here."

It was like one of those nightmares where you kept falling. And Abby had nothing to grab hold of.

CHAPTER 27

Abby sat in the primary negotiator's seat, earphones on. An invisible fist was clutching her heart, slowly squeezing.

"Are you up for this?" Will asked.

"Yeah," she whispered.

Will touched her forearm, and she drew away sharply. He let his hand drop and put on his own earphones.

She hit the call button. The phone rang. One ring. Two rings.

Her throat clenched. She wasn't sure she'd be able to talk once they answered. Perhaps she wasn't up for this. Will and Estrada were right; she couldn't negotiate like this. She couldn't even perform this simple handover. She glanced at the disconnect button. Maybe she should disconnect the call, take a walk, calm down, then call again. She almost did.

Third ring.

But they were paranoid in there, and calling them and hanging up wouldn't make them calmer. She couldn't afford to mess this up. She needed to do this right for Sam.

She shut her eyes, gritting her teeth.

Fourth ring.

What if they didn't answer? What if the person who answered wasn't Caterpillar? What if they already knew Sam was her daughter and threatened to kill her if she didn't comply with their demands? What then?

A click, and then a voice.

"Hello?" It was Caterpillar. Speaking quietly, probably so that he couldn't be heard by his friends.

"Hi, Caterpillar, it's Abby." Her voice came out as warm and natural as ever. Years of training had prepared her for this. Never let them know what you felt. Even now, barely keeping her wits, she slid into the conversation easily. She smiled, hoping that he would hear it in her voice. "I already have some good news. I have access to the police database, so I can research this thing thoroughly."

"Okay, good, what did you find?"

"Like we discussed before, it will take me a while to research this, and I can't do it from here. So I'm going to drive back to the station and start digging. We'll see what I can uncover."

"Wait!" Caterpillar raised his voice, sounding panicky. "We need you here to keep everyone away."

"I'm sorry, but I can't investigate this from here," Abby said.

"Find a damn solution! We need you to expose the truth about what happened."

Abby needed to rephrase his demand for him, and the words came to her, but a fraction of a second slower than usual. Nothing that Caterpillar would notice. But Will raised an eyebrow at the short silence.

She cleared her throat. "Your stress is understandable. You want me to find evidence of the truth, that the chief of detectives was involved in child trafficking from this school, because I'm the only cop who currently believes you. But you also want me to be here and ensure everyone's safety. And it's hard for you to put your trust in the police if there's no one here that you can rely on."

"Yeah, exactly, so you need to solve this."

"How do you suggest we solve this?" She'd stated the problem clearly, and had given him only one way out.

Now she needed him to take the bait and solve this for her.

This was going too slow. Caterpillar clenched the phone, frustrated. Everything was suddenly difficult, insurmountable. There was no way they could do this. Get this one cop to find the truth for them, while surviving long enough without the police storming in? Not to mention the teacher who was clearly about to die, and the cabal probably closing in with their agents, and Hatter making things worse, and Alma losing her trust in him, and . . . and . . .

He groaned, helpless.

"Hey, Caterpillar." Abby's voice in his ear, calm, warm. "You're doing great. I really appreciate how you're keeping everyone safe. We can do this together, okay? One thing at a time. Let's figure out how to move forward."

"Okay," he said, exhausted. "Okay, let me think."

He needed her to do this for him. The Watchers never had access to the resources that this cop had. There was no way around it. But if she left, who would prevent the cops and the bureau from storming this place? She was the only one he trusted. But could he trust her judgment?

He'd have to.

"Is there someone else who you trust, who could make sure that they all stay away?" he asked. "It has to be someone you have absolute faith in. Someone who would care about the lives of the hostages here more than anything. And you don't need to tell him what you're doing. They don't need to know all that. It just has to be someone who can make sure that these people out there stay away, no matter what."

"You're asking if I know someone who's trustworthy and good, who can be relied upon to keep everyone safe? Someone who can keep things here under control?"

"Yes."

"I know one guy who can do that," Abby said, no hesitation in her voice. "He's someone I work with. His name is Will. I've known him for a long time. He's one of the most honorable people I know. Everyone respects him; they'd listen to him. And he would never cooperate with anything that would put people at risk."

"Okay. Can you get him to come here and keep things under control?"

"Absolutely. I will contact him right now. What about you? How are things on your end? Everything under control?"

"Absolutely."

◆ ◆ ◆

Sam's head was spinning. She hadn't eaten breakfast and had barely drunk any water since she'd woken up. When her sugar levels dipped, she always felt nauseous and light headed. She leaned against Fiona, resting her head on her friend's shoulder, and took deep breaths to keep the nausea at bay.

In the adjacent room, Caterpillar was talking on the phone again, probably with Mom. She tried to listen but could hardly hear anything beyond faint murmurs.

It occurred to her that if she screamed right now for help, her mom would hear her. For a few seconds she imagined it, her mom speaking on the phone, hearing Sam's cries for help, rushing into the school, gun drawn, to save her daughter.

But that would not be how it played out. If she screamed for help, Hatter would hit her or, worse, shoot her. Mom would hear it but would not be able to rush in because it would put her and the rest of the hostages in danger. And everything would go to hell.

Still, what if she did try to send a message to Mom?

Once, when she'd been younger, Mom had been called to talk to a man who'd barricaded himself in his home with his wife and child and threatened to shoot them. Mom had talked to him on and off throughout the day. It took them twenty-two hours to get the man to surrender, and the wife and daughter came out unharmed. Sam had later asked her mom what she had talked about all that time.

And Mom told her that she'd listened. Because desperate people mostly wanted to be heard. And because information was the negotiator's oxygen. The more they knew, the better, Mom said. If they knew enough, they could form a solid strategy to resolve everything.

Mom needed information.

"Alma," she said, her voice alarmed and loud. "I don't think that Mr. Ramirez is breathing. I need to check him, okay?"

Alma, who was rummaging through one of the secretary's file cabinets, raised her head and looked at him. "He seems the same to me," she said hesitantly.

"He's been shot in the chest, and I think it pierced his lung," Sam said, raising her voice. "If this goes badly, he'll die! We need to get him help."

"Shut up!" Hatter barked from his chair.

"But, Hatter, you have to listen to me—"

"No one asked for your damn opinion!"

"There's six of us here," Sam cried, sounding desperate. "Even if you let him go, you'll have five hostages. And if you and Alma—"

"I told you to shut the hell up!" Hatter screamed, lunging from his chair, pointing his gun at her. "Do I need to shoot you to make that happen?"

It started with background mutterings, and Abby tried to ignore them, focusing on Caterpillar's words. During this call, it was Will's job to listen to the voices in the background.

But as the voices rose, she couldn't ignore them. Not any longer.

It was Sam. Shouting at someone. Arguing. Riling armed men, making them dangerous and unpredictable.

And then a man screaming, "Do I need to shoot you to make that happen?"

More shouts, and Caterpillar was yelling, "Stop that—don't move, don't any of you move."

"Caterpillar," Abby said, raising her voice. "It sounds like things are getting—"

"Don't shoot!" a woman screamed.

"Stop talking, shut up, you'll get us killed!"

"Put that gun down!"

"All of you, shut the hell up!" Caterpillar shouted.

"Caterpillar!" Abby was shouting herself. "Tell them to calm down! You should all calm down!"

The screams continued, but Abby couldn't parse what they were saying. Her breath was gone, a frosty chill spreading through her chest as her own last shout echoed in her mind.

She'd shouted at the subject. She'd told him to *calm down.*

Had anyone ever calmed down when someone told them to? Abby had never seen it happen, not in all the hundreds of crisis transcripts she'd read, and not in her lifetime. She knew that.

An angry person, when told to calm down, would get angrier.

Negotiators *never* said that. It wasn't in their lexicon. It was something she repeatedly taught other cops. *Never* ever *tell someone to relax or calm down.*

She tried to find her voice, to say something else, but it was gone. Her throat clenched shut. She blinked rapidly, trying to refocus on what was going on there. Her eyes met Will's.

He was staring at her, aghast.

Then Caterpillar barked into the phone, "I'll talk to you later. Just get that guy to come here."

And he hung up.

"Jesus Christ," Abby breathed.

"Abby," Will said softly.

"No." She raised her hand. "Don't. Please. Just . . . give me a moment."

She took off the headphones and stood up, dazed. Stumbled over to the board and stared at it. She needed to write some of this down. They had new information. They had . . .

That man had threatened to shoot Sam. And Abby, if anything, had made it worse.

She slammed the whiteboard with her palm, smearing the ink. "Damn it!" Her voice was all wrong, like a wounded animal's.

"I don't think he even heard you," Will said. "And it didn't sound like anyone had gotten hurt. You've done a good job with the switch. I'll have some trust when I call him."

"Yeah," she said hollowly.

"I'll call in a few minutes, make sure that they've calmed down . . . that everyone's safe."

"Yeah."

"I think Sam was trying to be heard. She was feeding us information. We now know two new names. We know how many hostages there are and what the situation with Carlos is. We know—"

"She shouldn't have taken that risk." Abby's voice trembled. "She should wait for us to do our job. What the hell was she thinking, doing that? What if they shoot her, Will?"

"They won't."

"You don't know that."

For a few seconds they were both quiet.

"I can't be here," Abby finally said.

"No, you can't," Will agreed.

"You need to get a different second negotiator. Put Tammi on it, but you'll need to get someone to fill her place. Maybe Elsbeth. Or Bradly. Bradly's good—"

"I'll take care of it."

"Okay."

"We'll get her out. We'll get all of them out. You can trust me."

Could she? Could she trust anyone with her daughter's life?

It didn't matter. She couldn't trust herself. Not anymore.

CHAPTER 28

Abby hesitated before finally knocking on Steve's front door. She'd wanted to stay at the school, but she didn't want to distract Will. It would only endanger Sam. So she'd forced herself to get in the car and drive away. And the only thing she could do was go and see Ben.

Steve opened the door. He looked terrible. Shirt rumpled, face pale, eyes bloodshot. Judging by his expression, she didn't look any better.

"Hi," Abby whispered. "Did you pick up Ben? Is he here?"

"I . . . yeah. I tried calling you several times, but you didn't answer. Sam's not answering her phone either. Where is she?"

"Sam's still . . . she's still there. At the school."

"Why? Why didn't you bring her with you?" His voice was sharp, frustrated. Any other day it would spark the rage that constantly simmered inside her. But not today.

"Steve." She lowered her voice, in case Ben was close behind him. "There's a hostage situation at school. A few armed men are holding six hostages inside the building. Samantha's one of the hostages."

His eyes widened with horror. "What? You told me she was all right—"

"Yes, at first we thought she was fine, but then it turned out that she was still inside."

"How could you not verify with your own damn eyes—"

Abby burst into tears.

She hadn't cried in front of him in over five years. It was a conscious decision. Steve had lost the privilege of that intimacy. When she'd confronted him about the affair, she hadn't cried, nor had she in any of their endless arguments later. Not when he finally left. And definitely not after that. Of course she'd cried when they'd split up, when she felt that her life was falling apart. But she'd done it in private. Never in front of him.

But now, there was no possible way to hold it back.

How *could* she not have verified with her own eyes that Sam was okay? She'd been there for *almost two hours* before finally finding out that her daughter was far from safe. And once she'd found out, her handling of it had been abysmal. Not to mention that the reason Sam had put herself at risk was probably because of things Abby had told her at one time or another.

"Hang on, Abby, please, um . . . come in." Steve led her inside. "Just . . . calm down. Okay? Stop crying."

Calm down. The irony of her ex using those same words that she'd idiotically shouted at Caterpillar would have made her laugh, if she weren't sobbing uncontrollably. She let herself be led to the kitchen, and slumped onto one of the chairs.

"Here, I'll pour you a glass of water, okay? And you just . . . try to breathe, okay?"

"Where's Ben?" she managed to ask.

"He's upstairs, watching TV."

"What did you tell him?"

"Nothing much." Steve handed her a glass of water. "Just that there was some sort of accident at Sam's school, but that you were there and that Sam was all right. And then I allowed him to watch *Microcosmos* on TV. Is Sam hurt?"

Abby shook her head and took a sip of water. "Not as far as we know."

Steve sat down in front of her. "What do they want?"

"I can't talk about it. But it's being negotiated. They're talking to us."

"But they'll let her go, right?"

"We're doing everything we can, Steve. We're very experienced in these kinds of situations." *That* was what he needed to hear. Abby wished that the same sentences could reassure her as well.

"So how long do these things usually take?"

She shrugged. "You remember when we were together and they'd call me. Sometimes it could be over in twenty minutes. Other times it could take hours." Or days. "I'm going to hug Ben, okay?"

"Yeah, absolutely." Steve looked shell shocked. Abby could relate.

She washed her face in the bathroom, making sure that her recent crying bout wasn't too obvious. Once she was satisfied, she climbed the stairs and went to Ben's bedroom. Steve had installed TVs in both their children's bedrooms, which Abby *hated*. They had endless fights over those televisions, but Steve wouldn't budge.

"Ben?" She opened the door.

Her heart skipped a beat.

Ben was sitting on the bed, staring at the screen. He wasn't watching his favorite movie, *Microcosmos*. He was watching the news. A reporter stood talking outside in the street, several police cars behind her, and in the background—Christopher Columbus High School.

Abby barged into the room, eyes searching for the remote. Not finding it, she yanked the plug, and the television went dark.

"Mom? What are you doing here?" Ben's big eyes went to her.

"I came to see you," she said breathlessly. "What were you watching?"

"I was watching *Microcosmos*. But when it ended, I saw Sam's school."

"Oh." Her mind was paralyzed.

"They said on the news that there was a shooting in the school."

Damn, damn, damn. "Yes, but we think none of the kids were hurt."

"Mrs. Browning says that if someone shoots in our school, we need to get under the desks until the teacher tells us to run outside." Ben looked at his hands. "We practiced it."

"I know, baby, I remember." Abby's breath hitched.

"Does Sam know to hide under the table? Did her teacher tell her?"

"I'm sure she did."

"Dad said that Sam is okay."

Abby hesitated. "Yes, she's okay."

"Is she here?"

"No. Honey, Sam is still in the school."

"Why?"

"Because there are some people there who won't let everyone leave."

"Why?"

"Because they're sad and angry."

Ben considered it. "Like the people you sometimes talk to at your job?"

"Yes, exactly like that."

"So are you talking to those people?"

"I did talk to them, earlier. And now Will is talking to them. He's very good at that."

"And when he's done talking to them, they'll let Sam come home?"

Abby blinked the tears away. "Yeah. But it might be a long conversation."

"Okay."

"Do you want a hug?"

"Okay."

She hugged him, pressing her cheek into his blond hair, inhaling deeply, drawing courage. She imagined pulling Sam into this hug, holding her kids together, never letting go.

"Mom, you're squashing me."

"Sorry." She drew back. "I'm going to talk to your dad now, okay?"

"Yeah."

"I don't want you watching TV anymore today, okay? You can read a book."

Ben nodded.

She stepped out of the room and went downstairs. Steve was still in the kitchen. He'd opened a beer bottle and was staring vacantly at the wall, peeling the bottle's label.

"Ben was watching the news when I came into the room," Abby said sharply.

"Oh shit," Steve said. "Every time it finishes streaming, it goes back to the news. I don't know why it does that."

"He saw the news about Sam's school, Steve. You can't let him watch the news in his room alone like that—"

"Do you want to argue about that now?" Steve interrupted.

Abby shut her eyes and took a deep breath. "No. I don't."

"Good. I'm sorry that he saw that. What did you tell him?"

"Just the most basic facts. A few angry and sad people won't let Sam come home. But we're talking to them."

"Sad and angry, huh?"

"Yup."

Steve peeled the bottle label completely and crumpled it. "Who's the negotiator?"

"Will Vereen."

Steve eyed her. "Wolverine, huh?" Steve always called her partner that. "Why aren't you there? When we talked earlier, it sounded like you were involved."

"That was before we found out that Sam was in there. I can't be the negotiator now."

"Why the hell not?"

Her throat tightened. "A negotiator has to be calm and empathic and patient. It can't be someone who's involved with the hostages."

"The hell with your procedures, this is our daughter in there—"

"I tried, Steve! I was talking to them, and I only made it worse. If I talk to them, it only puts Sam in danger."

Steve sipped from his beer, never taking his eyes off her. Abby leaned against the kitchen counter, exhausted.

"Is Will any good?"

"What? A good negotiator? He's the best."

Steve shook his head. "*You're* the best. You know that, right? You're the best negotiator in the NYPD."

Abby blinked in surprise. Steve telling her she was the best at anything was probably a first. "You don't know anything about crisis negotiators."

"I know they put you in charge of training. I know about that bank robbery a year ago, and about the Fletcher kid, and all those times you went out there when we were married, talking people off ledges and out of their barricaded houses or whatever. I remember, Abby, almost every single time. You'd go there, and tell me about it later. You're the best negotiator."

"Not this time."

"You still need to be there. Help Wolverine out. Tell him what to say."

Abby sighed. "I'll get in the way. It doesn't work like that. The primary negotiator needs to make the calls."

"Come on, how many times when you started out did you tell me that the primary negotiator made the wrong call. That you would have done it differently. That if he'd only asked you—"

"When I started out, I didn't know any better."

"Abby, no one can do this like you."

Abby rolled her eyes, exasperated. Steve couldn't wrap his mind around the idea that sometimes you had to step down. In Steve's world, you had to be the one who held the power, the one in charge.

Her phone blipped in her pocket, and she whipped it out, her heartbeat instantly spiking. Was it a message from Will? Was it over? Was Sam hurt?

No. The name on the message notification was Isaac. It took a few seconds for her to fully register what this meant. This wasn't a message from Isaac at all. This was a new message on her chat with the person who'd impersonated Isaac.

Sometimes we can't even trust the words that are cast into stone.

She blinked, the message jarring, confusing. It was a reply to what she'd written him the day before, she realized. When she'd sent him the memorial's photo. He was telling her that she was right.

"What is it?" Steve asked. "Is it Will?"

"No." She shook her head, shoving the phone into her pocket. "It's something else. It's not relevant."

"Oh," he said, deflated.

"I need to go. Don't let Ben stay in his room, okay? He's very upset, even if he won't let it show. You know how he is."

"Yeah, of course."

"And don't let him watch any news."

"I won't."

"I'm just saying, because they'll want to make it sound even worse than it is, and I don't want him to—"

"Abby, I won't let him watch the news." His voice was exasperated.

"Okay. Thanks, Steve."

"You'll call me as soon as you have any news?" His eyes were desperate.

"Of course."

He would wait for her call, and she would wait for Will's call. Two helpless parents, full of trepidation, with nothing to do but wait.

CHAPTER 29

Abby regretted going home the moment she opened the door. She had no idea what she was about to do besides stare at her phone, waiting for Will to call her, to tell her it was all over. She briefly considered going to the nearby drugstore to buy some cigarettes. She'd quit in her early twenties, but right now, smoking would keep her busy.

Keebles waddled to the entrance and tilted her head quizzically. She probably just wanted a snack, but it was easy to imagine that the dog was wondering where Sam was.

Abby shut the door behind her and went to the kitchen. She should eat. She hadn't eaten since the early morning. She grabbed a frozen bagel from the freezer and thawed it in the microwave. Once it was ready, she sat down with it and took a bite.

It was then that she realized that she couldn't swallow.

Yes, she wasn't hungry, but it wasn't just that. The thing in her mouth didn't register as food. It felt like dust. Her throat didn't work properly. She chewed and chewed, but couldn't get it down. Finally she spat it into the trash and tossed the rest of the bagel as well.

Then she let out a heaving sob. The fear was everywhere, a darkness that consumed her mind. She kept running her conversations with Caterpillar in her head, trying to judge the chances that he would lose it, shoot a hostage, perhaps her daughter.

She tried to remind herself that he painted himself as the good guy, that he wouldn't want to tarnish that image.

But other things that he'd said . . .

Tell them I will shoot the hostages if the chopper doesn't fly away.

We want to expose those bastards once and for all.

An unhinged man whose world was twisted almost beyond recognition. If things didn't go his way . . .

She got up and walked over to Sam's room.

Keebles was there, crouching in front of Sam's dresser, staring at something, her entire body rigid. Abby frowned. What was it? Could it be important? Maybe something that would shed a new light on all of this? If Sam kept something secret in her room, it could potentially help the negotiators. Heart pounding, Abby knelt and peered under the dresser.

Dust balls and something round . . . a pill?

An M&M. Keebles was staring at a discarded M&M.

Abby stood up, brushing her pants off, and noticed something on Sam's desk. A book. The book about the Wilcox cult that Norman had given her. She hadn't even realized that Sam had swiped it.

She picked it up, stared at the cover vacantly. This and the message she'd gotten from the Isaac impostor seemed as if they belonged to another life. Just a few hours ago she'd been struggling with the identity of the impostor. Perhaps another survivor. That other George. But it was impossible, because there had been fifty-nine dead and three survivors. Fifty-nine plus three equaled sixty-two.

Caterpillar's words came back to her. *Whatever you do or say, you're just following orders, right? But whose orders? What agenda are you actually advancing?*

She'd been thinking about those fifty-nine, thinking that maybe the police had gotten it wrong, that there were actually fifty-eight. But what made her think there was a total of sixty-two? Norman had said so. But he'd also told her that some of them were drifters. That people came and went. So how could he know there were sixty-two?

She'd been the one who supplied that number, when they'd talked on the phone, over thirty years ago. She'd told Norman that there were sixty-two of them, repeating what Moses had told her to say.

"Tell them about the gun." His finger pressing against her temple, just like a gun. "Tell them all sixty-two of us are together."

He'd even scribbled the number on a piece of paper, underlining it. She remembered holding the paper. Sixty-two. That was the only thing written on that paper. The only thing that really mattered to Wilcox. That the police would think there were sixty-two people in the compound.

But there were actually sixty-three.

That message the Isaac impostor sent. **Sometimes we can't even trust the words that are cast into stone.** She'd assumed he was telling her that she was right, that a name was missing from the memorial. But the text didn't mention anything missing. He was talking about the names that were *there*. One of the names on the stone didn't belong on it.

Wilcox's name.

She could imagine how it had played out. He entered the mess hall and waited. When he heard Abby latch the door from outside, just like he'd instructed her, he stepped into the kitchen and started the fire. Then he stepped out the back door and locked it from outside. During the ensuing chaos—the raging fire, with firefighters, police, and locals all trying to help, to control the situation—he slipped away.

Later, the police counted fifty-nine dead and three survivors. Sixty-two. When they asked for names, the kids and locals told them that there was someone named George, but the cops assumed they were talking about George Fletcher. They didn't know there was a *second* George.

One of the bodies was assumed to be Moses Wilcox. But it wasn't.

If she was right, Moses Wilcox was still alive, and he'd planned the horrifying massacre to escape. As far as the world was concerned, Wilcox was dead, and he could start anew, with no one searching for him.

She tossed the book back on the desk, and it landed with a thump, making Keebles jump. None of it mattered. None of this would get Sam back.

But maybe Steve had been right. If she was focused enough to figure out a plan that had been enacted by one twisted man, *thirty years ago*, she could still help the negotiation team. She could still help Sam. Sure, she couldn't negotiate, but negotiators thrived on information. And she could still dig information up.

She took out her phone and called Tammi Summers.

Tammi answered after only one ring. "Hello?" She sounded apprehensive.

"Tammi, any news?"

"No, nothing yet. Will talked to them, and it sounds like things calmed down, but they won't release any hostages, and they're refusing medical assistance."

Abby's heart sank. After a negotiator switch, things tended to slow down for a while, but she'd been hoping that Caterpillar would learn to trust Will. Apparently that hadn't happened yet. "Okay. How's the intel going?"

"Um . . . it's going pretty well. Those names that your . . . that we heard in the last conversation gave us a breakthrough."

Right. Sam had made sure to shout two names. Alma and Hatter.

"There's some other news," Tammi said. "Regarding the Watcher forum."

"What is it?"

"The first names of the hostages were posted by one of the users. Someone called Dormouse."

"*What?*" Abby's grip on the phone tightened. She lowered her voice to a whisper. "Tammi, if the Watchers find out that Sam is my—"

"I know, we're handling it. The members of the forum aren't convinced, and a few others claimed they have a different list of names, so there's a lot of confusion. And it's only their first names that were posted."

"But if this Dormouse published the names, it means that he's in contact with the Watchers inside. Or maybe he's one of them."

"He's not one of them," Tammi said. "I'm pretty sure I have an ID. I'm about to send cops to interview him right now."

"I'll do it," Abby said, leaving no room for argument. "I can do it better than anyone else. I don't want an inexperienced officer to bungle it."

"I don't know . . ."

"Ask Will. He'll say yes." At least, Abby hoped he would.

There was a short pause. "You'll have to drive out of the city," Tammi finally said.

"No problem." Relief flooded Abby. She could still help. And keep herself busy.

"Let me check with Will first, okay? I'll call you back in a few minutes."

"Okay." Abby hung up. And then dialed Carver.

"Abby." He sounded worried. "I heard that you and Will switched."

"Yeah. Listen, I'm helping our intelligence officer. I think they're going to send me to interview someone related to all this. It'll probably be a few hours."

"Oh. Okay."

Abby took a deep breath. "Can you come with me? I don't want to go alone."

CHAPTER 30

Why are there endless articles about fires in Australia? Who profits? Immediately after media interest in Colorado drones—coincidence?

Abby read the text twice, and then scrolled down, reading the replies. A lot of the posts in the Watcher forum started like that—a few questions, no immediate answer. And then replies pouring in, the Watchers suggesting theories, linking to articles or other threads that supported their ideas.

She knew the power of open-ended questions. It was one of the negotiator's best tools. An open-ended question got people talking, trying to think from different points of view. Phrase the question right, and you could manipulate people to suggest solutions for you, making them think it was all their idea.

Questions got people invested.

She skimmed the answers, getting a sense of the dynamics of the Watcher community, the different groups within the forum. Then she returned to the thread about the hostage identities, which she'd already checked several times. Tammi was right. Dormouse had posted a list of names, but he didn't have a lot of credibility in the forum, and some other members posted alternate lists of names. Was some of this counterintelligence work? An undercover fed could be sowing confusion. It was possible, though it seemed that the Watchers were able to sow a lot of confusion on their own. By now there were over fifty possible names and identities, numbering at least three celebrities and one politician. Good.

She tapped the phone screen to move on to the next thread. The car jostled, and her finger missed the tiny icon. She grunted in frustration.

"Sorry," Carver said. He sat in the driver's seat, eyes intent on the road. "We're almost there, so maybe it's a good time to put that down anyway."

She switched off the screen and glanced out the passenger window. She was sick with worry. Will had updated her twenty minutes earlier—there was hardly any communication with the people inside the school. No success getting them to allow medical assistance for the teacher inside. And no news about Sam. Penny, Abby's mother, had called her earlier, after hearing about the situation at the school. Abby had to tell her that Sam was in there. As much as she'd tried to reassure Penny, she'd heard the terror in her mother's voice, and it only served to escalate Abby's own fear.

"I'm trying to understand how these people think," she said. "What makes them tick."

"They're a bunch of idiot nutjobs," Carver suggested.

"There's more to it than that. And they're definitely not nuts. Most people believe some conspiracy theories. Does that mean we're all crazy?"

"Bullshit. Almost no one I know believes any conspiracy theories."

"Really?" Abby shoved the phone into her bag. "Do you believe that Elvis is alive?"

"Of course not."

"What about nine-eleven. Do you believe there was a government cover-up there?"

Carver snorted. "No."

"Glad to hear it. Are you certain that we know all there is to know about the murder of JFK?"

They drove in silence for a few seconds.

"Okay, hang on a second," Carver finally said.

Abby glanced at him, raising her eyebrows. "I'm just saying, we all know what happened, right? Oswald was a lone shooter. In your own words, a nutjob."

"Yeah, I'm not saying otherwise. But there are some questions that were never answered fully. If you read about it, you'll see that there are a lot of contradictions in the official story. So there might be some truth in *some* of the stuff people say."

"Uh-huh."

"I'm just keeping an open mind. That doesn't mean I believe in conspiracy theories."

"Two-thirds of Americans don't believe that we know the whole story about JFK, even though there's not a real shred of proof that indicates otherwise. You're in good company."

Carver rolled his eyes. "Gee, thanks."

"We like it when we notice patterns. Our brain is wired that way. The Watchers are not that different from you and me. They don't start out by saying that Michael Jackson was murdered by a shadowy government. They're people who see some stuff that makes them uncomfortable, or angry, or scared. Things that seem random and chaotic. And then someone offers them a perfect solution. These terrible things have a reason. They're caused by a small group of nefarious people. Here are some facts that can corroborate that. And you know what else? Here's some other stuff these assholes have done. And you can help us fight them."

Carver got off the highway, checking the navigation app on his phone. "It's still pretty dumb. I mean, five minutes' research online would show them that it's all bullshit."

Abby sighed. "Five minutes' research online might show them *anything*. Look, just remember when we talk to this guy that if you treat him as if he's stupid or insane, he'll clam up. We need his cooperation."

"How is he related to those people at the school?"

"Dormouse is the one who posted the list of hostages' names. The *correct* list, that is. So he's been in contact with them today after they entered the school."

"So we have his IP? Is that how we have his home address?"

"No. The forum is a Tor website," Abby said. Tor websites were what people called the dark web. Websites that maintained the users' anonymity. "But Tammi scoured all his posts. He said once that he lives a few hours away from Manhattan. One post mentioned that his dad had been arrested twice for what he called fake drug charges. On a different post he named his math teacher as a possible agent of the cabal. The teacher's name is Libby Hadden. Only two Libby Haddens in the United States, and only one living on the East Coast. Tammi talked to her; she teaches in the Monticello High School. And there's only one guy in the area of that school who was busted twice for drug charges in the past few years. Richard Fry. His son is Dennis Fry, whose math teacher is the same Hadden. He's our Dormouse."

"Nice job, Tammi."

That got a smile out of Abby. "Yeah. She's a great intelligence officer."

They drove through Monticello in silence. It was a peaceful place, one of those towns where you could find parking anywhere you wanted and traffic jams were somebody else's problem. The contrast to the havoc they'd left behind made Abby's heart squeeze. Sam was cowering in some room, a gun probably aimed at her, police cars surrounding the school, while Abby was dozens of miles away, driving past grassy streets and sleepy-looking shops.

The Fry home was located on a side street where tall trees lined both sides, their leaves scattered on the road, dappled with the last rays of sunlight. Rickety fences outlined the borders between the houses. Trash littered the street—papers, plastic bags, bottles. And when they parked the car in front of Richard Fry's house, they saw why.

The yard was littered with junk.

This was not just a neglected yard, with old toys or a few broken plastic chairs. This was a cultivated junkyard with separated sections of garbage—a pile of deflated balls standing next to half a dozen broken bicycles. A tower of pizza trays. A mountain of torn, dirty clothing. A large section of the yard was dedicated to old electric appliances—fridges and washer/dryers. They were lined up almost like a second fence, blocking the view to the rest of the yard. The metal fence was shrouded in plastic bags, cloth, paper—stuff that had tumbled in the wind from the collection of junk.

"Wouldn't want to be this guy's neighbor," Carver said.

"Yeah." Abby got out of the car. The odor hit her first. This street should have smelled like wet earth and trees. But instead there was a rotten stench in the air, of food gone bad, rust, and chemicals.

The gate was sticky to the touch, and its hinges creaked as Abby pushed it open. The path between it and the front door was only a few yards, but she had to walk slowly. Circling a few boxes full of screws, carefully shuffling between a stack of tires and a pile of glass bottles, some broken, their shards glittering in the sun.

She knocked on the door, Carver stopping a few steps behind her. After a few minutes she knocked again. The door opened a crack, a door chain keeping it from opening completely.

"Yeah?" An unshaven man peered at her through the crack, his eyes bloodshot.

"Mr. Fry?"

"Yeah?"

She showed him her ID, holding it so that her thumb hid the NYPD logo. "I'm Lieutenant Mullen; this is my partner, Detective Carver. Can we come in?"

"Did that bitch Paula complain again? Look, the stuff in my yard is my property. I got a legal right to keep my possessions."

"This isn't about any complaint," Abby said. "We want to talk to your son, Dennis."

"Dennis?" Surprise in his tone. "What did *he* do?"

"He didn't do anything," Abby said. "But he might know something regarding a few people we're looking into."

"Dennis doesn't have a lot of friends."

"We want to ask him a few questions, and then we'll be on our way."

Richard seemed to mull this over. Finally he said, "Okay, come in. But mind where you step."

He shut the door, unchained it, and opened it wide.

The house's interior was, if anything, worse than the yard. The room had a topography all its own—stacks and piles and mountains of junk, some going almost all the way up to the ceiling. The air had a density and texture to it, and Abby had to fight an impulse to cover her mouth and nose. She walked after Richard, doing her best not to topple anything. Richard guided her through, saying things like "Careful here" and "Mind your bag." Abby had to adopt a sort of sideways shuffle to move through the house. Richard himself seemed to navigate with ease, knowing where he could step, on which stacks of garbage he could lean. Halfway through the living room he paused, picked up a *National Geographic* magazine from one pile of newspapers, and gently placed it on another. Then, apparently satisfied that it was now tidy, he motioned Abby farther into the junk maze.

"His room's over here," Richard said. He pushed a door open. It moved only a bit—enough to push through—apparently blocked by something inside the room.

"Dennis?" Richard said, stepping into the room. "There are some people . . . oh shit!"

Hearing the urgency, Abby pushed through the door, nearly slipping on a stack of flyers on the floor. She glanced around the room, taking in the empty chair, the open window, the figure moving outside it. Dennis was making a run for it.

"Carver, he's getting away!" she shouted.

Behind her, she heard things crashing as Carver turned around, making his way back to the front door. Abby pushed past Richard, stumbling over a stack of clothes. She got to the window and leaped outside, narrowly missing a broken clay pot.

The boy was running toward the back fence, zigzagging between the pieces of junk. Abby pushed through after him, the clutter creating a misleading labyrinth. Dennis obviously knew his way, moving fast, jumping over metal and plastic and rotting wood.

Abby beelined toward him, smashing into a stack of plastic crates. Something liquid and oily spilled on her, spattering her glasses, but she ignored it, pushing through, clenching her teeth. A mound of garbage bags stood in her way, and she climbed up it, the bags ripping under her feet, uncovering old newspapers and moldy books. From the corner of her eye she glimpsed Carver, trying to make his way past the endless wall of fridges.

"The car," she shouted. "Block him from the other side!"

Dennis was at the fence, running alongside it. She saw what he was aiming for—a pile of stools he could climb to get over the fence to the street beyond. She climbed down the garbage-bag hill, and the unstable stack shifted underneath her, tumbling. She slipped, fell, got up. "Stop!"

Dennis wasn't about to stop. He was at the stools, climbing. One of the stools shifted, and he grabbed the fence, gained his balance, kept climbing. Jumping over the fence, body disappearing.

Abby got to the stools a second later. She climbed them, and the entire pile tumbled underneath her. She lunged upward, managing to haul her body over the wooden fence, the poles scratching her belly and legs. She slumped unceremoniously to the other side, then got back on her feet.

Dennis was running down the street toward a thick cluster of trees. She dashed after him. He was fast, but she was gaining on him now, unhampered by the junk maze.

And then Carver's car appeared, squealing as it rounded the turn in the road, blocking the way. Dennis stopped and turned around. Abby crashed into him, and they fell to the ground. Before Dennis could catch his breath, she flipped him onto his stomach, pulling his wrist back. He screamed in pain.

Breathing hard, Abby pulled his other wrist back. Carver was by her side, snapping the handcuffs on Dennis's wrists. Abby got off him and wiped her face. She looked at her fingers in disgust. Whatever had splashed her face earlier looked and smelled like curdled milk.

"Dennis Fry," she said. "Are you Dormouse?"

Carver lifted the boy to his feet. He was freckled and pale, his face smudged with dirt, his large brown eyes skittering back and forth, terrified.

"I didn't do anything," he said. "I didn't know they were going in there with guns, I swear!"

Abby took off her glasses, wiping the spatter of milk off them. "I believe you. We want to ask you some questions."

CHAPTER 31

It was obvious to Abby and Carver that they couldn't interview Dennis, a.k.a. Dormouse, in his home. Abby doubted they'd find somewhere to all sit down there, and she didn't want the stench and the oppressive towers of garbage to distract her.

Instead, they asked Dennis if they could buy him a late lunch at the local Wendy's. The alternative, Abby said, was a police station interrogation room. And Wendy's, she added, would have plenty of witnesses. This seemed to reassure Dennis. They weren't going to take him to a back alley and shoot him.

He wouldn't get into the car. They went to Wendy's on foot, after Abby had taken the handcuffs off his wrists. Carver went back to the house to ask Richard Fry if he wanted to be present when they talked to his son.

Dennis didn't seem surprised to hear that his father had declined.

"He only leaves the house early in the morning, when everybody's asleep," he said. "He hates being around people."

The kid seemed ill at ease in the spacious fast-food restaurant. He sat hunched, his arms and feet close together, as if to take up less space. Abby recalled his room, the junk his father collected closing in from all sides, limiting his personal space to the bare minimum.

He actively avoided glancing at a group of boys sitting at an adjacent table. They were about his age and probably went to the same school. In such a small community, it was likely they all were in the same class. They kept looking over, whispering to each other. Two of them sniggered. Abby gave them a long, cool look, and they turned away, still whispering to each other.

Carver went to the counter to order, and Abby stayed with Dennis, sitting across from him. His fighting spirit seemed to have evaporated. All that was left was fear.

"So tell me," Abby said. "Why did you pick the nickname Dormouse?"

He looked around furtively. Was he about to tell her that she had the wrong guy?

But then he said, "It was available. And we use names of characters from Lewis Carroll's books."

"Because the Watchers go down the rabbit hole, right?"

"Yeah."

"But why not go for Humpty Dumpty or Tweedledum?"

"Those names were unavailable when I joined the forum. And I didn't want to use something lame like adding a number to the nickname, you know? Like Cheshire54. So I figured I'd try the smaller characters. Dodo was taken, but Dormouse wasn't."

"When did you join the forum?"

His body hunched even tighter than before. "I don't know."

"You said all the good names were taken, so it wasn't right at the start, was it?"

"I guess not."

She smiled at him. She knew that none of the fear or impatience or anger that kept churning in her gut would show up in her smile. People thought you could tell a lot about someone from the way they smiled. And maybe it was true about most. Maybe it was even true for Abby, when she smiled at her kids or her friends.

But smiles were also useful masks. This smile was warm, and open, and earnest. It promised acceptance and safety. Only a *good person* could smile like that. Or a great liar. Which Abby happened to be.

Her smile was reflected in Dennis's body language. His shoulders relaxed. He leaned back a little. There was even a glimmer of a returning smile on his lips.

"Can you estimate?" she asked.

"I don't know. About a year ago."

Close enough. It was eleven months ago. His username's creation date was in his profile's details.

"What made you join the forum?"

"I saw this YouTube video, and they said some pretty interesting stuff. And they linked to the forum."

"What kind of stuff? What was the video about?"

When Abby taught classes, she always spoke about the 7-38-55 rule. When people talked, the words they said only accounted for 7 percent of how they felt. Tone was 38 percent. And 55 percent came from their body language. During a crisis, since she mostly talked on the phone or through a closed door, she only had tone and words—45 percent—to work with. But sitting here, face to face with this kid, she had all 100 percent, and she knew how to work it.

So when she asked about the video, he almost certainly couldn't perceive boredom, or skepticism, or impatience. He definitely wouldn't be able to notice that she was constantly thinking about her daughter, worrying about her, imagining the worst scenarios, desperate to check her phone for messages from Will.

All she gave Dennis was curiosity, and interest, and respect.

He was fourteen, and had no friends. He was desperate to talk to anyone who would listen. Not to mention that, like for many others, this was what conspiracy theorists loved best—talking about their passion.

She could almost see the moment when she unlocked him. The shift in his expression. The sudden widening of his eyes. The way he leaned forward.

"It was this guy, and he was talking about bullshit arrests," Dennis said, the words pouring out fast. "Look, no offense, I know that you're a cop, and I'm not one of those guys who think all cops are assholes, okay? But did you know that seventy-three percent of all arrests are completely bogus? That's why they always try to settle in court, because they *know* they can't make it stick. So they settle, and they never have to actually prove anything."

"Seventy-three percent? That sounds too high." Abby frowned.

"These are statistics that you can easily find online if you know where to look. You don't have to take my word for it. In fact, you shouldn't. Do your own research. Dig it up. Seventy. Three. Percent. So this guy was talking about it. Like, giving examples, and explaining why they did it, and showing proof, and I *knew* what he was talking about, you know?"

"How did you know?" She already knew the answer. So this was the hook for Dennis. His dad's drug charges.

"My dad was arrested *twice*, okay? For possession. And it's complete bullshit. Sure, my dad had a joint on him . . . but, like, half of the people here smoke pot. You don't see them get arrested, right?"

Probably not, but they didn't have the neighbors constantly complaining about Richard Fry's hoarding habits. Abby was willing to bet that Richard wasn't the cops' favorite resident.

"So this guy was saying that if we want to fight back, we should do some research. And that we can join this forum and read some stuff that other people found out. I didn't want my dad arrested again, because next time, they might have decided that I couldn't stay with him, you know? I didn't want to go live in some shithole foster home. Besides, it turns out that's how they get some of the kids."

"They? You mean the Circle?"

"Yeah. They get the parents locked up, and then the kids are supposedly going to some foster home or whatever, but they actually end up, like, being sold."

"From the foster homes?"

"No! They never even went to the foster homes. Some lady would show up, say she was a social worker, maybe she even had the right credentials, right? And she would take these kids, and some of them would just disappear. There's a lot of evidence of that happening."

Carver came over, placing trays in front of them. Dennis got a burger and a large Coke. Abby had told Carver she didn't want anything, but he now placed a chicken salad with some fruit in front of her. He'd gotten a burger for himself as well.

He sat down, and she gave him a brief look. She needed him to make himself invisible. Dennis was already retreating into his hunched form.

Carver gave them both an innocent smile. "Man, I'm hungry," he said, and unwrapped his burger. He took a large bite while looking distractedly out the large glass walls, leaning back, his posture suggesting distinct disinterest with their conversation.

"So you saw that YouTube video," Abby said. "And joined the forum, right? I bet they have a new-member thread. Did you introduce yourself right away?"

"No," Dennis said, unwrapping his burger. "I mostly just read the threads. Lurked, you know? An Alice."

"An Alice?" Abby asked, grinning. "What does that mean?"

"That's what we call newcomers who don't have a nickname. Alices, right? Because they haven't decided to go down the rabbit hole yet."

"Did you spend a lot of time reading those threads?"

"Not just reading the threads. There are a few really amazing Watcher YouTubers who posted, like, hundreds of videos." The words were flowing again. He was speaking as he chewed his hamburger, too excited to stop. "But it wasn't just Watcher stuff, right? Watchers aren't sheep. We don't let other people tell us what to think. So I read about all the sex trafficking, and the police corruption, and the people behind it. Once you start looking, you can see it everywhere. I spent, like . . . six or eight hours every day on it. Before that I used to play Fortnite every day, like, for hours. But that day I stopped like that." He snapped his fingers.

Abby let him keep talking, adding the odd extra question when needed. This kid could probably talk about this for ten hours straight. Maybe, if she had time, she'd even let him, build his trust. But she couldn't. She ate some of her salad, forcing down every bite with water. She needed the food, or she'd be useless. She ate and listened, while Carver did his chameleon act, blending into the background.

Finally, when he finished explaining about how the Circle controlled people through pharma, Abby cleared her throat. "Dennis, you know why I'm here."

The wariness came instantly back. She prayed that she hadn't misjudged her timing.

"Is it about that school?" he asked.

"Yes. Three of your friends are there. Caterpillar, Hatter, and, uh . . ." She frowned, as if trying to recall the third one. She let the silence stretch. People got uncomfortable with silence. They wanted it to go away.

"Red Queen," Dennis said miserably.

"Exactly." So Alma was Red Queen. "I know why they went there. In fact, I talked to Caterpillar earlier, and he explained all of it."

"You *talked* to Caterpillar?" Suspicion was etched on his face.

"Absolutely. If you can chat with him or call him, you can even ask him."

"Oh." There was something there. His eyes shifted sideways. But Abby was almost certain that she'd gained some of his trust by saying that.

She sighed. "I believe that your friends wanted to do the right thing. They thought there were kidnapped kids sold from that school, right? They wanted to help them. But things got out of hand."

"Yeah. They never intended for any of that to happen. They just talked about checking the place out, I swear."

"I believe you, I really do. Now, I want to resolve this without *anyone* getting hurt. As long as no one gets seriously injured, I can help your friends. I can speak for them, help everyone see their side of the story. But if someone gets shot . . ." She spread her hands. "It'll be out of my control."

"Okay. So why are you talking to me? You should be talking to the other cops."

"I think there's some disagreement between your friends about how to proceed. And I was hoping you could shed some light on it. I only talked to Caterpillar so far."

"I don't know what's going on there."

Abby nodded with a thoughtful look. He knew, of course. He was the one who'd posted the names of the hostages. But she didn't want to accuse him of lying and make him defensive. "You don't know."

"Yeah, I mean, I saw the news, but that's about it."

"Earlier, you said that your friends talked about checking out the school. Where did they say that?"

He tightened. "What do you mean?"

"Did you guys talk on the phone? Did you meet up?"

"Like, just in a private chat." He shrugged, trying to make it seem as if it were no big deal. But Dennis wasn't a good liar. His eyes skittered; his fingers went to his lips. Either he was lying, or talking about this chat was making him very uncomfortable.

"What sort of private chat? Do you talk there often?"

"I mean, occasionally."

"Why not talk on the forum?"

"I don't know."

"Dennis." She leaned forward, raising her eyebrows. "Your friends are in danger. And I'm really trying to help them. I need to know."

He hesitated, then said, "Look, a couple of months ago, something happened, and Caterpillar decided that we needed to create this chat, okay? Everyone knows that the feds and the police are reading the posts in our forum. Some of the members who post are actually fake profiles, used by the cops. So he figured we should start our own private chat. Just people that we trust, and who all live nearby."

"So it's a private chat for you, Hatter, Red Queen, Caterpillar, and . . . ?"

"And that's it," he said quickly. "Just the four of us."

"It's not a crime to be in a private chat," Abby said softly. "We want all the details so we can resolve this peacefully."

"There's this one other guy," Dennis said after a second. "Jabberwocky. But he didn't do anything; he didn't go to that school."

"So five of you in the chat."

"Yeah."

"And they've been posting messages there even today, after they entered the school." She inflected her voice downward, slow and firm. She was not asking; she was stating a fact. Time to get Dennis on board.

He shifted uncomfortably. "Yeah, just a few comments. Like, Red Queen posted about the hostages. But then . . . well, I posted about it in the forum, and Caterpillar told me not to share anything else, that they don't want any information to leak."

"Did they post anything else on the chat?"

"No. I mean . . . they're pretty busy."

"Did Caterpillar choose who joins the chat?"

"Yeah, I mean, Red Queen and Hatter were really good friends of his; they've known each other on the forum for more than a year."

"And you?"

"He said he was impressed with my analytical skills. I'd found several, um . . . codes in public announcements and stuff." He seemed wary as he said it, as if ready to be mocked, but Abby kept nodding, listening attentively. "And he knew I lived in the state, so that was that."

"And what about Jabberwocky?"

"I actually suggested Jabberwocky. Red Queen and Hatter weren't thrilled about it, but Caterpillar said that he thought Jabberwocky was all right."

"Why didn't Red Queen and Hatter like him?"

"It's not that they didn't like him; he's just a bit strange. He joined a while ago, but he kind of weirded everyone out. He kept wanting to meet people in person, which seemed like something an undercover cop would do. And it sometimes felt like he was trying too hard, you know? Like, he'd flatter people about their posts all the time. I don't know. I think he was clueless, you know? Like, he was trying to be nice. Anyway, he stopped doing that; it's no big thing."

"Did *you* meet him in person?"

"No."

"Why not?"

Dennis glanced down in embarrassment. "Because people in the forum don't know how old I am."

Abby nodded in understanding. "So this Jabberwocky lives in the area?"

"Yeah."

"How do you know?"

"Because I was thinking I might actually meet him, and he said he could meet me near his place. He gave me an address."

Abby let that hang, then said, "You mentioned that something happened to make Caterpillar want to form this private group. What was it?"

"I don't know. He wouldn't talk about it. But he said that he'd learned that you can't trust almost anyone, that there were agents everywhere. I got the sense that someone close to him turned out to be an agent."

"An agent is someone who works for the Circle?"

"Yeah."

"And you said it was a couple of months ago?"

"Yeah, it was a few days before Halloween. After that he changed. He got really intense, you know?"

"Intense how?"

"Before that he wasn't posting that much, and the things he posted were, like . . . memes and stuff. But whatever happened really changed him. He started talking about striking back and bringing the fight to the Circle. Whatever happened really messed him up, you know?"

Abby leaned back and took a deep breath. "Dennis . . . this chat. Is it active? Can we use it to talk to your friends? Can you use it?"

And there was that look again. That shifting in his eyes. A thought he didn't like. "No. There's no way."

"I know you want to protect your friends—"

"You don't understand! There's literally no way. When you showed up at the door, I left the chat. That's something Caterpillar kept stressing when we created it. That if, at any time, we think the Circle are there to get us, we leave the chat. That way, the Circle doesn't have our chat log, and they can't pretend to be one of us, you know? And we agreed that when someone leaves the chat, it's a sign. That he's burned."

He looked utterly miserable. He'd been cut off from his friends.

"Well, Caterpillar was definitely cautious," Abby said, hiding her disappointment. She wanted that chat. "I guess he didn't take any chances."

"Yeah. Like I said, I think someone close hurt him."

CHAPTER 32

May 12, 2017

"You know how I told you yesterday that Big Pharma and the FDA have a symbiosis?" Neal said.

"Yeah." Jackie smiled at him. "The cancer cure, right?"

"It's part of it. I mean, there are also HIV vaccines that they don't want us to know about, but obviously also the cancer cures. If we eliminate cancer, the entire industry of radiation therapy and chemo will collapse. Which is why they get the FDA to destroy any chance for those cures."

"I remember."

Neal glanced at her. Lately, whenever he looked at her, he was struck by how gorgeous she was. Right now, as they walked in the park, her chestnut hair seemed to almost shine in the sunlight. He loved how she moved, as if she had no care in the world, each step almost like a bounce. Gravity didn't seem to work on Jackie the same way it did for other people.

He loved talking to her.

"So it turns out that the pharmaceutical companies have another accomplice. Guess who."

"I don't know."

"Come on, guess!"

"I don't know." She laughed. "The police? The military?"

"The Mexican drug cartels."

"Whaaaat?" she shrieked, her eyes widening. "Come on." Her mouth, left slightly open, the sweetest thing in the world.

"I'm telling you. I watched this guy explain it yesterday. Big Pharma gets those people hooked on painkillers, then cuts off the supply, all at once. What are people supposed to do? They're already addicted, right? So they go for what's available at the closest street corner. Heroin. There's, like, a shitload of internal memos and anonymous sources from within those companies testifying to it. So the drug cartels pay a portion of their earnings to Big Pharma, who in turn hooks those people on painkillers *and* influences the DEA's strategies."

They walked in silence for a while.

"I haven't seen you this excited about anything in a long while," Jackie finally said. "Ever since you found these people, you're so *invested*. It's really great to see."

Neal nodded. He knew what she was talking about. The past two years had been rough. Jackie's miscarriage, then his mom dying, then losing his job. His life had seemed to spiral down the drain. He could hardly get out of bed in the morning. He'd spend hours staring at the TV, not even knowing what he was watching.

He first found out about the Watchers when a friend shared a post on Facebook. He'd been scrolling down his feed, and it caught his eye. The post caption was, *Is FEMA building a concentration camp?*

Was it? Confused, Neal clicked the link and read through the article. It wasn't very well written, and there wasn't a lot of information, so he googled *FEMA concentration camps*.

A lot of results there. And it wasn't like he had anything better to do.

Once he began reading, he couldn't stop. And then he found the videos. Talking not just about FEMA but about Big Pharma and child slavery and rising unemployment, and it struck a chord with him.

His mom had died from cancer.

He'd lost his job because it had been outsourced to India.

Things clicked together. It all made sense.

Now he woke up early every morning. Reading more, telling Jackie about it, animated, excited. It turned out he could fight back. He could help collect the evidence, find missing links, spot the patterns. One day, soon, the Circle, which was pulling the strings, would be exposed. And people like Neal would be the ones who did it.

The Watchers.

Now, after they returned home from their morning walk, Neal sat by the computer and entered the Watcher forum. Four new threads since that morning. The forum was active all the time, pulsing with information, debates, and arguments. Neal loved reading the threads, getting to know the members.

Each of those threads already had dozens of replies. He began reading them.

And then a new thread popped up. The topic was *Big Pharma influencing the DEA???* A member asking for any links proving it.

Neal's heart leaped. This could be his first post on the forum. He'd just watched the video this morning! And it would be a useful contribution.

Before he could change his mind, he dragged the cursor to the reply button. But it was disabled. He wasn't logged in. Because he had no user profile.

He tapped the register button, and the forum asked him for a nickname.

Recently, some members had been adopting names from Lewis Carroll books, because they were all going down the rabbit hole. He liked the idea. He hesitated for a second, then wrote *Caterpillar*, and clicked the "Check Availability" button.

A green check mark. The name was available. That would do for now. He'd decide later if he should keep it.

He registered, and posted the first reply as Caterpillar.

A minute later, his response had fifty-six views and three responses.

He was a part of the community.

CHAPTER 33

Caterpillar stared at his phone in disbelief.

He'd opened the cell phone's browser, navigating to the Watcher forum. Skimming the forum's threads about the Columbus High incident, his eyes landed on a short subject line: *High school shooting—classic hoax.*

The member suggested in his thread that the entire thing was fake—a collaboration between the police and the media to cast the Watchers in a bad light. A few other Watchers seemed to be intrigued with the idea, pointing out that it had been done before.

Hitting reply, Caterpillar furiously typed, *Are you saying that I'm in on the hoax? I'm on the third floor of the building, looking down at the damn cops. If you don't believe me, come over, join the party.*

He had to get the entire Watcher community and the public on his side. He needed proof about the trafficking. But they had found nothing in the school's paperwork. Alma was meticulously going through every file cabinet, with nothing to show for it. Where was it?

Or maybe the real question was, Who was it? The Circle had to have someone in the school's administration. Someone they could manipulate, whom they could use. Someone weak who would be easy to bully or bribe.

He eyed the principal, who was slumped against the wall. The perfect candidate.

Grabbing his gun, he marched over to the man. He aimed the barrel at the principal's temple.

"Who approached you?" he snarled.

The principal flinched, edging away from the weapon. "What?"

"Someone approached you. They wanted you to cooperate with their child-trafficking operation. Who was it?"

"I don't know what you're talking about. Please, I—"

"Whoever it was, they aren't here. *I* am. I'm going to count to five, and if you don't give me a name, I'll shoot. One."

"I'm begging you, no one approached me for anything! I'm the school's principal. I would never—"

"Two."

"Don't shoot me, please, you're making a big mistake."

"Three."

The man whimpered, raising his hand, as if it could protect him from the bullet.

"Caterpillar, that's enough," Alma said, voice trembling.

"Four."

"What will you gain by shooting him?"

It was one of the girls. Samantha. The one who'd bandaged Carlos. She looked at him, her eyes pleading. The question made him hesitate.

"Stay out of it," he said. "It's none of your concern."

"I'm just saying, what will you gain? It won't help those poor kids, right?"

"He's been working with some very bad people," Caterpillar said, his teeth clenched. "Who did things you can't even imagine."

"How do you know that he worked with them?"

"Because it makes perfect sense."

"It sounds like you aren't sure," the girl said slowly.

"I'm sure," Caterpillar said after a short pause.

"And suppose he did. What will shooting him gain?"

Who gains? The constant question that they always asked. The truth was, he wouldn't gain. He would lose his chance to force a confession from the principal. It would look bad. It might make the police storm inside. They'd have one less hostage.

He lowered his gun.

Hatter let out a snort. "Didn't think you had the balls, anyway."

Caterpillar whirled on the man. "You know I do."

"Why? Because you killed that Circle agent you keep talking about?" Hatter raised an eyebrow.

"Yes. That's exactly why." He turned to the principal, who shrank under his gaze. "I've killed before, Mr. Bell. Remember that. And I won't hesitate to kill again."

CHAPTER 34

"I don't think there's anyone home," Carver said, peering through the window.

Abby checked her phone again impatiently. She'd been doing it every few minutes on their drive to the address that Dennis had given them—Jabberwocky's home. She checked the forum constantly for updates, and had seen Caterpillar's comment appearing on one of the posts, furiously berating someone who claimed the entire thing was a hoax. Were Will and Tammi aware that the people inside were now commenting on the forum? Were they using this? She'd texted them the info. She was getting furious at Will for not sending her updates, even though she knew that he had good reasons—there was too much work for the negotiations commander in a crisis like this, even without needing to regularly update a frightened hostage's parent.

She vented her frustrations at the door, thumping on it with her fist.

"We can check with one of the neighbors," Carver suggested. "Someone might know when he gets home. They might even have a phone number."

"Yeah," Abby said, unsure. Something was off with this house. The windows were spattered with dirt, the garden full of dry leaves and weeds. Sure, Jabberwocky could just be a slob, but it didn't look like it.

The house seemed freshly painted. A shadowy row of dead rosebushes told a tale of a garden that had been tended regularly, a while ago.

An absence. He wasn't home, and hadn't been there for a while. Perhaps he'd gone somewhere for the holidays and hadn't returned yet.

A dead end.

"I'll go check," Carver said, walking away from the house.

Abby paced the dark porch. How long had Sam been in that school, trapped with three unpredictable, dangerous, armed people? Each minute wondering if she would get out of this alive, ever see her parents, her brother, her dog. Ever play her violin.

Abby's phone vibrated, and she took it out of her pocket and stared at the screen. It was a message from the so-called Isaac. The person she now believed was Moses Wilcox.

She swallowed, tapping the screen, the chat opening. She read and reread the message.

I know about Sam. She'll survive it, she's a fighter, it runs in her blood, just like it runs in yours. I can help.

The message seemed impossible. How could he know about Sam? Sure, the hostage situation was reported in the media, but the names of the hostages hadn't been released.

She'd stirred him from his silence the day before with her message, and drawn his attention to her and her family. He'd then found out about the shooting. He knew that Sam studied there. But how . . . ?

That damn Watcher forum. He must have somehow found out about it, and had been following the posts, just like the police were. He'd seen Samantha's name, and unlike the Watchers, he wasn't confused by the rest of the names that had been thrown around.

Moses Wilcox was a man who preyed on moments of weakness. He caught people when they were down, made them think he had the answers. Lured them in with beautiful words and sentiments.

Of course he would try to use this opportunity, when she was going through the worst experience in her life.

If her daughter weren't in danger, she would have replied, tried to get him to talk. Perhaps set up a meeting. But she couldn't afford to be distracted by that right now. Wilcox, or whoever it was, could wait.

Abby took a step back from the house. It was possible to find out the real name of the house owner through proper channels, or through his neighbors. Get his phone number, maybe his email address. It would all take too much time.

She flipped the doormat with her foot. Nothing underneath but dust. Stepping off the front porch, she walked over to the nearby rain gutter and rummaged in it. Wet leaves and mud. Nothing else. Turning away from it, she scrutinized the front yard patiently, squinting in the darkness.

There.

She crossed the yard and crouched by one of the rocks that lined a flower patch. If she hadn't known what to look for, she wouldn't have noticed it. It looked like any other rock. But she'd seen that rock before, several times. It was a modern wonder—a fake rock that you could buy in a store and hide your house key inside. The problem with good fake rocks was that there were just a few models out there. And all the rocks of the same model were identical. Many burglars knew how to spot them. And some cops did too.

She picked up the rock and slid it open, retrieving the front door key.

It was breaking and entering; there was no way to justify what she was about to do. She could lose her job. She could be arrested.

She didn't even hesitate.

She went over to the front door and unlocked it. The house was completely dark, and silent as a tomb. If she'd had any doubt about the last time anyone had stepped inside, she didn't anymore. The place had that distinct smell of a house that had been dormant for a while, musty and stale.

She flipped the light switch, took a look around. The living room was sparse—one couch and one armchair, a small coffee table with nothing on top but a thin layer of dust. An alcove was set into the wall to her right, holding a small pot, the plant inside shriveled to a husk. Next to it was a shelf with three framed photographs. They were all of the same girl—in the first she was perhaps Ben's age, sitting on a slide, smiling. The second was her a few years later, crouching by a flower in the field. In the third she was sitting across the table in a coffee shop, staring out a window. Was this Jabberwocky's daughter?

Abby stepped away from the shelf and crossed the room. A bookshelf with rows and rows of books stood by a desk. The surface of the desk was bare, except for a monitor, a mouse, and a cursor. The computer sat in a niche in the desk. It was clear that everything in the room had its place.

She went over to the library and scanned it. The conspiracy books were easy to spot—all clustered together, with titles like *The Biggest Secret* and *Controlled Demolition*. The rest seemed to be professional psychology books, about various topics. The name Sigmund Freud caught her eye, just because she recognized it. It seemed that all Freud's books were on the same shelf. And a bunch of books by Carl Jung nearby. In fact, the books were clustered according to author name. And it took her only a minute to realize that the entire shelf was alphabetized, as was the shelf dedicated to conspiracy theories.

She turned to the desk. It had three drawers, and she opened the top one. It had a bunch of letters, bills, and receipts. She retrieved a stack and thumbed through them.

Theodor Quinn. That was Jabberwocky's actual name.

"Jesus, Abby." Carver's voice made her jump. She turned around. He was standing at the front door, staring at her in shock.

"I just need ten minutes," she said.

"Are you insane? What if someone saw you enter? What if—"

"What if I find something that would help Will? What if it could save Sam? What if I hadn't gone inside, and Sam got"—she swallowed—"hurt?"

Carver stared at her silently.

"Ten minutes," Abby said again. "If you want, you can report me later. You don't need to be an accomplice in this."

She regretted saying it as soon as she saw the hurt on his face. But she had no time to make this right. She turned back to the desk, and opened the second drawer. A yearly planner sat on top of a few notebooks. Theodor Quinn was the kind of guy who'd have a detailed, meticulous planner. She picked it up and skimmed through it. It had surprisingly little inside. A few addresses, emails, and phone numbers of contacts. An occasional meeting or a list of tasks penned on different days. He wrote down appointments with the dentist, and a regular haircut every few weeks. Two notations that read *Lunch date—Georgia*. A few meetings with someone penned in as *Prof. Landsman*.

And then, on Saturday, May 25, after a completely empty week, a single notation: *7:30 pm—Interview with Caterpillar*.

The front door clicked shut behind her, and Carver joined her at the desk. He crouched and switched on the computer. She glanced at him, thinking that she should say something, tell him he should wait outside. Then, deciding she'd said enough, she turned back to the planner, and flipped through the pages slowly.

Sunday, June 9, another interview with Caterpillar. Then one more three weeks later. Then another one, two weeks after that. No interviews with anyone else, and the small number of other appointments he'd had before seemed to dwindle to almost nothing—no more haircuts, no more Professor Landsman. The meetings with Caterpillar accelerated. Every week, then even twice a week, no longer just on weekends. They were no longer annotated as interviews, but instead said *Caterpillar*.

October 29th—Caterpillar.

And then . . . nothing. The rest of the planner was empty.

"Abby," Carver said.

"Carver, you have to see this," she muttered.

"And you have to see *this*," Carver said.

She raised her eyes. Carver was staring at the screen. A desktop, the background image a lake. It took her a moment to realize what Carver wanted her to see. One of the shortcuts was a document named Caterpillar.

Carver opened it, the document appearing on screen. A small pop-up appeared, informing them that this document was last opened on August 20. Abby skimmed the first few sentences, quickly catching on to what this was. An interview summary with Caterpillar. She read through the first page quickly, the sentences becoming a blur.

Subject said that he was now down to four hours research a day . . .

. . . No prescribed medicine . . .

. . . showed little interest in talking anything beyond Watcher and Circle material . . .

"I don't think Jabberwocky was a Watcher at all," Carver said.

"No." Abby leaned forward, scrolling down the document. There were over thirty pages, detailing their interviews. "He was doing research."

"Do you think he was writing a book?"

"Or a paper. Maybe an academic paper. There's a Professor Landsman in his planner. We can check with him."

She stopped scrolling. Something had caught her eye. Theodor had marked a sentence in bold typeface.

Subject agreed to tell me his real name, Neal Wyatt.

"Neal Wyatt," Abby said aloud. Neal Wyatt was Caterpillar. This was the man who held Sam hostage.

CHAPTER 35

The constant red-and-blue flickering lights shone through the uncovered patches in the windows, reflecting on the wall. Sam stared at them, almost in a trance. Red, blue, red, blue. How far away were those police cars? A dozen yards? Twenty yards?

So close. And so useless.

It was a constant effort not to cry. Fiona's bouts of crying were bad enough. When Mr. Bell broke down and begged among sobs that they let them go, it became even worse. Sam could feel the tears loaded up in her tear ducts, just waiting for the signal.

Not yet, tears. Maybe in five minutes. Or ten.

The looming tears weren't the only physical issue, of course. She was tired, her body hurt, and she was desperately hungry and thirsty.

But more than anything, she needed to pee. She kept trying to shift to a more comfortable position. Soon, she knew, she wouldn't be able to hold it any longer. And if she wet herself, she was pretty sure those tears would start and never stop.

And through that fog of misery, she still managed to think of a plan. Well, not really a plan, but something. An attempt.

"I want to check Mr. Ramirez's dressing," she said aloud. "Is that okay?"

"What for?" Hatter snapped. In the past couple of hours he'd snarled constantly at both his associates, losing the shreds of self-control he still had.

"I need to check if it's inflamed."

He didn't say anything, and neither did Alma or Caterpillar. Alma was going through the secretary's file cabinet, reading through the paperwork, ignoring everyone around her. Caterpillar spent his time on his phone, tapping endlessly.

"Fiona, can you help me?" Sam said. "I might need you to hold him up."

Fiona blinked, as if snapping out of a dream. "Sure," she said listlessly.

They both got up and went over to where Mr. Ramirez lay. His breathing was weak, pink froth on his lips.

"He doesn't look so good," Fiona said, her voice trembling.

"Yeah, I need you to be brave for me, okay?" Sam said. "Just like that time in second grade, when we had that math test."

Fiona glanced at her, confused. Sam didn't meet her eyes, and instead unbuttoned Mr. Ramirez's shirt. She needed Fiona to get the hint, but her friend was unfocused and terrified. Maybe there was another way. She tried to think, but her head pounded. The time for those tears was probably now. She had no idea why or how she had held up so far. Her breath shuddered as she opened Mr. Ramirez's shirt. The dressing was crimson with blood, and it *did* look inflamed. Not that Sam had any idea what to do about it.

"It's bad, Sam," Fiona blurted.

"I know."

"Oh god, I think I'm going to be sick!" Fiona stumbled to the corner of the room, gagging, choking. She vomited noisily on the floor. Just like she'd done all those years ago, in second grade.

Her act had been so incredibly convincing that a second passed before Sam caught on to what had happened. All eyes were on Fiona.

Sam reached for Mr. Ramirez's bulky pocket, grabbing his phone, her heart thudding in her chest. She yanked it out, and it nearly tumbled from her fingers. Vaguely, somewhere far away, she heard Hatter cursing Fiona, disgusted, and Alma asking if she was okay, and still Fiona coughed and sputtered, crying. Sam shoved the phone into her pocket, breathing hard.

"You're going to clean that up!" Hatter was shouting at Fiona, who was trembling in the corner, spitting the remnants of her vomit.

"Hatter, leave the child alone," Alma said angrily.

"That *child* just stank up the room. I'm not going to sit here for hours with the stench of her puke everywhere."

"I'm sorry," Fiona said weakly.

"We're not going to be here much longer," Caterpillar said. "Just sit tight."

"That's what you said two hours ago!" Hatter shouted. "You know what? Why don't I talk to the cop instead of you? I don't think you've been doing a great job so far."

"I told you, that cop is looking into it!" Caterpillar raised his voice. "What are you gonna do? Call them and tell them you're going to shoot the hostages soon? That'll make things worse."

"Do you really think things can get worse?"

Sam rebuttoned Mr. Ramirez's shirt and sat back down in the corner, Fiona joining her a few seconds later. No one was looking at them. Could she use the phone now? She put her hand in her pocket, feeling it. No, there was no way.

The two men kept arguing, with Alma occasionally trying to edge in a word. Finally Sam got up again and walked over to Hatter.

He paused and whirled at her. "What?"

"I think we'd better have a bathroom break soon," she said in a low voice. "Or . . . I mean . . ." She stared at the floor, faking embarrassment.

Hatter watched her, saying nothing. He was enjoying this in some twisted way; she was sure of it. Good. Hatter was like a lot of the boys in school. Nasty when cornered, but as long as he felt like he was the boss, he could be reasoned with.

"Please?" That last word a broken whisper.

"I'll take them," Alma said.

"The hell you will," Hatter said. "What if they try to run off? Will you have the guts to shoot them?"

"I'll do it," Caterpillar said wearily. "We'll split them. I'll take the girls first, the men after that."

"Okay." Hatter shrugged. "Maybe find the janitor's closet and grab a mop to clean up here."

Caterpillar seemed about to say something, then shook his head. He turned to the rest of the group in the corner. "Let's go. Girls first."

They all stepped out of the room, Caterpillar walking in the rear, gun in hand. The phone felt like it weighed twenty pounds. Was its bulky presence visible through the cloth of the jacket? Would Caterpillar notice it? What if it tumbled out? The pockets in her jacket were crap; things fell out all the time. But she didn't dare stick her hands in them and draw any attention to their contents.

She slowed her pace, falling back beside Caterpillar.

"Thanks," she said softly. "For taking us."

"Sure."

"Alma told me that you were looking for kids who were being sold. For sex."

"That's right."

"I didn't know that even happened in this country. That's horrible. Why aren't the police doing anything?"

He let out a disgusted snort. "Because the police are in on it."

They reached the faculty bathrooms. Mrs. Nelson opened the door to the women's room, and they stepped inside. Caterpillar entered after them.

"You can wait outside the door," Mrs. Nelson said, looking disgusted. "We're not going to escape through the toilet."

Caterpillar's face remained impassive. "You can use the toilet with me in here, or not use it. It's your call."

Nelson turned away, shaking her head, and stepped into one of the two stalls. Fiona glanced at Sam.

"Go ahead," Sam said. "I'll go next."

Fiona entered the second stall.

"You said the police are in on it?" Sam asked Caterpillar.

"Yes. The people who do this have the police command in their pocket." Caterpillar turned to face Sam. His nose was still swollen, the bruises under his eyes getting darker. But at least he wasn't dripping blood like before. "And the FBI, and the military. And they all let kids, just like you, or even younger, get taken and sold, to be repeatedly raped by pedophiles."

"Oh god," Sam whispered, letting her breath catch. Forcing herself to think of Mom, and Dad, and Ben, outside. How she might never see them again. Glancing at the gun in this psycho's hand. Dredging up every bit of fear in her body, letting it all loose.

Her eyes watered, a single tear trickling down her left cheek. She didn't wipe it, let it roll down, sniffling.

Caterpillar cleared his throat, looking uncomfortable.

"I just never knew." She sniffled. "I can't even imagine what those kids are going through."

"And you shouldn't need to," Caterpillar said. He patted her shoulder clumsily. "That's why we're doing it. So that kids like you can be safe."

She smiled at him, curbing the reflex to flinch from his touch, another tear running down her face. "Thanks."

Water flushed, and Mrs. Nelson stepped out of the stall. Sam gave Caterpillar another teary look, and stepped into the stall, shutting the door.

Once inside, she took a deep breath, quickly wiping her eyes. She took out the phone from her pocket as she peed. It was switched off.

She turned it on, and it started up slowly. What should she text to her mom? As much information as possible. She had no idea what would be useful, so she'd tell her everything. Where they were, descriptions of all the nutjobs who were holding them hostage, descriptions of their guns. She had time; she could say she had an upset stomach. She could . . .

Oh god, what if the phone blipped when it finished the start-up? Her phone *always* did that when she turned it on in the morning, all the texts and notifications pouring in. And Ramirez would surely have missed calls and texts, from his worried wife, or kids, or whatever.

The phone was finishing its start-up. Panicked, she flushed, the loud sound of the toilet echoing in the stall. The phone blinked into life, and just as she'd suspected, it blipped. And blipped again, notifications showing up one after the other. Desperately, her finger ran along the side of the phone, searching for the volume button, pressing it, as the beeps kept coming, each one feeling as loud as a church bell. Finally, the phone vibrated as she managed to mute it completely. For a few seconds she didn't move.

Had Caterpillar heard the phone over the sound of the running water?

There was no knocking on the door. No angry shouting. He hadn't noticed.

But she didn't dare take her time now. Maybe he thought he'd heard something, and now he'd see that she wasn't getting out after she'd already flushed. He'd get suspicious, and might break down the door. And if he saw she was holding a phone . . .

She started a new message, fingers flying on the keyboard, tapping the message as fast as she could, not bothering to fix the typos.

"Are you done?" Caterpillar's voice vibrated in the bathroom.

"I think it's her period," Fiona said. "It might take her a few more seconds."

"Oh."

Thank god for Fiona. Sam finished tapping the message. What was her mom's phone number? She'd known it by heart—Mom had made her memorize it years ago—but who even remembered phone numbers anymore? Damn it, damn it!

She shut her eyes, recalling the digits, and tapped them into the screen before hitting send.

The message was out.

She shoved the phone back in her pocket, then hesitated. At some point someone would notice it. Or it would fall out. And if that happened, she would be screwed.

Instead, she wrapped the thing with toilet paper and dropped it in the trash. If she wanted, she could ask to go to the bathroom again. Especially now that Fiona had bequeathed on her that time of the month.

But she hoped she wouldn't need it. She hoped that in a few hours, she'd be outside and finally safe. And the thought of that made the tears flow again.

CHAPTER 36

"We can sit in here," Professor Landsman said.

Carver entered the room, looking around him. This room was obviously Landsman's private clinic. An armchair faced a two-seater sofa, a coffee table between them. A bookshelf had books with names like *Acceptance and Commitment* and *Communication Miracles for Couples*. On the opposite wall was a landscape painting, which Carver imagined was intended to form an immediate bond between any couple that came for therapy. No matter how much someone hated their spouse, they could still instantly agree that the painting was hideous.

"You said this has something to do with Mr. Quinn?" Landsman asked, sitting down.

Landsman, it had turned out when they called him, lived only a few miles away from Theodor Quinn's house. So they'd decided to talk to him in person. Of course, Carver had expected to talk to the man in his living room or kitchen, not in his clinic. When he conducted interviews, he was used to being the one dominating the room. Now, somehow, he was sitting uncomfortably on a couple's couch, while Landsman was leaning forward, intertwining his fingers, as if he were about to hear how Carver and Abby weren't spending enough quality time together.

Landsman had a thick black beard, bushy eyebrows, and an unruly mane. The amount of hair all over his face made him look more like a medieval czar than a couples' therapist. In fact, hair even grew in tufts out of his ears. Didn't it impede his ability to hear his patients' issues with each other?

"When I told you on the phone that we wanted to talk about Theodor Quinn, you didn't sound very surprised," Abby said.

Landsman nodded. "I'd thought that something had happened to him. I even emailed his daughter a few weeks ago, but she assured me that she'd talked to her dad, and that he was simply taking some time off."

"Why did you think that something happened to him?" Abby asked.

"Because I stopped hearing from him completely a few months ago."

"How do you know Theodor Quinn?"

"I used to be his counselor, when he was working on his PhD. Then, when that didn't pan out, he kept consulting with me."

Carver glanced at Abby, but she seemed to be momentarily out of it, her eyes glazed. This had happened several times throughout the day. Carver couldn't imagine what kind of horror scenario was currently running through her mind. He took charge. "Didn't pan out? What do you mean by that?"

Landsman scratched his neck. "He just wasn't cut out for it. It's a very difficult program."

"But even after it didn't work out, he stayed in touch with you?"

"He got in touch after a year. Said he was writing a book. It was related to the subject that he'd researched before during his PhD program. Social media addiction. Except he was approaching it from a different angle. He had a theory that there was a relationship between social media addiction and a tendency to believe conspiracy theories."

Carver leaned forward. "What sort of relationship?"

"Well . . . conspiracy theorists tend to have certain traits. Anxiety, a need to control their environment and impose order, self-absorption, narcissism, disagreeableness, paranoia—"

"I'm sure they don't all have those traits." Carver shuffled uncomfortably, thinking of earlier, when he and Abby had discussed JFK.

"Those are statistical tendencies. It doesn't mean that every person who believes a conspiracy theory shares all those traits."

"Yeah, he could actually have none of those traits. He could be an awesome person." He needed to stress the point. It was this couples' therapy clinic. It made him defensive.

"Um . . . right. Anyway, people who are addicted to social media also have some traits linked to them. Among other things, they tend to be more agreeable. Are you with me so far?"

"Yes."

"Theodor claimed that because in the modern era, conspiracy theories are spread using social media, there is a subset of conspiracy theorists who actually tend to be agreeable, and not disagreeable. To put it plainly, he thought some modern conspiracy theorists actually just want to go with the flow."

"Okay." Carver rubbed the bridge of his nose. Theodor's research sounded mind-numbingly boring. "And why did he contact you?"

"He wanted me to help him formulate effective questionnaires for his research."

"And did you?"

"I gave him some guidance, out of professional courtesy. We met a few times. But then he stopped calling. Before that, he would call me every couple of weeks. And then . . . nothing."

"When did you two last talk?"

"I don't remember. Maybe sometime during the summer. Maybe a bit later."

Carver shuffled on the couch uncomfortably. How did this guy's patients pay to sit here? It was one of the least comfortable couches he'd ever sat on. Would he and Abby joke about this in the future? *Remember how we went to couples' therapy a few months after we started dating? Ha ha.*

Probably not.

"What did he tell you about his progress in the research?"

"He was very excited about it. He'd apparently found a very large online community that matched his theory. He was making friends there, conducting interviews."

"Did he tell you who they were?"

"No. I never asked. I got the sense that he didn't want to divulge any information."

"Did he ever mention someone named Neal Wyatt?"

"Not that I recall."

"How about someone called Caterpillar?"

Landsman frowned. "Definitely not. I would have remembered *that*."

"Did he seem worried or afraid when you talked to him?"

"No, he mostly seemed very excited."

Carver drummed on the couch's armrest. "You said that he wasn't cut out for the PhD program. How so?"

"I'd really rather not elaborate. It's not my place. You should ask him about it."

Carver sighed. "Professor Landsman, I think it's admirable that you want to cover for your colleague. But we aren't here because Quinn got a speeding ticket. We have reason to believe that Quinn was in touch with some very disturbed people, and we suspect he might have been harmed. So I would really appreciate it, for Quinn's sake, if you could tell us everything. Why didn't he get his PhD?"

Landsman seemed to consider this. He glanced away, at the painting on the wall. "During his PhD, Quinn was running an experiment that was supposed to demonstrate his theory. Except the findings didn't support his theory. In fact, they contradicted it. So he manipulated the results. He fudged his interviews, asked leading questions, and finally also changed some of the data. I found out. And I decided to terminate the program."

Carver leaned forward. "What about his recent research? Do you think he manipulated the results there as well? Conducted interviews in a certain way to get a certain type of result?"

Landsman spread his arms helplessly. "I wouldn't know. But in my experience, people who do that once are very likely to do it again."

"So if he talked to these people—"

A sudden loud blip interrupted Carver's question. He turned to Abby, who took out her phone from her bag, checking the message. Her mouth snapped open, her eyes widening.

"What is it?" Carver asked, instantly thinking the worst.

Abby looked at him, an expression of pure fear etched on her face. "I got a message from Sam. From inside the school."

CHAPTER 37

They kept calling.

The phone's shrill ringing set Caterpillar's teeth on edge. He often answered it just to make it stop. And when he did, that guy Will was always on the other end of the line.

"Hey, Caterpillar," Will said. He sounded like that actor. What was his name? It was on the tip of Caterpillar's tongue. Had the Circle hired an actor to talk to him?

No, that made no sense.

"I asked you to stop calling unless there's any progress with what Abby is doing," Caterpillar said.

"That's what I'm calling about. Just to let you know that she's run into some red tape. No worries, Abby can handle it."

"Good."

"I'm worried about that guy, the one who got hurt? It seems like you're doing this for really good reasons. And once it's all over, we want that impression to stick. But it won't look good if he doesn't get the help he needs—"

"He's fine," Caterpillar said sharply, eyeing the man on the floor. He was pretty far from fine. Even if they got him a doctor now, Caterpillar doubted the man would make it. And the NYPD would be sure to let everyone know that the Watchers in the school had shot a teacher in cold blood.

Will was right; it was all about public impression. And Caterpillar wanted the people out there to know the truth. He wanted them to realize that he was the good guy here, fighting against insurmountable odds.

First, he needed Abby to do her thing, dig up the dirt on the Circle. Once that was public, they could get the man the medical assistance he needed.

"Let's think about it together," Will said. "Suppose you release that man to get the help that he needs. What's the best-case scenario?"

"Best case?" Caterpillar frowned. "Best-case scenario they treat him, and he survives."

"Survives?" Will echoed. "You mean that you're worried he won't survive?"

Caterpillar shut his eyes in frustration. "No, I told you, he's fine. It's just a scratch."

"It's just a scratch," Will said.

"Yeah. Look, he lunged at . . . someone, and got shot. But it's nothing serious, okay? You can trust me."

"You're an honorable guy; I know I can trust you," Will said. "So that's the best-case scenario, right? They treat him, he's fine, and we'll tell everyone how cooperative you were. Because you're doing all this to save lives, not hurt them."

"That's right."

"What's the worst that could happen?"

The conversations with Will went round and round. The worst that could happen was that the man would die, and the Circle would make it sound like it was the Watchers' fault. Or they'd trick Caterpillar, and as they tried to release the man, the NYPD would barge in, shooting all of them. Or it would turn out that Carlos was a Circle agent all along, and he was only faking a bad injury to get out and give the Circle all the intel he collected. Or—

"What do you think?" Will asked. "What's really the worst that could happen?"

"Look, he's fine!" Caterpillar snapped. "I need to check some stuff. Let's talk in half an hour."

He hung up the phone and massaged his forehead, allowing himself a moment of silence. The door to the adjacent office was shut, and beyond it lay havoc. A dying man, a bunch of hostages, the stale smell of vomit in the air, two fellow Watchers whose trust in him faded every minute.

How the hell had all this happened? He thought about all his decisions, moments in the past, bringing him to this point.

His gun shuddering in his hand, Carlos collapsing to the floor . . .

Hatter's eyes shining as he took one of the guns in the car . . .

Sitting by his computer, noticing two spelling mistakes in a single tweet . . .

He groaned as the memories flickered in his mind, jumping back and forth in time, a litany of choices, each of them pushing him closer to a trap of his own making.

His wife's face as she looked at him just before she left . . .

A hammer in his hand rising and falling, spattering blood and teeth fragments, his own eyes clouding with tears . . .

Digging in the yard at night, sweat running down his back despite the cold, the grave becoming deeper and deeper . . .

Purchasing three guns at the gun show, blurting that they were just for self-protection, as the stall owner smirked knowingly . . .

The two of them sitting in the living room, sharing a beer, and that moment they formed a friendship that would change everything.

"You don't need to call me Caterpillar. We're friends. You can call me Neal."

CHAPTER 38

Its Sam. Were in admin six hostages I think one is dying everyone hungry. Three ppl with handguns hatter—angry violent alma—mother looking for kids caterpillar—expose cabal killed before. Can't reply

"The message looks like she wrote it very fast," Will said.

"Yeah," Abby said, her throat dry. She took a sip of water, but it did nothing. With her daughter in danger, her body apparently lost the ability to absorb water.

They were back in the negotiation truck in front of the high school. They'd driven back as soon as they got the text, Carver flooring the gas pedal and Abby talking on the phone, alternating between Will and Tammi. Now that they were here, Abby had no intention of staying away.

"We assume that she managed to get a few seconds to herself with someone's phone," Carver said. "*Can't reply* probably means that she won't be able to answer the phone."

"Did you try calling or messaging back?"

"No," Abby quickly said. "If it's on her, we didn't want to put her in danger."

"That phone number is registered to Carlos Ramirez," Tammi said. "There's a very likely risk that someone else will call that number."

"I'm hoping Sam turned off the phone," Abby said, and emptied her glass. She tried to hide the tremor in her hand, but judging from Will's brief glance, he'd noticed.

"This message verifies a lot of what we already know," Will said. "Presumably Ramirez is the hostage who's critical."

"It sounds like this Hatter might be the most volatile of the three," Carver said. "You'll have to consider that even if you get Caterpillar to cooperate, Hatter might not go along."

"Sam said that Caterpillar killed before," Abby said. "That might mean that he's even more dangerous. If he thinks he'll end up spending a lifetime in prison, he's not likely to surrender."

"He definitely isn't cooperating at the moment," Will said. "I've had seven phone calls with him. He's kept all of them very short. Throughout all of them he showed little interest in accepting any assistance from us. He refused to discuss anything beyond our progress in digging up evidence regarding the NYPD's work with the cabal."

"Tammi, what do you have on him?" Abby asked. Those two words, *killed before*, made her gut tighten. Whom had Neal killed?

Tammi flipped through a stack of pages. "Once you gave me his name, Neal Wyatt, I managed to find a bit about him. He has very little social media presence. I found an unmaintained Facebook profile, and it's private. He's married to Jackie Wyatt, and she's not big on social media either. They live in Monticello. I'm working on getting his phone records."

"Anyone talk to Jackie?"

"She isn't answering her phone. A local cop went over to the house, and there was no one there. Their car was gone. A neighbor said that Jackie used to do morning jogs a few times a week, but they hadn't seen her for at least a month."

"Search warrant?" Will asked.

"Working on it."

Abby glanced at the whiteboard. Tammi had taped the sketches they had of the three armed Watchers. Under Neal's sketch was a photo of him taken through a crack in the window, his mangled nose giving his face an unpleasant, vile aspect. "What else do we have on him?"

"I read a lot of his posts on the Watcher forum," Tammi said. "He started out sort of meek; most of his early posts are one or two sentences long, usually aimed at reinforcing another member's theory without offering a lot of extra input. After a few months he began to be more dominant and came up with theories of his own. He presents his theories with a lot of references, which people like. It makes his posts feel more like facts and less like, um . . ."

"The deranged monologues of a lunatic?" Carver suggested.

"Yeah. I mean, that's not how these guys look at it. But his theories are generally considered more sound. He's clearly popular in the forum. He's also more charming and has a self-deprecating sense of humor. He posts a lot of memes. But his posts changed in the past two months. No more memes, no more jokes. He's a lot more critical of other members' theories, and his own posts have become much more radical."

"We're talking about people who think that some of our politicians are controlled by remote brain waves," Carver said. "So define *more radical.*"

"His theories are a lot more specific, pointing fingers at specific people, and he advocates action. It's no longer only about figuring out what the Circle is doing. It's about how the Watchers can start fighting back."

Abby nodded. She'd seen a lot of what Tammi described in her own foray into the forum. "And how do people react to his posts?"

"Most of these people don't really want to do anything risky. They're content to talk. There are always some people who suggest massive protests, but that's as far as it goes, usually. But there's a bunch of members who are on board. The names that kept showing up are Hatter, Red Queen, Dormouse, and Jabberwocky."

"Red Queen is Alma," Abby said. "Dormouse is a teenager named Dennis. We talked to him, and he's willing to cooperate with us, maybe even come over here and talk to these guys on the phone, if we decide it's a good idea. Jabberwocky is a former psychology student who's been researching the Watchers. He's been meeting Neal regularly. We don't know where he currently is."

"How are members reacting to what's happening right now?" Will asked.

"There's basically two camps in the forum. The majority are scared. They're saying that Caterpillar jumped the gun, and this will get the FBI and the police to look into the members of the forum. There was a group of members who already quit the forum, some leaving behind panicky messages along the lines of *this isn't what I wanted*. A few announced that they're moving to their safe houses, whatever that means."

"Probably remote cabins where they can hide under a blanket and wait for this to go away," Carver suggested.

"There's a small group who are excited. As you know, Caterpillar recently posted on the forum from inside the school, and these people are sure that the cabal is finally about to be exposed. Jabberwocky is constantly telling everyone not to give up. A few of the members formed a sort of half-assed protest, a few blocks away."

"We've seen it," Abby said grimly. They'd glimpsed the group as they drove past, men and women holding signs like DEATH TO THE CIRCLE and EXPOSE THE TRUTH, and of course the unavoidable SAVE THE KIDS. Which naturally referenced the imaginary kids being sold to sexual slavery from within the school, not the actual kids, her daughter among them, held hostage. Abby had been glad that Carver was behind the wheel so that she couldn't consider veering the car and running them over.

"Any progress in finding out Alma's last name?" Carver asked.

Tammi shook her head. "Not so far."

"We've debated giving the sketch and the photos to the media," Will said. "See if anyone identifies her. But we're worried that it might make the negotiation more difficult."

Abby understood the concern. It was likely that the three Watchers were following the reports on the media. Once the media got their teeth into these names, the Watchers would be served with a barrage of negative coverage that would likely destroy any hope they had of this nightmare ever ending.

"Abby, what about the interviews you mentioned?" Tammi asked.

"I'll forward them to you," Abby said. "I read through them on the way over. Theodor Quinn joined the Watcher forum in April as Jabberwocky. He made a few attempts to talk to members one on one, but any approach for an actual phone call or face-to-face meeting was received with a lot of suspicion in the forum, especially from a new member. Then, last June, he managed to convince Neal to talk to him on the phone. During the interview, Theodor tried to milk Neal about his childhood, but Neal wasn't forthcoming. Theodor did his best to appear as a fellow Watcher, which Neal seemed to have believed. Theodor writes here that Neal kept saying things like *us Watchers* and *we're even more alike than I thought* and kept asking Theodor for his own take on some Watcher theories."

"So as long as Theodor stayed focused on Watcher stuff, Neal was happy to play along," Will said.

"Exactly. And Theodor caught on. Next few interviews were all Watcher stuff, with Theodor acting like a new Watcher learning the ropes. Then things got friendlier. Up to that point, Theodor called him Caterpillar, but then Neal told him his real name. He opened up, telling Theodor about his parents, about how his father lost his job when he was a kid. He mentions Jackie in one interview, and said that they wanted a kid but that Jackie had a miscarriage. It sounds like they're becoming friends. They even meet at Theodor's home a couple of times. In the last two documented interviews, they stop talking about Neal's life and just talk about Watcher stuff again, in more detail. And that's the last documented interview. We know there were more, and that their frequency increased, but we have nothing that documents them. If we want more, we'll need a search warrant for Theodor's home, and I'm not sure we'll get it."

Carver glanced sharply at Abby but said nothing.

"Dennis told us that something happened to Caterpillar around Halloween that changed him," Abby continued. "That matches the change in behavior that we saw on the forum. And we know that Theodor and Neal met on the twenty-ninth of October. It's very likely that whatever happened during that meeting had a huge impact on Neal. We'll know more if we manage to find Theodor."

"I'm on it," Tammi said.

"Okay," Abby said, looking at Will. "How are you moving forward?"

"So far we were acting on very little information," Will said. "I've been addressing Neal by his nickname, mostly trying to get him to see that we were concerned about them, and that it wouldn't look well if anyone got hurt. It got us nowhere. Now it sounds like there was good reason. Neal isn't just looking for a way to get out of this. He wants to strike a blow at this cabal and expose them. According to the text from Samantha, he may have killed before. I need him to view me as an ally. To do that, I need to start getting him to talk about the facts. I think I can talk about his posts in the forum."

"I think you're right," Abby said. "He has a private chat for his secrets. Apparently the Watchers generally assume that there are members in the forum who are FBI and police anyway, so he won't view this as a hostile action if he learns that you've been reading posts in the forum. You can use me as backup. We told him I'm doing some digging, so I can surface up for a quick chat and an update."

"I don't want to do that," Will said. "It might muddy the waters. I want him to think of you as if you're out of the picture. If he gets the idea that he can talk to you, he'll stop talking to me."

"It really depends on how we do it," Abby said sharply. "I can say that—"

The rear door opened, and all of them turned to look at the new arrivals.

It was Estrada, the incident commander, and Baker from ESU, both wearing vests. Baker was wearing a helmet as well. Abby's heart lurched.

Estrada glanced briefly at Abby and frowned. Then he turned to Will. "Vereen, we came to let you know that we're moving in."

"What?" Abby blurted. "Now? But we've just had a huge breakthrough."

"I know," Estrada said, his eyes still on Will. "That's why we're moving. It's clear that Carlos Ramirez has very little time. The text you got reinforced that fact. The people inside have refused repeatedly to send him out or to agree to any form of medical assistance, and now we know that they've killed before. Waiting any more would end Carlos's life."

"I think it's a mistake, sir," Will said. "Statistically, given enough time, the vast majority of negotiations work much better than—"

"Given enough time," Estrada interrupted. "Like I said, in this case, we don't have time. Do you think you can get any results within ten or twenty minutes?"

Will clenched his jaw. Abby knew what Will knew. Negotiation never worked under time pressure.

"Breaking in might result in even more lives lost," Will said. "Baker said that the chances of doing this without casualties are low."

"Our chances improved a lot," Baker said. "We know where the security cameras are."

CHAPTER 39

"It's past my dinnertime."

Sam heard the words vaguely, beyond a haze of hunger and exhaustion, beyond the constant dull throb in her skull. For a second the sentence, and the snarky tone, seemed misplaced. It was something Dad would say. *It's past dinnertime, kids. Let's go get some pizza.* And maybe she'd argue that she'd rather get a salad or go to that Mexican place that Dad hated. And those complaints seemed so dumb now. What she would give to grab a pizza with Dad and Ben. Her brother would order a Coke, because Mom never let him, especially in the evening, and Dad didn't care. And Sam would remind him for the millionth time about that experiment with the tooth that they melted in Coke. An experiment she wasn't even sure really happened. Someone had told her it was just a myth. That pizza, the cheese dripping everywhere, would taste divine. And Ben would drink all the Coke and burp, and Dad would laugh, as if it were even remotely funny, and . . .

Her eyes were tearing up. They'd been doing that for a while now. Just crying and crying. She'd stop, and Fiona would cry, or Ray. Silent sobs because the one time Fiona cried too loud, Hatter went over and slapped her.

She wasn't even sure what she was thinking about.

Oh yeah. Someone had said it was past their dinnertime.

Hatter.

He checked his gun and shoved it in his belt. Then he went over to them and crouched by Fiona.

"Let's go, princess," he said. "Show me where the cafeteria is."

Fiona flinched, shrinking back. Hatter grabbed her arm, yanking her up. She let out a gasp, stumbling forward.

"I'll show you," Sam said hurriedly. "Fiona isn't well."

He fixed his gaze on her, his face expressionless. "Okay, doc. Lead the way." Standing up, he turned to Alma, who was sitting in the secretary's chair, staring at the security camera feed. "I'll go get us some food. If you see any movement at all, make sure you let me know, yeah?"

She nodded dejectedly, face pallid, hair disheveled. Earlier, she'd stepped into the principal's office, then returned twenty minutes later, her eyes puffy and bloodshot. Caterpillar seemed in control, and Hatter, if anything, was getting weirdly cheerful, but Alma was cracking under the strain.

Sam stood up, head spinning. She was weak with hunger. Had she ever gone an entire day without eating? Fiona was Jewish, and she fasted each year on Yom Kippur. She said it felt good, cleansing. Sam didn't feel cleansed at all. She was just weak and empty.

They stepped out of the room, Hatter tensing up as he checked the corridor. How did it feel for them to leave the room they were barricaded in? To walk around in a place they weren't familiar with, knowing the police could charge in at any moment? His nerves must be shot.

"The cafeteria is on the first floor," she said.

"Then I guess we're going on a little trip," Hatter answered. His voice seemed steady, casual.

"Earlier, I heard you say that you didn't even want to enter the school at first. Why did you change your mind?"

For a few seconds, Hatter remained silent. Then he said, half to himself, "Because it felt right."

"It felt right?"

"Yes. To come into this place, backed up by my friends. A gun in my pocket. It felt right."

Sam swallowed. She'd been hoping for another insane conspiracy conversation, Hatter telling her how he'd wanted to rescue imaginary kids from an imaginary fate. But she had to keep the conversation going, get to know this guy better, befriend him. "Why did it feel right?"

They came up to the staircase. Hatter paused, grabbing her arm, listening for a few seconds. "Why do you care, doc?"

"Just making conversation."

He leered at her. "Yeah? Why's that? You want to get to know me better?"

"I just thought . . . if I understood, maybe I could help everyone get out of this safely. Including you."

Hatter descended the steps, still holding her arm, dragging her with him. "Do you really believe this will end with no one getting hurt?"

Her heart skipped a beat. "Won't it? That's why Caterpillar is talking to the cops, right? He's looking for a way to end this."

"Caterpillar thinks that the NYPD will announce to the world that we were right all along. That they're corrupt and were helping some pedophiles purchase little kids. And then everyone would embrace us as the heroes that saved the day." Hatter let out a hoarse laugh, which echoed in the empty staircase. "And Alma thinks maybe we'll still find the kids stuffed in a locker or a basement somewhere."

"And what do you think?"

"I think that in a few hours, the cops will come in, guns blazing. And that we'll all be killed or arrested."

Sam glanced at him. His voice was impassive, as if they were talking about the weather.

"We can try and think how to avoid it," she said. "It doesn't have to happen."

They'd reached the bottom floor, and he paused again, looking warily around, before prodding her to lead on. "Who said I want to avoid it?"

She'd run out of words, a chilly realization creeping into her. Some people couldn't be reasoned with. Some people were already too far gone. Maybe her mom would know what to say to this guy. How to get him to back down. But Sam had no idea.

"Maybe this is where I want to be," Hatter said. "Maybe I can think of worse places to spend my last hours than in a school, with a gun and a certified doctor to keep me company." His hand slid off her arm, onto her back, creeping down. Sam tried to move away, but Hatter moved with her, his hand still there, a rough, vile touch. He reached her backside and squeezed it, his breath rasping.

Sam shied away. "Um . . . the cafeteria is right through this door." Her voice broken and terrified. No longer trying to figure out what made this man tick. All she wanted was to be as far away from him as possible.

Hatter leered at her, then walked over to the cafeteria's double doors. He opened one a crack and peered in.

"Well, this is going to be fun," he muttered.

Sam knew what he was looking at. The vast, empty space, lined with white rectangular tables. A sadistic design that almost seemed to be aimed at enhancing all the horrors of the high school social order. Were you the kid who sat alone at a table meant for six? Or maybe you were forced to choose daily who your cafeteria friends were? And would the people sitting around you notice what you ate, and how?

But, of course, that was not what Hatter was concerned about.

The entire cafeteria was lined with enormous glass windows, facing the schoolyard and the street. Where dozens of armed cops stood, waiting.

CHAPTER 40

"I thought we didn't have access to the school's security cameras," Will said.

"We don't," Baker said. "But we managed to get our hands on an old security footage backup from a few days ago. Using that, we managed to map out an entrance route that goes through the security network's blind spots. They won't see us coming."

Baker stood on the bumper of the negotiation truck as he explained it, the rear door open, police lights flashing in the darkness behind him. He clearly didn't intend for this to be a discussion. The decision was final. ESU was moving in. The negotiation team was no longer needed.

"You're not moving in from the roof?" Abby asked.

"No. We'll go through one of the doors, then go up the staircase."

"When?" Will asked.

"We want to move in as soon as possible. We're moving all the media trucks away first so that they don't film us going in." Baker glanced at Abby. "It's an easy path, and we'll catch them completely by surprise. There's almost no risk to—"

His radio crackled with a burst of static, and then a voice. "We have movement in the cafeteria."

Baker pressed the mic. "What kind of movement?"

A short pause, and the lookout answered. "Two figures. A man and a girl. He's holding a gun to her head."

Baker jumped off the bumper, disappearing into the night, followed by the commander. Abby was on her feet, running, before she even realized it. She leaped off the truck, the cold night air hitting her face. She spotted the two men as they moved toward the street corner. She chased after them, her feet hardly touching the ground, crisscrossing between cops and vehicles and makeshift barriers.

She caught up to Baker as he was looking through a pair of night goggles at the dark cafeteria. Abby tried to look through the dusty windows, but could hardly see anything beyond the faded outline of a few tables. Was that movement, or just her imagination? She was breathing hard, barely feeling the night's chill. Looking around, she spotted an ESU officer talking on the radio, a pair of night goggles strapped onto his forehead.

"Hey." She approached him. "Can I have those? For just a moment?"

She was already reaching for the goggles as she spoke. He frowned in confusion as she grabbed them, tugging the things off his head.

"Hey, hang on—"

She ignored him, pressing the goggles to her eyes, the world swimming into a haze of bright green, the cafeteria's interior clear as daylight.

And there was Sam.

Eyes open wide, lips twisted in fear, body limp and helpless. A gun held to her temple. She was led by a large man, whom Abby instantly recognized from the sketch—Hatter. He was shuffling backward, dragging Sam with him, using her as a human shield.

"I have a line of sight," someone said on the radio. "I can take him out."

Abby swallowed. She didn't know what she was hoping for. If he took the shot, an ESU squad would be inside the cafeteria in seconds, dragging Sam out to safety. She could be holding her daughter in her arms in no time, this nightmare behind them.

But what if he missed, hitting Sam? What if he didn't kill Hatter, who would shoot Sam in retaliation? And, a distant voice wondered, what about the other hostages? What would happen to them if the police opened fire now?

"Sir, should I take the shot?"

◆ ◆ ◆

Sam could glimpse the dark shapes of police officers in the street, outlined by the flickering lights. Hatter had his thick arm around her, and he was dragging her, the stench of his sweat everywhere. His gun muzzle dug into her temple, a constant sharp pain that made her whimper. Hatter was breathing hard as he moved, and every few seconds he would turn to face a different window. With her always in front of him.

His arm was inches away. If she bit him really hard, maybe he would let go. She could flatten herself on the floor, and let the cops deal with him.

Except he probably wouldn't let go. He would probably just shoot her instead.

He moved slowly through the room, never loosening his iron grip, never shifting the gun away from her head. It was cold and hard. Death was a fraction of a second away. The world seemed to fade, until there was nothing except for that gun, and the arm that held her, and that useless red-and-blue light, shimmering in the distance.

◆ ◆ ◆

"Negative," Baker said. "Don't take the shot."

The night goggles were snatched away from Abby, and Sam disappeared, replaced by darkness. Abby let out a soft cry, turning to reclaim the goggles. It was the man she'd originally taken the goggles from.

"What the hell?" He was staring at her, looking furious.

"Hey," Baker said, glancing their way. "Relax, Jones. She's with me."

Jones gave Abby another piercing look and left, the goggles in his hand.

Abby walked over to Baker, saying nothing. She didn't want to confuse him, not when the wrong word from this man could seal her daughter's fate.

Baker kept watching, tense. Time slowed down to a crawl, as Abby desperately tried to glimpse something, anything, in the murky cafeteria. Finally he lowered his goggles.

"They're gone," he said. "They went into the kitchen in the back."

"Probably getting food," Estrada said.

"We could move in when they show up again," Baker said after a second. "They're split up. One team can break through the windows in the administration wing on the third floor, and take out the two there. And we can take this guy out when he shows up."

"Do you think it's the right course of action?" Estrada asked.

Baker hesitated, then said, "I'll get the second team ready to go. We'll make the call when they step out."

◆ ◆ ◆

Sam stared forward as Hatter dragged her into the kitchen. He kicked the door shut, darkness enveloping them, the police cars disappearing from view. A second later he found the switch, the room filling with white fluorescent light. He shoved her away, and she stumbled, grabbing a nearby metal counter for balance.

Hatter looked around him, still breathing heavily. "Well, look at that," he said, approaching a stack of cardboard boxes. He opened the top one. "Turkey sandwiches! That's what you get for lunch?"

"Only on Wednesdays," Sam said weakly. She didn't let go of the metal counter. She wasn't sure her legs would hold her. Her heart beat wildly, and she could still feel the ghost imprint of the gun barrel burrowing into her temple.

"Wednesdays, huh? Lucky we didn't come here on a Thursday. Go check the fridge over there, see what we got." Hatter rummaged in the box.

She forced herself to do as he said, walking slowly over to the metal fridge at the far side of the room.

A knife lay by a stack of chopped cucumbers on the counter, left behind when the school was evacuated. The blade gleaming and sharp. A long knife that would cut deep.

She didn't pause, just kept walking, slightly altering course, raising her hand casually, letting it slide over the counter. Touched the knife handle. Tightened her grip, the knife heavy in her hand, the blade gleaming in the harsh light from above.

"Hey, doc?"

She whipped around, the knife hidden behind her back. Hatter stood a few feet away, two cardboard boxes under his arm, the gun aimed at her.

"Why don't you put down that knife?" he suggested.

The blade tumbled from her fingers, as if they were made of rubber. It missed her foot by inches and clattered on the floor. Hatter set the boxes aside on the counter, strode over, and then, his arm so fast it was a blur, he slapped her.

She screamed as she stumbled back, colliding with the fridge. Her cheek was on fire, her eyes cloudy with tears. Hatter kicked the knife away, his face expressionless.

He gestured at the fridge. "Open it."

She did, her hand trembling. It was stacked with chocolate milk cartons. Hatter picked up the cardboard boxes and walked over to her. "Hold these."

The boxes weren't too heavy. She balanced both in her arms, tears running down her face. Hatter opened the top box and tossed some of the sandwiches out onto the floor. He then took half a dozen chocolate milk cartons and shoved them into the box.

"Let's go, doc. We have what we came for."

◆ ◆ ◆

"There they are," Baker said, looking intently through the goggles. "They got some food from the cafeteria."

Abby couldn't see a thing. "Is Sam okay?" she blurted.

A short pause. "Yeah. She's carrying the boxes," Baker answered, and pressed the shoulder mic. "Team alpha, are you in position?"

The response came almost instantly. "Affirmative."

"Dodger, do you have line of sight on the target?"

The lookout answered a second later, sounding hesitant. "Negative, not yet."

Abby glanced at the buildings around her, wondering where he was positioned. In one of the apartments, looking out a window? On a rooftop, staring down his sniper rifle at Hatter and Sam as they moved through the cafeteria?

"That guy's getting jittery," Baker said. "I don't like it."

"I had him in my sights for a second," Dodger said. "But he keeps turning. It's a close call."

Don't. The words hovered on Abby's lips. Would he do it? Risk her daughter's life like that?

Don't.

Baker sighed. "Stand down. Team alpha, stand down."

Abby exhaled, a long, torturous breath, relief and disappointment intermingling. Her daughter was still alive. And she was being dragged away, a gun to her head.

CHAPTER 41

"This is looking even better," Baker told Estrada. "These people probably haven't eaten a thing all day. They'll be busy stuffing their faces when we go in."

Abby stood a few feet away, still staring at the dark cafeteria, her mind replaying the image of Sam being dragged through that dark space, a gun to her head. Her fists were clenched tightly, fingernails digging into her palms. She could almost see the vague outlines of Sam and Hatter still there, in the cafeteria, as if the image had been seared into her corneas.

"I got word that the media crews have all been cleared from 157th Street," Estrada said. "You can move in."

"We'll give that guy five more minutes to return to the admin wing," Baker said. "We don't want the two groups apart when we strike."

"Once they eat, they'll be a lot more rational," Abby said. "It'll be easier to negotiate with them, get them to stand down."

Estrada shook his head. "We've been trying all day. And a hostage will die if we don't get medical assistance to him soon. I agree with Baker; it'll be much safer to strike when they're eating."

"*Safer?* Is that your idea of—"

"It's not your call, Mullen. I know your daughter is in there. But if you can't let us do our job, I'll have you removed from the scene."

Abby's mouth snapped shut. Given time she could maybe convince Estrada that this was a bad, risky move. But like he'd repeatedly pointed out, they were out of time.

◆ ◆ ◆

A minute or two, and they'd be back with everyone else. That was all Sam could think about. Because suddenly, being in that room was almost *safe*. She could sit down next to Fiona, and keep her mouth shut like the rest of the hostages, until Mom would manage to negotiate a surrender. Her earlier plans, to befriend the Watchers, and to do what she could to help the police, all seemed incredibly stupid. In fact, maybe if they'd stayed in the music room like Ray had said, they'd still be there now. Safe.

Instead, she was being dragged through the hallways by Hatter, while the cardboard boxes jostled in her hands, feeling heavier and heavier.

"Let's stop here," Hatter said.

"What? The office is up those—" The rest of the sentence died as Hatter yanked her into an empty classroom.

The room was in chaos, chairs toppled over, backpacks, notebooks, and pens scattered everywhere. Hatter shut the door behind them.

"Put the boxes on the teacher's desk." He gestured with the gun.

Sam bit her lip as she did it. She stepped away, walking back to the far end of the room.

"I thought we could have a nice picnic after our trip," Hatter said. He opened the top box, took out a sandwich, and tore the plastic cover with his teeth. "You want one?"

Sam shook her head. "I'm okay," she whispered. "We should get those back. Your friends are waiting."

"They can wait a bit longer," Hatter said, chewing, a piece of lettuce dangling from his mouth. "I think we deserve a reward for what we did. Don't you?"

Sam lowered her gaze. Mom would have known what to say. She'd have known if she should smile, or laugh, or give him a piercing, angry look. Sam had no idea. In fact, she wasn't sure there was anything she could do. She was just a passenger on this nightmare train.

"You know, I think this is the first time I'm drinking chocolate milk since I left school," Hatter said, taking a carton out of the box. "I used to love this shit; I don't know why I never bought myself any."

He unscrewed the top and drank, the carton slowly crumpling in his hand. A trickle ran down the side of his mouth, but he didn't seem to notice or care. Finally he tossed the carton on the floor, chocolate milk spattering everywhere.

"You sure you don't want some?" he asked. "There isn't enough for everyone."

She gave her head another shake.

"Suit yourself." He put the rest of the sandwich on the desk and walked toward her. "So what do you say, doc? I got you this fancy dinner. I think we can take this date to the next level."

She backed away along the wall, eyes skittering, measuring the distance to the door, planning out her escape—toss a chair in his direction and run. Or leap over one of the desks and use it as a barrier, keeping it between them. Or maybe grab a pen and drive it into his eye before lunging outside.

But her body refused to respond, and the only thing she could do was backpedal, into the corner of the room, as Hatter lumbered closer.

◆ ◆ ◆

"Central, team alpha. We're ready to breach."

The voice came loud and clear through the radio in the command center. Abby stood in the corner, listening, body frozen with fear. She'd followed Estrada and Baker inside, and they let her stay. But she knew that a word out of place would get her kicked out. She wasn't even sure she could talk if she wanted to. Her throat was clenched so tightly it was hard to breathe.

A screen on the wall displayed the feed from the body cam of the ESU team leader. Abby's eyes were transfixed on the screen, where a man was placing some sort of breaching device on the door.

"How loud will the breach be?" Estrada asked.

"The device is hydraulic, so it's pretty silent," Baker said. "The loudest sound will come from the door's wooden frame splintering. They're on the far side of the school, on the bottom floor, so the people in the administration wing won't hear a thing."

"Okay, go," Estrada said.

Baker pressed the mic. "Team alpha, go."

The man on screen fiddled with some sort of remote. A second later the door buckled, then burst open. The man who'd breached the door grabbed the device, moving aside, and the feed on screen jiggered as the team moved in.

"See how they're sticking to the left of the hallway?" Baker said. "There's a single security camera there, and they're sticking to its blind spot. After that, they have a completely unmonitored path to the administration wing."

"It's all going to be over soon," Estrada said grimly.

◆ ◆ ◆

Caterpillar paced the room. What the hell was Hatter doing? He'd watched the man on the security feed as he stepped out of the cafeteria with the girl. She was holding two boxes, presumably full of food. And then, on the way back, they'd simply stepped into one of the classrooms, disappearing from view.

He could call him on the PA system, but the cops outside would hear him. He didn't want them to know what was going on inside. He didn't want them to think he was losing control over the situation.

He sat back down, searching for movement, willing Hatter to step out of the classroom.

"Caterpillar," Alma said, her voice urgent.

"What?" The woman was driving him insane, constantly searching through the students' files, looking for any mention of the kidnapped kids. Every few minutes she thought she found a coded message, or a hint, or a missing page. Didn't she get it already? The school would never keep a written record of their illegal acts in such an obvious place.

"Look at this." Her face was pale, terrified, as she handed him her phone. He took it and frowned at the screen. It was the Watcher forum, open on one of the threads dealing with them. A single post, all in caps.

THE POLICE JUST ENTERED THE BUILDING FROM THE BACK DOOR!!!!!

Caterpillar blinked, then checked the posting time. Less than a minute ago. The user was Cheshire_Cat_2. A solid Watcher who wasn't prone to hysteria or to all-caps posts.

"How does he know?" he shouted at Alma.

"He's protesting outside. He must have seen them!"

Caterpillar scanned the feed again, but there was nothing. What if they'd somehow hacked the security cameras?

"Shut the door, and lock it!" he yelled at Alma. "And get ready to shoot."

He pulled out his own gun, aiming it at the principal, his hand trembling. Damn it, not yet. Not yet!

A sudden sound from the school, loud and screechy.

"Attention, police! Call your people out, or I'm shooting the hostages. Do it now. Now!" It was Caterpillar, shouting on the PA system.

"They can see them," Abby blurted.

"That's impossible," Baker said. "We need to move forward. Our team is only thirty seconds away."

Abby stared at the jerky feed, the team still moving forward.

"But they're ready now; you won't catch them by surprise." She raised her voice, keeping it steady.

"Pull them out," Estrada said. "We can't risk it."

Baker took a deep breath. Then he hit the mic. "Team alpha, move out. Move out."

Hatter loomed over Sam, his face impassive. Foamy drool coated his lower lip, a trickle of it running down his chin. He touched her cheek, and she flinched, but she had nowhere to go.

"Attention, police! Call your people out, or I'm shooting the hostages. Do it now. Now!"

The screechy sound echoed in the room, and Hatter turned around.

Sam darted away, stumbling toward the doorway, heart thudding in her chest, a whimper lodged in her throat. She was out of the room, saw movement in the hallway. Figures running down the hall, away from her. She opened her mouth to shout for help.

A sudden iron grip on her arm. She was yanked back, a hand muffling her mouth as she tried to scream.

And then fingers on her throat. Squeezing.

Hatter slammed her against the wall, his hand still squeezing. She tried to scream, but there was no air, and all she managed was a broken croak. She fumbled at his hand, clawing at the fingers that were crushing her windpipe, trying to scratch his wrist. She kicked his ankle, a weak, helpless kick that he didn't even seem to notice.

His face was still impassive, vacant eyes staring at her with mild interest as she gasped for air, flailing, buckling.

Her lungs burned. Spots danced in front of her eyes. The world seemed to fade.

She couldn't breathe.

CHAPTER 42

Abby watched the screen as the ESU team ran out, no longer focused on staying quiet or on sticking to the security cameras' blind spots. It was a complete disaster. A botched attempt at an assault meant that all trust between the subjects and the negotiators was gone. Everything that she and Will had worked to build, swept away within minutes. Negotiating a surrender seemed less likely than ever.

The rear door of the command center opened. It was Tammi, breathing hard, her vest askew and half-open.

"Sir," she said. "Caterpillar is on the phone with Will. It doesn't sound good."

Abby was already out the door, dashing to the negotiation truck, leaping inside. Will sat at the negotiation station, his headphones on.

"It's understandable," he was saying. "It seems like the police acted in bad faith. It must be very stressful to—" He paused and glanced at Abby, his face grim, as the man on the other side of the call ranted at him.

"I should never have agreed to this!" Caterpillar stood in the principal's office, screaming, his gun wavering, still pointed at the hostages through the doorway. "I was an idiot to trust you."

"Caterpillar, so far we managed to avoid anyone getting hurt by working together," Will said. "You kept things under control in there, and I really appreciate it. You're an honest man—"

"A lot of good that did me," Caterpillar snarled. His heart was hammering hard. A few seconds ago he'd spotted the team of cops on the security camera feed, running out of the building. He couldn't believe they were that close to storming in and finishing them off. If Alma hadn't glimpsed that forum post when she did . . .

"We're still not sure what happened here," Will said. "We think it might have been a different group, perhaps the FBI. I'll talk to some people, figure this out. But meanwhile—"

"Meanwhile, you tell your people that they messed up," Caterpillar said. They'd forced his hand. He had to take a firm stand, make them see that they couldn't try that again. "And that has consequences."

He hung up, and marched out of the room, aiming his gun.

Squeezing the trigger.

◆ ◆ ◆

The strength was leeching away from Sam's body. Her flailing hands were clawing weakly at something—she wasn't even sure what.

A sudden loud explosion vibrated, somewhere nearby.

The grip on her throat loosened, and she gasped for air, letting out a wheezy cough. She collapsed to her knees, gulping air desperately, her entire body shaking. She stared at the floor, at her hands, as they swam into focus. Her neck throbbed, and her head pounded, and she was about to be sick.

But she was still alive.

A strong grip on her forearm, pulling her up.

"Come on, doc," Hatter whispered in her ear. "And if you try to scream, if you even whisper, I'll splatter your brain all over the wall. Do you understand?"

She nodded weakly, unable to talk.

He dragged her outside the classroom, and she stumbled, her feet still numb and shaking. Up the staircase, tripping, hitting her knee, pain blazing, more stairs, empty corridors. A locked door. Hatter pounding on it, shouting for them to open up, that it was only him. The lock clicked, the door opened, Alma standing in the doorway, face slack and pale. The sound of crying, someone saying "oh god oh god oh god," over and over and over. It was hard to focus, blotchy spots still dancing in front of Sam's eyes, as she looked around the room dizzily. Saw the blood spatter.

Caterpillar stood above Mr. Ramirez, his gun pointed down. Mr. Ramirez's head was . . . it was . . . there was blood, and fragments, and . . .

Sam turned away and threw up bile.

Mr. Ramirez was gone.

◆ ◆ ◆

"Shot fired. I repeat, shot fired."

One shot. Abby had heard it from inside the negotiation truck. Just after Caterpillar had told Will that there would be consequences.

They'd just executed one of the hostages.

"Call them," she said. "Ask them what happened. Who they shot. Call them! Ask them who they shot!"

She lunged at the station, punching the buttons, dialing the principal's office. "Let me talk to them! They'll talk to me! We need to know who they shot!"

Someone grabbed her, pulled her away, shouts around her, someone saying, "Get her out of here," as she bucked and struggled.

"Who did they kill?" she screamed as they pulled her outside. "Who did they kill?"

CHAPTER 43

"... but how? How did they get in?"

"... must have missed them ..."

"... were watching the security cameras, ask Alma. Alma! Snap out of it ..."

"... oh god oh god oh god ..."

"... shut the hell up ..."

"... have to get him out of here ..."

"... call them, and tell them ..."

"... where were you when this all happened? Why didn't you come back ..."

"... took a little detour ..."

"... maybe you let them in ..."

"... get that gun out of my face ..."

"... Alma! Get a grip ..."

Sam curled against the wall, palms to her ears, eyes shut because if she opened them, she would see the spatter, and all that blood, and those little pieces ... she coughed and vomited again, more bile; she had nothing to throw up but water. They were all screaming and waving their guns, and she was sure that at any moment someone would shoot again.

The door was shut and locked again, and they were trapped once more, with that awful smell of vomit and blood and sweat.

Her neck throbbed, and her head hurt. Her body was completely drained, as if the terror of the past hour had leeched every little bit of energy out of her. All she could do was keep her hands on her ears, keep her eyes shut. More than anything, she needed to keep her eyes shut.

"One of them is an agent. We have to pull out their teeth. We need a pair of pliers. Do you know where the janitor's closet is?"

"Are you insane? Pull out their teeth?"

"They have tiny microphones, in their teeth, so that the Circle can listen. That's how they knew. They knew you were gone."

"They knew I was gone because they saw me through the windows in the cafeteria, you moron."

"We should pull out their teeth. Just to make sure. I know which; I have the sketch."

"We don't have microphones in our teeth! Please let us go."

"Shut up, damn it!"

Someone touched her. She flinched, but it was a delicate touch, not like Hatter's iron grip and probing fingers. A gentle caress.

She opened her eyes. It was Fiona. She'd crawled over to Sam, and now took her hand, their fingers intertwining. Sam let out a whimper, buried her head in Fiona's chest. Another heaving sob. She shuddered as her friend caressed her hair, saying nothing. There was nothing to say. And it was dangerous to talk.

She should never have talked to Mom like she had the night before. They might never get to talk again. This would be Mom's last memory of Sam—her daughter calling her a liar.

She thought about the night of the fire, all those years ago. Mom trapped in the burning compound with her parents and the rest of the congregation. Flames rising all around her. Sam now had a glimpse of what she must have felt all those years ago. The helplessness. The terror. The room had probably been full of smoke. Sam touched her bruised neck. It would have been impossible to breathe.

"Tell me where the janitor's closet is."

247

"Listen, we're not opening a dental shop here, okay? If you want, we can lock them in another room."

"What if the cops come back? We need them nearby."

"We keep one here. If the cops show up, we're all screwed anyway. And we need to get this body out of here too. Jesus, did you have to shoot him in the head? What a mess."

"How did the cops get in?"

"We'll figure it out. Let's get those people out of here. God, I wish we could open a window; this place stinks."

"You two, get up."

Sam tightened, clutching Fiona's jacket. She couldn't move.

"You deaf? Get the hell up."

Fiona caressed Sam's hair, leaning toward her ear. "Sam? We have to go, okay? But I got you. You can keep your eyes shut and hold my hand, okay? You think you could do that?"

Sam nodded. Fiona gently helped her stand up, and Sam squeezed her eyes shut even more, because if she accidentally opened them, if she saw what had happened to Mr. Ramirez . . . god, those empty eyes.

"Move, doc." Hatter's voice close by. "Or do you need me to move you?"

"Come on, Sam." Fiona tugging her, one step at a time, the smell of blood slowly diminishing. But still there. She could still feel it. Just like she could still feel the ghosts of Hatter's fingers on her throat. The memory of the gun barrel digging into her temple.

One step at a time. Eyes shut. Trusting her friend to lead her.

CHAPTER 44

Abby leaned on the hood of Carver's car, shivering in the cold, watching the protesters across the road. There were already dozens, shouting at the cops, chanting about the Circle, about child slavery, about the new world order. A few media crews were filming the protest, commentators talking with the mob in the background. She wanted to feel angry at these people, wished for a burning rage. But she was numb with fear, and her mind had no room for any other emotion.

"Here." Carver approached her and handed her a large, steaming paper cup. "Drink this. It's tea."

"Thanks," she whispered and sipped from it. The cup warmed her hands. It was a small relief.

"They're saying one of the protesters warned the Watchers inside," Carver said.

It took her a few seconds to parse the sentence, wrestle meaning out of those words that had been strung out one after the other. Her mind was stuttering; she could hardly pull it together.

"Yeah, I know," she finally said. "It was posted on the forum."

"You read the post?"

"I read all the posts," she said, taking another sip. "I'm hoping that one of the people inside will post about the hostage they executed."

Six hostages. Her daughter one of them. A one-in-six chance, a toss of the die. She pushed the thought away. Should she check the forum again? Maybe there was a new post. A dim part of her brain registered the irony. Her biggest hope for information came from a forum that constantly spread twisted lies and nonsensical accusations. She shut her eyes, listening to the protesters.

"Our children are not for sale!"

"Stop the Circle of death!"

"The blood of the Messiah must be freed!"

"Down with the cabal!"

"The new world order will not rise!"

"It looks like the protest is growing," Carver said.

"It's catching on," Abby said. "The Watchers are confident that there are actual people from the cabal here, and they want to find them. One of the protesters said that when the ESU team came out, they were carrying something that looked like a child. And two networks went live, interviewing the protesters. There are more of them coming. There's an actual bus picking people up to join the protest. It's all over the forum."

"Maybe you should stop reading that," Carver said gently. "The forum is being monitored by Tammi, and by the FBI. If they find out anything about the hostages, you'll know."

Abby raised her eyebrow. "Okay, so I'll stop reading it . . . and do what? Go home, get some sleep?"

"You could get in the car for starters. I'll put the heater on."

She felt like she was falling apart. She tried to collect herself again. She needed to be strong. "You know," she said, "Sam found out yesterday about Wilcox. I kept it a secret all these years. And now she knows."

Carver looked at her, saying nothing, the curling steam from his cup intermingling with his foggy breath.

"I liked to think that I kept it a secret from her to protect her, you know? From all those terrible things in my past."

"That makes sense."

Abby shook her head. "But it's bullshit, right? I knew she'd find out eventually. Maybe I just didn't want my kids to see me like *that*. A massacre survivor. Someone who grew up in a cult. It was just me being selfish."

Carver cleared his throat. "Could be a bit of both. You wanted to protect her, and you didn't want her to see you differently. Doesn't sound so selfish to me."

Abby took a big gulp from the tea, which was getting tepid fast. "And now she ended up in the same situation, just like I had been as a little girl. In the midst of a police siege, barricaded with dangerous people with a twisted perception of reality."

"It's not the same." Carver shifted closer to her. "You had no one looking out for you. But she has you out here."

Abby crumpled her empty cup. "If she's even still alive. If they . . . if they haven't shot *her*."

"We don't even know that they shot a hostage."

"They did."

"And *even* if they did, they would have shot one of the older hostages. Not one of the kids. These people think of themselves as the heroes, right?"

She shrugged. She had no idea what they thought or felt anymore.

Carver placed his arm around her, pulling her toward him. She let herself lean into his body, take comfort from his presence. What would she have done if he weren't there with her today? As impossible as it sounded, the day would have been much worse. She would have completely fallen apart. She shut her eyes, losing herself to the sensation of him holding her for one second.

Her phone rang. She pulled away from Carver and took it out, staring at the screen. Steve. The ringing intermingled with the shouts of the protesters. With them in the background and her gut-chilling terror for Sam's life, talking to Steve right now seemed impossible. Her finger hovered above the decline button.

But what if Ben needed her?

She answered the call. "Hello?"

"Abby?" Steve's voice, tired and tense. "What's that noise?"

"Nothing. Just some people in the street."

"Okay. Any news about Sam?"

Yes. A hostage had been shot. Their daughter might be dead right now. And just before, Abby had seen her hauled across the school cafeteria with a gun jammed against her head. "No news yet. We had eyes on her about half an hour ago. She looked unhurt."

"That's good news." Steve sounded relieved. "Any progress with the negotiation?"

"Will's working on it. How's Ben?"

"He's okay. I mean . . . it's hard to tell, really. You know how Ben is."

She knew. When Ben was scared, or sad, or angry, he closed up, like a snail, retreating into his own mental shell. He spoke in monosyllables, and his face became blank, his emotions betrayed only by a slight tremor in his lips. Usually Abby could sense what he was feeling, could coax him out of it. But Steve was completely useless in that regard.

"Is he asleep?"

"No . . . he won't go to sleep. I tried reading him three different bedtime stories. He just sits in his bed."

"Put him on the phone."

"Okay, hang on."

She listened as Steve gave Ben the phone, telling him to talk to Mommy.

"Hi," Ben said.

"Ben, sweetie, are you going to sleep?"

"Yeah."

"Dad told me you're staying awake. It's really late; you should sleep."

"Okay."

Abby sighed. "Tell you what. I bet you'd like to see Jeepers and Pretzel before you go to sleep, right?" Other kids snuggled with their teddy bears or puppies. Ben snuggled with his pet tarantula and snake.

A slight pause, and then, "Yes, I need to talk to them."

"What do you want to talk to them about?"

"I need to tell them about Sam. Jeepers is probably worried, and I need to tell him that she'll be okay."

"Yeah." Abby wiped a tear.

"Pretzel misses Sam too."

"I know, sweetie. That's a good idea. Put Daddy on the phone."

Steve's voice came back on. "Hey."

"Listen, I know it's a lot to ask, but can you take Ben to—"

"Absolutely. I'll take him right now. If I manage to get him to go to sleep at your place, I'll sleep on the couch."

"Thanks, Steve." Abby tensed as she noticed Tammi walking over. "I have to go."

"Okay, bye."

She hung up, and scrutinized Tammi, trying to read the young officer's body language. Her body was hunched against the cold, and she looked miserable. Was it because she was bringing Abby bad news?

"Hey," Tammi said, stepping close enough that she could talk without being overheard.

Abby leaned closer; it was hard to hear her with the protesters shouting in the background. "Do we know—"

"They killed Ramirez," Tammi said. "They shot him. Not Sam. Sam's okay."

Abby exhaled, feeling the fear morph in her gut, switching from one kind to another. The binary alive-or-dead terror replaced with the now-familiar fear for her daughter's safety.

"So Sam's definitely okay?" Carver asked.

"Yeah," Tammi said. "Will called Caterpillar. He managed to get it out of him. The other hostages are fine."

"So what's the plan?" Abby asked.

Tammi looked at her sadly. "We're mending the broken trust. Estrada won't have you talking to the Watchers. I think Will would have considered it, but Estrada won't hear of it."

Abby nodded, unsurprised. After her hysterical scene, Estrada would have to be insane to let her get on the phone with Caterpillar.

"There's another development," Tammi said. "I found Jackie Wyatt."

It took Abby a second to catch on. "Neal's wife?"

"Yeah. I got her phone details from one of her Facebook friends. I just talked to her. She's staying at her mom's place in the Bronx. Will wants to bring her here, talk to her."

"I'll pick her up," Abby blurted.

"I thought you'd want to." Tammi touched Abby's arm. "That's fine. Pick her up; get her straight here. Just . . . don't make me regret it, okay?"

CHAPTER 45

Jackie was waiting by the window, staring at the road outside, fists clenched. Once the patrol car showed up, all hell would break loose. Mother would ask why they were there, and Jackie would have to tell her that they were there to pick her up. And Mother would freeeeeeak out, because if there was something she would never in a million years let go unused, it was an opportunity for drama. Why were they here for Jackie? Because of Neal? She'd told her, repeatedly, that he was no good, and why couldn't Jackie listen? What would the neighbors think? Paula from next door always asked why Jackie wasn't working, and now she'd think that Jackie was a criminal. Did Jackie want her mother to die of a heart attack before her grandchild was born? Was that it?

Mother's dramatic episodes always came in the form of questions, delivered in shrieks, with no time to formulate answers.

Jackie was so deep in her imaginary predictions of what her mother would say that when they showed up, parking in front of her house in a *regular* car, she almost didn't realize it was them. But then they stepped out, a man and a woman, and even though they weren't in uniform, you could sort of sense that they were cops. It was the way they carried themselves. Well, at least it was for the man. The woman seemed too small, and pale, and tired.

Jackie lunged from the window to the door, opening it before they had time to knock.

"Bye, Mother, I'm going out! Don't wait up!" she yelled, already stepping outside, the cops staring at her in surprise.

"Where are you going this time of night?" Mother shouted from her bedroom.

Jackie was already shutting the door, because answering her mother's questions always gave birth to more questions.

"Hi," she whispered at the man. "I'm Jackie."

"Okay." The man showed her his badge, as if there were any doubt. "I'm Detective Carver. This is Lieutenant Mullen."

Detective Carver was an attractive dude, if you were into that sort of thing. He had that "man make fire" kind of look, with his broad shoulders, and his height, and that scar on his chin that you could imagine he got in a fight, even though he'd probably gotten it while shaving. But Lieutenant Mullen, she was . . . she was something else. There was an eeriness about her, like she was about to explode, or maybe she'd already exploded, and this was what remained. And behind her blank face there was something that Jackie knew well. It was a deep, carnal fear.

But then Mullen blinked and shook her head, as if focusing, and smiled at Jackie. Jackie had gotten it wrong. Mullen's expression was kind and warm and perfectly calm. Jackie was a good judge of character, and this woman had her shit together. She was cool. Maybe, if circumstances were different, they could be friends.

"Hey, Jackie," Mullen said. Her voice was soft. "You can call me Abby. Let's get in the car."

Jackie nodded and followed them, but then slowed down as she reached the car. It wasn't that she was afraid, not really. But anyone who'd spent the past couple of years with Neal would have been wary to step into a car with a couple of cops. All the stories he'd told her came back, the people who disappeared, and the murders the cops didn't even bother to hide, simply claiming that it was a justified shooting, as if there could be such a thing. And she didn't even realize that she'd listened all that closely until she had to step into the car and suddenly could imagine how one day she would be one of those stories. How she'd entered the car, and it had driven off, and no one had seen her since.

"You can sit in the back," Abby told her.

"Um . . . maybe we can do this here?" Jackie said. She tried to be assertive, because Neal always said that they could smell weakness, but her voice was too high, and it didn't really sound like a statement so much as a plea.

Abby smiled again, and brushed a stray lock of hair from her face, tucking it behind her ear. She had surprisingly large ears, and with her small, delicate face, it almost made her look like a mouse. A kind, sweet mouse. "It must be difficult to get in a car with two cops sitting in the front, in the middle of the night. I'll sit in the back beside you, okay? Would that make it easier?"

Jackie found herself smiling back. Really, it was impossible not to. "Okay, thanks."

She slid inside, and Abby sat beside her. Jackie glanced back as they drove off, and saw that the light in Mother's bedroom was on. She quickly looked away.

"Is it true, what the woman on the phone told me?" she asked. "Is Neal . . . one of those armed men at that high school?"

It was like asking if the sun rose at nighttime or if dogs could talk. It was impossible. She had her issues with Neal, and she'd been furious at him, and worried, but . . . this? Barricading himself in a school? With kids as hostages?

"I'm afraid so," Abby said. "How long have you been married to Neal?"

"Six years," Jackie said. "But we lived together before. I've known him for a long time. And this . . . what you're saying, it's not my Neal."

"It's not your Neal?" Abby asked.

"No. I mean, I know he has crazy theories, but he would never do that. He's a good guy."

"I believe you," Abby said. "I spoke with him on the phone, and he sounds like a very good guy who just ended up in a bad situation."

"That's exactly right! If you only knew him . . . he never used to be obsessed with all that Watcher stuff. He was this lovely . . . decent guy."

"And then what happened?" Abby asked.

Jackie sighed. She'd tried to explain it before, but people didn't understand. Most of them just thought that Neal had lost it. But it wasn't like that. It wasn't like that at all.

"We had a rough patch. He lost his job. And his mom died. And we had . . . some other issues. So he was home all the time, watching TV, doing nothing, just so sad and angry. We argued a lot. And then he found those guys, right? The Watchers. And he was really excited. It was like getting Neal back." Her voice trembled. She swallowed, shaking her head.

"He found something that made him feel good, that gave him purpose," Abby said.

"Yeah. He would talk again. Like, he'd spend a whole hour explaining about this stuff that he found out. And he had new friends, which actually sounded really nice. People who wanted to make a difference. I know that a lot of what the Watchers say is a bit . . . out there, but there's crazy stuff in the world that everyone knows about, right? Like that CIA MK-Ultra program? I actually saw a documentary about it. So Neal and his friends, they're just open to ideas and don't believe everything they're told. That's not a bad thing."

"That's not a bad thing," Abby agreed.

"And the thing is, it didn't become his entire life, you know? Sure, at first he'd spend hours on the computer, researching and stuff. But then after a month or two he calmed down, and he'd read about it a couple of hours a day and chat with his friends. That's it."

"It was his hobby," Abby said. "I get it. My kids spend a lot of time on their hobbies. As long as they still do their schoolwork and meet friends, I think it's great. Much better than staring at the TV."

"Yeah," Jackie said. "I was happy about it. He found something that really interested him."

"Did he involve you in it?"

"He tried to a few times, you know? Like, he wanted me to create a user profile on that forum, but I wasn't really into that. Like you said, it was his hobby, but it wasn't mine. And he got it; he wasn't an asshole about it—I mean, I had my hobbies that he didn't care about, like gardening and running. And I was happy to hear him talk about it. You know how sometimes you listen to someone you love talk, and you're just happy to see how enthusiastic he is about it?"

"Oh yeah." Abby grinned. "You should hear my boy talk about his pets. So . . . what happened then?"

"Well . . . this summer he spent more time on it again. Like six, seven hours a day. He'd go to sleep really late. And it was all he talked about. Like, nonstop."

"Did he mention anything specific?"

Jackie shook her head. "It sounded like the usual stuff. But it came pouring out, you know? He was getting angry about how we're being controlled by the Circle . . . that's what the Watchers call those people who run everything. He was meeting his Watcher friends three or four times a week, coming home in the middle of the night. And then he lost his job again. Which didn't surprise me at all, because he was hardly sleeping, and he was on the computer or his phone all the time."

She wiped a tear away, and looked out the window.

"Did he know you were pregnant?" Abby asked.

Jackie looked at her, surprised. Her belly hardly even showed under her coat, and she definitely hadn't mentioned it. How did she know? Was it like Neal said? Did her doctor sell her medical info to the Circle, who informed the police? Was that how this woman knew that—

"When I was pregnant, I used to put my hand on my stomach when I was riding in a car," Abby said. "Just like you're doing. It's a mother thing." She grinned at Jackie.

Jackie smiled back, relieved. That made sense. Then the smile faded away. "I didn't tell him. At first, I didn't want to get his hopes up. We lost a . . . I had a miscarriage. Back when things were rough. But then I got worried that Neal wouldn't be able to be a proper father. Eventually, I decided to take a break. And it was also a sort of ultimatum, you know? *Get your shit together, or I'm gone.* We loved each other; I thought it would be good for him."

"When was that?"

"A few months ago. Just before Halloween. He was about to go to another of his meetings, and I packed a bag and let him know I wouldn't be there when he came back."

"How did he react?"

"He . . . it was bad. We got into a really bad argument. And I left."

"So you left around Halloween," Abby said. "And then what happened?"

"He never called me. *I* ended up trying to call *him.* I missed him. But he didn't answer my calls. I texted him, and he answered back and wrote that for my own protection, it was better if I stayed away. Really paranoid stuff. So I figured I'd go and see him. I went over to our house. But . . ." She shut her eyes, covering her mouth, wishing she could go back in time, do things differently.

"You went over to your house," Abby said. "And what happened?"

"He didn't answer the door. All the blinds were drawn. And he'd changed the locks. I couldn't get in."

CHAPTER 46

October 29, 2019

It was the suitcase that really drove the knife into his back. A suitcase they'd used on their honeymoon, for that wonderful week in Mexico. And again, for the trip she'd always dreamed about to the Grand Canyon. And for their fifth anniversary in Florida. It was a suitcase that Neal had always associated with wonderful memories.

And now she'd packed this suitcase in secret, to leave him.

It was a large suitcase, and the way she dragged it made it clear that it was heavy. It wasn't an overnight bag she was taking with her. And it didn't take half an hour of angry packing. This had been planned in advance, and long term.

The way she talked also felt planned in advance. An endless monologue about how he wasn't there anymore. She was living with a stranger. When she talked to him, it was like having a conversation with a dark, stormy cloud.

Usually when Jackie tried to explain something important, she searched for words; she stuttered and mumbled. But not this time. This speech had been practiced.

The question was why.

"Why are you doing this?" he blurted.

She blinked. The question had punctured her speech balloon. "Because . . . what I just said. I feel like you're not even there—"

"Bullshit! You wouldn't leave because of that. Someone turned you against me. Was it your mother? It was your mother, right? She's always hated me. What did she say? Did she offer you money? Or did she threaten to write you out of her will? Is that it?"

Jackie's eyes welled up. "Neal, it's not because of my mother. I'm unhappy. I need you back. The old you. Not this . . . obsessed, angry—"

"Was it *them*?" The thought shot out of his mouth before he had time to think it through.

"Them?" Her tone shifted. The hurt gone, replaced by a different, sharper edge.

"Did someone contact you? Threaten you? Blackmail you? Or did they offer you anything to—"

"You think I'm leaving you because of . . . of . . . a group of shadowy men?" Her eyes widened. "Are you insane? Why would they even . . . you know what? Forget it."

She turned to the door, dragging the suitcase behind her.

"You're not leaving." He was out of his chair, hand grabbing her forearm. Clenching hard.

"Don't touch me!" she shrieked, yanking her arm away.

He wanted to slap her then, something that had never crossed his mind before but seemed almost impossible to stop now. In fact, his hand was already moving.

He slammed it into the wall instead, the sudden pain emptying his mind of everything for a few seconds. He vaguely saw her leaving, shutting the door behind her.

Stumbling to his computer, he tried to dig for an explanation. Why? Why had she left? Jackie would never leave him like that. His instincts had been right on the mark. This had the stench of the Circle all over it. This was aimed to distract him from what he and Theodor were doing. That was what this was all about. They must have found out somehow.

He clicked the forum shortcut and created a new thread. The subject was *CIRCLE TARGETING OUR FAMILIES NOW.*

The words poured out. *My wife just left, and it was clear from her behavior that someone else had been organizing this for some time. We've been happy together, this came completely out of the blue. Or maybe she's been acting for a while. Had she been spying on me for someone else? If so, any of you whose identities I know might be at risk. I am sorry, I should never have told her about any of this. But the question remains, why did they tell her to leave? I thought back to the recent divorces within our members. Three divorces in just the past few months. And that horrifying custody hearing that White_King went through. That's higher than the average divorce rate.*

He paused, searching for divorce rates, added the link to the post. He always backed his posts with facts.

And those are the ones we know of. How many of you are going through breakups that haven't told the group? I'm not judging, but we need to know. If this is something that the Circle are doing. If they're turning our families against us, making them into agents . . .

He paused, staring at the screen.

There was a pattern there; he felt it.

Except there wasn't.

Here was something he knew, more than anything. Jackie would *never* let herself be a pawn of the Circle. She wouldn't let them turn her against him.

The pieces fit. He could think of all these moments that he couldn't explain in her behavior. And this explained all of them. That day she'd decided to go running, even though it was raining outside. And that evening she kept checking her phone. And that time she took a phone call outside the house, like she didn't want to be overheard. And that one time, ten minutes ago, when she'd left him without a warning. It could all be explained if she was working for the Circle.

But there was no way.

He deleted the post and closed the browser window. Something inside his mind broke.

A phone call jarred him out of it. He glanced at the screen. Jabberwocky.

"Hey," he said, trying to control his voice.

"Hi." Theodor sounded cheerful. "Listen, I wanted to ask you, can we meet half an hour later? I have a few things I need to tie up here."

"Yeah, um . . . look, I think I won't make it today. I'm feeling kinda shitty; I think I might have caught a stomach bug."

"That's too bad, man," Theodor said. "You sure? We can make it short."

"Yeah, I think I need to rest. I'm not up for that drive. You know."

"Why don't we do it at your place?" Theodor said.

"My place?"

"Sure! I never saw your place. You always come here. I'll grab us a six-pack on the way."

"Fine," Neal said, clenching his jaw. "Come on over."

"Great!" Theodor said. "What's your address?"

CHAPTER 47

"So what do you think happened?" Carver asked Abby.

They were parked around the corner, away from the majority of the police force, away from the command center and the negotiation truck. The basketball court stood between them and the school. The chain-link fence, high enough to stop any wayward balls, made the structure look like a prison in the darkness. Or maybe it was just Carver's mood. Throughout the day he'd felt helpless and frustrated. Thinking and rethinking of those moments within the school. What if he'd moved quicker, sooner? Would he have made it in time to save those hostages? Or maybe just get Sam out?

"What?" Abby asked after a few seconds.

"Jackie told us that she'd left Neal just before Halloween. We know that's the last time Neal and Theodor met. And it sounds like Neal took the breakup pretty badly. Became angrier, right? Wanted to take the fight back to the Circle or whatever. Why?"

"I don't know," Abby said tiredly.

"Theodor was researching the Watchers, right? And Neal was his main subject." Carver let it hang.

"Right," Abby finally agreed. "And according to Landsman, Theodor would be happy to manipulate his research to get the results he wanted."

"Neal would have been upset when they met. And easy to manipulate."

"You think Theodor used Neal's mood after the breakup to . . . what? Match up with his research paper?"

"He was in a volatile state. Maybe Theodor saw an opportunity there."

"Maybe he was already manipulating him," Abby said, turning to Carver. "Jackie said that he'd been getting more and more obsessed with the Watchers for a few months before Halloween. And he and Theodor began meeting around that time. Maybe these two things are related."

"The frequency of their meetings kept accelerating," Carver said. "And it doesn't sound like Neal knew that he was a subject for a paper, right? Theodor was acting as another Watcher."

"Yeah." Abby chewed her bottom lip.

"Could it help the negotiation? If that was the case?"

"Anything we know could help," Abby said. "Maybe, if Will makes Neal realize that he's acting because Theodor was manipulating him, that could impact Neal's behavior. He'd be more susceptible to surrender."

"What about Jackie?"

"What about her?"

"Would Will let her talk to Neal?"

"Maybe." Abby frowned. "It's always tricky, letting spouses talk in these kinds of situations. This is already a very tense crisis. Letting them talk might add a lot of unknown issues into the mix. And Jackie is not a negotiator. Will would have to brief her regarding what she can and can't say. And if Neal is suicidal, it makes things worse."

"Why?"

"Suicidal people often want to talk to their loved ones before killing themselves. It could push him over the edge."

Carver nodded. "But he didn't sound suicidal."

"No. And there's the pregnancy. The future is a fantastic leverage for negotiators. We want people to have hope. And an unborn child is as hopeful a future as can be. It could be a game changer."

"So would you let him talk to her? If you were the negotiator?"

Abby sighed. "I don't know."

Carver took her hand in his. It was chilly to the touch. Was Abby cold? Could she even sense if she was warm or cold, or hungry, or tired? Or was she entirely consumed by the gnawing worry for her daughter?

He gave her hand a slight squeeze. "Would you let Neal talk to Jackie?"

"Yeah," Abby said after a short pause. "I think I would. But I'd probably wait for the search of their house. They might find something that could be relevant."

As soon as they had dropped Jackie at the school, Tammi had gotten the address to Neal and Jackie's home from her and sent cops over to check it out. They didn't even need a search warrant. Legally, it was still Jackie's home, and she gave them permission.

Carver sat in the dark, holding Abby's hand, saying nothing for a long while.

"Look," Abby said.

Carver blinked. He'd almost fallen asleep. "What is it?"

"They're pushing back the protesters."

She was right. Despite the late hour and the night's chill, the protest had grown. Now a group of uniformed police officers was pushing them back.

"This'll only make it worse," Carver said. "They'll start saying that the police are hiding something."

"I don't think there's anything that wouldn't make it worse."

A sudden shift in the crowd made the police officers push harder. A cop was shouting through a bullhorn while people in the crowd screamed. Someone fell.

"Oh shit," Carver said, and stepped out of the car. He sprinted toward the crowd. More screams. Someone hit a cop with his protest sign. A woman broke through and, to Carver's horror, ran toward the school.

"Stop her!" Carver shouted, but his voice was swallowed by the din. Another cop was chasing the woman, yelling.

"My child is in there!" the woman screeched. "My child is in there!"

Carver was now running as fast as he could, wind shrieking in his ears. He had to grab the woman and pull her away before someone accidentally shot her. She was already at one of the school's entrances.

Carver stared in disbelief as she pulled the door open. It took him a second to realize what had happened. The woman had gone for the door that the ESU breached two hours before.

And now she disappeared into the school.

CHAPTER 48

"There's someone inside."

The words made Caterpillar sit up in surprise, blinking. Had he been dozing? It seemed impossible to fall asleep in this situation, when every minute could be their last. But after they'd locked most of the hostages away and had eaten the sandwiches that Hatter got from the cafeteria, an unusual silence settled between them. It was possible he'd nodded off.

"Who is it?" he asked, rushing over to Alma, gun in hand. Hatter joined them as well.

She pointed at the screen. "Look."

He watched the security footage as a woman crept down one of the hallways, her body tense, head darting left and right.

Caterpillar gritted his jaw, aiming his gun at the principal, who still sat in the corner of the room, his hands now bound behind his back. He snatched the PA mic from the secretary's desk. "Attention," he barked into the mic, hearing his voice echo outside. "Get out of the building, or I shoot the principal. Get out. Now!"

The woman on screen paused, looked up, and then kept walking.

Caterpillar strode over to the principal, pulling him to his feet. He dragged the man to the desk and shoved the mic in his face. "Tell her!"

"Um . . . this is Henry, the school's principal." The man's voice trembled. "They have a gun to my head. Please do as they say."

"She's not turning away," Alma said, alarmed.

"Maybe she's not taking us seriously enough," Caterpillar said. His trigger finger tightened.

"Wait, don't," Alma said. "We don't know who she is—"

"Who do you think?" Hatter snarled. "She's a cop. Shoot him. She'll get the message."

"What if she's that woman you talked to earlier?" Alma said urgently. "Abby? What if it's her?"

Caterpillar hesitated. Could it be? The woman didn't seem armed. In fact, she didn't even look like a cop. She was dressed in a plain shirt and jeans, her hair swept back in a simple ponytail. Was this Abby?

The phone in the principal's office rang.

"Shoot the asshole," Hatter said. "I'll go get the other hostages."

"Answer the phone," Alma said.

"Please," the principal mumbled. "She's just one woman. There's no reason to—"

"Shut up!" Hatter punched the man in the stomach.

The principal folded, gasping. Alma screamed something at Hatter, and the phone was still ringing while the woman . . . just walked, moving from one security camera to the next.

Caterpillar ran to the principal's office and picked up the phone. "Hello?"

"Caterpillar, I'm glad you answered." Will's voice. Low and measured. "The woman that entered the building is not a cop. We think she's a parent of one of the kids you're holding inside."

"Bullshit," Caterpillar said. "How did she enter the building?"

"She broke through the police barricade. I imagine things are getting heated there, but we should try to keep this under control."

Will could be lying. She could be a fed in plain clothes. Or a Circle assassin, there to dispatch the problem once and for all.

"Well, what do you want me to do about this?" Caterpillar snarled.

"Let's figure this out together," Will said. "She's clearly emotional, and we don't need that tension in there, right?"

"Caterpillar, they're posting about this in the forum," Alma called. "They're saying that this woman broke through the police lines. They posted a video."

"She's no threat to anyone," Will was saying.

Caterpillar wanted to smash the phone to pieces. Was it really a parent? Or an assassin? Or something else entirely? If she was an assassin, she wouldn't care if he shot the hostage. In fact, she would probably kill the hostages herself, removing any evidence.

He hung up and stepped out of the room, ignoring the phone as it rang again.

"Where is she now?" he asked Alma.

"Camera fourteen." Alma pointed at the screen.

That meant nothing to him. The woman seemed to have stopped, and was looking at something outside the camera's view. Caterpillar tried to figure out where in the building she was, but had no idea.

"I know where that is," Hatter said. "I'll go and get her."

"I'll go with you," Caterpillar said quickly.

"You should stay here, talk to your friends on the phone," Hatter answered, walking toward the door.

"You'll need backup," Caterpillar said. He didn't want Hatter left alone with that woman. He didn't want Hatter alone anywhere.

Hatter shrugged. "Fine. Let's go."

He unlocked the door and stepped out, Caterpillar following close behind. As they stepped through the empty hallways, the hair rose on the back of Caterpillar's neck. Throughout the day, the tension between him and Hatter kept growing, and now, Caterpillar had no idea what the man would do. What if he wasn't leading them to the woman at all? What if he was taking Caterpillar somewhere quiet, out of view, so that he could finish him off without Alma knowing? Maybe Hatter was already working with the cops, or the Circle, or that unknown woman.

Caterpillar had been betrayed before. That time, he had been lucky. This time, he would be prepared.

In fact, it was better to finish this now.

He raised the gun, aiming at the back of Hatter's head, trying to stop his hand from trembling. One shot was all it would—

"There," Hatter said in a soft voice.

The woman they'd seen on the security footage stood in the hallway, staring through an open door, her face transfixed, mouth agape.

"Don't move," Caterpillar said aloud, his gun barrel shifting, aiming at the woman. "Hands on your head."

She glanced at him. Her face seemed blank, hardly registering the gun aimed at her. Slowly, she placed her hands on her head.

Hatter marched over and grabbed her hands, yanking them behind her. Caterpillar took a few steps toward them, to see what the woman was looking at.

It was nothing. Just a storage room, with a snowblower, a lawn mower, some metal containers. He slammed the door shut and turned to the woman, his heart hammering in his chest.

"Who the hell are you?" he spat.

"I'm one of the kids' mothers," she said hurriedly. "I wanted to come in and get her. That's all!"

"That's all?" Caterpillar stared at her in disbelief. There was something weird in her expression. Eyes glazed, mouth slack. Did she have some sort of mental disability? "Which kid?"

"Samantha," the woman said. "I'm Samantha's mom."

CHAPTER 49

Sam sat with her back against the wall, knees hunched to her chest. She stared tiredly at the claustrophobic space the four of them were in—the school's sports storage room—where Hatter had locked them more than an hour before. It was actually a relief to be locked away from the three armed maniacs. Her world had been reduced to the three people who shared this space with her—Ray, Fiona, and Mrs. Nelson, the secretary. Mr. Bell had remained behind, in the office, with their captors.

It was also a relief to be away from Mr. Ramirez's body, from his vacant, dead expression. Even though she could still see his face whenever she shut her eyes.

A sharp clang made her start, her heart leaping. She focused on Ray, who was holding a hockey stick.

"I told you to put that thing down, Ray," Sam snapped in frustration.

The space was cramped—with all the gear inside, all they had left was a tight, long strip of floor for them to sit on. And the tiny room had felt even closer since Ray had found the hockey sticks and begun swinging one of them around.

"Instead of yelling at me, grab another one," Ray said disgustedly. "At least I'm trying." He took another practice swing, hitting one of the metal shelves. It clanged again, and they all winced.

"Ray, I swear to god, if you do that again, I'll grab one of those and try it on you!" Fiona shouted.

"I keep telling you, this is our opportunity," Ray said. "When they come for us, they won't all come together, right? It'll be just one or two of them. If we're all ready with these, we can catch them by surprise and—"

"And they'll shoot us," Sam said tiredly. They'd gone through this three times already. "Because they have guns. And you have a stick. And I know that you think you're a big scary man, but you're still just fourteen. And these guys . . . they're strong." The memory of the hand gripping her neck flashed in her mind again. It was still tender to the touch. Fiona had told her it was bruised.

"We should really try to sleep," Mrs. Nelson said.

They'd spread a bunch of exercise mats on the floor. They had just enough room to all lie down, though it'd be cramped, like sardines. They'd have to lie down in couples—two to a mat. Fiona and Sam had figured this out, and clustered together instinctively. If they went to sleep, Ray would be spooning Mrs. Nelson. Perhaps that was why he was so adamant about forcing his way out.

"We can't sleep," Fiona said. "What if the police come to get us out? We need to be ready. This can't go on for much longer."

Sam raised an eyebrow. "Can't it? The siege on the Branch Davidians lasted almost two months. A few years ago, a guy grabbed a boy and dragged him to a bunker, and started a standoff that lasted a whole week. And there was an incident in an Amish school that took . . ." She realized they were all watching her, horrified. "A while. Anyway, these things take time. We need to be patient."

She swallowed, her throat dry. She wished they'd left them some water. Caterpillar had given them a box with a few sandwiches and chocolate milk cartons, but those were long gone. And Sam would have gladly exchanged her chocolate milk for a glass of water.

"What if they just . . . leave us here?" Fiona asked.

Sam reflexively looked around the room, imagining staying there for days. Nothing to eat or drink. Nothing useful in the room, just stacks of Hula-Hoops, large net sacks full of various balls, foam rollers, and, of course, Ray's dumb hockey sticks.

"They won't," she said, trying to reassure them. "And besides, I was talking out of my ass. This is not a bunker or whatever; it's a school. And they're just three people; it's not like they can—"

The lock rattled, and Sam whirled to face it, crawling away from the door, imagining Hatter at the other side. Coming for her. Nowhere to run. Suddenly she wanted a hockey stick, or anything that could help her fight.

The door opened. Hatter and Caterpillar. And someone else. A woman.

"Hey, doc," Hatter said. "Guess who came to join you?"

He pushed the woman inside, and she tripped on the edge of the exercise mat, falling to her knees. The door slammed shut. The sound of the key turning in the lock echoed in the silent room.

The woman lifted her eyes, staring at them, blinking slowly.

"Are you okay?" Sam asked.

"It's you," the woman whispered. "It's really you."

Sam frowned. "I . . . do I know you?"

The woman shut her eyes. "'I looked and heard the voice of many angels, numbering thousands upon thousands, and ten thousand times ten thousand,'" she said softly.

"She's crazy," Ray said, his voice trembling.

"That's a verse from the book of Revelation," Mrs. Nelson said.

"Who are you?" Sam asked. "How did you end up here? Are you a cop?"

The woman's eyes snapped open. "My name is Deborah. Father sent me to you."

"Father? You mean . . . my dad?"

The woman grinned at Sam, her eyes widening. Ray was right. She was crazy. She leaned forward and touched Sam's foot. Sam pulled it back quickly.

"'Behold,'" the woman whispered. "'I send an angel before you to guard you on the way and to bring you to the place that I have prepared.'"

CHAPTER 50

Twelve hours after she'd been removed from her role as the primary negotiator, Abby found herself once again in the command center, with the rest of the task force. She had absolutely no idea why. Will had simply called her and told her to come over, that they were about to start a meeting, and that Estrada wanted her there. Perhaps they wanted her to talk with Caterpillar again? She doubted it, but couldn't figure out any other reason.

There was a certain way they looked at her that set her teeth on edge. They peered at her from the corners of their eyes, some of them almost imperceptibly leaning away. She knew that stare, the one you saw people in the street giving to a homeless person sitting in the corner. Or the way someone might glance at a person with a deformity. As if their misfortune, or tragedy, were infectious, and a direct look might make you catch it. She was the mother whose daughter was in the building. Who had been seen hauled along with a gun against her head. But, of course, she was also their peer who worked alongside them, and they had a hard time wrapping their minds around it. It made her realize that Carver hadn't done that. Throughout the day, he'd been straightforward and solid. She wished she had him in the command center by her side.

"Okay." Estrada leaned forward on the table. Despite the fact that he'd been managing the crisis for over twelve hours, he seemed alert and energetic. "Quick update. Because of the information leak from civilians to the hostiles in the school, we widened the cordoned-off area. I got extra manpower from adjacent precincts to maintain it. No one will be allowed to set a damn foot here without getting permission from me. So if any of you want to bring in anyone new, I'll need to know about it beforehand. I assume that come morning, you'll want some personnel switched around so people can rest up. Give me a list of all the names."

Will and Baker nodded. Abby gritted her teeth. It was the right call to start working in shifts, but it was another reminder of what they all felt. This thing could stretch out much longer than a single day.

"Baker, where are we at?" Estrada asked.

"After the failed attempt to breach the door, we have to assume that the people inside will take measures to make sure we don't catch them with their pants down again," Baker said. "So for now we ruled out another breach from that direction. We're back to our original scenario, breaching in from the windows after rappelling from the roof. But we still need to practice it. And it's best if we wait before doing it. Right now, they are on their toes."

"We have"—Estrada glanced at his wristwatch—"five and a half hours until dawn. And then it's off the table."

"I don't think we should do it tonight. Not unless it is a last resort. Earlier we acted out of time pressure. To save Carlos Ramirez. Now it's too late for that."

"Okay, so we're back to the negotiation table. Where are we at?" Abby turned her eyes to Will.

"Not good," Will said. "As could be expected, the trust and rapport we established with the people inside is pretty much gone. The conversations I had with Neal were short and angry. If this continues, we might have to switch negotiators again."

Abby cleared her throat. "I could try to talk to him—"

"No." Estrada's voice was sharp and final.

She didn't press the point. So that wasn't why they'd called her. Then why was she there?

Will pressed forward. "Our ace in the hole is Jackie. I'm planning on putting her on the phone with Neal, to mend some of the trust, and to give us some emotional leverage. But I need him to calm down soon. We also have a worrying update regarding the search of their home." He opened a thin brown folder, took out a photo, and placed it on the table. "This is a photo the Monticello cops sent us from the house. This stain was hidden under the carpet."

Abby glanced at the photo. It depicted a wooden floor and an enormous dark stain. There was no doubt in her mind what it was. Dried blood.

"Our own forensics are on their way, but it'll probably take some time until we have confirmation," Will said. "Still, it looks like someone bled there pretty severely. And that jibes with the message we got from Samantha Mullen about Neal killing before. Obviously, we won't let him know we found out about this, because it'll only make it much more unlikely for him to surrender."

"Did they find anything else in the house?" Abby asked.

"They're still looking," Will said. "They'll let us know."

"What about the recent development?" Estrada asked.

Everyone turned their eyes on Abby. She blinked, surprised. "Um . . . what?"

Estrada picked up a remote and aimed it at a large screen on the wall. A video began playing. It showed the woman who'd breached the barricade earlier running into the school. The footage was rough, the camera juddering, and there was a lot of screaming in the background, but Abby could hear the woman shrieking, "My child is in there!"

"Do you know that woman?" Estrada asked Abby.

"It's not Fiona Brock's mother," Abby said. "I know her well. I don't remember meeting Ray Miller's mom, so I'm guessing—"

"I talked to Ray Miller's mom," Estrada said. "It's not her."

"Is there still a student who's unaccounted for?" Abby asked.

"Abby," Will said. "I talked to Caterpillar about that woman twenty minutes ago. And he told me it's Samantha's mom."

Abby stared at him, feeling as if the entire world were tilting. "What . . . did he . . . why would he say that?"

"That's what she told him," Will answered. "They're holding her with the rest of the hostages."

"I thought that maybe it's a relative of yours," Estrada said. "Someone attached to Sam who—"

"I've never seen this woman before in my life."

"We have some better footage of her," Estrada said. "A local network is doing a piece about the protesters, and they've been filming them on and off for a while. She's been standing with them for hours."

He opened a new video on screen. The protesters standing across the street from the school, holding signs, shouting and chanting. They were mostly men, and the woman was easy to spot. She was shouting angrily, both hands raised, looking like the other protesters. It was impossible to hear her over the collective din.

"She doesn't look like a parent," Abby said. "She looks like one of the protesters. A Watcher."

"Then why wouldn't she identify herself as such when she entered the school?" Will asked.

Abby shook her head. It made no sense.

"This is from even earlier," Estrada said, starting a third video. Only about a dozen protesters this time. Just one woman. The same woman. And this time, the camera focused on her, giving Abby a clear shot of the woman's face as she shouted. She seemed about Abby's age, maybe a bit older.

"You sure you've never seen her before?" Estrada asked again.

"Yeah, I'm sure . . ." What was the woman shouting? "Can you raise the volume?"

He did as he was asked, the small space in the command center filling with the shouts of the angry protesters.

"The . . . blood . . . Messiah . . . freed . . ," The woman's voice, higher than the voices of the rest of the protesters, could be singled out.

"'The blood of the Messiah must be freed,'" Abby said. "I heard her earlier. That's what she's shouting."

"Yeah," Baker agreed. "That's what I heard. She's just one of those psychos. And they're playing some kind of game with us."

Abby stared at the screen. "But the Watchers don't really involve religion in their conspiracies. There's never a mention of a Messiah."

"They believe in a sort of approaching apocalypse, right?" Estrada said. "Maybe some of them also believe in a Messiah."

The woman raised her hands above her head as she shouted. Not shaking her fists, but more like a prayer.

Abby's gut clenched as something familiar on the screen caught her eye. "Pause it," she said urgently.

He did, and Abby scrutinized the frozen image, the woman's hands.

"What is it? You recognize her?" Estrada asked.

"Those scratches on her hands," Abby muttered, heart pounding hard. "See them?"

"Oh yeah. I see it," Estrada said. "She hurt her hands somehow."

Abby looked at the numerous scratch marks on the woman's hands, visible even from a distance. "I've seen this before. These are the kinds of marks you get when you scrub your hands with a metal scrubber." She knew those scratches very well. Knew how they felt. Her hands had looked just like that when she was younger.

"What? Why would she do that?"

"She might be a member of a religious cult."

"You said the Watchers aren't religious."

"And they're not a cult," Abby said. "I don't think she's a Watcher. She's something else."

That message she'd received from the fake Isaac. From the man she suspected was Moses Wilcox. Was he behind this?

Had this happened because she'd stupidly messaged him the day before?

"Is there anything we can do about this?" Estrada asked, looking at Will.

"I don't think so," Will said. "Whoever this woman is, we should treat her as another hostage until we know better. We definitely don't want to add mixed signals about her to my conversations with Caterpillar. Things are confused enough as it is."

Will was right. Even if Moses was playing some sort of game, there was nothing they could do about it. Not now.

"Okay. Thanks, Abby," Estrada said. "We'll update you once anything crops up. Um . . . like I said before, we want to tighten things here and leave only relevant personnel at the scene. I would feel better if you go and be with your family. They need you."

Abby nodded numbly and got up. Their eyes were all on her as she got out of the command center, shutting the door behind her. Then she took out her phone and opened the chat with "Isaac." Reread his last message.

I can help.

She tapped an answer, shaking with fury. Raising his name from the grave. Pointing in accusation.

Moses, was that you? Did you send that woman?

She sent the message, then waited. Would he ignore her again?

No, there it was. The indication of a response being written. Three dots, appearing and disappearing, reappearing again. On and off, on and off, he sat somewhere tugging her strings, formulating an answer.

Yes.

It had taken him almost a minute to write that. What had he typed and then deleted? An apology? A presumptuous explanation? A long and winding Bible quote? She gritted her teeth, a dozen responses coming to mind. But she had no time for a dialogue with this ghost from the past. And no way to predict his reaction to anything she said. She shoved the phone into her pocket. Later. She would deal with him later.

Carver was waiting for her in his car. She slipped inside and shut the door.

"What was that all about?" Carver asked.

Abby filled him in. She saw her own shock mirrored in his eyes.

"I'll call Will in a bit," she said. "Tell him that she was sent by Moses Wilcox. Will knows . . . about me."

"Okay. Do you want me to take you home?"

"No." She couldn't stomach the idea. "Um . . . you should probably go home. I'll drive myself. It's a pretty long drive."

"Uh-huh." Carver raised an eyebrow. "Where do you need me to take you? No bullshit, Abby."

Abby smiled at him tiredly. "Neal and Jackie's house in Monticello. They found a bloodstain there. I want to take a look." There was something about Neal that didn't click for her. Something that didn't fit. She needed to dig deeper, to figure it out. Maybe then she would know how to get him to stand down. How to end this and get her daughter back.

Carver switched on the engine. "Do you have an address?"

"Yeah." It had been typed in the corner of the photo Will had shown them.

"Okay. Then let's go."

CHAPTER 51

The stain on the hardwood floor told a grim story. It was a misshapen thing, with smears in several directions, and colors that ranged from black to a faded brown. A wide strip of the stained floor was scratched, and Carver knelt by the scratches, inspecting them. He'd seen this kind of thing before.

"Someone tried to clean up the blood," he said.

The CSU detective, Ahmed Nader, was swabbing a segment of the stain carefully. "That's what it looks like."

The bloodstain covered a large portion of the floor in Neal Wyatt's living room. Carver straightened and looked around him. If not for the stain, it would have been a cozy space. A single couch in front of a small TV. A few potted plants, all lush and green. A round coffee table. All of it spotlessly clean and organized, which made the stain seem even more grotesque.

A large carpet had been rolled up and set against the wall. A uniformed cop was measuring the distance between the couch and the bloodstain.

"Are you the one who found the bloodstain, Officer?" Carver asked him.

The cop nodded. "You can call me Mitch. Yeah. I mean, at first we were just looking around, because of the search warrant, and it said to look for papers and guns and stuff, so I wasn't looking for stains, right?

But you know how sometimes you can step into a room and just feel like something is off? It's like a sixth sense sometimes. And I sensed it as soon as I stepped into the room—bang, like there's a radar in my head going bleep-bleep-bleep. So I tried to figure it out. I told Paulie—that's my partner—I told him, 'Is there something weird here,' and he said, 'Nuh.' But I couldn't shake it off, that weird feeling in my head. And then I saw the carpet was placed really weird. I mean, this room is sorta tight, everything in its place. But the carpet, it didn't cover all the floor, but it was placed against the wall. And the radar in my head was going faster, like bleep-bleep-bleep-bleep-bleep. So I move the carpet, and what do I see?"

"The stain?" Carver suggested.

Mitch pointed at him with the measuring tape, grinning happily. "The stain!"

"Nice catch."

"So I was thinking, this isn't just a coffee stain, right? And I had a dog once, and it peed on the floor—I got a floor like that, and the pee, it messed the floor up. But it didn't look like that. Plus, there's no sign of a dog here, right?"

"No dog here," Carver agreed. "We'd have noticed a dog."

"Exactly! So I said, 'Paulie, dude, I think that's a bloodstain.' And then we reported it." He seemed sad at the anticlimactic ending of his story.

"Carver," Abby called him.

"I'll be glad to hear more about it later," Carver told Mitch.

He went to the bedroom, where Abby was standing beside a large dresser, with the aforementioned Paulie.

"What's up?" Carver said.

"Look what we found," Abby said, her face grim. She held a small brown wallet in her gloved hand.

Carver took the wallet from her and looked inside it, finding a driver's license. The name on the license was Theodor Quinn.

Aside from the driver's license, the wallet had a single credit card, a member card for a library in Middletown, and a photo of a young girl whom Carver quickly identified as the same girl who appeared in the photos in Theodor Quinn's home.

"Where did you find this?" Carver asked.

"Bottom drawer," Paulie said.

Carver opened it. It was full of underwear and socks. "It was just here?"

"Under the socks," Paulie answered. He clearly didn't share his partner's penchant for exciting stories.

Carver shut the drawer, then glanced at Abby. "What do you think?"

"I think things don't look good for Jabberwocky," she said.

Carver nodded. "Found anything else?" he asked Paulie.

"We have a laptop," Paulie said. "It's password protected. Also some bullets."

"Where'd you find the bullets?" Carver asked.

"In the garage, in a metal box."

"Can you show me?"

Without saying a word, Paulie led him to the garage, and pointed at a metal case on one of the shelves.

Carver flipped the case open. Like Paulie had said, it contained five boxes of .357 bullets. One of the boxes was open. Carver picked it up, emptying it into his hand. Five bullets. The box had originally contained fifty. Three Watchers in the school, three guns, fifteen bullets each.

He put the bullets back and looked around. The garage, like the rest of the house, was organized nicely. Paint cans on one shelf, cleaning supplies on the next, a toolbox and a drill on the bottom shelf. A rake, a hoe, and a shovel placed in the corner.

Carver frowned, examining the gardening tools closely. The dirt on them was easy to notice in the spotless space. All the gardening tools had seen recent action. Including the shovel.

"Hey, Paulie, did you guys check the yard?"

"Nope."

Carver stepped out of the house and went to the backyard. The yard light was dim, not enough to see anything properly. Carver clicked on his flashlight, scanning the ground slowly with its beam. A well-maintained lawn, and surrounding it, despite the cold, flower beds containing tiny drooping white flowers. Carver narrowed his eyes, stepping closer.

"Huh, those are nice," Mitch said behind him. "Didn't know you could grow flowers in the winter like that."

"These are snowdrops," Carver said. "My mom plants them every year during autumn."

"Every autumn, huh? My parents never bothered with flowers. We lived on the third floor, so no yard, you know. I guess maybe we had a few flower pots around the house. I don't really remember. You looking for something there?"

"Well, I think the radar in my head is going bleep-bleep," Carver muttered.

"Yeah, I know *that* feeling. Can't ignore the radar in your head. It's almost like a sixth sense sometimes. I feel like not all cops have it. I don't know if Paulie has it. If he did, he never said. But I got it."

Carver let the flashlight beam hover above a flower bed on the far side. The snowdrops there were all dead. "What's your sixth sense telling you now, Mitch?"

"It's, uh . . . telling me that something is off."

"Yeah?" Carver walked over to the flower bed, looking closely. The nearby snowdrops were a bit limp as well. "What do you think is off?"

Mitch looked over his shoulder. "The dude who lived here didn't take good care of these flowers."

"Well . . ." Carver crouched, inspecting one of them. "The rest are fine, right? And these get the same sunlight as all the rest. So what's wrong with this patch?"

"Maybe he poured something here. Like bleach or something. I once tried to water a houseplant with water from a bucket that I used to wash the floor. Because I figured, catch two birds with one stone, right? I get to clean the floor *and* water the plants at the same time. Except the flowers died. And I figured out that it was the soap in the water that killed them."

"Maybe," Carver allowed. "Though he's been looking after this yard really well. Sounds weird that he'd be so careless. But you know what? You're right. I bet this patch of ground here is different. That would explain it. If the ground is acidic, it kills off plants."

"Yeah?" Mitch asked hesitantly.

"You know what sometimes makes the ground really acidic?" Carver straightened. "Decomposing bodies."

"Yeah? That's . . . oh. Oh!"

"What's your radar doing now?"

"Oh man, it's going super fast."

"Yeah."

Carver went back to the garage to grab the shovel. He returned to the dead patch in the garden and began digging carefully. The ground crumbled easily under the shovel. Too easily.

It only took ten minutes for him to encounter a shred of cloth. Scraping the ground around it, he uncovered a rotting, dead hand.

CHAPTER 52

Like most cops, Abby'd had her fair share of waking people up in the middle of the night. Typically, it was an intimate act, saved for someone close: a child with a bad dream, a lover searching for a hug, or perhaps a cat acting out one of its unexplainable rituals. It was stepping into that twilight zone between dreaming and wakefulness, when deeply buried fears or hopes were scratching the surface of a person's consciousness. And all the armor that people wore during the day—the well-chosen outfit, the delicate layer of makeup, the carefully maintained hairstyle—was gone.

It felt like reading someone's secret journal.

Theodor Quinn's daughter, Georgia, managed better than most. She'd put on a cozy purple bathrobe and made sure to ask to see a badge before unlatching the door. Even now, in her early twenties, she managed to retain that innocent, childlike look that Abby had seen in the photos in Theodor's home.

When they told her it was about her father, asking to come in, she opened the door wider and stood aside.

"My roommate is asleep," she said, her voice just above a whisper. "Let's talk in the kitchen."

She led them to her small kitchen and took a seat in one of the chairs by a bare wooden table. They sat in front of her. Someone had doodled on the table's surface with a pen. A long, curvy line that kept looping and twirling.

"What happened?" Georgia asked. "Is my dad hurt?" A slight tremor in her voice.

"Ms. Quinn," Carver said. "Has your father been missing?"

"Not that I know of. I heard from him on Sunday."

"Did you talk on the phone?"

"Nah. My dad doesn't really do phone calls. The only time he calls is on my birthday, and even then he tries to make it short. Listen, cut to the chase. Did something happen? Has he been in an accident or something?"

"We're not sure yet," Abby said. "We found your father's wallet."

"You come here in the middle of the night because you found my dad's wallet? Did you try calling him?"

"Yes," Abby said. "His phone is offline. According to the phone company, it has been offline for a while."

"How do you talk to your dad?" Carver asked.

"We chat on Telegram. That's how he likes to communicate. Chats and emails."

"When was the last time you saw him in person?"

"I don't know. A few months ago. Hang on." She stood up and walked off, then returned a minute later with her phone and a pack of cigarettes.

"Of course you'd show up in the middle of the night two days after I decided to quit smoking." Georgia put a cigarette between her lips and lit it. She shut her eyes and inhaled deeply.

"Sorry," Carver said.

She let out a plume of smoke. "Yeah, whatever. I wouldn't have managed anyway. So you were asking when was the last time I saw my dad." She placed the cigarette loosely in her mouth again and started fiddling with her phone. "We met for lunch in September."

"Is it usual for you not to meet your dad for months?"

"We have a complicated relationship." Georgia expelled a cloud of smoke from the corner of her mouth. "Look, I don't know what this is about, but I have no idea where my dad is. In the morning, I'll write him and tell him you have his wallet, okay?"

That body that they'd uncovered in Neal Wyatt's backyard. Badly decomposed, crawling with bugs, its face completely mangled. The medical examiner estimated that it had been in the shallow grave for at least a month, probably more. Theodor Quinn wouldn't be coming for his wallet anytime soon.

Until they formally identified the body, they had to tread gently. But this couldn't wait.

"Ms. Quinn, we're here because your dad was in touch with some people who are related to the—"

"To the hostage situation at that high school?"

Abby blinked in surprise. "Yes. How did you know?"

Georgia inhaled from her cigarette, then tapped the ash into a dirty coffee mug. "I saw it on the news. They're those Watcher psychos, right? I was wondering if my dad knew any of them."

"You knew about his interest in the Watchers?"

"Oh yeah. He couldn't stop talking about them. He was writing this amazing paper. He might get a book deal. He was working on that thing for hours every day. It was going to be his magnum opus. Blah, blah, blah. I've heard it all before. My dad loved to talk about his amazing future accomplishments." Georgia shrugged. "And then he just lost interest."

"He lost interest?" Abby asked.

"Yeah. Last time I met him, I asked how his research was going, and he said he'd decided to drop it. He was a bit embarrassed about it. Told me he got these people all wrong."

"He got them all wrong?"

"You're like my therapist, the way you keep repeating my sentences back to me. Yeah, that's what he said. He didn't want to talk about it, but I got the feeling that he felt ashamed, which was weird."

"Why was it weird?"

"Because shame wasn't something that usually bothered my dad. He had no problem manipulating people or using them when he needed to. He could see when someone was vulnerable and use that for his own agenda. I know it sounds strange coming from me, but if you were in my shoes, you'd know."

Abby knew the kind of people Georgia was describing quite well. "That talk you had . . . you said it was in September?"

"Yeah. It's not unusual. My dad does it all the time. He gets completely obsessed with some project. He thinks it's going to be this amazing thing that'll make him famous, that'll carve his name in the history books. But then halfway through he becomes impatient and cuts corners, or changes the project completely, or loses interest. That's pretty much how he does everything in life. That's practically how he handled being married to my mom. He shifted from being a loving husband to a certified asshole in about a week." She dropped the cigarette stub into the mug. "Anyway, my dad stopped researching them about four months ago, so I doubt he has anything to do with those psychos in the school."

"Are you sure he didn't keep meeting with them?" Carver asked.

"Not that he told me. Why would he?"

"Did you notice any shift in his behavior these past months?"

She shook her head. "Not really. But like I said, I haven't seen him; we were only chatting and emailing these past few months. And frankly, shifts in behavior are not anything unusual in my dad."

Abby nodded, thinking of her own chat with Isaac. Years of chatting with someone, assuming you knew who he was. Later finding out that he wasn't, that he was someone else entirely. That boy, Dennis, had befriended the Watchers, not telling them he was in fact a fourteen-year-old boy. These online chats were like a digital fog, hiding the person you talked to behind a cloud of LOLs and emojis and GIFs. Whom had Georgia been talking to these past months? Probably Neal himself.

Abby let Carver take the lead with the interview as he asked Georgia about her father's acquaintances, his murky past in academia, anything he might have told her about the Watchers he met. She listened distractedly, knowing that they were both thinking the same thing.

Theodor had been researching the Watchers, focusing on Neal as his subject. During his interviews, he manipulated Neal, making the man sink deeper and deeper into the Watcher conspiracy world. And then, at some point, he decided to change tack. Maybe, like Georgia said, he'd just lost interest. Or maybe he wanted to shift the direction his research was going.

And when he met Neal, straight after Jackie had left the man, Theodor saw that Neal was vulnerable. And he figured he'd use it somehow. But it backfired. Whatever happened between them that night ended with Neal killing Theodor and burying him in his backyard.

And then, for whatever reason, Neal began pretending that he was Theodor. Chatting with Georgia. Posting on the forum and in the chat room as Jabberwocky. All the while getting more and more angry and desperate. Until it had culminated in him stepping into Sam's school with a gun in his pocket.

CHAPTER 53

Caterpillar sat in the principal's office, the door half-closed. He peered through the crack in the door. The principal was slumped against the wall, looking worn. Hatter sat on one of the chairs, head resting forward on his chest, a sliver of drool hanging from his chin. Alma was still wide awake, her eyes bloodshot, staring at the screen. She'd become convinced that the police were about to storm in at any moment. She was alternating between watching the security cameras and reading the posts on the forum.

Caterpillar took out his cell phone and opened the forum. In the past hour, the pace of the posts had slowed down to a trickle as the majority of the Watchers went to sleep. There was still an occasional post from one of the Watchers in the protest outside, or from the few European Watchers who were still catching up on the latest events.

Caterpillar logged out of his account. The username on the top right part of the screen changed to *guest*.

He tapped the log-in button and entered the other name he used.

The username changed again from *guest* to *Jabberwocky*.

He went through a few threads, quoting this post or that, agreeing or suggesting alternatives. He took care to congratulate the member who'd warned them about the police attempt to enter the school. That kind of behavior should get as much praise as possible. Then he tracked some of the members who were saying that the entire siege in the school was a terrible mistake. He created a new thread in which he suggested that these members were actually Circle spies and agents.

Jabberwocky, as far as the other members in the forum knew, wasn't one of the besieged Watchers. He had no skin in this game. When he said that he thought someone should organize a few live cameras to constantly film the NYPD's actions, the other Watchers responded. Many figured it was a good idea. One of them said he could get there in the morning to try to set this up.

The principal's phone rang, and he quickly grabbed it.

"Hello?"

"Hey, Caterpillar, how are you hanging in there?" It was Will again.

"We're okay, but I'm starting to think that you and Abby aren't going to keep up your side of the deal."

"You have to be patient; these things take time. We're still looking into it. We're just two people. If you are okay with us bringing in more men, there are a few people that I think we can trust—"

"No. No way. The NYPD is rotten to the core. Just you and Abby, no one else."

"Then you'll have to be patient. Meanwhile, there's someone here who wants to talk to you. Someone that you already know."

"Is it Abby? Did she find anything?"

"Hang on, I'll put her on."

A moment of silence followed, Caterpillar waiting, tense, jaw clenched tight.

"Hi. Um . . . it's me."

It wasn't Abby's voice at all. Caterpillar listened to the woman on the other end of the line, his heart racing.

"Honey? It's Jackie. I know that . . . that you probably don't want to talk to me. But Will here thought that we should talk. Because there's something that I should have told you a while ago. I'm sorry I haven't said it sooner; maybe it could have prevented all this." She sniffed, her breath shuddering. "Neal . . . I'm pregnant. I found out a few months ago. We're going to be parents. And . . . I want our boy to meet his daddy, okay? I want us to have a family. Will said that if you cooperate—"

Caterpillar put down the phone, ending the call. He could hardly breathe.

When it rang again, he didn't answer.

CHAPTER 54

A sudden blip jolted Abby, making her jump in alarm, heart thudding. She'd fallen asleep. She was in Carver's car, and something heavy and warm was covering her. Carver's trench coat. He'd probably placed it over her when he'd realized she was sleeping.

She massaged her aching neck as she looked blearily around her. Carver was in the driver's seat, head leaning against the window, eyes shut, his mouth slightly ajar. She looked at him for a few seconds, simply drawing strength from his presence beside her.

Their car was parked by a sign that clearly stated that there was no parking there. To her side, she could glimpse bare, skeletal trees in the darkness and, farther away, the water.

When they'd come back from the interview with Georgia, something had kept niggling at her, something that didn't align properly. It was as if she'd constructed a puzzle and was left with only one piece in her hand, except that it didn't fit in the gap. And instead of figuring out where she'd gone wrong, she'd hammered the piece in by force. She wanted to fix it, to think it through. But as they got closer to the school, her mind was filled with the static of fear and helplessness. So she'd told Carver to keep driving, to find somewhere she could figure it out. And then she must have fallen asleep.

She recognized where they were now. MacNeil Park, just a few blocks from her home. When the kids were younger, she and Steve would take them here almost every weekend. Sam loved it; she'd put on her Rollerblades and spin around the park over and over and over. How long since they'd been here last? When had they stopped coming here, and why?

Something had woken her up. Her phone. She took it out of her pocket and glanced at the text, rubbing her eyes.

It was from Tammi. **Neal hung the phone up when we put Jackie on the line.**

She frowned at the message. Something there. Something important. A truth, hovering out of reach.

She stepped out of the car and shut the door behind her but regretted it almost instantly. As freezing as it was in the car, outside it was worse. That cold that settled in the streets just before dawn. It seeped through her multiple layers, chilling her to the core. She wrapped Carver's coat tightly around her and walked over to the walkway around the park, dialing Tammi.

"Hey," Tammi answered, her voice drained, exhausted. "I wasn't sure if you were sleeping, but I thought you might like to be kept in the loop—"

"I do, thanks," Abby said. "Did Will get an explanation from him?"

"No. He answered the phone once, and told Will not to call again. Then he stopped answering the phone completely. We've been trying every fifteen minutes. We're starting to consider alternatives."

Abby sighed, frustrated. "If Neal had only talked to her for a bit, found out she's pregnant—"

"She managed to tell him she was pregnant. He hung up after that."

Abby was stunned. "He hung up on her after learning she was pregnant?"

"Yeah."

She thought back to everything she knew, assembling and reassembling . . .

"Abby, are you there?" Tammi asked.

Abby blinked. "Yeah . . . just zoned out for a second. Thanks for letting me know. Keep me posted if anything changes, okay?"

"Sure."

Abby hung up. Shoving her hands in the coat's pockets, she turned to face the East River, hunching her body in the cold. The sky was getting lighter, dark blue shifting into purple, the waves lapping gently at the rocky shore. She leaned on the frozen handrail, staring at the horizon.

This didn't fit. Just like what had bothered her before—the garden at Neal's house, where the body was buried. So well tended. Even the ground over the grave had those white flowers on top of it. Hadn't Jackie told them that she was the one doing the gardening? Yes, she had. She said that Neal showed no interest in it. But according to what Jackie said, she'd left Neal at the end of October, more than two months ago. And from everything they theorized, it was *before* Neal had killed Theodor and buried him in the yard. Had Neal decided to take up gardening, to keep up with what Jackie had done so far? It was possible.

Or maybe Jackie had lied. Had she returned to their home since she'd left? Was that it?

"How are you doing?"

It was Carver. He joined her and stared at the sea, his body braced against the cold. Abby quickly opened the coat, about to offer it to him.

"No, I'm fine, keep it," he said, waving it away. "It's not that cold."

"It's freezing," Abby said.

"I'm fine. What are you thinking about?"

"Just . . . trying to wrap my head around something. Jackie talked to Neal on the phone. She told him she was pregnant. And he hung up on her."

"Huh." He frowned. "So it made him angry. Maybe he didn't want kids? Or maybe Jackie was unfaithful, was that it?"

Abby shook her head. "He'd want to know more, right? This is a guy who constantly looks for the truth. And even if he felt angry, he wouldn't just hang up. He'd yell at her, or say he'd done it all for her. He's trapped in an impossible situation, feeling as if every moment might be his last. He would want to talk to her. She's probably the person who's closest to him."

"Maybe."

"You think I'm overthinking this?"

He shook his head. "I had a thought that was bothering me too."

"About Jackie?"

"No. Actually it's about Theodor. Georgia told us she saw him in September, and he'd told her he'd lost interest in the Watchers."

"Right."

"But we know he'd been meeting Neal more and more frequently, until *October*. His planner was full of meetings with Neal. Why would he do that, if he'd lost interest in them?"

Abby thought about that planner. About their interview with Georgia. "She didn't say he lost interest in the *Watchers*. She said he lost interest in the research. And that matches the interview summaries we found in his computer. He stopped summarizing his interviews around August."

"Okay. So he was still interested in the Watchers, or in Neal, but he lost interest in the research."

Abby looked at him, and then gasped. It all clicked.

"Carver, he got *more* interested in the Watchers. He bought into their conspiracy theories."

Carver snorted. "Seriously?"

"Think about it. His personality matches. Remember what Landsman told us? The traits associated with conspiracy theorists? A need to control their environment—his house was in meticulous order, everything in its place, books sorted alphabetically. Georgia said her father was self-absorbed, disagreeable, narcissistic. And Theodor told Georgia he'd gotten the Watchers all wrong. Neal probably converted him. He really began to believe the Watchers were right. His meetings with Neal became even more frequent, two or three times a week. They *both* got more invested in the Watcher alternative world."

"Okay . . . suppose he did."

She needed him to see it, to make sure it wasn't her mind playing tricks on her. "Now, think it through. Georgia said that she and her dad only chatted."

"Right. And in the past two months it was probably Neal chatting with her, pretending to be her dad, just like he's pretending to be Jabberwocky on the forum."

"Wouldn't you notice if the person you chatted with was completely different?"

"Not necessarily . . ." Carver hesitated. "You didn't, right? When you thought you were chatting with Isaac."

Abby clenched her jaw. "It's not the same. I've been talking with Moses from day one. Sure, I was fooled, but the person I talked to never changed. His chatting style, the topics we talked about, his mannerisms—they were consistent."

Carver thought about it. "Neal probably read through their chat, and tried to emulate her dad's style."

"That's what I figured . . . but why would he do that? Why not just stop communicating? Why go to all that trouble?"

Carver squinted. "What are you getting at?"

Abby could hardly breathe. "Think about that day, in October. Jackie leaves Neal, tells him he has to get his shit together if he wants her back."

"Right," Carver said. "Straight afterward Neal meets Theodor and tells him about it. Theodor says something that pisses Neal off. He loses it, kills Theodor, and buries him in his yard."

"And then decides to pretend he's Theodor . . . ," Abby said slowly. "Chatting with Georgia, while ignoring Jackie completely."

Carver stared at her. She could see it sink in, the understanding. It had been in front of their faces all along.

"That garden in Neal's house," Abby said. "It was so well tended. There were even flowers planted on top of the grave. But Jackie told us she was the one who did the gardening, not Neal. And you know who else had a meticulous garden?"

"Theodor Quinn," Carver said.

"That's right."

"Neal didn't kill Theodor and pretend to be him," Carver said. "It was the other way around."

Abby exhaled, heart beating wildly. "Neal must have said something that angered Theodor somehow."

Carver nodded. "Maybe he told Theodor that he wanted to stop dedicating his life to the Watchers, because it was destroying his actual life."

"Theodor killed Neal, buried him in his garden, and embraced his online nickname, Caterpillar," Abby said. "Neal has been dead for over two months. That's why he won't talk to Jackie, and why he avoided her, even changing the locks."

"That fits. We know that he began sounding like a different person in the forum. More aggressive. With grander gestures. A man who wanted to beat the cabal once and for all."

"He sounds like a different man in the forum because *he is a different man*. A man who wants to be famous. Who wants his name etched in the history books."

Carver shook his head. "But . . . Tammi would have noticed, when she did her background check. We have photos—"

"The best photo we have of him right now is with a busted nose and bruised face. And in the interviews, Neal told Theodor that they were even more alike than he thought, remember? He was referring to their appearance—they look similar."

"And Hatter and Alma have never seen him before, so they had no way of knowing that it wasn't him."

"You remember what Dennis told us? Hatter and Alma didn't even want Jabberwocky in their private chat. They didn't trust him. But Caterpillar said he trusted him."

"Of course he did," Carver said. "By that point Theodor was both Caterpillar and Jabberwocky."

Abby clenched her jaw, dread crawling inside her. "Theodor now knows that Jackie is waiting for him outside. Surrendering to the police would mean that the entire thing would be over. The other Watchers will find out he isn't the person he said he was. He probably understands that once that happens, we'll look for Neal. And find him."

Carver looked at her, saying nothing.

"Caterpillar will never release the hostages," Abby said. "Negotiating with him is pointless."

CHAPTER 55

October 29, 2019

"I don't understand," Theodor said again.

Neal offered him another beer, but the man shook his head. Neal's own head was spinning. He'd drunk four . . . no, five beers since Jackie had left.

"Jackie means everything to me," he said. "What we're doing . . . maybe it's important—"

"Maybe?" Theodor snapped. "We're the only ones in the struggle. If we give up, the Circle will be free to do whatever—"

"Yes," Neal said impatiently. They'd been arguing in circles for what felt like hours. "Fine. It's important. But as far as I'm concerned, if I lose Jackie, they've won, okay? They've taken Jackie away from me."

"All the more reason you should fight them! If they're targeting our homes, they should pay a price. We have to strike back."

"They're not . . . haven't you been paying attention? She left me because I've been neglecting her. For months!"

"No, I don't think she did. You're a good guy. You love her. You should ask yourself why she *really* left. Was it because she was forced to? Maybe they scared her? Threatened to kill both of you if she didn't leave?"

Neal wanted to nod. To say that Theodor was right. It would be so easy to go with it. Theodor gave him an easy out. It wasn't Neal's fault at all. Neither was Jackie to blame, really. They were both victims. He *should* be angry. He should be vying for revenge . . .

But that wasn't it. Jackie wouldn't have done it. She would have told him. They would have found a way to face it together. Just like they did when she had a miscarriage. Like when they almost lost their home. Like they used to do with everything.

And there it was again. If it was so easy to find "proof" that Jackie had left him because of the Circle, what else had they gotten wrong? Perhaps one of the assassinations the Circle had supposedly enacted? Or the Circle alliance with Big Pharma? If you started dismantling it all, what was left?

"What if we're wrong?" he said tiredly. He regretted inviting Theodor over. He wished he could go to bed.

"Wrong about what?"

"About . . . a lot. I don't know. You remember that discussion a couple of days ago, about the debunking video?"

A popular YouTuber posted videos supposedly debunking Watcher theories. He'd present a Watcher core belief, such as the cabal's connection to the Weinstein scandal. And he'd start picking it apart. And the Watchers on the forum spent endless hours nitpicking those videos, dismantling his so-called proofs. Debunking the debunker. They all had a blast.

Except . . . a lot of it came down to *We can't trust any police sources, because the police are corrupt.* And *We can't believe anything the Department of Justice says because we've proved that it has been infiltrated by the Circle.*

And a lot of their own proof relied on things other Watchers said. And there was a huge problem with *that.*

"What about it?" Theodor said.

"I don't know if you remember, but at some point, we were talking about something that Senator John Argyle said, and someone pointed out that we've proven that he was a cabal agent. It's, like . . . established."

"Yeah, of course."

"I'm the one who proved it," Neal said. "A year ago. It was my biggest win."

Theodor frowned. "So what?"

"It's not true."

"What do you mean?"

"I mean, it might be true; I don't know. But when I came up with that theory, that's all it was. A theory. He'd said something about streamlining FDA procedures, and it got my attention. And then I found a few articles of stuff he did. I posted about it on the forum, linking all the articles, and everyone talked about it. A day later, they were already convinced I was right. Like, one hundred percent convinced. Hell, *I* was convinced. But there wasn't any concrete proof. It was just a theory. I know, because I came up with it."

Theodor stared at him, saying nothing.

"It felt good to believe that I'd figured it out. And it would feel good to believe that Jackie left because the Circle scared her off. So maybe both things are wrong. Maybe a lot of what we believe is wrong."

He was feeling sleepy. Too many beers.

"I should post about it. We should all ask ourselves what's true."

"No," Theodor said firmly. "You were right about John Argyle. It wasn't just a made-up theory."

"It's made up. Trust me. It's bullshit. All we believe is bullshit."

"They got to you, didn't they?"

"What?" Neal gaped at Theodor incredulously.

"The Circle. What did they tell you? What do they have on you?"

"Are you even listening to yourself right now?" Neal lunged from his chair, his fists clenched. "Get the hell out."

Now Theodor was standing as well. Getting in his face. Shouting. Pushing him.

Neal stumbled back. He'd had too much to drink. He flailed his arms, trying to regain his balance. But he couldn't.

◆ ◆ ◆

So much blood, and it kept spreading, leaking all over the floor, crimson and sticky and horrifying. Didn't they say you had to keep pressure on the wound? Except the blood was leaking from Neal's head, and should you really apply pressure to a hole in someone's skull? Besides, Neal was lying on the floor, and people always said you shouldn't move anyone who'd fallen because of potential spinal injury, but the blood was spreading, it was everywhere, and now he stepped in it, and left a bloody footprint, and smeared it, and it really was everywhere. Neal was sobbing . . . no, wait, it was him. He was sobbing—deep, heavy, panicky sobs, because Neal wasn't making *any* sound and his eyes were open, staring at the ceiling in a way that felt so damn empty and hollow and terrifying.

"Neal," Theodor said again. Not for the first time. He'd been calling his friend, over and over, and there was no response.

He had to call an ambulance, except there was something in all that blood and that terrifying stillness that made him think there was no point in calling anyone, because Neal was gone, gone, gone. And when they came and saw the blood, and his footprints, the questions would start—*How did this happen,* and *Why didn't you call us immediately*—and what could he say? What could he really say? That Neal had tripped? That he didn't call them because he thought at first that it wasn't a big deal, that Neal would get up in a minute and kick him out?

Had Neal tripped? Perhaps they'd shoved each other first? He couldn't remember, it was hazy, and all that blood was freaking him out, because there shouldn't be so much of it, and it was just everywhere, smearing, and now he saw that he had some on his sleeve and on his pants, and there was a tiny spatter on the table—why the hell would that wooden coffee table, and its firm, deadly corners, even be there?

Had *he* done it? No, there was no way.

Theodor never just *did* anything. He always thought things through. And he would *never* do anything like this. It wasn't his fault. They'd been arguing and Neal pushed him, so he pushed back. Neal had reacted badly. Theodor was only trying to help, but Neal had completely lost it. Why had he reacted like that?

Because he'd realized that Theodor had discovered the truth. That was the only explanation. Theodor had figured out that Neal had switched sides.

He was an agent.

What would've happened if Theodor hadn't been quick enough to stop him? Neal would never have let him leave this house alive. Not knowing what he knew. This had been an act of self-defense.

He still had a hard time believing it. Neal's betrayal. The sudden violence. It was too much. How should he handle this? Perhaps he should leave. Except he'd left his fingerprints and footprints everywhere. And the Circle must already know that he was meeting with Neal.

In fact, they would be wondering why they hadn't heard from their agent. They'd check the GPS tracker that they placed within all their agents. They'd check the audio footage. And they'd investigate.

He had to be fast.

They were coming.

He stumbled around the dark house, eyes darting frantically, sobbing in fear. How long did he have? An hour? Maybe less. And he knew what they'd do to him when they got there. He tried not to think about it, but he knew. He'd heard enough testimonies, seen enough photos. *Please, God, don't let them get to me.*

He found Neal's toolbox on the top shelf in the garage. As he pulled it, the lid opened, a screwdriver tumbling, hitting his head. Hissing in pain, he set it on the floor. He rummaged inside, the rattling of metal objects echoing in the dusty space. *Come on, come on . . .* He upended it on the floor, the loud crashing noise making him wince. Did anyone hear it? The neighbors? A random passerby, already calling the police? Or maybe *them*?

There! He grabbed the pliers, and ran out of the garage, heart thudding in his chest.

First to get the GPS tracker out. He knelt on the floor, trying to recall the schematics that he'd memorized. But it was difficult to concentrate, his breathing erratic, his mind filled with all the things they'd do to him when they got here. The burns. The mutilations.

He took a deep breath, forced himself to focus. This was the moment to prove himself. To show what he was worth. Hours of training, of memorizing, of preparing for this moment. He now remembered.

Theodor pulled Neal's chin, forcing his mouth open. Pinching the hidden tracker with the pliers, he yanked, tearing it out of its socket. Trembling, he got up, went to the bathroom. When he tried to drop it into the toilet, he dropped the pliers instead. *Damn it, damn it!* He fished the pliers out, flushed the tracker.

Now for the microphone.

As he was trying to reach the microphone, something flickered in the darkness. A patch of white light, a cell phone. He picked it up, and stared at the screen. A new message.

Red_Queen: Caterpillar, you there?

Caterpillar was not his name; it had been Neal's. But online aliases were the costumes they all wore to muddy the waters, camouflage their scent. He had to answer, to mislead anyone who was listening, watching, making notes.

He knew Red Queen; she was a member of the forum. Was she also a double agent? He didn't think so, but he couldn't be sure.

Finger quivering, he typed, I'm here. His finger left a smear of blood on the screen, a red, sticky stain. His DNA and fingerprint.

Red_Queen: Did you see the thread they posted earlier? About those kids?

He wanted to smash the screen, to yell at Red Queen that this was not the time, that they might be coming, that he could be compromised. Instead he forced himself to tap the answer, calm, short, no spelling mistakes.

Caterpillar: Busy. Will check later.

He turned off the screen, grabbed the pliers again. Turned back to Neal's inert body.

Which one was the mic?

CHAPTER 56

When Sam opened her eyes, the first thing she saw was that strange woman, Deborah, sitting there on the edge of the mat, staring at her. Her lips moved silently, as if in prayer.

She was freaking Sam out.

What time was it? In the windowless storage room, it was impossible to tell, and Sam didn't have a watch. The rest of the group seemed to be asleep. Fiona lay by Sam's side, eyes closed, looking peaceful for the first time since this had started.

Very gently, Sam sat up, scooching her feet away from Deborah. For some reason, she was afraid the woman would touch her, grip her clothes. When she'd first shown up, Deborah had mostly spouted cryptic biblical passages. But when pressed repeatedly with questions, she'd stopped responding, shut her eyes, and begun praying, ignoring the people around her.

"You don't have to be afraid of me," Deborah spoke softly. "I'm here to help you."

Sam swallowed. "I'm not afraid. How did you get inside the school?"

Deborah smiled at her mischievously. "I ran inside. The police breached the door, and then left it open."

"Which door?" Sam asked breathlessly.

Deborah considered it. "The one in the back, next to the fenced basketball court."

Sam nodded. Next to the art classroom, on the first floor. If they had an opportunity to escape, they could get there easily. "Why did you come here? You said something about my dad earlier. Are you one of his colleagues? Or his students?" Dad was a big shot math professor at Columbia, and his students often looked up to him. Would one of them be so devoted that they'd enter a hostage situation for him? It sounded insane.

Deborah shook her head, the smile plastered on her face. "Not your dad. *Father.*"

A priest, then. That explained the prayers and the Bible quotes. "But why did he send you to protect me?" Sam tried to think of any priests she knew.

"Because you're the blood of the Messiah."

The woman was deranged. "I'm not. You got the wrong person."

"It's you. I can see it in your eyes. When we leave, I will take you to meet Father. He will make you see."

Sam decided to change tack. She had enough troubles without this religious fanatic stirring things up. "Okay, I believe you. But for now, I don't want you to—"

The lock clicked. Sam instinctively drew as far away from the door as possible. Beside her, Fiona raised her head, blinking.

It was Hatter and Alma in the doorway.

"We figured you need a bathroom break," Alma said. "Two at a time."

"I need to go," Fiona said, rubbing her eyes.

"Me too," Sam said quickly.

"I'll go," Deborah said. "I also need to wash myself."

"Just two," Alma repeated. "You two. The girls."

"No," Deborah said. "Samantha and I will go together."

"It's okay. I'll go with Fiona." Sam got up and gingerly made her way to the door.

"No!" Deborah grabbed her leg.

Terrified, Sam kicked her leg free, accidentally stepping on Ray, and stumbled out of the room. Fiona followed her, while Deborah shot to her feet and tried to join them. Before anyone could talk, Hatter slammed the door shut, and locked it. Muffled thumping came from within.

"Let me out!" Deborah screamed.

"What the hell is wrong with her?" Hatter asked sharply.

"I think she's just scared," Sam said. "We all are." She looked around her. Through a window in an adjacent room, she glimpsed the brightening sky. It was dawn. They'd been in the school for almost twenty-four hours.

"I'll take them to the bathroom, then come back for the secretary and that other woman," Alma said.

Hatter stared at his gun, his jaw clenched tightly.

Alma led them down the hallway, toward the closest bathroom stalls.

"Um . . . can we go to the bathroom that we went to yesterday?" Sam asked.

"Why?" Alma asked, frowning.

"I need to wash my face and have a drink. And the sinks in the bathroom here don't work well. No water pressure."

Fiona seemed to tense up in confusion, but her expression stayed blank, a bit sleepy, masking her surprise.

"Yeah, sure," Alma said. She turned around, leading both of them toward the bathroom next to the secretary's office.

"How are *you* handling all this?" Sam asked. "It's been a long night. It must have been difficult."

"It's been . . . incredibly challenging." Alma's voice broke. "I miss my kids."

"It must be hard, staying apart from them for so long," Sam said. "I've been having a hard time being apart from my baby brother. When I see him again, I'll hug him for, like . . . forever."

Alma smiled at her, but Sam saw no hope in that smile. Alma couldn't imagine the same for herself. She wasn't there. And Sam had no idea how to get her there.

But she knew who would be able to do it.

"Did you try talking to the police?" she asked.

"Caterpillar talked to them. He's working on getting us all out safely."

"What if *you* try to talk to them? I heard that it was a woman Caterpillar was talking to, right? She might respond well talking to another woman."

"It's not a woman anymore. It's a guy. And Caterpillar talks to them. We work together." Alma tensed up, her jaw clenching.

"Absolutely. It's understandable. You're a team."

Alma said nothing to that. Sam scrambled to figure out something else to say, to get her talking again, but they were approaching the bathroom, and she had nothing. She was exhausted from trying to find the right thing to say in this impossibly volatile situation. She yearned for the peace and quiet of her own bedroom, with nothing but Keebles and her violin to keep her company.

When they stepped inside the bathroom, Fiona went for the stall on the left—the one where Sam had left the phone. With no other option, Sam lunged forward, nudging her friend aside as she entered the stall, locking the door behind her. Had Alma noticed her aggressive behavior?

She took out the bundle of toilet paper from the trash and unwrapped it. Then she turned the thing on, hoping that it was still muted. As the screen blinked to life, the phone vibrated with notifications. It wasn't beeping, but in the quiet bathroom, Sam felt like the vibration could be heard.

She bit her lip as she stared at the thing. She could write another text to her mom, trying to pass on information about Deborah, and about their own location.

But that would mean that afterward she would go back to the sports-equipment storage room. With Deborah, the fanatic. With Caterpillar and Hatter looming beyond the door.

So instead, she punched in her mom's phone number, and dialed.

Her mom answered immediately.

"Hello?" A breathless, hopeful voice. Sam teared up as she heard her. She wanted to sob. She wanted to cry to her mom, tell her everything, ask her to come and save her.

Instead she opened the stall door, the phone held toward Alma.

Alma's eyes widened, her face twisted in horror as she realized what Sam was holding. She raised the gun in her hand.

"Hello?" Mom's voice buzzed from the phone.

"The woman on the phone is the cop Caterpillar was talking to before," Sam said to Alma. She kept her voice calm and firm, holding the woman's gaze as she offered the phone to her. "You can talk to her now. You *should* talk to her now. In private."

For a second Alma stood there, her gun aimed at Sam, while Sam pointed the phone back at her in a bizarre standoff. Alma's expression was almost plaintive, as if she was begging Sam to end the call.

"Just talk to her," Sam said again. "I think she'd understand what you're going through better than anyone."

Her heart was in her throat, but she didn't dare move, didn't dare even blink. She hoped Fiona had the common sense to stay in the other bathroom stall, to keep out of sight.

Finally, Alma lowered the gun, and took the phone from Sam's outstretched hand, as if it could explode. She put the thing to her ear.

"Hello."

CHAPTER 57

For a few seconds, Abby had heard her daughter speaking. Even though Sam wasn't talking directly to her, it was enough to drown Abby in a tidal wave of emotions, knocking her breath away.

When the woman answered the phone, she could hardly collect herself in time to answer.

"Hello?" the woman said again, confused.

"Hi," Abby said automatically. "I'm Abby. Who am I talking to?"

She already knew whom she was talking to. It had to be Alma. But when in doubt, she always preferred to give the person on the other side of the call the sensation of control.

"Um . . ." The woman hesitated. "You can call me Red . . . um . . . my name is Alma."

And now Abby was walking briskly to the car, Carver by her side. They had to get to the school as fast as possible, had to do this from the negotiation truck. She needed another negotiator to listen in on the call, someone to write down the intel; she needed a record of this phone call. She needed her team.

"Hi, Alma, I'm glad to finally talk to you." She kept her breath steady, despite the quick march. "It's been a very tense night for all of us, and you're probably very scared. Tell me a little about what's going on there."

"I'm not sure . . . I'm with these two girls; I took them to the bathroom. We're doing a bathroom break, taking two at a time."

"That sounds like a good idea." The wind whipped at Abby's face as she walked. Did the woman hear the waves? Abby wished she could mute all the background noise. "The most important thing for me is that everyone stay safe. And it sounds like you feel the same. Are you hurt?"

"N-no. I'm just tired, and scared."

"It must be very frightening for you." They reached the car, Carver hurrying to open the door for her. Abby slid into the passenger seat. "What about the two girls with you? Are they okay?"

"Yes. They're fine. One of them handed me this phone. I don't understand where she found it."

"I'm glad that you have it now, and that we can talk. Is there anyone else with you there?"

"Maybe." The woman became cagey, probably realizing that she shouldn't give away too much.

Carver started the car and mouthed *school*, his eyes questioning. Abby nodded at him. He drove them down the street. They weren't far, and it was still early in the morning. It would take only minutes to get there.

"How did you get into this, Alma?" Abby asked.

"I never thought this would happen. We were trying to help these kids . . . are you the woman Caterpillar talked to earlier? He said you were investigating this for us. He said you were trying to dig into the police involvement in the kids' kidnapping."

"That's true, but it's a long process. I have to be honest with you—this kind of investigation will take time, Alma, especially because I'm working alone. It might take a while before I get any—"

"How much time?"

It was time to get rid of that false hope. It seemed that as long as the Watchers in the building felt like Abby might deliver their redemption, they wouldn't budge.

"It might take months."

"Months?"

"That's why I'm glad I can talk to you. We need to put our heads together and think this through. I know you only wanted to help these kids, and I really appreciate it. I'm a mother, and I have two kids."

"I'm a mother too." Alma's voice cracked.

Abby smiled so that the smile would reflect in her voice. "I'm really happy to hear that, Alma. There are kids there with you right now, and it's very reassuring to know that a mother is keeping them safe. It must be difficult to be away from your kids for so long."

"It's . . . it's terrible. They must be so worried."

"I'm sure they are. How old are your kids?"

"Ten and eleven."

"Oh, that's amazing. One year apart, huh? I could never do that. Mine are fourteen and eight. You know, I just spent a few days away from them on a work trip, and it was incredibly tough. It must be so much harder for you. But imagine how wonderful it would feel to hold them in your arms after this."

"If I ever see them again."

"Alma, I promise you, mother to mother, that I'll do everything I can to help you get back to your children. But we have to work together."

"Oh god, they'll be wondering where I am. I need to get back."

They were arriving at the school. The majority of the protesters had left, thank god, with only a few crazies still marching with signs. Carver drove to the cops blocking the road, and waved at them. They must have recognized him, because they let their car pass.

"I want to keep talking to you on the phone; is that possible?"

A small pause. "I don't think so. Caterpillar . . . he's the one talking to the police. We agreed he should do the talking. But I can tell him that you called."

"Why would it bother Caterpillar that you're talking to me?"

"He just . . . he prefers to do it. And I trust him. I have to go."

Carver parked the car, and Abby stepped out. If Alma hung up now, she might not have a chance to talk to her again.

"Wait, Alma, this is important. Why do you trust Caterpillar to do this for you?"

"I've known him really well for a long time." Alma's voice sharpened. "We're good friends."

"Oh, you've met before yesterday?" Abby walked over to the negotiation truck, and yanked the rear door open. She hopped inside, frantically signaling to the confused, bleary-eyed Will and Tammi to stay quiet.

"I've . . . I've known him online. For a long time. You wouldn't understand."

"I have a friend from childhood, and I've stayed in touch with him for years without meeting him." Abby waved Will over, and he hurried to her side. Abby held the phone so that he could hear the conversation as well. "So I definitely understand how close online friends can be. I believe you that you're close to Caterpillar, and that in your experience, you can trust him implicitly."

"I really have to go."

"Just one more question, Alma. If you've known him for so long, did you notice any sudden change in his behavior, say, in the past two months?"

There was a silence at the other end. She'd touched a nerve.

"Me and my friend chat every day," Abby said. "We talk about our families; we have these private jokes—you know how it is. It's probably similar with you and Caterpillar, right? Except maybe you noticed something strange about him lately. Maybe he didn't remember something you told him. Or he used acronyms he never used before. Or he doesn't send you the same emojis or GIFs as he used to. Almost like he changed overnight."

"I don't understand what you're talking about."

"The Caterpillar you knew so well isn't the same person you've been talking to for the past two months," Abby said, her voice calm and firm, stating a fact. "If you'll think about it, you'll realize I'm right. He is a completely different person."

Will stared at Abby in shock, and she gave him a look, a nod, hoping that he would trust her.

He nodded back.

Abby took a deep breath. "I'm really sorry, Alma, but you can't trust this man."

CHAPTER 58

"You've been handling yourself well so far," Abby said. "Taking this call was smart; you clearly have good instincts. When was the first time you noticed that something changed in Caterpillar's behavior?"

It was a gamble, trying to convince Alma that a person she considered her friend was someone else entirely. Abby would never have tried it with a random person off the street. But Alma had been in the Watcher forum for more than a year. She was trained to think outside the box, to suspect everything and everyone. And to see patterns, even when there were none. And in a strange, ironic twist, it would make it easier to convince her of a true, real-life conspiracy of one.

Or not. Perhaps Abby had it wrong. Alma could view her as an outsider, and her sense of kinship with the other Watchers would be too strong to break. Abby prayed that wasn't the case.

"I . . . you're wrong," Alma said. The hesitancy in her voice was hard to miss. There was already something on her mind. "I trust him completely. He's been under a lot of stress. His wife left him."

"That would explain anger," Abby said. "Or sadness. But would it explain a strange forgetfulness? Sudden change in opinions? What is it you've seen?"

"There was . . . it was nothing. I should really go."

"I'm sure it wasn't nothing. It sounds like it bothered you. What was it?"

"You know that book *The Very Hungry Caterpillar*?"

"Of course." Abby smiled, shifting her tone. Lighter, friendlier. A conversation between two moms. "It was my son's favorite."

"My kids loved it too. And I used to joke with him about it. Like, on a Saturday, I'd write, um . . . Caterpillar that he must be so full after eating a cake and an ice cream and a pickle . . ." Alma's voice faded.

"And a lollipop," Abby said. "And a watermelon."

"Right. Exactly. And he would post a funny GIF of someone emptying whipped cream into his mouth or something. But I said something like that a month ago, and he just . . . didn't get it. He said that he just ate a small breakfast. But it's nothing—maybe he was tired of that joke, or he wasn't in the mood."

"Did he sound like he was tired of the joke?"

A small pause. "No. It sounded like he was confused."

Abby and Will exchanged glances. The seed of doubt had been planted. The schism between Alma and her associates was growing larger by the second.

◆ ◆ ◆

"Open this door! Let me out now!"

The woman's screams were getting on Hatter's nerves. She had a screechy voice that kept drilling and drilling into his skull. And that tone, as if she were in a position to make demands.

He pounded on the door with his fist. "Shut the hell up, you dumb bitch!"

But she didn't. She kept screeching. He heard the muffled voices of the people inside with her, trying to calm her down, begging her to be silent. The boy asked her if she wanted to get them all killed.

Did she? It was a damn good question. Hatter was partial to the idea. They had enough hostages even without the ones in the storage room.

Where the hell was Alma, and the two girls? How long could it possibly take for two women to piss?

Princess and the doc. Now, those two he would definitely rather keep alive for now. Princess, she was just like every other stuck-up bitch in high school. Daddy probably bought her a damn pony every Christmas, delivered in a brand-new sports car, because why the hell not. The kind of girl who would walk around with cleavage that went all the way down to her pierced belly button, and then later complain if some guy checked out the merchandise.

But Doc? She was something else. Everyone's best friend, that one. All smiles, and fluttering eyelashes, and demure glances. And when your back was turned, bam, she'd stick that knife into you. She thought he was too dumb to notice, but he had her figured out. He'd met her kind too. Like that woman who'd complained about him at Walmart. And that girl in Spanish class who—

"Open the door right now!"

Right now? *Right now?*

Yeah, he could open the door right now. No problem at all. He turned the lock and yanked the door open.

The crazy bitch lunged at him. Fingers curved, nails scratching at his face, digging, probing for his eyes, as she let out a high-pitched scream. He stumbled back, shouting in pain, his fist sinking into the woman's gut. She let out a gasp, folding in two, and he jerked his knee up, into her face. A satisfying crunch. She toppled to the floor, her fighting spirit gone. Well, too bad. His fighting spirit was very much still there.

The saying went that you shouldn't kick a man while he was down, which didn't match Hatter's own experience. He found that it was when he was down that everyone around him did the majority of the kicking. And it was about time to do some kicking of his own.

His first kick hit her in the face, which was now spattered with blood. The second kick hit her between the legs, making her emit another heaving gasp.

Movement from the storage room. He glanced inside, saw the boy holding a hockey stick limply. As he glared, the stick toppled from the kid's hands, dropping to the floor.

Hatter aimed his gun at the boy. "Go ahead," he snarled. "Pick it up."

The boy shook his head, a wet stain spreading on his crotch. Pathetic. Hatter's face burned, and that familiar rage filled him, so pure that it was almost like happiness. His finger twitched on the trigger. For a second he almost shot the boy.

Instead he let his arm drop.

And squeezed the trigger, shooting the woman curled on the floor.

The sound of the blast stole Alma's breath away. A shot. Had the police stormed in while she was distracted on the phone? Had they shot Hatter, or Caterpillar? Or was it one of her associates, firing their own gun?

She drew away from the bathroom door, already raising her own firearm against anyone who might enter.

"Alma? What was that?" Abby asked, her voice worried but still somehow steady.

"I don't know." Alma's voice was strangled. She was dizzy, about to fall. "Did the cops enter the building? Was it one of your people?"

She leaned against the wall, her eyes darting from the bathroom door to Samantha to the stall door from which the other girl—Fiona—had just stepped out. Alma pointed her gun at Fiona, gestured for her to join her friend.

"No one here entered the building," Abby said. "Are you hurt? Or any of the girls with you?"

"No." She couldn't trust this woman. She couldn't trust anyone. She was on her own. The tears filled her eyes, but she couldn't afford to break down. Not now. Later, when she was on her own. "It was the cops, wasn't it? They shot one of my friends. Are they coming to shoot me? I have girls . . . hostages with me! You tell them that if they enter, I'll . . ." She couldn't even say it. Shoot the girls? The hostages? She would never do that. She'd known that from the moment it all started. The gun in her hand was nothing but a prop. A lie.

"Alma, I promise you, no one is coming. It sounds like you're under a lot of pressure. We need to think together—"

Alma hung up, and shoved the phone into her pocket. She turned to the girls. "Let's go."

"Maybe we should stay here and wait," Samantha said. "To make sure it's safe."

For a second, Alma was struck by how similar Samantha sounded to that woman on the phone. Both of them steady and calm, despite the situation. Even their intonation was similar.

"No." Could they see how the gun trembled in her hand? Did they realize they could walk away, and she could do nothing to stop them? "We're going back to the equipment room."

She gestured at the door, taking a step toward them. For a second, they almost seemed as if they were about to refuse. But then they relented, walking in front of her. Samantha opened the door, and froze.

Hatter stood in the doorway.

"There you are," he said. "I thought you might have gotten lost."

"We were just coming back," Alma said. There was something wrong with Hatter's expression. His eyes seemed . . . dead. Fear crawled into her gut, her throat, down to her legs, making her knees buckle. "What was that sound we heard before?"

"I had to shoot the doc's mom," Hatter said. "That's why I'm here. Doc, your mom's hurt. She needs your medical expertise. She's in the nurse's office. Let's go. Alma, you can take Princess here back to the other hostages."

"We'll come with you," Alma blurted. She didn't know why she'd said it, but she couldn't leave the girl alone with Hatter. Not right now, not the way he looked at her.

"No," he said. "We're fine."

She was about to argue. There was no way in hell she would let him do anything to that—

The phone in her pocket buzzed. Its humming was loud and clear in the silent hallway, and Alma instinctively put her hand over it.

Hatter clearly noticed. He raised an eyebrow, staring at her.

"Alma," he said, his voice becoming a whisper, a vehement, dangerous hiss. "What is it you have there?"

She swallowed. "I'll take Fiona to the room with the others," she said, her voice trembling. "You should take Sam to her mother."

Hatter's mouth twisted in a mocking smile. "Yes. That's a good idea."

CHAPTER 59

Sam could hardly see where she was going through the tears in her eyes. Hatter was dragging her down the hallway, his gun at her waist, occasionally digging into her body. The nurse's office was a few steps away, but the way there seemed endless. The stench of his sweat was clogging her nostrils, and she kept thinking of the night before. His hand on her throat. His vacant eyes as he squeezed, stealing her breath.

He opened the door to the nurse's room, and pushed Sam inside. She stumbled, nearly falling to the floor, and grabbed the small cot to steady herself. Her eyes scanned the confined space, but Deborah wasn't there. She turned to face Hatter.

He shut the door, locking it.

"Where's Debo . . . my mom?" she asked. She sounded strange in her own ears. A different, broken, scared child.

"She's where I left her." He licked his rubbery lips. "I don't think you can help her, doc. It's all about to end anyway. The only thing any of us can do is try to enjoy our final moments together."

Sam took a step back. But there was nowhere to go. "When this ends . . . I could tell them that you tried to help us. If you take me to her, I can bandage her, save her. You won't be charged with murder—"

"You know what's strange?" Hatter asked. "If I could go back in time . . . I would do it all over again. All of it."

"All of it?" Sam asked. If she could keep him talking, it would all be okay. As long as he was talking, he wasn't doing anything else.

"Yes. All of it." He pointed the gun at her head. "Take your clothes off."

"Wait—"

"We're done with the first-date conversation, doc. I took you out to a nice dinner, showed you around town. Now it's time for my fun to start. Strip. Now."

Sam's lips trembled. Her body was paralyzed with fear. Her eyes darted to the door, which was locked; there was no way out. No one to save her. Not her mom, not the dozens of cops who were less than fifty yards away, not Alma or Caterpillar. She tried to tell herself that she could get through this, that it would end quickly and she would get over it. But it felt like the end. She couldn't, she just couldn't—

"Doc, you don't want me to do it for you, trust me," Hatter growled.

"My mom is a cop," she blurted. "She's out there."

He frowned, confusion flashing on his face. "That dumb bitch is a cop?"

"No! She was just pretending. My real mother is Lieutenant Abby Mullen. She's with the negotiation team. My full name is Samantha Mullen. You can google her, you'll see. And I can show you my Facebook page, I have pictures of her." She was babbling now, desperate. "She's the one Caterpillar was talking to. And Alma. They were both talking to her. I can give you her phone number, you can talk to her yourself. You can trade me for a getaway car, they won't stop you. She's my mom, I swear, just check. You don't want to do this. You can get out of here and disappear. You can—"

"Shut the fuck up!" His roar made her start, and she let out a whimper.

He stared at her for a long while, his blank face telling her nothing. What was going on in the mind of this monster?

"You know what, doc?" he finally said. "I think I believe you. I was wondering where you got your cocky attitude, and now I know. And if you're really a lieutenant's daughter, they'll give me anything I want. Mommy wouldn't risk her precious child, would she?"

"Do you want to call her?" Sam asked weakly.

He let out a snort. "Call her? Nah. I think we're done with phone calls. Let's go outside and meet her, right now."

◆ ◆ ◆

For a few seconds, as Hatter walked away with Samantha, Alma was planted in place. The phone was still buzzing in her pocket, but she made no move to answer it. Fiona was sobbing silently.

It was clear from Hatter's behavior that he knew Alma was hiding something. That he'd heard the humming of the phone's vibrations in her pocket. But what really scared her was that he didn't seem to care. As far as Hatter was concerned, they weren't a group anymore, working together against a common enemy.

And if he had gone his own way, all that was left was Caterpillar. And she didn't know how she felt about that. Because what Abby had said was true. Caterpillar had changed a couple of months ago. Almost instantly, in a single day. And it wasn't just the shock of the breakup with his wife. In fact, the Caterpillar that she'd known wouldn't have written off his wife so easily. How many times had he told Alma how lucky he was to have found his wife? The one good thing in his life. Often mentioning her with affection.

And then, when she left, nothing. Didn't even say that he missed her.

She walked toward the storage room, leading Fiona. The girl followed obediently, looking exhausted and miserable. Alma almost wanted to tell her that if she wanted, she could go.

Instead she said, "Wait. Not there. Let's turn around."

Fiona didn't even ask why.

They returned to the secretary's room.

Caterpillar was standing by the desk, his eyes glued to the screen. The phone was ringing in the principal's office, but Caterpillar made no move to go answer it. In the corner, the principal was slumped on the floor, pale, eyes sunken and drained.

As they stepped inside, Caterpillar didn't even look up. He just said, "Hatter shot one of the hostages."

"He told me," Alma said. "You should talk to the police. We should start negotiating a surrender."

That got his attention. He lifted his gaze from the screen, frowning. "But they haven't even admitted their connection to the Circle."

She wanted to scream at him. To scratch his eyes out. Didn't he get it? It was over. "They'll storm inside if you don't talk to them. Please. I want to see my kids again."

"You will," he said distractedly. "But first we need to use this. The Watchers are depending on us. We'll never get another opportunity like this again."

The constant ringing of the phone was driving her mad. Back at home, when the phone rang, she would often shout, "Will someone get that?" But here, there was no one to shout for. If Caterpillar didn't answer, she would have to. And she didn't think he would let her.

The phone in her pocket began buzzing again too.

"Please," she said again. "My children need me. Kevin. And Olivia. You know how Olivia can't handle being apart from me."

"Olivia will see you soon," Caterpillar said. "I promise."

"Right." Alma's throat went dry. Her kids weren't named Olivia and Kevin.

Caterpillar knew that. She'd mentioned her kids to him several times. He knew their names. He used to ask her about them. He'd ask about Frances's allergies. Or if Kyle had any big games anytime soon. That was, before he broke up with his wife. He'd stopped asking about them, and after that Alma took care not to mention them, because it felt tactless, like rubbing her perfect family life in his face.

But he used to know their names.

"I'm going to return Fiona to the storage room," she said. "I should probably take Mr. Bell, as well."

"No," Caterpillar said resolutely. "I want him to stay with me."

"Okay," she said hurriedly. "I'll just take Fiona."

"And find Hatter on your way back," Caterpillar said. "I saw him enter the nurse's office with the other girl. I want us all to plan our strategy today."

"Sure," Alma said, already halfway out of the room. "We'll be right back."

◆ ◆ ◆

Abby dialed the number again, the ringtone chiming in her ear, thinking about the shot they'd heard, reminding herself that there was no way it could have been anywhere near Alma, that Sam was with Alma, Sam was still safe. *Come on, Alma, pick the hell up, come on, come on.*

"He's not answering," Will said, sliding the earphones halfway off. "Maybe I should try the number for Alma. She might pick up for a different number."

Abby nodded hesitantly. "Okay, we can—"

The ringtone in her ear abruptly stopped. "Hello?" Alma's voice, half-whispering, frightened.

Abby signaled to Will. "Hi, Alma, I'm glad you answered. Where are you?"

"I'm in the bathroom again. If I . . . if I come out with the hostages, can you give me immunity? Like, in court?"

"We can look into it, Alma," Abby said. Will stood by her side, listening in, his eyes shining with excitement. "In any case, I can guarantee that I'll testify in court about your cooperation. That kind of thing goes a long way with the judge."

"I want to see my kids again."

"If you come out, I can promise you that I'll do all I can so that you'll see your kids today, okay?"

"I didn't hurt anyone. The girls and the rest of the hostages can testify to that. I just wanted to help those poor kids."

"It sounds like you were caught in a bad situation. We'll do everything that we can to help you. But we need you to get those hostages out."

"Yes, they're in the storage room. I'll go there right now."

Abby took a deep breath. She had to make sure they did it right. Even the smallest misunderstanding could end in disaster. She went over to the school's blueprints, hanging on the wall. "Okay, so the hostages are in a storage room. What floor?"

"Third floor. It's the sports-equipment storage room."

Will tapped on the room that she specified. The closest stairway wasn't far, but . . .

"Alma, where are Hatter and Caterpillar?"

"Caterpillar is still in the secretary's office. And Hatter went to the nurse's office." Alma's voice broke as she said that. She was obviously terrified; she was two-timing her associates.

Abby examined the map. If she went to the closest stairway, she would have to go past the admin wing, where Hatter and Caterpillar were. No way.

"We'll need you to take the hostages to the stairway on the southern part of the floor, next to the choir room, okay? Do you know where that is?"

"No."

"The girls know where that is. They can take you there. Once you get to the bottom floor, go to the exit by the art room. I want you to let me know when you get there, okay? It's important; I want everyone to be ready so that there'll be no misunderstandings." The last thing they needed was for some jittery cop to shoot Alma as she tried to step out and surrender.

"O-okay."

"But tell them to go there through the hallway that doesn't go by the admin wing, okay? Don't go anywhere close to the secretary's office."

"Yes. Oh!" Alma sounded startled.

"What is it?"

"I just reached the storage room door. There's blood here."

Abby tensed. "Blood?"

One of the phones at the far end of the negotiation command center rang. Will dashed over, glancing at the display. He turned to Abby and mouthed, *It's him.*

◆ ◆ ◆

Staring at the security camera feed, Caterpillar realized that everything was slowly falling apart.

First Hatter had shot that woman. Then he'd dragged one of the girls into the nurse's office. By that point it was clear that Hatter's intentions were very far from Caterpillar's. His guts twisted, thinking of what Hatter was doing to that girl in there. An underage child, like the ones the Circle was trafficking. All those sexual jokes and memes Hatter occasionally posted on the forum didn't seem just "immature" or "out of place" anymore. The man was a predator, pure and simple.

And then Caterpillar noticed Alma walking down one of the corridors with the other girl, looking around her nervously. *Holding a phone to her ear.* Talking to someone. Probably the police. Or maybe directly to the Circle.

Caterpillar swallowed. The end was coming; he could smell it. But he wouldn't wait for it sitting down.

"Get up!" he barked at the principal.

The man cringed, and Caterpillar had to yell at him a second time and aim a gun at him to get him to move. He dragged him into the man's office, grabbed the landline, and dialed. Will would tell him he had to keep things under control. Or let him talk to Neal's ex-wife again, which Caterpillar had no intention of doing. No. There was only one person he wanted to talk to right now.

The line clicked as Will picked up.

"Caterpillar, thank you for returning my call—"

"I have a gun to the principal's head," Caterpillar said. "If you don't give me Abby's phone number, I'll blow his head off."

"I'm not sure I have it on me. What do you—"

"I'll count to five. If you don't give me her number, this man dies." This time, he was going to follow through.

"Caterpillar—"

"One." Caterpillar dug his gun into the principal's skull. The man let out a frightened sob. He was a Circle agent anyway; the kids were about to be sold from *his* school.

"It sounds like you're under a lot of pressure—"

"Two." He wouldn't waver. If they didn't let him talk to Abby, he would die knowing that he had come close to bringing the Circle to their knees. All the Watchers would know.

"I need a bit more time to find her number—"

"Three." Perhaps he should have said he'd count to ten. But changing his mind now was impossible.

A silence from the other side of the phone. Was Will checking his address book, looking for the number? Or telling the cops to break in? If they did, Caterpillar was intent on shooting.

"Four." His finger tightened on the trigger. It was all about to end. He gritted his teeth, steeling himself.

"Caterpillar, it's Abby. I'm here."

Her voice caught him completely by surprise. "I didn't know you were over there," he said dumbly.

"I just got here." She sounded out of breath. "Will said you wanted to talk to me. And I also have some things we should discuss."

CHAPTER 60

Abby tried to settle her beating heart as she adjusted her earphones. "It sounds like you had a tense night."

"I'm barely hanging on here." He sounded terrified and angry. "You told me I could trust Will. He *didn't* keep things under control. The police stormed inside."

"I heard; I'm sorry about that. But I'm here now." Will was talking urgently on his phone, updating ESU about Alma's surrender and hostage release. "I appreciate the fact that you kept things mostly under control at your end."

She imagined her daughter hurrying through the hallways, leading Alma and the rest of the hostages to the exit. Perhaps, in a few minutes, Abby would be holding Sam in her arms. She tried to concentrate on the conversation. She had to buy time for Alma to leave, and keep Caterpillar from killing Henry Bell.

"What about what you promised you'd do?" Caterpillar asked sharply. "There's been no admission of guilt from anyone in the NYPD. And I didn't hear a word from you throughout the night."

"I'm sorry; I had to cut through a lot of red tape and do some serious digging." She glanced at Carver, who was standing silently in the corner of the narrow space, listening in. She motioned him over.

"What did you find?"

What did he want to hear? Should she straight up lie, tell him about the corruption she'd unearthed?

No. These guys weren't really interested in answers. They wanted questions.

"I found a lot of strange coincidences," she said. Carver crouched by her side. She grabbed a pen and a piece of paper, and jotted, *Go and be there for Sam when she gets out.* He nodded and walked away, stepping out of the truck. Abby shut her eyes, focusing on the conversation. "There are gaps in the chief of detectives' calendar. Four hours, twice a week, with no explanation. His secretary couldn't give me straight answers about these gaps. From everything I could dig up, it's related to the DAS system. Does that make any sense to you? Why would he spend so much time on the DAS system?"

The Domain Awareness System collected footage from over eighteen thousand security cameras in the city, archiving them in a huge digital database, which was later analyzed by a machine learning algorithm, as well as detectives. It was frequently criticized for violation of privacy, and Abby was sure it would grab Caterpillar's attention.

"The DAS?" His voice shifted. Anger intermingled with excitement. "There were some theories we had about that, but I never thought it was directly related to the Circle."

Her own cell phone rang. Alma. She hit the mute button on the console as Caterpillar said something about the connection between DAS and the NYPD's underwater drones.

She glanced at Will. "Are ESU in position?"

He gave her the thumbs-up.

It was time.

◆ ◆ ◆

Alma walked behind the three hostages, hardly breathing. She'd spent a large part of the past twenty-four hours watching the security camera feed. She knew that somewhere on that split screen, they could be seen. Without intending to, she raised her head, searching for the camera.

Were Caterpillar and Hatter watching her as she betrayed them? Was one of them sprinting through the school, gun in hand, intent on stopping her?

If so, it was too late. There was the exit.

"Okay, wait," she said. "They told me to call before we step out."

She took out her phone and called Abby. It took the woman a few nail-biting seconds to answer the call.

"Hello?" Abby's voice.

"I'm at the door."

"Good job. All of you stand back from the door. Are you armed?"

"I . . . I have a gun, but I haven't used it."

"Okay, I'll need you to put the gun on the floor and kick it toward the door. Then put your hands on your head. Let the hostages go first. Then walk toward the door. There'll be armed officers in vests outside, so don't get startled; they won't hurt you. We want everyone to get out unhurt, okay?"

"Yes."

"Let's do it."

Alma hung up the phone. Then she placed the gun on the floor and kicked it, but hit it with her heel awkwardly, and it just spun two feet and hit the wall. The teenage boy glanced at the gun and tensed.

"Ray, don't you dare," Fiona said. "The police are going to open that door, and if you're holding a gun—"

The door burst open.

Alma watched as the three hostages ran outside, someone shouting at them to move. Slowly, as if in a dream, she put her hands on her head and stepped forward. The cops stood in full gear waiting for her as she approached them. Tears were running down her face.

As one of the cops grabbed her, pulling her hands behind her back, she realized she wasn't afraid at all, or angry, or sad. She didn't care about the Circle, or the fact that the Watchers had failed to expose their sex trafficking operation. Perhaps she wasn't really a good Watcher.

All she felt was relief.

◆ ◆ ◆

Sam felt as if her arm were being held in a vise. Hatter was gripping it hard, dragging her down the hall, muttering instructions at her.

"When we step out, you don't say anything except *please do what he says*, you got that? You tell them to get your mom over and to do whatever I say."

She nodded, afraid to even speak.

"And you stay very still. If you struggle, I'll shoot you and we die together. I don't mind dying. Do you believe me?"

She nodded again.

"I'll ask for a car, and when they get me the car, you get in with me. Again, you don't struggle."

"You can trade me for a car," she whispered.

Impossibly, his arm tightened even more, and she whimpered in pain.

"Do you think I'm an idiot? The moment I let you go, they'll shoot me down. No. We step out together; we drive off together. You and me are going on a honeymoon, doc."

She lowered her gaze to the floor, feeling sick. Then something caught her eye. A smear of blood. Not entirely surprising, in the wake of the violence of the past twenty-four hours. Except this smear seemed fresh. And there was another one. And a few steps later, some splattered drops.

"I'm going to hold you very closely in front of me," Hatter said. "With a gun to your temple, so you better be on your best behavior, or . . ." He slowed down, and stopped talking.

Blood spattered the floor by an open door, and a crimson handprint was smeared on the wall. Hatter paced silently close to the door and then, with a sudden kick, opened the door wide, aiming his gun inside the room.

It was just a storage room, with a lawn mower, a snowblower, and some tins. There was no one there, and clearly nowhere to hide.

"What was she looking for here?" he muttered.

"Who?"

He didn't answer, just kept staring into the storage room.

A sharp, loud beeping noise began screeching all around them. It startled Sam, her heart lurching. Hatter's grip on her arm loosened slightly as he stared around him in confusion.

She had only a fragment of a second to act. Almost reflexively, her knee shot up, sinking into his groin.

She'd imagined doing that countless times throughout the night. Picturing it in vivid detail, practicing the motion in her mind. And now, with the gun pointed away from her, with his attention elsewhere, she'd seen her one chance.

She threw all her fear and hate into that one kick, and when it connected, she sensed she'd done it right. Hatter let out a wheezing gasp as he folded in two, and she was already running, knowing that she had only a few seconds before he shot her down. She dashed to the nearest corner, zigzagging like they'd been taught, and then the gun exploded behind her. Once, twice, and she was around the corner, and she thought she wasn't hurt, she wasn't sure, but there was no time to check, so she kept on running as the shrill beeping carried on around her. When she saw the smoke ahead, she understood what it was.

The fire alarm was ringing.

CHAPTER 61

The tension that had been building for the past twenty-four hours erupted all at once. Carver ran down the street as shrill fire alarms blared from the school. Officers in full gear were shouting around him, their voices momentarily drowned out by the chopper flying overhead. Members of the media were all struggling at the edge of the police barricades to get footage, cops stretched to prevent them from coming too close, yelling at them through a bullhorn. The air smelled of smoke.

And then he spotted them. The bedraggled hostages, tended to by medics, looking dazed and shocked. Carver beelined to them, jostling his way past a group of ESU officers. He ran past a woman whose head was being bandaged, past a teenage boy who was shivering uncontrollably as a nurse was covering him with a blanket. A girl was sobbing, sitting on the edge of an ambulance as an officer tried to console her, holding her hand gently.

Where the hell was Sam?

A group of ESU cops suddenly dashed down the street. Carver caught snippets of shouted conversations.

". . . another hostage, it's the principal . . ."

". . . still unaccounted . . ."

". . . stand by for the signal . . ."

". . . ready on the roof . . ."

He stopped a medic who was rushing past him.

"Where's the other hostage?" he shouted. "Samantha Mullen. She's fourteen!"

The medic shook his head. "Those are the three I saw. Maybe another team has her."

Carver turned away and ran over to the sobbing girl. She seemed to have calmed down a bit, but her lips still trembled, and she sat huddled and miserable.

"Hi," he said, trying to be as gentle as he could while still being heard over the noise in the background. "You're Fiona, right?"

"Y-yeah."

"Fiona, where's Sam?"

"She didn't come out with us." She started crying again. "The other guy had her."

"Which other guy?"

She tried to answer but she was hyperventilating, and now a medic was pushing him away, shouting angrily at him.

Carver whirled around. There. That woman sitting inside a patrol car, in the back. Looking just as shocked as the rest of them. He instantly identified her from her portrait. This was Alma, the Red Queen.

He rushed to the car, flashing his badge to the patrol cop in front. "I'm Detective Carver. I need half a minute with her. Just half a minute."

The man nodded hesitantly, and Carver yanked the door open. The woman sat with her hands cuffed behind her back.

"Alma, I'm Detective Carver," he said. "Where's Samantha?"

"Hatter took her," she blurted. "I'm sorry, I couldn't stop him. He took her to the nurse's office."

Someone was shouting about a fire. They needed to evacuate the building.

Carver dashed past the ambulances, the medics, the cops, and into the school.

◆ ◆ ◆

"What the hell is that?" Caterpillar screamed into the phone. "Did you do this?"

"We didn't do anything," Abby said. "Can you tell me what's going on in there?"

"It's the fire alarm," the principal blurted. "The fire alarm is ringing."

"Did the cops set fire to the school?" Caterpillar roared into the phone.

"No, of course not. We don't want anyone to get hurt," Abby said. She sounded anxious, her calm demeanor fading away.

"Maybe you don't, but the Circle does. They want to eliminate all the witnesses," Caterpillar said. He could already smell smoke. Or was he imagining it? It was impossible to tell. "You tell them they just killed the principal. I would have let him go, Abby, but when they set fire to the school, they sentenced him to—"

"Theodor, wait."

The name caught him completely by surprise, and his mouth snapped shut.

"You're almost there," Abby said. "The truth is at our fingertips. Why else would this happen?"

She was right. The Circle wouldn't have done something so radical as setting the school on fire unless they thought that he could destroy them.

"You've been fooling them for months," she said. "And it's your time to finally expose them. Whatever it is, you've figured it out. Do you know what they're trying to bury? It's not just the sex trafficking. It's something much bigger. You must have found it."

Had he?

He had. She was right. The DAS system. The school. The trap they'd all stumbled into. Alma's surprising backstabbing. He saw the pattern.

"Yes," he said, talking louder over the screeching fire alarm. "You're right. We were so blind, I see it now. It's all a big—"

"Wait! Give me a moment," Abby said. Then, her voice away from the phone, he heard her shout, "Everyone out! You too, Tammi, outside. Close the door behind you. Now, damn it!"

Somewhere in the background, something slammed.

"Sorry," Abby said, her voice softer. "I didn't want *anyone* to overhear. I wasn't sure where their alliances lie."

"Okay," Caterpillar said. "I was starting to say . . ." He became quiet.

"What is it?" Abby asked.

"Hang on." He put the phone down, and led the principal outside the room.

"Try to leave, and I'll shoot you in the back, you got that?" he hissed at the man.

The principal nodded, trembling.

Caterpillar returned to the principal's office, shutting the door. "Sorry, I had to make sure I was alone as well."

"Are you alone now?" Abby's voice was hushed, conspiratorial.

"Yes. What I realize now is—"

The window shattered into a million pieces. Something exploded, and now he could hardly see, his ears ringing, faint figures pouring into the room, and someone grabbed him, flattening him to the ground, hands behind his back. He screamed in despair. Victory had been snatched from his hands.

The Circle had won.

◆ ◆ ◆

Abby sat still in the primary negotiator chair, listening as the ESU officers shouted, glass shattering and furniture breaking in the background. And then, faintly, a shout: "Clear!"

Barker stood by her side, talking into his shoulder mic. "Team alpha, is the hostage unhurt?"

The radio crackled. "This is team alpha. He's in shock, but he appears to be unhurt. We're escorting him outside now."

Abby pulled off the headphones, letting them drop to her neck, feeling the tension ebb away from her body. It was done. Henry Bell, the last hostage remaining, was now safe.

Barker placed a hand on her shoulder. "Fantastic job. I didn't think you could get him to separate from the hostage."

Abby nodded, whirling her chair. Will grinned at her, his headphones still on.

"I wasn't sure I'd manage it either," Abby said, her voice barely a whisper. She took off her headphones, and walked over to the truck's rear door. According to reports on the radio, Alma was already in custody, all the hostages safe. Carver was probably with Sam right now.

She opened the door, blinking at the bright light. The sun had come up while she'd been inside, its rays glaring off the school's windows. The fire alarms were still ringing, and black smoke billowed from a window. In the distance, she heard the sirens of the approaching fire trucks. Someone was shouting for people to grab fire extinguishers.

She looked around her, searching for her daughter. Walking slowly toward the ambulances, her eyes scanning the people around her. The medical crew. The dazed hostages.

Her footsteps quickened, her heart pounding. Where was Carver? Where was Sam?

◆ ◆ ◆

The smoke got thicker as Sam ran down the hallway, and soon, she saw the source. Thick clouds of smoke were billowing from an open classroom door. She barely slowed down, and knowing that Hatter wasn't far behind, she ran through the smoke.

The room was on fire. Sam glanced briefly inside, through the smoky haze, saw the desks and the chairs burning. Even the floor was on fire. The heat from inside was unbearable. She turned her head to the side, half-blind, coughing. Kept on running, leaving the roaring flames behind. It made no sense. Why would they set the school on fire while they were inside?

It didn't matter. She was almost at the library, which had an emergency door. Maybe she could get out from there.

She was now stumbling rather than running, her lungs burning from the smoke she'd inhaled, eyes stinging and full of tears. Just a few more steps. The library was up ahead. She had no idea if Hatter was behind her, couldn't hear anything beyond the shrill fire alarm, beyond her own coughing. She didn't dare look back.

She barged through the double doors, which swung shut behind her. The fire alarm was muffled here, as if the cardinal rule of silence in the library applied even to that.

Deborah was slumped by the librarian's desk.

Her shirt was bloodstained, and a trickle of blood ran from her lips as well. She lifted her head as Sam entered, and her lips moved, as if she was trying to say something. Sam hurried to her side, knowing that she might have only seconds before Hatter barged in.

"Can you stand?" she asked urgently. There was a sharp stench around Deborah, but Sam's nostrils were clogged with smoke, and she couldn't quite pinpoint the source of it.

"Fire," Deborah whispered.

"I know." Sam didn't dare move the woman. But the emergency door was right there across the room. "Wait here, I'll get help."

She shifted when Deborah grabbed her wrist. The woman's grip was surprisingly strong.

"Fire," Deborah said again. "'He will baptize you with the Holy Spirit and fire.'"

That sharp smell. Gasoline.

A tin canister lay on its side by the woman, its lip still dripping. The wall-to-wall carpet all around them was soggy.

It was Deborah who'd set the fire in the classroom. Did she intend to set fire to the library as well?

There was something clenched in the woman's other hand.

A lighter.

"The fire cleansed the Messiah once," Deborah croaked. "It can cleanse us."

Sam yanked her arm, but the woman held on.

"Wait," Sam said, panic rising in her throat. "You said that Father sent you to protect me. Don't do this. This isn't what he wants, right?"

Deborah blinked, her lips moving without making a sound. Sam tugged her arm again, but the woman's grip was vicious.

"Don't be scared," Deborah said. "The trial of fire makes us stronger. Our purity will be our shield. Only the wicked need to fear the flames."

She raised her other hand, and switched on the lighter.

It sparked, but no flame ignited.

"Let go!" Sam screamed. She pulled hard, but it seemed that Deborah was using all her strength to hang on with her bony fingers.

"We shall be reborn from the flames!" She grinned madly.

She clicked the lighter again, and this time, the little flame flared up. Deborah shifted, bringing the flame closer to her shirt.

Sam half stood, still bent as the woman held on to her wrist. She kicked the woman hard in the face. A crunch and a groan, and Sam was free, stumbling back, realizing that there were other soggy patches on the carpet. Deborah had poured gasoline all around her before she'd collapsed.

The madwoman touched the flame to her clothes, and instantly burst into flames. Sam stumbled back, fire rising everywhere. She lurched to the far corner of the library, momentarily safe from the blaze. The woman was screeching terribly now, rolling back and forth on the carpet, setting more of it on fire. Books were burning, the heat rising around Sam.

She dashed to the emergency door and pushed it.

The door was locked.

CHAPTER 62

Sam shook the door once, twice, letting out a scream of frustration as she tugged on it a third time, the heat of the flames stinging her back, the room turning hazy with smoke, the fire crackling, and somewhere in the background still that blaring fire alarm, or was it Deborah's screaming—they were intermingling, almost indistinguishable.

Sam turned around. The center of the library between her and the double doors was now in flames, Deborah's inert body hardly visible in the middle of the blaze. Sam dashed sideways, around the fire, back to the double doors, embers flying around her, smoke in her lungs; she had to get out of this inferno—

The door opened.

Hatter, snarling in anger, the fire casting a hellish glare on his face. And then a smile.

"What's cooking, doc?" he roared, then let out a snorting laugh, and another, immensely pleased with himself. He raised the gun.

Sam darted into one of the aisles as the gun blasted. Again. And again. She was running crouched, shielding her head from the fire, from the shots. She glanced back and saw that Hatter wasn't even aiming at her. He was shooting everywhere. At the ceiling, at the aisles, at Deborah's burnt body.

But now he was coming after her, the gun at his side. He didn't want to shoot her. He wanted to kill her with his bare hands.

She zigzagged through the aisles, the smoke so thick she could hardly see where she was going. Somewhere in the room something crashed, a shower of sparks and burning pages flying everywhere. Her throat burned and she kept coughing, holding her jacket over her face. Behind her, Hatter was laughing, or screaming, or crying—it was impossible to tell.

She no longer knew where she was in this maze of books, but there were flames everywhere, and when she accidentally touched a metal shelf, it burned her fingers, and she let out a scream that turned into another endless cough.

A bookshelf collapsed behind her. Glancing around, she saw only flames. But ahead, through the smoke, she spotted the faded blue of the library's double doors.

She forced herself to move, holding her breath, until Hatter shifted into view, blocking the way.

The fire roared behind her. Her eyes darted around, but there was nowhere left to go. And Hatter was lumbering over to her down the aisle, indifferent to the flames. Another shelf collapsed, a shower of embers and sparks falling from above. Sam screamed and crouched, but Hatter just kept walking as they landed on him, still shining with deadly heat. The edge of his sleeve was now on fire, but still he kept on coming, a different flame blazing in his eyes.

He reached her and yanked her up by her hair. She was coughing and screaming, and then nothing, because his hand tightened on her throat, and there was no more air.

Black spots danced in front of her eyes as she stared at his face, twisted with malice. She recalled how he'd told her that he wouldn't have changed a thing. This was what he wanted. Around them, the fire blazed higher, burning page fragments tumbling from above like snowflakes, the smoke turning everything dark, or perhaps the world became dark because there was no air; she was fading away.

A shot and another—he was shooting again . . . but no, his gun was aimed at the floor, and his eyes were widening in surprise and pain, his grip gone, and Sam inhaled deeply, the smoke burning her lungs.

Hatter tumbled to the floor.

Behind him, almost invisible in the gray smoke, stood Jonathan Carver.

The girl slumped to the floor like a rag doll. Carver holstered his gun and hurried to her side. The heat was intolerable. He had to get her away from the flames. He scooped her, hefting her to his shoulder. Then he turned around, carrying her through the billowing smoke to the double doors.

As he got closer, a tall bookshelf collapsed sideways, showering burning embers around it and blocking the way. Something stung Carver's arm, and he hurriedly brushed away a red-hot shimmering ember from his sleeve.

His lungs and throat burned. He had to get them out of there soon. Smoke inhalation could kill them just as the flames could. Whirling around, he barely glimpsed the other door, the emergency exit light above it. The carpet between them and the door was burning in many sections, but he saw no other way to do it.

Sam coughed on his shoulder, twisting sharply. He adjusted her, trying to hold her as high as possible.

"Sam!" he shouted. "I'm about to run for the door. I got you, but you have to stay still, okay? Don't struggle." He ended with a series of coughs.

She seemed to relax. Carver steeled himself and strode as fast as he could through the burning room. He spotted a blackened figure lying in the flames but didn't slow down, kept going. A fire blazing ahead of him. He shifted so that Sam was protected by his body from the flames.

Walked right past it, his sleeve smoking, a part of his shoe starting to burn. He dragged it on the floor, killing the flames, kept moving, he could hardly breathe, the flames were turning his face into a crisp, Sam was completely inert, he hoped she was okay, couldn't check, couldn't see anything, not even the door.

A wall. How had he ended up here? Where was the damn door? He coughed and retched, turning around. Left or right? Maybe he'd veered too far to the right. He turned left, stayed close to the wall as he took one step and another. And another. The strength slowly fading from his body with the lack of oxygen.

There! The door. He touched the doorknob, and pulled back, hissing. It was boiling. Shifting his sleeve to protect his hand, he grabbed the knob again and turned it. Rattled the door.

Locked.

No time to mess around. Gently he set Sam against the wall. Her eyelids fluttered.

"Just one second, Sam, hang on for me, okay?"

She nodded faintly.

He took a step back, and launched a kick, narrowly missing the doorknob. The door burst open, and at that moment the fire roared as a mass of oxygen flooded into the room, feeding the flames. Carver's back was burning, but he ignored it; scooping Sam, he lunged out of the library, leaving the inferno behind.

Already he was surrounded by people. Someone was yelling at him to stay still as they slapped him, killing the multiple blazes on the back of his shirt. He still held on to Sam, blinking, taking in lungfuls of air, and then he saw a small blonde woman running toward him, and he smiled at her, feeling that he might collapse soon, but it would really be nice if he could stay standing for just a few seconds more.

Someone helped Sam off his shoulders, and now the girl was in Abby's arms. And Carver stood by, grinning, because everything was finally all right now.

CHAPTER 63

Abby kept touching Sam. Caressing her hair, taking her hand, giving her yet another hug. Sam never once told her to stop.

She sat on the edge of the ambulance, an oxygen mask on. They wanted to take her to the hospital, but Sam wouldn't go, not even when Abby said she would come with her. She said over and over that she just wanted to go home. Finally, exasperated, the medic placed the mask on Sam's face and gave her some space.

"How are you feeling?" Abby asked for the fourth . . . no, fifth time. "Blink once for *good*, twice for *bad*, three times for *Mom, you're annoying me*."

Sam blinked three times.

"Almost back to normal, then." Abby squeezed Sam's hand.

Now that Sam was safe, the life-threatening danger gone, all the anxieties that had waited for their turn during the past twenty-four hours bloomed in Abby's mind. Sam had gone through a hellish, violent experience. She'd seen several people die terribly. From what Carver had said, she was being strangled by Hatter when he'd saved her. The bruises on Sam's neck told the same story. Beyond the physical injuries, Abby was fully aware of how harmful such a traumatic event could be.

She didn't let the worry show. Sam would need support and patience from her mom. And Abby would give her just that.

"Oh, look who's here." Abby touched Sam's shoulder and pointed.

Steve had been let into the cordoned-off area and was looking around him, seeming lost and confused. This wasn't his scene, surrounded by firefighters and cops and blaring sirens. Abby waved to him, and as soon as he noticed her, a smile materialized on his face, and he ran over and hugged Sam, tears in his eyes.

"Just watch her mask, Steve," Abby said.

Relief was etched on his face. They'd just gotten their daughter back.

Finally he drew back. "How are you feeling?" he asked Sam.

Sam rolled her eyes.

"We'll take her to a doctor later for a full checkup," Abby said. "But it looks like she'll be fine."

Steve exhaled. "Okay."

"Is Ben at school?"

"No, he hardly slept last night. I left him at your house with Gina."

Gina was Steve's niece, and he occasionally used her as a babysitter for Ben. Abby's issues with that were many, because Gina let Ben eat as much candy as he wanted, didn't really care if he watched TV past his bedtime, and often talked in a way that wasn't fitting for an eight-year-old's ears. But then again, Steve let the kids eat as much candy as they wanted, didn't care if they watched TV past their bedtime, and often talked in a way that wasn't fitting for *anyone's* ears. So there was that.

The medic came over and took off Sam's mask. "How are you feeling?" he asked, examining her eyes. "Do you have a headache? Shortness of breath?"

"Not really." Sam's voice was raspy.

The medic glanced into her nostrils with a small flashlight. "Well, it could have been much worse. But you should go see a doctor to be safe."

"Can I go home, see my brother, and have a shower?" Sam pleaded.

"We live really close by," Abby said.

The medic shrugged. "Okay. Just don't wait too long with it." He took one last look at Sam, and walked away.

"Where's Carver?" Sam asked.

"They took him to the hospital," Abby said. "He had a few burns, and he also inhaled a lot of smoke, like you."

"Burns? Is he okay?" Sam asked in alarm.

"Yes, he's really fine. It was nothing serious."

"Who's Carver?" Steve asked.

"He's Mom's—"

"He's a detective who helped out and saved Sam's life," Abby interrupted. "He ran into the fire and got Sam out."

Sam's eyes glazed; her jaw clenched. It was obviously too early to talk about it. And Abby knew that Carver hadn't just saved Sam from the fire.

"Well, I'll definitely talk to him and thank him myself," Steve said. "Maybe we should get him flowers and a thank-you note or something."

"We should *definitely* do that," Sam said brightly. "He'd love to get flowers from you, Dad. And I'm sure Mom can find out his phone number, right, Mom?"

Abby would have been annoyed, except that it was such a relief to see her daughter enjoy her own mischief. She found herself grinning at Sam. "Yeah, I probably can."

"Okay." Steve frowned. He wasn't thick, and could usually sense when someone was putting him on. "Come on, I'll take you home."

"My car is actually still here," Abby said. "I'll drive on my own."

"Oh." Steve's face fell.

"But I'd love it if you could grab breakfast for all of us on the way," Abby said.

Spending any amount of time with Steve wasn't Abby's favorite thing. But Sam needed both her parents right now.

"No problem! Starbucks or Dunkin' Donuts?" Steve asked.

"Those are the only options?" Abby raised an eyebrow.

"Dunkin' Donuts," Sam said.

"You want to come with me and pick your donuts?" Steve asked Sam.

"Sure, Dad. Because I really want to go somewhere smelling like a campfire and looking like a war refugee." Sam shook her head.

"Oh, good, your sarcasm isn't hurt either," Steve said dryly. "I'll see you at your mom's place." He gave Sam another long hug and walked away.

"Okay." Abby touched Sam's arm. "Let's go home."

CHAPTER 64

It seemed incredible to Abby that there was traffic in the streets. Rationally, she knew that this was rush hour, and everyone was on their way to work, a typical morning in the city. But after what Sam and she had gone through in the past twenty-four hours, it seemed right for people to take a day off, spend time with their families. It was like sitting in a restaurant after you'd finished your meal, just waiting for the check, staring at all those people around you eating, as if they had a reason to be hungry. Didn't they know how stuffed you were?

She glanced at Sam worriedly. Her daughter was staring silently out the passenger window. Abby ran the backs of her fingers down Sam's hair, letting her know that she was there.

"Mom," Sam said. "You know that woman, Deborah, who came inside? The one who set herself on fire?"

"Yes," Abby said. Sam had told her about it briefly before, not going into details. Abby had her own theories about it.

"She kept talking about the Messiah. And about me. Like she was my guardian angel."

"She seemed to be a religious fanatic," Abby said. "We'll definitely look into her past."

"Yes, but . . . she knew who I was. She instantly recognized me. She said I was the blood of the Messiah. That she could see it in my eyes."

"It must have been very upsetting."

"She freaked me out. She said that she would take me to see some sort of priest."

The car lurched as Abby hit the gas pedal too strongly. "What priest?"

"I don't know; she didn't say." Sam let out a long breath. "She tried to set us both on fire. She said the fire would cleanse us."

"I'm just glad Carver managed to get to you in time." Abby's voice trembled.

"Her screams when she burned . . ." Sam wiped a tear. "Why would she do that? Why would anyone do that to themselves?"

Abby sighed. "People sometimes make terrible mistakes."

Sam leaned her head on the window. "Is Fiona okay?"

"I haven't seen her, but they told me she's fine. And Ray and Mr. Bell too. Mrs. Nelson apparently has a mild concussion."

"Did they arrest Caterpillar and Alma?"

"Yes."

"Alma didn't want all of that to happen. Do you think she'll go to prison?"

"Yes. But I'll make sure that the prosecutor knows she cooperated with us in the end."

"I wasn't sure if I should give her the phone."

Abby caressed her daughter's hair again. "I think you probably saved a few lives."

"I couldn't save Mr. Ramirez." Sam's lips trembled.

"You did more than anyone could expect, sweetie. You saved more lives than any of us outside the school. You have no idea how proud I am of you."

"Okay." Sam sniffed. "I want to see Ben."

"We'll be back home in ten minutes."

"Okay."

Sam shut her eyes, leaning her head against the window. Abby smiled at her, then nearly ran into the car in front, which had stopped too suddenly. It would be incredibly dumb to have an accident after everything. She forced herself to focus on the road.

Abby's phone rang, startling Sam. Abby answered it. "Hello?"

"Hi, Abby, it's Gina." Steve's niece's voice was shrill, coming from the speakerphone.

"Hey, Gina, we'll be home in about ten minutes."

"Oh, good, Ben still hasn't woken up. He'll be so glad that you're home. And your father is here."

"He is?" Abby smiled in surprise.

"Yeah. He wants to take Ben to the park for a bit. He's really nice."

Something in the way she said it drove a jolt of alarm into Abby's mind. She talked as if it was the first time she'd met him. "Gina, is my mom also there?"

"No, just your dad. I hardly recognized him; I think last time I saw him was at your wedding. But, I mean, you can't mistake him, right? You two are so similar."

They obviously were not. Abby was adopted, and her dad was as different from her as could be. And what was he doing there without Mom? As a matter of fact, how did he even know to go there? When they talked the previous day, Abby told her parents that Ben was at Steve's.

"Gina, he didn't already take him to the park, right?" Abby asked, the fear tainting her voice.

"No, that's why I called. To make sure it's all right. Ben is actually still sleeping. Your dad is waiting outside."

"Lock the front door and go to Ben's room right now. Don't let him out of your sight."

"Okay, what's wrong?"

"Just do it, right now. Don't let that man take Ben anywhere. Don't let him into the house. He's not my father."

"Okay, I'm going." Gina's voice trembled.

"Mom, what is it?" Sam asked.

"Gina? Did you lock the door?" Abby switched on the siren, flooring the gas pedal.

"Um . . . yes. I'm going to Ben's room right now."

"Okay, I'm hanging up. I'll be there in a few minutes." She hung up.

"Mom, what's going on?" Sam asked in alarm.

"Sweetie, grab my phone from my bag and dial 911." Abby hit the horn repeatedly, clenching her jaw. She veered to the opposite lane, drove past two cars, then had to swing back as a car in front of her honked and flashed frantically.

"Why? Who is it at our house?"

"I don't know. Not Grandpa."

You two are so similar.

For a second she thought of her other father. The one in the newspaper clipping.

You two are so similar.

But that was the thing. They weren't similar either. Abby had taken most of her looks from her mom. And her biological father was dead; she was sure of that. Then who was it at her house? Not her dad.

She instantly recognized me. She said I was the blood of the Messiah. That she could see it in my eyes.

Sam had Abby's eyes.

That woman had said that the blood of the Messiah must be freed. She'd been talking about Sam. She wasn't just talking about someone descended from the Wilcox cult.

"Nine-one-one, what's your emergency?" A woman's voice blared from her phone's speaker.

"This is Lieutenant Abby Mullen." Abby swerved to avoid hitting a motorcycle. A long honk. Sam screamed in fear. "I need a patrol car to drive to my home address. I think there might be an intruder there."

She gave dispatch the address. Red light. She slowed down despite herself, wishing Sam weren't in the car with her. A school bus drove past, and Abby hit the gas, the car lurching between the bus and a pickup truck, which stopped violently, breaks screeching.

The blood of the Messiah.

They were minutes away. She blazed through their neighborhood, siren screeching, wishing she could go even faster. She thought of Ben, lying in his bed, and that man outside, that stranger, who wanted to take him to the park. Her teeth clenched tightly as they hurtled down the street, the world a blur.

Finally, they reached home. Abby hit the brakes, one of the car's wheels hitting the curb. She breathlessly stared out the window. The house seemed dark. No movement inside.

"Stay in the car," she said.

"Mom, what's going on?" Sam whispered.

Abby looked around the street, searching for any sign of that man Gina was talking about. Nothing. "I'll handle it, sweetie. Just stay in the car. Lock the doors."

She grabbed her phone, stepped out of the car, and gently shut the door, making sure it didn't slam. She put a hand on her holster as she crept to the front door. She tried the doorknob. Locked.

After unlocking the door, she stepped in, holding her breath. Stepping lightly, she went straight for Ben's room. The door was shut.

She flung it open.

Ben was sitting on his bed, looking sleepy and confused. Gina stood by his side, eyes tearstained. She held one of Ben's thick illustrated encyclopedias, hand stretched back as if she intended to throw it at anyone who came through the door. Her body sagged in relief when she saw Abby.

"I didn't let him in," Gina blurted. "He knocked and rang the doorbell, but I didn't let him in."

Abby nodded and glanced through the window at the street. Sam was still in the car, waiting, pale with fear.

There was no one else there.

CHAPTER 65

Abby lay in bed, in the dark. To her left and right, the dormant forms of her children, their breathing heavy in their sleep.

The day had been chaotic, even if she ignored the events of that morning. Reassuring Gina, talking to the cops who showed up. Then Steve arrived, with a box of donuts and a horrified expression. She had to somehow manage it all, then take Sam to the hospital to get her checked, which meant Steve and Ben tagging along because no one wanted to be left behind, and Sam burst into tears twice in the hospital, and Steve kept asking about that man who had shown up at their house, and Sam kept asking to see Fiona, and . . .

It had been a hectic day.

Neither Ben nor Sam had wanted to sleep alone, and somehow they'd both ended up in Abby's bed. Which was *just fine* with her. Because frankly, she didn't want to take her eyes off either of them ever again. They would just stay in her bedroom. *No more school, kids, Mom is too terrified to let you out of her sight.*

She sighed heavily. She'd thought she'd fall asleep too. Her sleep deprivation was dangerously close to the stage of hallucinations.

But she couldn't sleep. Not yet.

Carefully, she pried Ben's hand off her. She slowly got up and crept out of the room, glancing back at the kids. Her two beautiful kids.

She sat by the dining table and opened her chat with Moses Wilcox on her phone.

Slowly, she tapped on the phone. You came by my house today.

She watched as the chat indicated that he saw her message. Would he deny it? Or would he say he'd just wanted to visit?

Whatever he wrote, it essentially didn't matter. She wanted his answer because it would give the cyber team something to work with. They would be able to figure out his approximate location. In fact, even by opening the chat just now and seeing her message, he'd probably done enough. They would get him.

Still, she wanted to see what he would write.

A few minutes went by. She stared at the screen so hard that when she shut her eyes, she could still see its rectangular imprint, framed in the darkness. He wasn't about to answer.

The phone began ringing.

She opened her eyes, startled, nearly dropping the phone. A video chat.

Getting up, she stepped out of the house, the phone still ringing in her hand. She walked to her car, slid in, shut the door. The phone still rang.

She slid her finger across the screen. A face materialized.

She remembered Moses the way a seven-year-old remembered a figure of authority. Bigger than life. Powerful. Scary. The face that appeared on screen was not that. His long hair had gone silver, and wrinkles lined his face. He wore glasses now. But the eyes behind those glasses were the same, piercingly sharp. Like a predator's eyes. And they made her feel like prey.

"Hello, Abihail," he said.

She needed to keep him talking. The more he talked, the easier it would be to find him. They would have more information to use.

"Hello, Moses," she said. Not the trained, calm voice of a negotiator. The strangled, panicky voice of a seven-year-old girl, afraid of her almighty preacher. "I'm . . . I'm glad you called."

He narrowed his eyes. "Are you?"

He was far from stupid, and she'd told him on their chats numerous times throughout the years, assuming he was Isaac, how she despised Moses Wilcox.

"Yes." She was regaining her self-control. She wasn't seven. She wasn't in his clutches anymore. He'd called, which meant he wanted to talk to her. "We have a lot to talk about."

He nodded thoughtfully. "How is Sam?"

"She's okay. Sleeping. She told me she met someone you knew. A woman named Deborah."

He seemed satisfied at that. "A very devout woman. You would have liked her. Where is Deborah now?"

Abby was almost sure he knew the answer to that. "She's dead. There was a fire."

His face remained impassive. "Ah. 'He will baptize you with the Holy Spirit and fire.'"

Bible quotes were Moses's armor, and he loved hiding behind them. If she asked him what it meant, the conversation would devolve into a religious discussion that he would dominate by twisting the meaning of verses to match his own needs. She briefly contemplated going down that road. It would definitely keep him talking. But she would get nothing out of that conversation. And there were things she needed to know.

"Why did you send Deborah to that school?"

"I didn't send her anywhere, Abihail. She volunteered. I told her that my granddaughter was in trouble, and Deborah immediately said she would try to help. She was a resourceful woman."

There it was. He didn't skirt around it. Abby took a long, shuddering breath.

"Is she really your granddaughter?"

"What do you think?" Moses asked.

What *did* she think? Her biological mother had joined the Wilcox cult when she was in her twenties. What would Moses Wilcox do with an attractive young woman who would do anything he said?

You two are so similar.

They were. She saw it. Same eyebrows, same chin. Same eyes.

As a child, she'd always known that her destiny was to bear Moses Wilcox's descendants, who would be the warrior angels that protected the survivors of the apocalypse. She'd always assumed it meant that she was supposed to marry him and have his children.

But perhaps any child she had was *already* Moses's descendant.

"I think you called me Abihail for a reason," she finally said.

He smiled at her, looking pleased. "Yes. That's exactly right."

Abihail. In Hebrew, it meant "my father the brave." And, of course, a narcissist like Moses would never give that name to another man's child.

"You're my father."

"Of course I am. And now that we finally get a chance to talk, isn't there something you want to say to me?"

What did he want to hear? This was what this phone call was all about.

"I don't know," she said carefully. "I haven't seen you for so long; there's so much to talk about."

"Why don't we start with First Thessalonians chapter five, verse eighteen," he said sharply, his eyes narrowing.

Another test, one she'd inevitably fail. "I've been neglecting my Bible studies. Haven't quite found a teacher to match you," she said.

"Let me refresh your memory." He was getting angrier, raising his voice. "'Give thanks in all circumstances; for this is God's will for you in Christ Jesus.'"

He wanted her to thank him. The idea was so preposterous she nearly let out a snort. But it didn't really matter. She thanked psychos and tweakers and abusive husbands all the time. Thanked them for talking to her on the phone, thanked them for not killing the hostages, thanked them for losing their shit just a little and not a lot. *Thank you* was one of the cheapest phrases in her arsenal.

"Thank you, for helping me survive that night in the fire," she said. "And for teaching me. And for sending a woman to protect and save Sam. And for listening to me and providing me comfort through all these difficult years."

The way he smiled. So full of satisfaction. She had to curb her reflex to roll her eyes.

"You're welcome," he said benevolently.

"It was you who came by the house earlier, right?"

"Yes. But unfortunately, you weren't there."

He was never looking for her. He'd known she'd be away. "I heard you wanted to take Ben for a walk in the park."

"I wanted to meet my grandson."

"And Sam told me that Deborah said she wanted to take her to see you."

For a second he remained silent. Then he smiled at her. "They're my grandchildren, Abihail. They belong with my flock."

She could feel her self-control dissipating almost instantly. A surge of anger intermingled with fear washed over her. "You stay away from us, you son of a bitch," she snarled. "If you ever set a foot near us, I'll kill you. You got that?"

He blinked, surprised. She gripped the phone tightly, wishing she could shove her hand through and grip his scrawny neck.

"Beware the fire that burns within you, my child," he finally said. "For it will consume you whole."

He shifted, and she realized he was about to hang up the call. Quickly, she pressed the phone volume button, coupled with the power, hearing that satisfying click of the phone's screenshot. A fragment of a second later, the call went dark.

She tapped her screen, opening her images. The most recent image appeared on top, a blurry image of Moses Wilcox. The image caught him when he was blinking, one of his eyes shut, his mouth curved in a half-mocking smile. It made him look like a demented imp.

"I'm coming for you, you bastard," Abby whispered at the image on her phone.

CHAPTER 66

After two days in jail, Caterpillar couldn't figure out why he was still alive.

At first, when the police had burst into the room, he was sure it was the end. They would either shoot him on the spot or take him to a dark room somewhere and execute him. Sure, they would later claim he'd "committed suicide" like Jeffrey Epstein or Johnny J. And even if people suspected the truth, they'd have no proof. Caterpillar would be gone, the truth once again swept aside.

Except instead, they booked him, and put him in jail . . . with other people.

Which was when he realized he was about to be assassinated by one of the inmates. He endlessly tried to assess who the agent would be. That big guy with the swastika tattoo on his neck? The fat, bald Latino guy who kept eyeing him from the corner? No—it must be that apparently harmless thin man shivering on the cot, just biding his time, waiting for the right moment.

He hardly slept, staying alert, preparing himself for the inevitable assault.

But whoever the assassin was, he must have figured out that Caterpillar was ready for him. The attack never came.

He talked to Georgia on the phone. She wanted him to get an attorney, but why would he? They would never let him walk. He had no doubt that he would be tried by a judge the Circle chose, in front of jurors the Circle would pick. The prosecutor would be their agent, and even Caterpillar's own defense attorney would probably be under the Circle's thumb.

No, best keep his money for Georgia, instead of wasting it trying to squirm free within a corrupt system.

And now they were taking him in front of a judge, for his arraignment. He had a court-appointed defense attorney. A gray-haired woman whose lips pursed disapprovingly when they talked, as if she already knew he was a lost cause. Which he was.

They led him into the court, hands cuffed in front of him, armed guards everywhere. He glimpsed Georgia in the crowd, glanced at her briefly. Her eyes were puffy, her hair in disarray. His heart twinged at seeing her like that. It hurt that she had to pay for her father's cause, even if it was just and right.

The judge stepped in, a severe man with a mole above his lip, and they all rose. The judge stared at him, and Caterpillar looked back, knowing that each knew who the other was. Did the judge smirk, or was it Caterpillar's imagination? How much had they given him to throw Caterpillar away for the rest of his life?

The judge read the case number, a series of numbers that Caterpillar hoped someone was noting down. A fellow Watcher, checking to see if the number was a code or just random digits that meant nothing. He said it was the case of *The People v. Theodor Quinn*, and maybe it was true, because it was him against a very small, shadowy group of people. And then his own defense attorney said they were "waiving the reading," just like that. Caterpillar had known it from the start: she was one of them, and they were all working together to rush the process, make him disappear.

He waited for the judge to ask him how he pleaded, but to his surprise, that didn't happen as he expected. The judge asked, "How does the defendant plead?" and *his own attorney* answered for him, saying that he pleaded not guilty. And now they were already talking about timelines, and notices, and motions. They were about to rush him out without letting him utter a single word.

He looked behind him. There were a few people there, and two of them watched him intently. One of them, a woman with curly brown hair and a pink sweater, mouthed something.

The Circle cannot reach us.

A Watcher. Here with him.

He cleared his throat. "Um . . . I didn't plead yet."

The judge stopped talking and eyed him dispassionately. "Your defense attorney said you pleaded not guilty."

"Don't I get a say in it?"

Now his defense attorney was leaning over, whispering frantically in his ear. But he ignored her, standing up.

The Circle had underestimated him. And they would regret it.

"The DAS system is connected to eighteen thousand security cameras, spread throughout the city," Caterpillar said aloud. "And in the last ten years, the NYPD has acquired six submarine drones. But is it really the NYPD in charge of all these capabilities? And is it really only in New York? Or are similar systems hooked up all over the United States?"

Someone was shouting at him, his defense attorney pulling his sleeve, an armed guard already making his way over to him.

"How are the surveillance networks related to Christopher Columbus High?" Caterpillar was screaming now. "Why did the police set fire to it? Think of its exact location! Why did they set an ambush for two Watchers? That's right, *two* Watchers, because the third was a double agent! What's connecting all these together?"

He was being dragged out of the court, and he stared at the pews in the back, at Georgia and his fellow Watcher.

"Do your research!" he yelled. "Who gains? What's their endgame? Don't take my word for it! Do your research!"

Someone slammed him against the wall, but he didn't care. Even if they killed him now, it was too late. In an hour, his fellow Watchers would understand what he'd understood. The extent of the Circle's conspiracy. And they'd do everything they could to expose the Circle, to stop them once and for all.

The Circle cannot reach us.

He grinned as they led him away and muttered, "They can't stop what's coming."

CHAPTER 67

It was Steve's weekend with the kids, and after almost a whole day without seeing them, Abby felt like a rubber band, stretched to the point of breaking. Sure, she'd called Sam twice, once pretending to be unable to find the remote control to the TV, and a few hours later not even trying to pretend anymore, just calling to hear her voice, make sure that everything was all right.

But it wasn't the same as being with them. Looking at them with her own eyes.

Sam had already been complaining that Abby was looking at her "like some creepy weirdo." And she probably didn't even know that Abby sometimes crept into her room at night, just to verify she was safely in her bed. Because it was true: Abby really was some creepy weirdo, stalking her own daughter.

But now, her kids were in one of the places in New York Abby couldn't go to uninvited. Her ex-husband's home. Yeah, sure, she could invite herself in, but the sheer amount of patronizing commentary from Steve was keeping her away. He'd already mansplained to her twice about PTSD, *and* had suggested that she go to a therapist to discuss what had happened "just to be sure." Naturally, when she'd asked him if he'd seen a therapist, he'd just stared at her in confusion.

Staying home was also difficult, because the kids' rooms were so empty. Unless one counted the dog, spider, snake, chameleon, and vivarium with the crickets. But Abby didn't.

So she'd gone to Carver's.

Part of her still wanted to take it slow, to keep him at arm's length. She'd gone through *so much* in the past few months that she felt like her mind had been trampled by a herd of buffalo. She told herself she was just going to eat dinner and spend a comforting evening with him.

He opened a bottle of wine after dinner as they sat on the couch, and she drank a glass. And another. A third one would mean that she wouldn't be able to drive home.

"You know," Carver said, "my sister told me this amazing story about whales today."

"Which sister?" Abby asked. "You have, like, a bazillion."

"I have four sisters. But when I say I talked to my sister, I always mean Holly."

"What would you say if you talked to, um . . ." She tried to recall the other ones' names. "Dana?"

"I'd say I talked to Dana."

"Why? Is Holly your favorite?"

Carver frowned. "No, I just talk to her the most . . . you're interrupting my story."

"Sorry." Abby emptied her second glass.

"Okay. So they talk in different frequencies."

"Your sisters?"

"What? No. Whales. Whales talk in different frequencies." A small smile curled his lips, and Abby was momentarily distracted by the beautiful shape of his mouth, the crinkles at the corners of his eyes that gave him a warm expression. He was only a few inches from her, and the heat from his body radiated against her skin. He wore a sweater of thin wool that looked deliciously soft. Her knee touched his, her skirt riding up just a little.

It took her a moment to realize what he'd actually said, and that she was staring at him. "Whales. Right."

Amusement danced in his eyes. "They call each other from dozens of miles away. That's how they find each other in the ocean. Different whale species use different frequencies so they don't get their wires crossed. So one whale calls, and then the others answer."

She didn't want to leave here. She wanted to stay and listen to him talk all night. The warm light in Carver's apartment gave his tanned skin an even more golden look. She found herself leaning toward him. "I might have another glass."

"Of course." He smiled at her, lifting the bottle to pour it for her. His arm brushed against hers, and she licked her lips.

"Where was I?" he asked.

"Different frequencies."

"Right. So scientists recorded this one whale. Really deep in icy waters. And he calls out in a completely different frequency than anyone else. So none of them ever answer him. *Ever.* He swims in that cold dark ocean. Calling out for someone to be his friend. Or someone to fall in love with. But no one ever answers him."

"That's so sad."

"Yeah. Are you crying?"

"No." But a tear was running down her cheek, and she wiped it away. She took a large sip.

She spent her days figuring out what other people wanted. Choosing her words and her tone carefully to make them feel safer and calmer. But this night was about what *she* wanted. What she needed.

She could feel the wine settling in her mind, coating all those jagged edges, muffling them. And more than that . . . right now, it was her way of making a decision in that most subtle of ways. Definitely too many glasses of wine to drive. Sure, she could take an Uber, but . . . even better, she could not do that. And really, if she was honest with herself, she'd come here prepared to spend the night. She didn't put on the good silky black underwear for just any occasion—and certainly not with a matching bra.

She leaned a little closer into Carver, her arm against his merino sweater. She felt completely safe with him, and yet she still felt a chill in her chest. "You know, I could have gotten the whale to talk to the others better."

The corner of his mouth quirked. "You could?"

"Yeah, I don't know if I ever told you, but I'm a pretty good negotiator. I can get almost anyone to talk to me."

"Really?" He lowered his voice, his face moving closer to hers. "How would you do that?"

"Well, first of all, I'd listen. And I'd repeat his words to him, to make him feel like he was being heard."

A line formed between his eyebrows, and he looked as if this were the most serious topic in the world. "So he would say *mmmmmmmmmmmmmmmm.*"

"Is that your whale impression?"

"Mind your tone. It's a perfect impression." When he smiled, the tiny scar on his chin shifted just a bit, giving his grin a sort of sexy, devilish twist.

She took a large sip from the wine, her head already spinning a bit. Its taste rich and silky as it rippled on her tongue. "Right. So I would say *mmmmmmmmmmmm* back to him. You know, repeating his words. I might rephrase them a bit, for a positive context, like this: *mmmmmmmmmmmmm.*"

"But in the right frequency."

"Definitely. I talk to everyone in the right frequency. It's a basic negotiator principle."

Carver's green eyes sparkled. "What then?"

"I'd ask him an open-ended question. To get him to elaborate."

He nodded. "So you'd say something like, *Do you like fish?*"

Abby had the strongest urge to reach out and touch the side of his face, but she kept her hand around the wineglass. "No. That's a yes-or-no question. That kills the dialogue. I'd say, *Why are fish important to you?* Or, *How can I help you with fish?*"

He shifted closer to her, seemingly entranced. "And what then?"

She put her glass on the table, then turned her body toward his. "Then," she whispered, her face just inches from his, "I'd find out what he really wanted."

He placed his glass on the table and turned back to face Abby. He slid his hand around the back of her neck, and pressed his lips against hers. It started out tentative, as if they were both unsure how the other one felt. Then Abby found her mouth opening, her tongue sweeping in to brush against his. He caressed the back of her neck as he kissed her, his other hand on her waist.

As the kiss deepened, Abby found herself wanting to press her body against his.

Her pulse raced, and she slid her fingers under the soft wool of his sweater.

She pulled away from the kiss with a nip to his lower lip, moving her hands up his abs. She pulled his sweater all the way off, and her eyes roamed over his body. "I want you," she whispered.

His gaze lowered to her shirt, and he started to unbutton it. Abby's breath shallowed at the feel of his hands grazing her breasts as he took it off. When he'd pulled the shirt off completely, she reached behind her back to unhook her bra. She leaned back, lying on the couch, and she pulled him on top of her. Her legs wrapped around him as he pressed his mouth against her neck, kissing her. He trailed heated kisses down her throat, her chest.

But she needed more of him, and she reached down to unbutton his pants, pull off his underwear. He slid his hands under her skirt, pulling off her good silky underwear that she didn't put on for just any occasion. He moved in closer, kissing her deeply. As they intertwined, for the first time in ages her mind was empty, aside from that all-encompassing, sweet desire.

CHAPTER 68

The book aisle seemed endless. Sam was running as fast as she could, not knowing where to go. She only knew what she was running from. He was behind her; she could hear his labored breaths, smell his stench, and when he would catch her, his hand would tighten on her throat, and she wouldn't be able to breathe. Fire licked at her feet, the books around her burning, a short, crazed laugh behind her, she tried to run faster but he was gaining on her, and the aisle was getting narrower, now she couldn't even run, she was squirming through the burning books, a hand pawing her from behind—

Sam sat up in bed, breathing hard, reflexively hitting the night-light, switching it on. She'd been going to bed with the night-light on every night lately. But Mom kept switching it off after she fell asleep.

Not that there was a lot of sleep going on. Ever since that horrifying day, Sam hadn't managed to sleep through an entire night. The psychologist said it was expected. And anyway, she was doing better than Ray, who couldn't even enter the school building.

It would have been fine, if she could only play the violin. But she couldn't. The first time she'd tried, her heart raced, and she could hardly breathe. The next few times weren't much better. And now she didn't even want to touch it. Two weeks without playing the violin. She used to think that would happen only if she broke all her fingers.

Her psychologist had her write down all the things she was avoiding, grading the anxiety levels they caused. The list lay on her desk, where she constantly tweaked it.

Playing the violin—7

Going to school in the morning—3

Going to the school cafeteria—9

Wearing a turtleneck sweater or a necklace—6

Sitting in a classroom when the door is shut—4

Going to the music room at school—10

On and on the list went. Supposedly she could break down the activities to train herself. For example, holding the violin without playing it was merely a four on her anxiety list, so she could do that a few times a day. Which was its own special kind of torture.

Right now she tried to do her breathing exercises. Last night she'd managed to fall back to sleep within a few minutes. But the recent nightmare was too raw and vivid in her mind; she just couldn't calm down.

Some nights she dragged her mattress to Ben's room and slept there. Here was something that didn't scare her any longer—his snake and spider. She didn't mind them one bit. But tonight she couldn't bring herself to do it, to face Mom's sad look tomorrow when she saw that Sam had spent another sleepless night. *No. Better to just lie here until morning.*

She stared at the ceiling, thinking of that moment when Deborah had grabbed her. That grip on her wrist. She played it over and over in her mind.

It was then that she noticed that she was humming. Three quick notes, over and over. She tried to figure out which song she was humming, but no, it wasn't any song that she knew. She was humming that moment, that grip, the icy fear in her chest, her own attempt to tug herself away.

It had a tune.

Surprised, she conjured the image of the cafeteria, Hatter dragging her, the police looking at them helplessly from outside. That unbearable minute had a rhythm in itself. And a single clear chord.

She sat up, throwing her blanket off. Keebles, who lay asleep in the corner of the room, raised her head, then let out a deep sigh and went back to sleep, already used to Sam's erratic nighttime activities. Sam got out of bed and grabbed her violin.

Her electric violin wasn't completely silent, but when it wasn't plugged into the speakers and the door was closed, it could barely be heard outside her room. Which was probably for the best, if she wanted to play at two in the morning. She plugged it into her headphones and placed it under her chin. Her heart was thudding, fear and excitement intermingling in her chest.

Where to start? She pictured those first moments, when they'd heard screaming outside the music room. The beginning of it all.

Yes, that moment had a shape too. She tugged her bow across the strings, an angry, violent tune cascading through her earphones. No, it had gotten lost somewhere between her mind and her fingers. She conjured the image again. Faster tempo, irregular, a series of jarring, sharp notes. She tried once more, getting it closer this time.

She kept going, picturing those tense minutes fraught with fear and uncertainty, not knowing if they should keep hiding or leave the room. Dense music in a chaotic tempo, and then . . . a long pause. Almost too long, tugging at anyone who listened, a reflection of what she'd felt, listening desperately at the door, hearing nothing. Followed by a flurry of notes, chasing each other, the final buildup before they opened the door.

She was breathing heavily when she was done. Her entire body was shaking.

And then she played it again.

She recorded the entire thing. Two minutes and thirty-six seconds of music from her own mind. She tried to write the notes down on paper. She'd never composed anything before, had no idea how to go about it. The process was strange and reversed, like slowly removing food from your mouth and placing it on your plate until it was full. She'd play a few notes, try to understand what she'd just played, write it down. Then she would try to play what she'd written down to see if she'd gotten it right. Little by little she got the whole thing written.

Three thirty in the morning, and she still couldn't fall asleep, not because she was scared but because she was excited. She took out her phone and messaged Fiona that most frequently messaged word in the history of chats.

Awake?

Both of them were hardly sleeping, and she wasn't surprised when Fiona answered. Yup. No sleep

I'm sending you something. A piece I wrote

Sam sent Fiona the audio and then almost instantly regretted it. Fiona would say it was horrible. Or she'd say that she knew this song; wasn't it from a Green Day album? Did Sam really think she'd come up with it? It was a well-known song. Or she would say it was trite. Or she'd say it was really nice, which was even worse. Or she'd—

Sam, this is amaaaaaazing! Did you write this???

Sam grinned. Yeah. Just now.

What's it called?

What was it called?

It's called "No Way Out."

She watched the chat window as the three dots appeared, then disappeared, then reappeared again.

I think this needs drums

Sam could hug Fiona right now. She checked the time. Twenty past four in the morning.

Well, we have a few hours until school starts.

CHAPTER 69

Today was better. Abby was sure of it. Although Sam's eyes had still been sunken and bloodshot, there was a bounce in her step that Abby hadn't seen for quite a while. And she had her violin case on her shoulder when she'd left for school. Abby allowed herself a moment of hope.

She needed to get to work; she was already late. But instead, she went to the garage and uncovered the large board hanging on the wall. She took a step back, examining the articles, the photos, her own written notes. That common photo of Moses Wilcox from all those years ago, obtainable with a quick Google search, taped on top. Next to it, she'd taped the blurry image from her phone. Moses, gray haired and wrinkled.

It had taken her a few days to get the warrant to retrieve the location of his phone from their video chat. He'd called her from Stewartstown in Pennsylvania. The local police asked around, but no one recognized the man in the photo. In her screenshot, it seemed like he was sitting in a tiny wooden room. The corner of a bed could be glimpsed behind him. She'd assumed it was from a local motel or Airbnb, but so far they hadn't located it.

She planned on going there herself sometime soon.

The phone he'd used to talk to her had been turned off, and he didn't turn it on again. He didn't check the messages she left on their chat, and ignored her attempts at calling him. He'd effectively disappeared.

The board was a bedlam of leads and attempts to trace the where-abouts of Moses Wilcox ever since the night of the Wilcox Cult Massacre.

Names and contact details of people who'd furiously denounced the police's actions that night and lauded Moses as a saint. Had one of them been hiding him in those days after the fire? Witness statements that the police took that seemed to hold significant clues—a sighting of someone running through a field that night. A stolen car from Ayden in North Carolina that reappeared three days later in Virginia. The addresses where Abby and Eden used to send letters, supposedly to Isaac but in truth to Moses.

Another section of the board was dedicated to Deborah. Abby had photocopies of the NYPD's investigation into the woman's identity. They didn't find a lot. No confirmed identity, no previous criminal record. A few photos, a sketch, and accounts of things she'd said to the hostages.

But Abby had begun ignoring all these leads, instead focusing on the fires.

The first one she'd encountered almost by accident. A house that had burned down in a town that matched an address Abby had sent letters to as a teenager. A man died in the fire, and his wife disap-peared. The police suspected arson. The neighbors testified that in the week before, they'd seen groups of strangers coming and going at strange times. And they constantly heard someone talking. Mostly just one voice, talking and shouting for hours on end. Abby could almost imagine it. Moses Wilcox standing in the living room of that house, preaching to a new flock. Telling them how the devil resided in germs, that they had to wash their hands all the time. That the apocalypse was coming, and God had chosen him as the Messiah. That, like Deborah had told Sam, the fire could cleanse their sins away.

She'd been looking into databases, making phone calls to police departments all over the country. Searching for other strange arson cases that seemed to be related.

She found five. Their photos now lined the bottom of the board, charred remains of structures. She didn't add the photos of the burnt bodies, in case Sam or Ben accidentally found the board. Two of those fires she'd marked with an asterisk. Indicating another peculiarity she'd encountered during her research.

Now she might have a sixth one. She held the photograph she'd printed out in her hand, a phone number written on the back. She dialed the number.

The phone was answered almost immediately by a cheerful-sounding woman. "Good morning, this is the Bloomington Police Department. How can I help?"

"Hi," Abby said. "I'm calling about the arson case in Ireland Grove from a year ago. I think I have information pertaining to the case. Can I talk to the detective in charge?"

The woman asked Abby to wait a moment, which ended up being four moments. Then she transferred her to Detective Dacosta. He sounded suspicious and cranky, but that was fine; Abby could easily handle suspicious, cranky men, and within ten minutes of talking, they were practically best friends. He gave her the info. A lot of it matched. Groups of strangers hanging around. A witness recalled that she'd been invited to some kind of mass prayer the week before the fire, something about the "flames of heaven." She didn't attend. Dacosta promised he'd send Abby some details she was interested in.

"You know," he said, "you're not the first one interested in this case lately."

There we go again. Abby took a blue marker and drew an asterisk on the photo of the burnt house. "Oh, really?" she asked. "Who else was interested?" She already knew who it was.

"The feds called a while back. They said it was related to an ongoing investigation. They left a phone number, in case I found out anything else."

Interesting. In the previous instances, the cops she talked to didn't have any names or numbers for her. "Can you give me the number?" she asked.

"Sure." He gave her the phone number. "The name was Agent Caldwell."

Abby thanked him and hung up. She taped the sixth photo to the board. Then she dialed the number.

"Hello." A sharp, impatient feminine voice answered the phone.

"Hi," Abby said. "Is this Agent Caldwell?"

"No, Caldwell isn't here. What's this about?"

"I was calling to talk to him about a case he's investigating . . . it's related to the arson case in Bloomington—"

"Caldwell isn't investigating that case anymore."

Another suspicious and cranky person. It was wearing thin. "I think I have some information about that case, and two other cases—"

"I'm sorry, who is this?"

"I'm Lieutenant Abby Mullen from the NYPD."

"Okay. What information?"

Something in the woman's voice was getting on Abby's nerves. Typical fed. Haughty and presumptuous. "Are *you* the agent in charge of the case?" Abby asked.

"I'm not an agent."

"I want to talk to the agent who's in charge of the case."

"I'm in charge of the case."

Abby sighed inwardly. The woman was impossible. "I was told that this was an FBI investigation."

"It is, Lieutenant Mullen. You've reached the Behavioral Analysis Unit of the FBI."

The BAU. Abby frowned. What were *they* doing looking into these fires? "Who am I talking to?"

"I'm Dr. Zoe Bentley."

"Nice to meet you, Dr. Bentley." Abby tried to make her voice as agreeable as she could, which demanded quite an effort. "I have reason to believe that the arson cases you're investigating are connected."

"Okay." Dr. Bentley didn't sound surprised. "Why do you think they're connected?"

"I think they're related to a cult I'm investigating."

"A cult?" Bentley's voice shot up in astonishment.

"Yes. There's evidence that—"

"Mullen," Bentley said. "You said you're from the NYPD?"

"That's right."

"We aren't investigating arson. We're investigating a series of murders. And it definitely sounds like we need to talk."

ACKNOWLEDGMENTS

As an author, my job is to rummage in my own imagination, memories, and thoughts and come up with ideas. These ideas are unruly and feral, and need to be physically forced onto a page with what we authors like to call "words" and "sentences." This process can be messy and, in my case, downright bloody. And it would be impossible without a lot of help.

My wife, Liora, is always by my side. One day I walked out of my writing room, dazed and confused, telling her, "I think I wrote something really weird. There's a bunch of people, and they're nick-named after *Alice in Wonderland* characters, but they attack a school with guns, and I don't know what I'm doing." She gently asked me for my unfinished draft, read through it, and then said, "Yeah, this is good; I want more." And that was all I needed to hear. She's the first person I brainstorm my ideas with, she's the first one to read my drafts, and she's the one I go to when I get that feeling that *this is not going to work*, which happens with each and every book. I can't imagine doing this without her.

My editor, Jessica Tribble Wells, brainstormed this book with me. Among other things, she was the one who pointed out that Samantha has to be one of the hostages. Her editing notes did a fantastic job helping me flesh out Caterpillar, as well as Abby's own turmoil, and they made this book shine.

Christine Mancuso read the finished draft, despite her discomfort with my descriptions of poor Deborah's demise. She gave me invaluable notes throughout the book and helped me nail the final chapter with Abby and Carver.

My parents, Haim and Rina Omer, both read my finished draft as well. It took me twenty-four years after I began writing, but I can finally receive notes from them without stomping my foot, going to my room, and slamming the door behind me. Which is fantastic, because they had some crucial notes that made this book significantly better.

Figuring out how a negotiator handles a crisis is difficult, and research could only take me so far. O. Shahar patiently sat with me for hours, walking me through the various techniques, and later also simulated a tricky sequence with me. Many of the clever tricks Abby pulled are thanks to him. And thanks to Yaron Lior for introducing us.

My developmental editor, Kevin Smith, did a fantastic job working with me to flesh out Abby and to make the moment of the big reveal really shine. It's always a pure pleasure working with him.

My agent, Sarah Hershman, has been working with me ever since I started writing mysteries, and without her belief in my books and me, this book would never have seen the light of day.

And above all, thanks to all my wonderful readers, for reading my books and making my dreams come true.

ABOUT THE AUTHOR

Mike Omer has been a journalist, a game developer, and the CEO of Loadingames, but he can currently be found penning his next thriller. Omer loves to write about two things: real people who could be the perpetrators or victims of crimes—and funny stuff. He mixes these two loves quite passionately into his suspenseful and often macabre mysteries.

Omer is married to a woman who diligently forces him to live his dream, and he is father to an angel, a pixie, and a gremlin. He has a voracious hound, five equally voracious chickens, and an unknown number of hamsters. A turtle also occasionally shows up in his yard. Learn more by emailing him at mike@strangerealm.com.